THE HANNE WILHELMSEN SERIES

Dead Joker

A Hanne Wilhelmsen Novel

Anne Holt

*Translated from the Norwegian
by Anne Bruce*

SCRIBNER

New York   London   Toronto   Sydney   New Delhi

To Tine

SCRIBNER
An Imprint of Simon & Schuster, Inc.
1230 Avenue of the Americas
New York, NY 10020

First Scribner trade paperback edition February 2018

SCRIBNER and design are registered trademarks of The Gale Group, Inc., used under license by Simon & Schuster, Inc., the publisher of this work.

For information about special discounts for bulk purchases, please contact Simon & Schuster Special Sales at 1-866-506-1949 or business@simonandschuster.com.

The Simon & Schuster Speakers Bureau can bring authors to your live event. For more information or to book an event, contact the Simon & Schuster Speakers Bureau at 1-866-248-3049 or visit our website at www.simonspeakers.com.

Manufactured in the United States of America

1   3   5   7   9   10   8   6   4   2

The Library of Congress has cataloged the hardcover edition as follows:

Names: Holt, Anne, 1958– author. | Bruce, Anne, 1952 April 22– translator.
Title: Dead joker : a Hanne Wilhelmsen novel / Anne Holt ;
Translated from the Norwegian by Anne Bruce.
Other titles: Død joker. English
Description: First Scribner hardcover edition. | New York : Scribner, 2016. |
Description version based on print version record and CIP data
provided by publisher; resource not viewed.
Identifiers: LCCN 2016021062 (print) | LCCN 2016018495 (ebook) |
ISBN 9781501123290 () | ISBN 9781501123269 | ISBN 9781501123290 (ebook)
Subjects: LCSH: Murder—Investigation—Norway—Fiction. |
GSAFD: Detective and mystery stories.
Classification: LCC PT8952.18.O386 (print) | LCC PT8952.18.O386 D613 2016 (ebook) |
DDC 839.823/8—dc23
LC record available at https://lccn.loc.gov/2016021062

ISBN 978-1-5011-2326-9
ISBN 978-1-5011-2327-6 (pbk)
ISBN 978-1-5011-2329-0 (ebook)

PART 1

1

The knowledge that he had only seconds to live made him finally close his eyes against the saltwater. Admittedly, he had felt a touch of fear as he'd thrown himself off the soaring span of the bridge and leaped into the air, but when he hit the fjord, the impact had not caused him any pain. He had probably broken both arms. His hands, glistening gray-white, were at a peculiar angle. He had attempted to swim a few involuntary strokes, but it had been useless, his arms ineffectual against the powerful current. All the same, he felt no pain. Quite the opposite, in fact. The water enveloped him with surprising warmth. He felt himself being dragged down into the depths, becoming drowsy.

The man's anorak swayed around his body, a dark, limp balloon on an even darker sea. His head bobbed like an abandoned buoy, and he finally stopped treading water.

The last thing the man noticed was that it was possible to breathe underwater. The sensation was not even unpleasant.

2

A short time earlier, the woman on the floor had been ash blond. You couldn't tell that now. Her head had been separated from her body, and her midlength hair had become entangled in the fibers of her severed neck. Also, the back of her head had been smashed. Her dead, wide-open eyes seemed to stare in astonishment at Hanne Wilhelmsen, as if the chief inspector were a most unexpected guest.

A fire was still burning in the hearth. Low flames licked the sooty black rear wall, but the glow they cast was faint and had a limited range. Since the power was cut and the dark night pressed against the windows like an inquisitive spectator, Hanne Wilhelmsen felt the urge to pile on some more logs. Instead, she switched on a flashlight. The beam swept over the corpse. The woman's head and body were clearly parted, but the short distance between them indicated that the decapitation must have occurred while the woman was lying on the floor.

"Pity about that polar-bear skin," Police Sergeant Erik Henriksen mumbled.

Hanne Wilhelmsen let the shaft of light dance around the room. The living room was spacious, almost square, and cluttered with furniture. The Chief Public Prosecutor and his wife obviously had a fondness for antiques, though their fondness for moderation was less well developed. In the semidarkness, Hanne Wilhelmsen could see wooden bowls, painted with flower motifs in traditional folk style, side by side with Chinese porcelain in white and pale blue. A musket was hanging above the fireplace. Sixteenth century, the chief inspector assumed, and had to stop herself from touching the exquisite weapon.

Two painstakingly crafted wrought-iron hooks yawned above the musket. The samurai sword must have hung there. Now it was lying on the floor beside mother-of-three Doris Flo Halvorsrud, a woman who would not celebrate her forty-fifth birthday, an occasion barely three months ahead. Hanne continued to search through the wallet she had removed from the handbag in the hallway. The eyes that had once gazed into a camera lens for the motor vehicle bureau had the same startled look as the lifeless head beside the hearth.

The pictures of her children were in a plastic pocket.

Hanne shuddered at the sight of the three teenagers laughing at the photographer from a rowing boat, all clad in life jackets and the elder boy brandishing a half-bottle of lager. The youngsters looked alike, and all resembled their mother. The beer drinker and his sister, the eldest, had the same blond hair as Doris Flo Halvorsrud. The youngest had been on the receiving end of a drastic haircut: a skinhead with acne and braces, making a V-sign with skinny boyish fingers above his sister's head.

The picture was vibrant with strong summer colors. Orange life jackets nonchalantly slung over bronzed shoulders, red-and-blue swimsuits dripping onto the green benches of the boat. This was a photograph telling a story about siblings as they rarely appear. About life as it almost never happens.

As Hanne put the photo back, it occurred to her that they had seen no sign of anyone else apart from Halvorsrud since they'd arrived. Running her finger absent-mindedly over an old scar on her eyebrow, she closed the wallet and scanned the room again.

A half-open door revealed a cherry-wood kitchen occupying what had to be the rear of the house. The picture windows faced southwest, and in the light from the city below the heights of Ekebergåsen, Hanne Wilhelmsen could make out a good-sized terrace. Beyond that stretched the Oslo Fjord, mirroring the full moon as it swept across the slopes above Bærum.

Chief Public Prosecutor Sigurd Halvorsrud sat sobbing in a barrel chair, his head in his hands. Hanne could see the reflection of the log fire in the embedded wedding ring on his right hand. Halvorsrud's pale-blue casual shirt was spattered with blood. His sparse hair was saturated with blood. His gray flannel trousers, with their sharp creases and waist pleats, were covered in dark stains. Blood. Blood everywhere.

"I'll never understand how a gallon of blood can spread so much," Hanne muttered as she turned to face Erik.

Her red-haired colleague did not answer. He was swallowing repeatedly.

"Raspberry candies," Hanne reminded him. "Think about something tart. Lemon. Red currants."

"I didn't do anything!" Halvorsrud was convulsed with sobs now. He let go of his face and flung his head back. Gasping for breath, the well-built man succumbed to a violent coughing fit.

Beside him stood a trainee policewoman wearing overalls. Uncertain of how to behave at a murder scene, she was standing at attention in an almost military pose. Hesitantly, she gave the public prosecutor a hearty slap on the back, to no noticeable effect.

"The worst thing is that I couldn't do anything," he wheezed as he finally succeeded in regaining his breath.

"He's damn well done enough," Erik Henriksen said softly, spitting out some flakes of tobacco as he fiddled with an unlit cigarette.

The Police Sergeant had turned away from the decapitated woman. Now he stood beside the picture window with his hand on his spine, swaying slightly. Hanne Wilhelmsen placed her hand between his shoulder blades. Her colleague was trembling. It could not possibly be from the cold. Although the power had gone off, it had to be 68 degrees in the room. The smell of blood and urine hung in the air, pungent and acrid. Had it not been for the technicians—who had arrived at last, after an intolerable delay—Hanne would have insisted on ventilating the room.

"Not so fast, Henriksen," she said instead. "It's a mistake to draw conclusions when you know nothing, so to speak."

"Know?" Erik spluttered, sending her a sideways glance. "Look at her, for God's sake!"

Hanne Wilhelmsen turned her face to the room again. She placed her arm on Erik's shoulder and leaned her chin on her hand, a gesture that was both affectionate and patronizing. It really was unbearably hot in there. The room was more brightly lit now that the crime scene examiners had begun fine-combing the vast space, centimeter by centimeter. They had barely reached the body yet.

"Anyone who is not meant to be here must leave," thundered the most senior of the technicians, sweeping a flashlight beam across the floor toward the hallway with repetitive, commanding movements. "Wilhelmsen! Take everyone out with you. Now."

She had no objections. She had seen more than enough. She had allowed Chief Public Prosecutor Halvorsrud to remain seated where they'd found him, in a carved barrel chair far too small for his bulky frame, because she'd had no choice. It had been impossible to converse with him. And there was a chance he might behave unpredictably. Hanne did not recognize the young trainee on duty. She did not know whether the girl was capable of dealing with a public prosecutor who was in shock and who might have just decapitated his wife. As for herself, Hanne Wilhelmsen could not leave the corpse until the crime scene examiners arrived. And Erik Henriksen had refused to be left alone with Doris Flo Halvorsrud's grotesque remains.

"Come on," she said to the Public Prosecutor, holding out her hand. "Come on, and we'll go somewhere else. The bedroom, maybe."

The Public Prosecutor did not react. His eyes were vacant. His mouth was half open and its corners wet, as if he were about to vomit.

"Wilhelmsen," he suddenly rasped. "Hanne Wilhelmsen."

"That's right," Hanne said with a smile. "Come on. Let's go, shall we?"

"Hanne," Halvorsrud repeated pointlessly, without standing up. "Come on now."

"I did nothing. Nothing. Can you understand that?"

Hanne Wilhelmsen did not answer. Instead, she smiled again and took the hand he would not give her voluntarily. Only now did she discover that his hands were also covered in dried blood. In the dim light, she had taken the traces they had noticed on his face for shadows or stubble. She let go automatically.

"Halvorsrud," she said loudly, sharper this time. "Come on now. At once."

The raised voice helped. Halvorsrud gave himself a shake and lifted his gaze, as if he had suddenly returned to a reality about which he understood nothing. Stiffly, he rose from the barrel chair.

"Take the photographer with you."

The trainee flinched when Hanne Wilhelmsen addressed her directly for the first time. "The photographer," the girl in overalls repeated with little comprehension.

"Yes. The photographer. The guy with the camera, you know. The guy snapping pictures over there."

The trainee looked down shyly. "Yep. Of course. The photographer. Okay."

It was a relief to close the door on the headless corpse. The hallway was pitch-dark and chilly. Hanne took a deep breath as she fumbled for the switch on her flashlight.

"The family room," Halvorsrud mumbled. "We can go in there."

He pointed at a door just to the left of the front door. When the light from Hanne's flashlight illuminated his hands, he stiffened.

"I did nothing. That I could . . . I didn't lift a finger."

Hanne Wilhelmsen placed her hand on the small of his back. He obeyed the slight prod and led the two police officers down the narrow corridor to the family room. He was about to touch the door handle, but Erik Henriksen beat him to it.

"I'll do that," Henriksen said quickly, squeezing past Halvorsrud. "There we go. You stay there."

The photographer appeared in the doorway, though no one had heard him coming. He glanced wordlessly at Hanne Wilhelmsen through thick glasses.

"Do you have any objection to us taking a few photos of you?"

Hanne asked, looking at the Public Prosecutor. "As you know all too well, there are lots of routine procedures in cases like this. It would be great if we could get some of them out of the way here, before we go to the station."

"To the station," repeated Halvorsrud, like an echo. "Pictures. Why is that?"

Hanne ran her fingers through her hair and caught herself experiencing an impatience neither she nor the case merited.

"You're splattered with blood. We'll take your clothes for examination, of course, but it would be helpful to have some photos of you wearing them. To be on the safe side, I mean. Then you can get washed and changed. That'll be better, don't you think?"

The only response Hanne received was an indistinct hawking. She chose to interpret that as agreement, and nodded at the photographer. The Public Prosecutor was momentarily bathed in the blue-white glare of a flashbulb. The photographer issued a series of brisk orders about how the Public Prosecutor should pose. Halvorsrud looked resigned. He held out his hands. He turned around. He stood sideways against the wall. He would probably have stood on his head if someone had asked him to.

"That's it," the photographer said three or four minutes later. "Thanks." He disappeared just as silently as he had arrived. Only the buzzing noise of film being rewound in the camera housing told them he was returning to the living room and the repulsive subject he would be working on for the next hour or so.

"Then we can go," Hanne Wilhelmsen said. "First of all, we'll find you some clothes, so that you can get changed once we get to the station. I can come with you to the bedroom. Where are your children, by the way?"

"But, Chief Inspector," Sigurd Halvorsrud protested, and Hanne could see for the first time something resembling alertness glittering in his eyes. "I was there when my wife was murdered! Don't you understand? I did nothing—"

He plopped down into a chair. Either he had forgotten the blood on his hands or else he couldn't care less. Regardless, he rubbed the bridge of his nose vigorously before running his hand several times over his head, as if making a futile attempt to bring himself some comfort.

"You were there," Hanne Wilhelmsen said slowly, without daring to look at Erik Henriksen. "For the record, I have to let you know that you don't need to make a statement without—"

Hanne Wilhelmsen was interrupted by an entirely different man from the sobbing, brand-new widower who, until a few minutes earlier, had been sitting like an overgrown schoolboy in a barrel chair beside his wife's beheaded remains. This was the Chief Public Prosecutor Sigurd Halvorsrud she had known previously. The sight made her shut her mouth.

His eyes were steel gray. His mouth was no longer a shapeless hole in his face. His lips stretched across unusually even teeth. The wings of his nose quivered slightly, as if he had caught the scent of a truth he suddenly found too good to share with others. Even the arrogant little toss of his head, crass and abrupt, with his neck jutting forward, happened so quickly that Hanne Wilhelmsen fleetingly thought she must be mistaken.

"I wasn't just there," Halvorsrud said lamely, in a low voice into empty space, as if on second thought he had decided to wait until a more appropriate juncture to return to his former self. "I can give you the name of the killer. And his address, for that matter."

The window was open a crack, even though it was only March and it looked as if spring had been seriously delayed. An ammonia smell wafted into the room, and a cat wailed so suddenly that everyone jumped. In the glow from a garden light beside the gate, Hanne could see that it had started to snow in soft, sparse flakes. The trainee wrinkled her nose and moved to close the window.

"So you know the . . . Was it a man?"

The Chief Public Prosecutor ought not to say anything. Hanne should not listen to him. Hanne Wilhelmsen was obliged to convey Sigurd Halvorsrud to police headquarters at Grønlandsleiret 44 as speedily as possible. The man required a lawyer. He had to have a shower and clean clothes. He needed to get away from this house where his wife lay dead and mutilated on the living room floor.

Hanne ought to keep her mouth shut.

Halvorsrud did not look at her.

"A man," he said with a nod.

"Someone you know?"

"No."

The Chief Public Prosecutor finally looked up again. He caught Hanne's eye, and what followed was a silent contest that Hanne could not interpret. She could not figure out the expression in his eyes. She was perplexed by the conspicuous shifts in the Public Prosecutor's behavior. One minute he was totally absent, and the next his usual arrogant self.

"I don't know him at all," Sigurd Halvorsrud said in a remarkably steady voice. Then he got to his feet and let Hanne follow him up to the first floor to pack an overnight bag.

The bedroom was spacious, with double doors opening on to a small balcony. Hanne's hand automatically slid over the light switch by the door. Amazingly, the six lights recessed in the ceiling came on. Sigurd Halvorsrud did not react in surprise at the upstairs lights actually working. He had pulled out two drawers in a tall green chest. Now he hunched over them, apparently rummaging aimlessly among underwear and shirts.

A gigantic four-poster bed dominated the room. The footboard was intricately carved, and the carpenter had made generous use of gold leaf. A virtual sea of cushions and quilts lent the room a fairytale character, an impression intensified by three oil paintings on the wall depicting scenes from Asbjørnsen and Moe's famous nineteenth-century Norwegian folktales.

"Can I help?" Hanne Wilhelmsen asked.

The Public Prosecutor was no longer rummaging around for something he could not find. His hand was clutching a silver-framed photograph displayed alongside five or six other family portraits on the green-lacquered chest of drawers. Hanne Wilhelmsen wasn't even sure if the man was still breathing.

She crossed the room and stopped two paces from Halvorsrud. As she'd anticipated, the picture was of his wife. She was on horseback, with a young child straddled between her and the pommel. The child looked nervous and was clinging to his mother's arm, which was angled protectively across the youngster's shoulder and stomach, like a seat belt. The woman was smiling. In contrast to the face that had stared expressionlessly at Hanne Wilhelmsen from the pale-pink driver's license, this photograph revealed that Doris Flo Halvorsrud had been an attractive woman. Her face was cheerful and guileless, and her strong nose and wide chin suggested an appealing tenacity rather than a lack of femininity.

Sigurd Halvorsrud held the picture in his right hand, his thumb pressed against the glass inside the embossed frame. His finger went white. Suddenly the glass cracked with a faint snap. Halvorsrud did not react, not even when blood began to pour from a deep cut on his hand.

"I don't know the man who killed my wife," he said. "But I know who he is. You can have his name."

The woman and child in the photograph had almost disappeared, lost beneath the splintered glass and dark blood. Hanne Wilhelmsen took hold of the picture and coaxed it out of the man's grasp. She replaced it gently on top of the chest of drawers, beside a silver hairbrush.

"Let's go, Halvorsrud."

The Chief Public Prosecutor shrugged and went with her. Drops of red were dripping from his injured thumb.

3

Journalist Evald Bromo had always enjoyed working at *Aftenposten*. It was an excellent newspaper. At least to work for. You avoided most of the adultery stories in the tabloids, and the pay was good. Now and then he even got the chance to immerse himself in a topic and study it in depth. Evald Bromo had worked on the financial pages for eleven years and usually looked forward to going to work.

But not today.

Evald Bromo's wife put a plate with two pancakes on the table in front of him, sandwiched with butter and smothered in maple syrup, just the way she knew he liked them. Instead of launching himself greedily at his breakfast, he took a tight grip of his knife and fork, absent-mindedly tapping them tunelessly on the tabletop.

"Don't you think?"

He flinched and dropped his fork on the floor.

Evald Bromo's wife, Margaret Kleiven, was skinny, as if the childlessness she had never come to terms with had eaten her up from the inside. Her skin seemed too large for her slight body, making her appear ten years older than her husband, even though they were the same age. They had never discussed adoption, so Margaret Kleiven had dedicated her life to discharging her duties as a high school teacher to the best of her ability and to treating her husband as a substitute for the child she had never had. She leaned over him and tucked his napkin more neatly into his shirt collar before retrieving his fork.

"Spring's obviously late this year," she repeated, mildly irritated, as she pointed insistently at the pancakes. "Eat up now. You're late."

Evald Bromo stared at his plate. The syrup had run down the sides and the butter had melted, and now everything was mixed together in a greasy mess around the edges of the pancakes, making him feel nauseous.

"I'm not very hungry today," he mumbled, pushing the food away.

"Aren't you feeling well?" she asked anxiously. "Are you coming down with something? There's such a lot going around just now. Maybe you should stay home."

"Not at all. It's just that I didn't sleep too well. I can get something to eat at work. If I'm hungry, I mean."

He forced a faint smile. Sweat was pouring from his armpits, even though he had taken a shower that morning.

He stood up abruptly.

"But, darling, you *must* have something to eat," she said firmly, placing her hand on his shoulder to make him sit down again.

"I'm going," Evald Bromo snarled, pulling away from her unwelcome touch.

Margaret Kleiven's narrow face became all eyes; her mouth and nose disappeared, creating an overpowering sense of gigantic gray-blue irises.

"Relax," he said, attempting a smile. "I may have to go to a meeting at . . . a meeting. Not sure, you see. I'll phone, okay?"

Margaret Kleiven did not reply. When Evald Bromo leaned across to give her a routine goodbye kiss, she drew back. He shrugged, muttering something she could not catch.

"Hope you feel better soon," she said in an injured tone as she turned her back on him.

Once he had left, she nevertheless stood staring at him until his back vanished behind their neighbor's overgrown hedge. She rubbed the curtains with her fingers, and it occurred to her in her distraction that they needed a spring cleaning. It also struck her that her husband's back had become thinner over the years.

When Evald Bromo knew his wife could no longer see him, he halted. The chill spring air jarred on a decayed molar as he opened his mouth and took a deep breath.

Evald Bromo's world was about to be shattered. It was all going to happen on the first of September. He would have the spring and the summer, but then right at the beginning of autumn, everything would be over. For Evald Bromo the coming six months would be blighted by pain, shame, and fear at the thought of what lay ahead.

His bus arrived, and he grabbed the one vacant seat before an old woman could reach it. He never usually did that kind of thing.

4

Evald Bromo was not at work. Out of habit, he had gotten off the bus on Akersgata at his usual stop, between the government tower block and the Ministry of Culture. He didn't even shoot a glance in the direction of *Aftenposten*, situated fifty yards down the street; instead, his feet had almost automatically taken him up to Vår Frelsers graveyard.

The graveyard was silent. The occasional high school pupil hurried along the network of paths to make it in time for the first class of the day at the nearby Cathedral School. Despite the signs bearing stern reminders about using a leash, a stray dog was sniffing among the graves. The mongrel, black and burly, was wagging its tail madly at everything it found. The owner had to be the equally burly man in an equally black coat who was leaning on a lamppost reading a newspaper.

Evald Bromo was freezing.

He opened the zipper of his leather jacket and loosened the scarf around his neck. Suddenly he felt ravenous. He was thirsty too, come to think of it. He sat down on a grimy bench beside a gravestone whose inscription was no longer legible and removed his gloves, placing them neatly by his side. He was plagued by thoughts about how cold he felt and how tormented with hunger and thirst he was. He conjured up images of food and recalled the sensation of ice-cold water filling his mouth after a long run; he felt the liquid progress from his palate down his throat. He decided to take off his jacket all the same.

Now his teeth were chattering.

He had received two emails. One anonymous and with a meaningless address: pokerface@hotmail.com. The other signed "Someone who never forgets." Forgets what?

Perhaps it was possible to trace a Hotmail address. Perhaps there were records of that kind of thing. Evald Bromo knew very well that the police sometimes had problems obtaining permission from Internet service providers to check where an email might have originated. It must be even worse for an ordinary citizen. He had decided to enlist the help of a colleague who knew considerably more than he did about electronic communications, but when it came to it, he could not bring himself to ask. When he'd felt the color rise in his cheeks, he had instead asked about searching an archive he had not been able to access.

Worst of all, however, was the thought that these emails were stored somewhere in *Aftenposten*'s colossal IT system. When they'd pinged onto his screen, he had opened them and read them twice before deleting them. He'd wanted to escape them, to get rid of them. Only after he had deleted the second one, the one that had arrived yesterday morning and had put him into a state of total panic, had it dawned on him that both emails were retrievable. Evald Bromo vaguely remembered receiving a circular a few months earlier. Since he hadn't really understood what it was about, he had only skimmed it. But he had noted its warning that IT staff might, for technical reasons, occasionally need to access employees' private mail. And that deleted documents could remain in the system for some considerable time.

Evald Bromo was a good journalist. At the age of forty-six, he had still not tired of it. He lived quietly, with a limited social circle and an apparent concern for his elderly mother that was touching. Over the years he had obtained a rudimentary education in economics, taking the odd accountancy qualification and correspondence school course. Enough to satisfy pertinent questions. More than sufficient to find weaknesses wherever they might lie, as a good business journalist should. Evald Bromo's approach was as thorough in his work as it was in his hobby of building model boats, something that had developed into a time-consuming obsession.

Building boats and writing were about the same thing.

Attention to detail. Fastidiousness. Just as every tiny detail had to be exactly right on a ship, from the cannon balls to the stitches on the sail and the drapery on the figurehead, so the stories he covered also needed to be correct. They might be critical, or presented from a particular point of view, but they were always meticulous. Everything in order. Everyone having a say.

Evald Bromo had only one real weakness.

Certainly there were sad aspects to his life. His father, who had died in a drinking binge when Evald was only six, had haunted his dreams ever since. However, his mother had done what she could for the boy. These days she lay in her decrepit shell of a body with a brain that had short-circuited long ago, but Evald Bromo derived a quiet pleasure from his almost daily visits to her nursing home. His marriage to Margaret Kleiven had never been a bed of roses, but at least it offered comfort. For the past fourteen years he had been looked after and given food and peace and quiet.

Evald Bromo's weakness was little girls.

He could not remember when it had started. It had probably always been like that. In a sense, he had never grown out of them. Giggling, gum-chewing girls with pigtails and long stockings under short skirts had swarmed around him that spring when he was twelve years old and had been given 500 kroner by an aunt. Eventually the girls grew bigger, but Evald Bromo did not keep up with them. He could never forget what one of them had given him in return for fifty shiny coins, behind the gymnasium and sworn to secrecy.

As a youth, he had buried his urges in work and exercise. He ran like a rabbit; for an hour before anyone else had risen, and usually for two hours in the early evening. The legal training he embarked on fell through after one and a half semesters. The hours he spent in the reading room, head bowed over books that did not interest him in the slightest, became unbearable. They provided too much room for thoughts he was reluctant to acknowledge. Evald Bromo ran: he ran like a madman, away from college and away from himself. At twenty-two years of age, in 1974, he arrived at a temporary post with the *Dagbladet* newspaper. And the running he was so fond of became fashionable.

On his twenty-fifth birthday, Evald Bromo became a criminal.

He had never had a girlfriend. His only sexual experience with another person was the one he had bought for fifty kroner coins threaded on a string when he was twelve and a half years old.

When he was double that age, he was aware of the difference between right and wrong. The young girl who had run away from home could not have been older than thirteen. She was begging for money when he staggered home after attending a celebration in town with a group of people who might be called friends. The girl received 300 kroner and a pack of cigarettes. In return, Evald Bromo got five minutes of intense pleasure and endless nights of regret and remorse.

But he had made a start.

He always paid. He was really generous, and never used force. Sometimes it amazed him how easy it was to find these youngsters. They were lost, superfluous in a city that closed its eyes to them as long as they did not hang around in gangs. And they didn't. Not these ones. They were alone, and even though they used makeup to look older, Evald Bromo possessed an expert eye when it came to what was hidden underneath those skintight blouses and bras stuffed with cotton. He could determine a girl's age almost to the exact month she was born. He shopped for illegal sex for a period of six years. Then he met Margaret Kleiven.

Margaret Kleiven was quiet, thin, and small. She was friendly. She was the first grown woman to show more than a sisterly interest in him. Sexually, she demanded very little. They married after three months' acquaintance, and when Evald Bromo slipped the ring on her finger, the emotions he felt were hope and relief. Now someone would keep him under control. Everything would be much more difficult, and finally simple again.

He had never been unfaithful. He did not regard it as such. When by chance he came across an address in a porn magazine he found lying around at work, the temptation was too great. It seemed safe. The arrangement cost far more than picking up strays in the street, but he could keep the home he shared with Margaret clean. Over the years, there had been new addresses in other shady magazines and also, from time to time, even younger girls, but he had always kept himself to a boundary of ten years old. That's where he said stop. What he was doing was wrong, terribly wrong, and it became worse the younger the girls were.

He was never unfaithful.

He bought sex once a month.

First and foremost, he was a journalist, and he built model boats.

Evald Bromo was forty-six years old and skipped work for the first time in his life. The morning rush hour had subsided, and one or two little birds seemed to believe that spring had already arrived. There was a smell of wet earth and an indefinable scent of the city, and he was chilled to the bone.

On the first day of September, *Aftenposten*'s chief editor would receive an envelope in the post. It would contain a video recording and five photographs of Evald Bromo and a twelve-year-old girl. The email had not included any demands. No threats. No exit routes of the type, "If you don't give me this, then . . ." Just a plain statement of fact. Short and sweet. This will happen. September the first.

Evald Bromo got to his feet, stiff with cold. He put on his jacket again and tied his scarf.

There was nothing he could do.

He could only wait. He had six months left.

5

Oslo Police Station had changed its name. At one stage during an endless series of reorganizations, the massive, sprawling gray building at Grønlandsleiret 44 had been renamed Oslo Police District Headquarters. No one really understood why. District police forces were merged with urban police forces, and all the good-natured rural officers were made accountable to police chiefs with law degrees and gold braiding on their shoulders. After the merger, police stations were no longer to be found in Norway. Instead there were district headquarters.

The change of name had not had any visible effect. Oslo Police District HQ seemed just as uncomfortable with its surroundings as Oslo Police Station had always been. On its eastern side stood the old Oslo Prison, formerly a national institution for long-term prisoners and now downgraded to a mere county jail on account of changing circumstances and a lack of financial resources. Grønland Church loomed on its western flank, defiantly and patiently awaiting visitors in an area of the city where half the residents were Muslim and the other half had barely seen the inside of a house of prayer since they were christened. The optimism that had infused the rest of Old Oslo and seen house prices double in the space of a year had never reached the hill on which the Police District HQ was located, with the main road, Åkebergveien, tucked in behind it.

"A station is and will always be a station," Hanne Wilhelmsen said emphatically, slinging a case folder into a corner. "Since I began in the police force, this place has been reorganized a zillion times. Don't touch those!"

She made a lunge for the man who, having leaned over her, had already nabbed four chocolate bananas from a blue enamel bowl on her desk.

The man helped himself to three more.

"Billy T.!" Hanne said furiously, slapping him so hard on the backside of his tight jeans that it sounded like an explosion. "Leave them alone, I said! Anyway, you're starting to get really fat! Gross!"

"Comfort padding." Billy T. grinned, giving himself a smack on the belly before sitting down in the visitor's chair. "I'm getting so much good food these days."

"Which quite simply means you're getting real food," Hanne said tartly. "Instead of all the junk you've lived on for as long as I've known you. I've loads to do, as a matter of fact."

She cast an encouraging glance in the direction of the door he had just slammed behind him.

"Fine." Billy T. beamed, picking up the *Dagbladet* newspaper that lay on a shelf under an overflowing ashtray. "I'll wait. Hell, you've started to smoke again!"

"Not at all," Hanne said. "Having a cigarette now and again certainly doesn't mean that I smoke."

"Now and again," Billy T. mumbled, already immersing himself in an article about new motorbikes coming out that spring. "That means once in a while. Are those butts there a whole year's worth?"

Hanne Wilhelmsen did not answer.

The man who sat reading a newspaper while discreetly picking his nose on the opposite side of her desk looked larger than ever. Billy T. had measured six foot seven in his stocking feet since he was eighteen. He had never been slim. He would soon turn forty and in the past six months must have put on 45 pounds. It looked as though the extra weight had also done something to his height. Even when seated, it was as if his shape had no actual beginning or end. He filled the room with something Hanne could not quite figure out.

Hanne leafed through a well-thumbed textbook on criminal law, pretending to read while she stole secret glances at Billy T. through her bangs. She ought to get a haircut. He ought to go on a diet.

Hanne Wilhelmsen had long ago given up trying to work out her relationship with Billy T. He was definitely her best pal. Over the years, they had fallen into a modus vivendi like that of a symbiotic old married couple, using a bickering, sarcastic tone that vanished in an instant if one realized the other was being serious. Hanne caught herself wondering how close they really were. In recent months she had started to question whether she was capable of being close to anyone. Apart from brief, transitory moments.

Something had happened between Hanne and Billy T. late one Thursday evening five months earlier. When she closed her eyes, she saw him lurching into her apartment, drunk as a sailor. The entire block must have heard him when he roared in delight that he was going to marry the mother of his soon-to-be fifth son. As he had never lived with any of the mothers of his first four boys, this called for a celebration. Cecilie, Hanne's live-in partner of almost twenty years, had welcomed Billy T. with coffee strong as dynamite, gentle admonitions, and heartfelt congratulations. Hanne had fallen silent, feeling both wounded and aggrieved—emotions that had still not quite dissipated. The realization of what was really bothering her hurt far more than the actual prospect of losing someone she thought she would have to herself for the rest of her life.

"Have you thought about your speech?" Billy T. asked suddenly.

"Speech?"

"The wedding. The speech. Have you thought about it?"

There were still almost three months to go. Hanne Wilhelmsen was to be best woman but did not even know if she could face going.

"Look at this," she said instead, throwing a folder containing Polaroid pictures across the desk. "Warning: graphic violence."

Billy T. threw the newspaper on the floor and opened the file. He pulled a grimace Hanne could not recall seeing before. Billy T. had grown older. His eyes were more deep-set than ever, and the laughter lines below them could be maliciously likened to dark bags. His shaved head was no longer a statement; he could just as easily have lost his hair. Even his teeth, visible when his lips contracted in disgust at the photos, bore signs that Billy T. would turn forty that summer. Hanne let her eyes slide from his face down to her own hands. The winter-dry skin was not improved by the hand cream she plastered on three times a day. Fine lines on the back of her hand reminded her she was only eighteen months younger than Billy T.

"Fucking hell," Billy T. said, banging the folder shut. "I heard about the case at the morning meeting, but that there . . ."

"Nasty," Hanne sighed. "He may have done it himself."

"Hardly," Billy T. said, kneading his face. "No one's going to get me to believe that Chief Public Prosecutor Halvorsrud has gone berserk with a samurai sword and attacked his own wife. No fucking way."

"Hasty conclusion, if I may say so."

Hanne Wilhelmsen scratched her neck irritably. Billy T. was the eighth police officer in the past few hours who, without a scrap of prior knowledge, had nonetheless come to a definite conclusion about the case.

"Obviously he could have done it," she said flatly. "Equally, he may well be telling the truth when he says he was threatened with a gun and therefore sat completely paralyzed while his wife was massacred by a madman. Who knows?"

She wanted to add, And who cares? Another sign that she was ready to move on. The worst thing was that she had no idea where to. Or why everything, in some vague, undefined way, was in flux. Something had entered her life that meant she could no longer muster the required energy. Or perhaps it would be more accurate to say that she could not be bothered. She had become quieter than before. Grumpier, without really wanting to be. Cecilie had begun to scrutinize her when she thought she would not notice. Hanne could not even take the trouble to ask what she was staring at.

There were four brisk knocks at the door.

"Come in!" Billy T. thundered, breaking into a broad smile when a policewoman with a huge stomach waddled into the cramped office. "My wife-to-be and my new son!"

He pulled his colleague onto his knee.

"Have you ever seen a more beautiful sight, Hanne?"

Without waiting for a reply, he rubbed his face against the police-woman's bump and embarked on an incomprehensible mumbled dialogue with the child inside.

"It's a GIRL," the heavily pregnant woman mouthed to Hanne without making a sound. "A GIRL!"

Hanne Wilhelmsen began to laugh involuntarily.

"A girl, Billy T.! Are you going to be daddy to a girl at last? Poor, unfortunate baby girl!"

"This guy only makes boys," Billy T. said, tapping her smock with his finger. "And this, my friends, this here is my son. The fifth in a row. Sure as shooting."

"What can I do for you?"

Hanne Wilhelmsen made an effort to disregard Billy T. Police Sergeant Tone-Marit Steen made a wholehearted attempt to tear herself away. Neither of them succeeded.

"Billy T.!"

He pulled a face and scowled at Hanne. "Goddamn it, you're so bad-tempered these days! Do you have PMS morning, noon, and night, or what? Get a grip on yourself, woman!"

His grimace transformed into a smile directed at Tone-Marit as he wriggled out of the chair and made himself scarce.

"What was it he was actually after?" Hanne asked, spreading her hands demonstratively.

"Haven't a clue," Tone-Marit said, sitting down with a groan she tried to conceal. "But I've got something for you. That guy who was supposed to have beheaded Halvorsrud's wife—"

"Ståle Salvesen," Hanne said briskly. "What about him?"

"Well, the man the Public Prosecutor insists—"

"I know who you're referring to." Hanne interrupted her in an irate voice. "What have you found out?"

"Dead."

"*Dead?*"

Hanne Wilhelmsen was aware that no one had caught Ståle Salvesen since she had initiated a search for him the night before. He was on a piece of paper in front of her.

Age: 52 years. Marital status: Separated. Employment: In receipt of disability benefit. One grown-up son. Address: Vogts

gate 14. Income: 32,000 kroner in 1997. No capital. No other
relative apart from his son, living in the USA.

Two patrols had been to Torshov to look for Ståle Salvesen at three
o'clock in the morning. As he was not at home and his apartment was
in fact unlocked, they had paid an unofficial visit inside. Cheerless
place, but tidy. Bed made. No Salvesen. Out-of-date milk in the fridge.
The compressed information had materialized in a special report
attached to the printout from the data register.

"What do you mean by 'dead'?" Hanne said, her tone needlessly
sharp; the previous night's information that Salvesen could not be
found had given her a secret hope that Sigurd Halvorsrud had actually
told the truth.

"Suicide. He jumped into the sea last Monday."

"Jumped into the sea?" Hanne Wilhelmsen felt an urge to laugh. She
had no idea why.

"It was a . . . Oops!" Tone-Marit touched her stomach and held her
breath.

"Just practice contractions," she gasped after a while. "A hiker saw a
man throw himself off Staure Bridge just before eleven o'clock on
Monday night. The police found Salvesen's old Honda nearby.
Unlocked, with the key in the ignition. There was a suicide note on the
dashboard. Straightforward stuff, four lines saying that he couldn't
stand it any more, et cetera, et cetera."

"And the body?"

"Not found yet. The currents are unpredictable in that spot, so it
could take some time. Salvesen may well have died in the fall. The drop
would have been over 65 feet."

A fire alarm wailed.

"Nooo!" Hanne Wilhelmsen screamed. "I'm damned fed up with
these false alarms! Damned fed up!"

"You're fed up most of the time," Tone-Marit said calmly, getting to
her feet. "Anyway, there might well be a fire."

In the doorway, she turned to gaze at her superior officer. For a second it looked as though she was about to say something more. Then
she shook her head almost imperceptibly, and walked off.

6

"This doesn't look too good," Hanne Wilhelmsen said in an undertone, pouring more coffee into the handleless mug in front of Chief Public Prosecutor Sigurd Halvorsrud. "You can see that, can't you?"

Halvorsrud had spruced himself up considerably. He was freshly showered and smooth-shaven, and he was even wearing a tie, despite his temporary place of residence being an uncomfortable holding cell. He nodded wordlessly.

"My client agrees to being held in custody for one week. By which time this misunderstanding should have been cleared up."

Hanne Wilhelmsen raised her eyebrows. "Honestly, Karen—"

An indistinct expression in Karen Borg's eyes made Hanne shift in her chair. "Miss Borg," she corrected herself. "Take a close look at this."

Hanne placed a sheet of paper with a handwritten list of bullet points in front of Halvorsrud's lawyer. She tapped her forefinger against each point in turn, itemizing the reasons the police had for remanding Halvorsrud in custody for significantly longer than a week.

"He was present at the crime scene when—"

"He was the one who called the police."

"Could I be allowed to continue without interruption?"

"Sorry. Go ahead."

Hanne Wilhelmsen took out a cigarette. Halvorsrud had driven her to go through three cigarettes during the formalities so far, and at that particular moment Hanne could not care less that Karen had developed a talent for sanctimoniousness since becoming the mother of two children.

"Halvorsrud was in fact on the spot when the murder was committed. His fingerprints are all over the place. On the sword, beside the body . . . everywhere."

"But he *lives*—"

"Miss Borg," Hanne said, clearly and emphatically, as she got to her feet.

She stood by the window of the office she had recently been assigned. The room did not feel like her own. She did not belong there. It contained hardly a single personal item. The view was not the one she was used to. The trees lining the avenue leading out from the old main entrance of the prison were still bare. A soccer ball rolled slowly along the gravel path, though there was not a child in sight.

"I suggest," Hanne Wilhelmsen began afresh, out of habit sending a smoke ring up to the ceiling, "that I be allowed to complete my exposition. Then you can have your say. Without interruptions."

She wheeled around to face the other two. "Okay?"

"Okay," Karen Borg said, flashing a smile as she touched her client's arm. "Of course."

"In addition to what I've just mentioned, there's the fact that Halvorsrud invokes a . . . an invalid alibi, so to speak. He claims that it was a certain Ståle Salvesen who abused and murdered his wife. Ståle Salvesen, however, died on Monday."

"*What?*" The Public Prosecutor launched himself forward, banging his elbows on the surface of the desk.

"Ståle Salvesen's not dead! Definitely not! He was at my house . . . He killed my wife last night! I saw it with my own eyes. I can—"

He rubbed his tender arm and looked at Karen Borg as if expecting his lawyer to vouch for his story. Help was not forthcoming. Karen Borg twiddled an unostentatious diamond ring and cocked her head as if she had misheard what Hanne had said.

"Ståle Salvesen took his own life on Monday night. At least everything indicates that. Eyewitnesses, his car parked just beside the bridge he jumped from, a suicide note."

"But no body," Karen Borg said slowly.

Hanne looked up. "No. Not yet. It will turn up. Sooner or later."

"Perhaps he's not dead," Karen Borg said.

"You're quite right, of course," Hanne said calmly. "But in the meantime there's not a solitary speck of evidence that your client is telling the truth. In other words . . ." She stubbed out her cigarette with a pang of conscience. It was her sixth that day. She should not have started again. Definitely not. ". . . one week is not enough time. But if you'll accept two, I'll work my butt off in the next two weeks."

"Fine," Halvorsrud said firmly, without reference to his attorney. "I relinquish my right to appear at a preliminary hearing. Two weeks. Okay."

"With a ban on letters and visits," Hanne Wilhelmsen added quickly.

Karen Borg nodded. "And with the minimum possible press

coverage," she said. "I notice the newspapers haven't picked up the story as yet."

"Dream on," Hanne muttered, before continuing. "I'll try to find a mattress for you, Halvorsrud. We'll have another, far more comprehensive interview tomorrow, if that's acceptable."

Karen Borg tucked her hair behind her ear in a compliant gesture. An officer was summoned over the intercom, and when he had closed the door behind himself and Halvorsrud, Karen Borg remained where she was.

"I haven't seen you in ages," she said.

Hanne smiled briefly and began to save some nonexistent item on her computer. "Too much to do. Both Cecilie and me. And what about you? How are the children doing?"

"Fine. And you?"

"Okay."

"Håkon says something's bothering you."

"Håkon says a lot of strange things."

"And a lot of sensible things too. He notices things. You and I both know that."

Six months earlier, Håkon had finally become a public prosecutor. The nomination had come late, later than for most police lawyers, who were promoted as a matter of routine. Sooner or later. It was just a question of being patient. Year after year. Case after case. The vast majority found themselves better-paid and less onerous jobs in the space of two or three years. Håkon Sand had held out, eventually earning a kind of respect, if not exactly admiration, from those in the higher echelons of the prosecution service. Not least for his work with Hanne Wilhelmsen and Billy T., who had both protested vehemently at losing their most police-friendly lawyer. However, Håkon Sand could not endure any more. He had shuffled green folders and walked the linoleum corridors of Grønlandsleiret 44 for nine years before finally being able to stuff his family photographs and a beautiful bronze statuette of the Goddess of Justice into a cardboard box and move to C. J. Hambros Plass 2B. As the crow flies, it was barely a mile away, but he had disappeared without a trace. Now and again, he phoned for a chat, most recently only a couple of days earlier. He had suggested lunch. Hanne had not had time. She never had time.

"I thought you'd become the champion of the disadvantaged and everyone's friend," Hanne said sharply. "What's made you take on the case of his scornful highness Halvorsrud?"

"Friend of the family. Of my brother, to be more specific. Besides, you said it yourself: Halvorsrud's in quite a weak position. What's really wrong with you, Hanne?"

"Nothing."

Hanne made a genuine effort to smile. She drew up the corners of her mouth and tried to drag her eyes along with them. They filled up. She looked from side to side with her eyes wide open, aware her smile was about to morph into a grimace that would reveal something of what she would not speak about. Of what she could not speak about.

Karen Borg leaned across the desk, very carefully placing her hand on Hanne's. Hanne pulled hers away, more as a reflex action than deliberate rejection.

"It's nothing, really." She tried to brush it aside as the tears began to roll.

Karen Borg had known Hanne Wilhelmsen since 1992. The early days of their friendship had been pretty dramatic: together they had been sent whirling into a murder case that had later turned into a political scandal of rare proportions. It had almost cost Karen Borg her life. Håkon Sand had rescued her from a burning cottage at the very last moment. When they had subsequently moved in together and had children, Hanne and Cecilie had become close friends of them both. Seven years had elapsed since.

"I've never seen you cry, Hanne."

"I'm not actually crying," Hanne Wilhelmsen corrected her as she wiped away her tears. "I'm just so worn out. Tired, somehow. All the time."

Snow began to fall again. The enormous, frisky flakes melted as soon as they touched the windowpane, and Hanne was not sure whether it was because of the snow or her tears that the shapes in the park outside were merging into an indistinct image in shades of gray.

"I wish it was summer soon," she whispered. "And warm. If only the weather was warmer, then everything would improve."

Karen Borg did not reply. It occurred to her that even the most intense heat wave ever would not help Hanne Wilhelmsen. Nevertheless, she could not restrain herself from checking the time.

The daycare center would close in fifteen minutes. Hanne still didn't say anything, and instead simply rocked to and fro in her chair, snapping her fingers. The feigned smile was still fixed like a mask on the lower part of her face, and tears were still running down her cheeks.

"We'll talk again, then," Karen Borg said, rising from her seat. "Tomorrow, ten o'clock."

She felt uneasy as she hurried along the third-floor gallery, yellow zone. And she had no idea what she was going to cook for dinner.

7

The current had carried Ståle Salvesen's mortal remains to the mouth of the fjord. Where the fjord met the sea, eddies had developed that toyed with the corpse for as long as they could summon the energy. When they'd grown tired of this, they'd forced it down to the seabed.

An old fishing boat, about 50 feet long, lay at a depth of 100 feet. It had lain there since one rough winter's night in 1952 and had long been a favorite haunt of amateur divers. The binnacle was gone. The solid oak wheel had been removed in the sixties by a young diver. There were no pots and pans left. All that remained was the shell of a boat with no glass in the windows of its pilot house.

Ståle Salvesen was no longer wearing his windbreaker. The water had wrenched it off him, and it now lethargically washed over the pebbles on the shore a bit more than a mile north. However, he still had his boots on. They were firmly attached, as if by vacuum suction. When Ståle Salvesen's right leg was dragged by the current through the pilot house, the shaft of the boot got caught on a hook no one had taken the trouble to remove.

He resembled a four-armed starfish as he swayed in the cold March brine.

8

She had sensed it as soon as they walked up the garden path, the heels on her winter boots slightly too high for the coarse gravel, and Billy T. swearing as he buttoned his well-worn leather jacket against the bitterly cold snow.

"There's something here," Hanne Wilhelmsen said decisively to Billy T. "I know there's something here."

"Four guys have searched the house for three hours now," he protested. "Zip. Zilch. Nothing. The most suspect thing we've found is a dishcloth that's in need of bleaching, according to Karianne, and two copies of *Cupido* magazine under the boy's bed."

"Where *are* they actually?"

"Who?"

"The children. Where are they, and who's looking after them?"

"Oh, the children. The eldest is on a school trip to Prague. The two younger ones are on a vacation in the sun with some aunt or other. Thank God for that, to some extent. It's good they weren't here last night. Everything's under control. Clergymen and psychologists have been sent on package vacations here, there, and everywhere, with the government footing the bill. We expect the kids will be brought home over the weekend."

"Poor devils," Hanne mumbled as she hunkered down in front of the fireplace in Public Prosecutor Halvorsrud's living room. "You can interview them. Since you've got such a way with children."

"Well, some children. They're teenagers, you know."

"It was actually two fuses that blew."

Hanne stood up stiffly, aware that her left foot had gone to sleep. She stamped it softly on the floor as she gazed at a female police sergeant she could not recall having seen before.

"By themselves? I mean, in the ordinary run of things? Overload?"

"It's difficult to say," the Sergeant said with an eagerness that Hanne allowed herself to be annoyed by. "The fuse box is the modern kind. With circuit breakers. You know—the kind you just flick up and down. Of course, someone may have deliberately blacked out the ground floor."

Evening was approaching. Hanne felt she was reaching the stage when it would be impossible to get to sleep without the help of pills.

She had once been able to whiz through three days and nights with only an hour's nap now and again. That had changed now too. One night without sleep, like last night, and her body called time only a few hours into the next day. She stifled a yawn.

"As far as the computer in the study is concerned," the woman in the doorway continued, "there's something . . . something odd, you might say."

"Odd?" Hanne glanced at the Sergeant and repeated, "Odd. Okay, what's so odd about it?"

"It's completely blank," the woman said, blushing.

"Which means?"

"Well, it means . . ." The woman squirmed. The burning in her cheeks did not let up. But neither did she. "It's odd when a computer that looks fairly well used, with a grubby keyboard and fingerprints on the screen, doesn't contain anything at all. Nothing. Not a single text file. The hard disk is absolutely empty of anything other than the software."

"This is Holbeck, by the way," Billy T. said, suddenly thinking it a good idea to introduce her. "She's just arrived from Bergen Police District. Hanne Wilhelmsen!" His hand swept through the air in Hanne's direction.

"Mmm," Karianne Holbeck said with a smile. "Very good. Should I take the computer with me for a closer check?"

"Can you do that without damaging anything?"

Hanne Wilhelmsen's knowledge of computers extended just as far as was necessary to write a document and store it.

"No problem," Karianne assured her.

"She was in charge of IT in Bergen," Billy T. whispered, loudly enough to ensure that Karianne could hear. "What's more, she's been on loan to the finance police at Økokrim precisely because she knows those machines inside out."

Hanne nodded impassively, but checked herself and shot a smile in the direction of her new colleague. It was too late. Karianne Holbeck had already vanished to pack up a computer that showed every sign of having been well used but nevertheless contained nothing whatsoever.

"One more visit to the basement, and then we'll call it a day."

"Okay then," Billy T. said, sulking as he trudged after Hanne into the hallway and down the stairs.

The basement smelled of laundry detergent and old rubber tires. A long corridor with four doors along one wall opened out into an orderly laundry room. The washing machine and drier bore the ultra-expensive Miele trademark. The dirty laundry, lying on a brown Formica worktop, was sorted into different bundles: whites, colors, and delicates. The walls and floor were tiled, and the room appeared remarkably clean.

"There's nothing here, at any rate," Billy T. said, scratching his crotch. "Besides, I get a crick in my neck down here."

Ignoring him, Hanne entered the adjoining room. If the laundry room was clean and tidy, this space was much more chaotic. It had clearly been a kind of hobby workshop—a carpentry bench and tools on the wall indicated as much. But it must have been a while since anyone had done any meaningful work in there. Two old bicycles were propped against the gable wall and three sets of worn car tires were stacked on sheets of brown cardboard, making it difficult to see the floor. In one corner there was a dusty bottle surrounded by old clothes and boxes containing what looked like tattered paperbacks, a tricycle, and the undercarriage of a baby's carriage from the eighties.

"This place doesn't exactly look as if it's been thoroughly searched," Hanne Wilhelmsen said, landing a kick on a black plastic bag.

Seven beetles scurried off at top speed to find a new hiding place.

"I did tell them to search the basement one more time," Billy T. said crossly. "But we've got people to do that, Hanne. It's not necessary for a chief inspector to grub around in the dirt, for fuck's sake."

"You didn't say that."

"What?"

"You didn't say that they should search the basement again. What's that?"

Without waiting for an answer, she picked her way over to the tricycle. Leaning forward, she extracted something Billy T. could not see.

"And what have we here?" she asked as she straightened up. "A medicine cabinet. A very *old* medicine cabinet."

"An *open* medicine cabinet?" Billy T. asked, half interested.

Hanne Wilhelmsen's hands, encased in plastic gloves, very gently picked the simple lock using the pocketknife Billy T. had handed to her. Then she held the cabinet out to her colleague as if it were a treasure chest.

"You can have the honor," she said. "Open it."

Neither of them had expected anything at all. Although Hanne Wilhelmsen's instinct had told her that something would reveal itself if they examined the Halvorsrud family villa in sufficiently minute detail, the contents of the shabby medicine cabinet still left her speechless for almost half a minute.

"Jesus," Billy T. spluttered at last.

"You can say that again," Hanne replied.

The cabinet, approximately 20 inches high by perhaps 15 inches wide, no longer contained any shelves. They had been removed to make room for fat bundles of banknotes wrapped in plastic, and what looked like fifteen to twenty computer disks. When Billy T. cautiously lifted the topmost wads of money, even more became visible.

"It'll be quite interesting to hear what our friend in the back yard has to say about this," Billy T. commented, lifting one of the bundles of notes to his nose, as though already keen to sniff out the answer.

"Billy T.!"

Karianne Holbeck stood breathless in the doorway.

"Look at this! I thought it would be a good idea to go through the trash . . ."

Hanne Wilhelmsen thrust her lower lip forward ever so slightly as she tossed her head in appreciation.

". . . and this was lying there." Karianne Holbeck seemed unsure who should receive the sheet of paper. Billy T. helped solve her dilemma.

"An application for legal separation," he said, reading further down the form, noting the smears of coffee grounds and something that had to be egg yolk.

"Signed by whom?" Hanne asked, directing her question to Karianne Holbeck. "I've spoken to Halvorsrud four times since last night, and he hasn't said a word about any divorce plans."

"By Doris Flo Halvorsrud. Only her. The column where the spouse's name should appear is blank. But the worst thing is the date. Or the best thing, I suppose. It depends who you're rooting for, I guess . . ."

Karianne smiled self-consciously and blushed again.

"Doris signed this paper yesterday. It must have been one of the last things she did. Before she . . . before someone decapitated her."

Hanne stood up straight, noting that Karianne Holbeck would benefit from losing 10 or 15 pounds.

"This is a lot to take in all at once," she said with a placid expression. "It looks as though we ought to expedite tomorrow's interview with Sigurd Halvorsrud. And I need to know what's on these disks. Without delay."

It was the afternoon of Friday, March 5, and the hour was approaching five-thirty.

9

"Billy T. insisted," Hanne Wilhelmsen said, intoxicated with sleep. "He wanted to do the interview himself. Everybody needs sleep, he said. Even Sigurd Halvorsrud. And I need a break, he told me."

She had dozed off with her feet on the table. A glass of red wine had tipped over, waking her.

Cecilie Vibe got up to get some paper towels. "Sensible," she said absentmindedly as she attempted to contain the damage to two books engulfed by the spreading pool of red liquid. "Put your feet down, then."

Hanne Wilhelmsen stretched out on the sofa, covering herself with a throw she pulled right up to her neck.

"Don't let me fall asleep here," she slurred.

Cecilie Vibe refilled the glass, switched off the TV, and moved a chair so that she could keep an eye on the woman asleep on the sofa. She did not enjoy the red wine. She had not enjoyed her dinner either. Nor had she for a long time now. Hanne had not even noticed that Cecilie had dropped almost 10 pounds in less than a month.

At some point, she would have to tell her. Two days had gone by. The doctor who had given her the results was an acquaintance from college. Someone she had never really liked. It had been just as difficult to make eye contact with him then as it had been before. He had tugged his earlobe roughly and mumbled into his coffee cup. Cecilie had fixed her gaze on her colleague's right ear, overwhelmed by the feeling that time was passing inordinately slowly.

When she left the hospital, the weather had not changed. The snow that barely an hour earlier had chased her in through the automatic doors of the oncology department cut through her just as sharply when she reemerged. But this time she did not notice. A blob of chewing gum on the wet asphalt had completely captured her attention. It became a globe, a bauble, a ball. A tumor. Eventually, an aide hauling empty beds had chided her, urging her to get going. She had no idea where to go.

Cecilie Vibe had a malignant tumor the size of a tennis ball on her colon. The probability was that it had been there for some time, though it was too early to tell whether it had pushed its way through the intestinal wall and forced itself into other organs. Perhaps. Perhaps not.

She put down the empty wineglass and filled it with fresh, cool spring water from a bottle, watching as it took on a faint trace of color from the wine dregs. She swirled the pastel-pink water around and around as she tried to think about what they might do that summer.

Cecilie had not posed a single question to the man with the bright red earlobe. She had none, just then. Later, she had looked up all the databases she could access from her office. Then she had wept as she walked all the way home.

She should have told Hanne this evening.

Hanne knew nothing. Even that morning six weeks earlier, when Cecilie had discovered blood in her stools and acknowledged for the first time a cold dread at the thought of how listless and out of sorts she had felt for some time, Hanne had been distant and unobservant. Her alarm at the discovery on the toilet paper, her longing for it all to be a mistake—perhaps her period had got muddled and come early— had made Cecilie flush it away as quickly as possible and then brush her teeth with excessive vigor. There was nothing to talk about. Not then. It was definitely nothing. Just a lot of unnecessary fear that Hanne had not noticed, even though it encased Cecilie like a shell as she stood in the bathroom, naked and completely invisible to Hanne; she had not even said goodbye when she left.

And then it turned out that there was something after all.

Hanne had been ready to drop when she got home at quarter to eight. For once she had babbled like a brook, maybe in order to stay awake long enough to eat something. Hanne chattered away about a headless corpse, a man who had jumped into the sea, and a public prosecutor who needed to prepare himself to spend years behind bars. About motherless teenagers with their father in jail, about Billy T. becoming ever more unbearable in his obsession with his forthcoming wedding. About the new office Hanne simply could not get accustomed to, and about the new exhaust for her Harley that had still not arrived.

There had not been space for a story about a tennis ball with threatening tentacles that lay somewhere inside Cecilie's stomach. There had been no space for Cecilie at all on this short, shivery spring evening.

Hanne was snoring softly.

Suddenly she moaned and flipped over toward Cecilie, her mouth open and her face upturned. Her right leg had settled along the back of the sofa, and her left arm was hanging helplessly just above the floor. She looked uncomfortable. Cecilie put Hanne's arm back carefully alongside her body before pouring herself some more water.

Hanne's bangs were too long, concealing one of her eyes. Her brown hair had developed faint traces of gray, and Cecilie was surprised not to have noticed this before. The lashes on her one visible eye twitched, the minuscule movements indicating that Hanne was dreaming. One corner of her mouth filled with spit, which slowly formed a dark stain on the cushion under her cheek.

"You look so small," Cecilie whispered. "I wish you could be a bit smaller."

The doorbell rang.

Cecilie was startled. Hanne Wilhelmsen did not move. Afraid that the doorbell would chime again, Cecilie rushed to the front door and snatched it open.

"Billy T.!" she exclaimed, realizing how long it had been since she'd experienced such instant, simple pleasure at seeing someone. "Come in!"

Then she hushed him by putting a finger to her lips.

"Hanne's sleeping on the sofa. We can sit in the kitchen."

Billy T. peered into the living room.

"No," he said firmly, crossing the room and moving the coffee table in order to get closer.

Billy T. lifted Hanne Wilhelmsen as if she were a child who had fallen asleep in the middle of a forbidden thriller on TV. Her weight felt comfortable against his rib cage. The faint scent of wine on her breath combined with day-old perfume prompted him to kiss her on the forehead without a moment's thought. Cecilie opened the doors, and Billy T. managed to put Hanne to bed without her showing any sign of waking up.

"I've never come across that in a grown-up," Billy T. said softly as he stood scrutinizing Hanne while Cecilie tucked the quilt around her. "Not waking when they're carried, I mean."

Cecilie smiled, gesturing that they should leave.

"Something's bothering her," Billy T. said, staying put. "Do you know what it is?"

Cecilie Vibe tried to avoid his eyes. They were too blue and familiar and saw too much. Cecilie wanted to leave the bedroom, step away from the sleeping Hanne and the stuffy smell of bedclothes and sleep. She wanted to go to the living room, open another bottle of wine, talk about movies they hadn't seen and guest lists and what the new baby was going to be called. She did not succeed in moving a muscle. When she finally raised her head, he was the one who pulled her close.

"What in the world *is* it with you two?" he whispered, putting his arms around her. "Are you having a crisis, or what?"

Billy T. sat with Cecilie until almost four o'clock on Saturday morning. When he left, Cecilie felt a prick of conscience that Hanne had not been the first to know. At the same time, she felt relieved and filled with something almost resembling optimism as she solicitously undressed Hanne before snuggling underneath the quilts herself.

"I think I'll sell the Harley," Hanne murmured, half asleep, cuddling up close to her. "It's about time I grew up."

10

Chief Public Prosecutor Sigurd Halvorsrud looked in remarkably good shape. His clothes were clean and his shirt freshly ironed. A diamond set in white gold glittered on his red-and-green tie. Only the suggestion of a slapdash shave said something about his current circumstances. His complexion was clear and his color surprisingly good for the time of year. His entire appearance might have seemed offensive to souls more delicate than Billy T., given that his wife had been murdered two days earlier and he himself was charged with her homicide.

However, there was something about the eyes.

They were bloodshot and completely lifeless. Although the man made an effort to retain some kind of dignity in the way he sat—very straight, and with the somewhat renowned jutting of the chin—he was betrayed by the look of despair in his eyes, which he tried to keep to himself.

Billy T. ran his fingers around the inside of two cups before filling them with coffee from a thermos.

"Black?"

"With sugar, please."

The Public Prosecutor's fingers were steady as he helped himself to two sugar lumps from a cardboard box. Billy T. took one himself and dipped it in his coffee before popping it between his lips.

"Karen Borg will be here shortly," he said, sucking the sugar lump noisily. "Should we wait for her, or just start right away?"

"We can start," Halvorsrud said, clearing his throat quietly. "If she's just around the corner, so to speak."

"This Ståle Salvesen," Billy T. began, taking a slurp of coffee to wash down the remains of the sugar. "How do you actually know the guy?"

Confused, Halvorsrud looked at Billy T. "But," he said, thumping down his coffee cup, "I was told he's dead. He . . . From what I understand, he committed suicide. So why are you asking?"

Billy T. helped himself to two more sugar lumps, dipped them in his cup, and placed them on his tongue. "We don't have a body yet," he said as he sucked them. "Plus, I understood from Hanne Wilhelmsen you're quite insistent that it was Ståle Salvesen who killed your wife. So you say. So I'm asking you about Ståle Salvesen. Okay?"

Halvorsrud ran his hand over his scalp, just visible through his thin, grayish-blond hair. It looked as though he doubted the value of continuing to assert that a dead man had killed his wife while he had sat there watching. It looked as though he doubted most things.

"I don't understand it," he said, trying to swallow a belch with his fist against his mouth. "Excuse me. Of course you don't believe me. But I *know* it was Ståle Salvesen who stood there in my living room. He was there—"

He raised his cup to his lips and swallowed twice, striking himself on the breastbone, and excusing himself yet again.

"Ståle Salvesen was there for some time. It's difficult to say *how* long—you lose your sense of time under such circumstances. Or so I assume. At least I did. But I'm in no doubt that it was him. He—"

"But how did you know that?" Billy T. interrupted. "How do you know a guy on disability benefit who lives in public housing in Torshov?"

Karen Borg entered the cramped office and stared in surprise at the policeman.

"Billy T.," she said sharply, "I thought Chief Inspector Wilhelmsen was to—"

"Sleeping," Billy T. said with a smile. "You have been too, I see! Busy morning with the children?"

Karen Borg smoothed her hair shamefacedly, attempting to brush away a splash of chocolate spread from her taupe-colored skirt. The stain simply grew larger. She stared at it momentarily, sighing softly, before sitting on the empty chair without opening her folder of documents.

"How far have you gotten, then?" she said with a strained smile.

"I'm attempting to find out how Halvorsrud knows a solitary man whose income is less than fifty thousand kroner." Billy T. yawned. "It's not so easy, I tell you. Do you want an antacid, Halvorsrud?"

He fished out two loose tablets from a box of paper clips.

"Thanks," the Public Prosecutor muttered as he swallowed them both with a gulp of coffee.

The whump-whump of a helicopter circling low over the city forced its way into the room. Billy T. leaned over to the window and squinted up at the sun. For the first time in several weeks, it was making a half-hearted attempt to thaw the wintry, frozen streets of Oslo, but that did not last long. The yellow chink in the sky retreated behind a heavy gray cloud, and the helicopter disappeared in a westerly direction.

"Ståle Salvesen was once a very successful businessman," Halvorsrud said aloud, glancing at his attorney. "In the eighties. He was chief executive of a promising IT company, Aurora Data. Salvesen was a typical entrepreneur, you might say. No education at all, but knew everything there was to know about software. In fact, for a while Aurora Data was in danger of being bought up by Microsoft. Since Salvesen was the majority shareholder, that did not materialize. He wanted to run the whole show himself. The guy had vision, I'll grant him that. The company was ahead of its time, and had developed a—"

Halvorsrud scratched the back of his hand before finally directing his gaze at Billy T. "I don't know much about that kind of thing. I knew it all then, of course, but I don't remember it so precisely. It was something or other to do with the Internet, in any case. A . . . browser? Have I recalled that correctly?"

He gave a slight shrug and examined a chip in the table in front of him. His finger ran to and fro across the rough surface.

"Then came the financial crisis at the end of the eighties. New companies, quite successful until then, toppled like dominoes. Aurora Data found a way through, oddly enough."

"Why do you say that?" Billy T. asked. "You said yourself the company was on a sound footing."

"Not sound, exactly. Impressive. Promising. Enormous potential. But even all that was no guarantee against catastrophe. That Aurora survived all the same was due first and foremost to a breakthrough with another software program. As far as I remember, it was specially designed for news editors—television, radio, and the press. Then Aurora was listed on the stock exchange."

Billy T. was a man who basked in his own weaknesses. The colossal figure bragged about everything he could not do or did not know. He never apologized for asking for explanations about the most obvious things. When TV journalist Anne Grosvold became queen of the screen, turning her trademark hard-hitting naiveté into a widely admired art form, Billy T. had hung a color photo of her on his bulletin board. There she stood, buxom and bright, with her arms flung wide as though bestowing her blessings upon Billy T. and his increasingly audacious trumpeting of his own self-declared lack of knowledge. There was only one thing he refused to admit: he did not have a clue about finance.

Billy T. had only a vague idea about what it meant to be listed on the stock exchange. He grabbed a pen from a lidless soft drink can and noted down the expression on a pink Post-it note.

"Okay," he said impassively, biting the tip of the ballpoint pen. "And then?"

"Being listed on the stock exchange involves a great deal. Increased supervision, for one thing. More attention, you might say. From the outside world."

Until that point, Billy T. had listened with lukewarm interest. Ståle Salvesen was a subject that had to be aired but would most probably be tucked away in a closet once the job was done. Ståle Salvesen was a pathetic recipient of state benefits who was dead into the bargain, and

Halvorsrud was not telling the truth. But now it looked as if there was something there. Salvesen had a history. He had not always lived in a two-room apartment with four items of food in the fridge. Ståle Salvesen had been a highflier only a decade ago.

"Ten years isn't long," Billy T. said absentmindedly.

"I beg your pardon?"

"Continue."

"I got to know Ståle Salvesen in 1990. That is to say . . ." Halvorsrud took out a pack of cigarettes and held it up to Billy T., seeking permission.

"Smoke away," Billy T. mumbled, without consulting Karen Borg.

"I didn't exactly get to know the man. In fact I've never met him. But he was charged in an ugly case. Insider trading. And more."

Billy T. scribbled down "ins. trade" on the pink sticky and poured himself more coffee.

"Salvesen's son—I've forgotten his name—at that time was studying economics in the United States." Halvorsrud pressed on. "He made an extremely favorable and very considerable purchase of shares in a company of which his father was chairman of the board. *Not* . . ." He emphasized the word. ". . . *not* Aurora Data. Another company. Immediately after the share acquisition—only a matter of days—it came to light that the company had made a lucrative deal with a multinational based in America. The shares suddenly doubled in value. That's when we entered the picture."

"Økokrim, which investigates financial crimes," Billy T. commented.

"Yes. I had just taken up a post there."

For the first time, Billy T. could discern the suggestion of a smile on the Chief Public Prosecutor's face. Halvorsrud had swum against the tide. After many years as a successful commercial lawyer, an expert in tax and company law and therefore in how to make money, he had made a clean break and entered the public sector. From earning around five million kroner a year, he had taken his unique skills and used them to investigate financial crimes, for remuneration that, to Halvorsrud, must have seemed like small change. Above the desk in his office hung a brass plate he had received as a gift from the colleagues he left behind, engraved: "It takes one to know one."

"We started to dig. And we found things. When you begin to investigate someone who has worked his way up from nothing to riches in only seven years, there's almost no limit to what you can find. Irregularities. Violations of the law."

"How much did he get, then?"

"Get?"

"Yes," Billy T. said impatiently. "How much jail time did he get?"

Halvorsrud smiled again, a stiff-necked, almost scornful sneer.

"We never indicted him."

Billy T. was about to point out how untenable it was for the Public Prosecutor to spread spiteful gossip about a dead man only to admit that the case never became serious enough to end up in court. Then he checked himself. More times than he wanted to remember, he had been in a similar situation himself. Guilt was obvious, but evidence slight.

"Which doesn't mean the man was innocent," Halvorsrud added, as if Billy T. had been thinking aloud. "It'll always be my opinion that Ståle Salvesen should have been convicted. But—"

"Fine," Billy T. said. "Understood. Been there myself. But things didn't go particularly well for Salvesen even so, then? Something must have happened, I mean. From a four-wheel drive to a bike in barely ten years . . ."

"Haven't the foggiest idea," Halvorsrud said tartly. "The case was shelved because of the lack of evidence in 1996. By then it had been . . . Well, we hadn't done much with it in the previous few years, as it were."

Billy T. did not make any effort to conceal a long-drawn-out yawn, and his jaw cracked. He let rip a stifled fart, hoping no one noticed. To be on the safe side, he leaned over to the window and opened it a notch.

Cases like Salvesen's were common. An almighty commotion for six months or so. The police upending every stone and turning every tiny scrap of information inside out, before the whole thing petered out slowly and quietly. The folder would be left lying at the bottom of a pile somewhere, the only reminder the occasional contact from a brash lawyer working himself into a frenzy on behalf of his client. In the end, the case would be dug out again, get stamped and signed with the code indicating the matter was being dropped, and then be consigned to the archives.

"When did you stop working on the case?" Billy T. asked.

"Sorry, don't remember. In '91, maybe? Don't really remember."

"In 1991," Billy T. repeated. "And the decision not to prosecute didn't come until '96. What did Salvesen do in the meantime?"

"As I said, I don't know."

"How did you recognize him?"

"Recognize him?"

"You say you've never met the guy, but all the same you've no doubt it was Ståle Salvesen who killed your wife. How—"

"The newspapers," Halvorsrud interrupted in a dejected voice. "The case was given due mention. Besides, I had seen pictures of him before then as well. As I've now told you repeatedly, the man was a success. He had grown older, of course, somewhat . . . thinner, perhaps? His hair, at least. But it was him."

"Did he say anything?"

"When he murdered my wife?"

Halvorsrud's voice momentarily turned falsetto. He swallowed noisily, shaking his head faintly as he peered inside his coffee cup. It was empty. Billy T. showed no sign of offering him more.

"He didn't say anything, in fact," Halvorsrud continued. "Not a word. One minute the lights went off, and the next, Salvesen was standing in the living room doorway aiming a gun at both of us. A revolver. Or . . . a pistol. Yes, it was a pistol."

He shivered, and Karen Borg reached for the coffee thermos.

"Would you prefer water, perhaps?" she asked softly.

The Chief Public Prosecutor shook his head ever so slightly, and produced another cigarette. He sucked the filter end frantically, and his left foot tapped the table leg in a nervous, monotonous rhythm.

"And then?"

"Then he forced me down into the chair. The barrel chair. My wife tried to talk to the man, but I . . . I said very little, I think. It was as if . . . When he grabbed the sword, I passed out for a second or two. I think. I don't really remember . . . I—"

"How detailed do we need to be, Billy T.?" Karen Borg fingered the chocolate stain, her gaze switching between the policeman and the Chief Public Prosecutor.

Billy T. stretched out to close the window. The helicopter had returned. The rotor blades were spinning at an angle as it flew low over the harbor basin at Bjørvika; then it tilted back and accelerated rapidly toward Police HQ at Grønlandsleiret 44. There was a deafening racket overhead. Then the noise slowly dwindled as the helicopter finally decided on a northerly course.

"What do you think about the new opera house, Halvorsrud? Should it be located in Bjørvika or Vestbanen?"

Halvorsrud stared at Billy T. Something resembling rage had rekindled in his dull gray eyes.

"I beg your pardon?"

"For my part, I don't really care. Opera's best on CD. We'll go into all the details. Right down to the most minuscule facts you can think of."

These last comments were directed at Karen Borg.

"We've spared your client from having to go through the details for thirty-six hours now. It's about time we got to the bottom of this. Don't you agree?"

Sigurd Halvorsrud crossed his legs and nodded.

"He went berserk. I don't entirely know how to explain it. He hit her on the head with a flashlight. And then—"

"Was it his own flashlight?"

"Pardon?"

"Was it Salvesen's own flashlight? Had he brought it with him?"

"Yes. He must have. We don't have one like that in the house. Not as far as I know, at least. Black." The Chief Public Prosecutor used his hands to measure out something about 10 inches long. "My wife collapsed in front of the fireplace, and I could see that the back of her head was bleeding badly. Then he took down the sword. Salvesen. He took the samurai sword and—"

Billy T. listened in fascination. Initially he had insisted on doing the interview to spare Hanne Wilhelmsen. It was a sacrifice for him to spend a Saturday doing unpaid overtime as well. The weekends were when he had access to his children, and even though Tone-Marit was patient—almost fanatically so—with Billy T.'s four sons, it was best not to tempt fate. Their wedding was only three months and one more child away.

However, the case had started to interest him. Or rather, Sigurd Halvorsrud had captured his attention. The actual murder case—the most macabre execution Billy T. had ever come across—was dramatic enough. But Billy T. had been on the police force long enough not to succumb to fascination without good reason. A homicide was a homicide. This was a case like all others: a case that should and must be solved.

Sigurd Halvorsrud, on the other hand, was something special.

Billy T. found himself believing the man.

It seemed absurd.

Everything pointed to Ståle Salvesen being dead. However, the body had not turned up. Ståle Salvesen could have arranged it all. For all Billy T. knew, Salvesen could be sitting in a bar in Mexico right then, sipping a tequila sunrise as he enjoyed himself on the proceeds he had stashed away when he was living in clover, having realized that the good guys were starting to breathe down his neck.

Despite their still being miles away from understanding why in the world Salvesen would want to take Doris Flo Halvorsrud's life, the story about Ståle Salvesen appeared paradoxically and almost provocatively credible. Sigurd Halvorsrud swallowed and turned pale, stammered and made mistakes, recalled little, and then thought of details such as that Ståle Salvesen had a mole, or perhaps it was a wart, on his right cheek, just above his mouth. On two separate occasions, Billy T. had noticed that the normally arrogant, self-assured man had been about to burst into tears. But he had pulled himself together, brushed imaginary specks of dust from his jacket sleeve, cleared his throat quietly, and continued his story. Halvorsrud was behaving like someone who was telling the truth.

"You've made it hellishly difficult for yourself," Billy T. said finally, glancing at the clock.

It was twenty to one.

"So you sat for more than an hour and a half staring at your wife's body before you rang the police? *An hour and a half?*"

"Something like that," Halvorsrud said in a low voice. "I don't remember, of course, but I've calculated that it must have been. Afterward. It didn't seem so long."

"But why on earth did you do that?" Billy T. flung out his arms, knocking over the can filled with pens and pencils. They clattered down on to the table, where they lay like a game of pickup sticks that no one could be bothered to play.

"I . . . I don't honestly know. I was in shock, I should think. I was thinking about the children. I was thinking about . . . our life together. How it had been. How our lives had turned out. I don't entirely know. It didn't feel like such a long time."

Billy T. understood what Halvorsrud had spent an hour and a half doing. If he was telling the truth. Which he probably wasn't, if you gave credence to the evidence in the case.

"You couldn't understand why you hadn't intervened," Billy T. said, hearing how harsh that sounded. "You were deeply and sincerely ashamed that you had let a man hurt your wife without your lifting a finger to stop him. Probably you wondered whether this was something you could live with. You couldn't imagine how you were going to explain to the children what had happened. For example. Am I right?"

Halvorsrud gasped for air, staring intently into Billy T.'s eyes; his gaze contained a mixture of deep shame and fresh hope.

"Do you believe me?" he whispered. "You sound as if you believe me."

"It matters zip-zilch-nothing what I believe. You know that only too well."

Billy T. rubbed his neck with one hand and retrieved a folder from the second-to-top drawer with the other, slapping it down on the desk in front of him without opening it.

"I find your story interesting," he said tersely. "But it'll be even more interesting to hear your explanation about the application for legal separation we found in your trash. Signed by your wife, and dated March 4. The day she died. The very day someone murdered Doris."

For the first time, Halvorsrud's face developed a deep-scarlet tinge. His gaze dropped to his lap, and he brushed his trouser leg like a man possessed.

"I didn't know that. I didn't know that she had actually . . . I didn't think our recent trifling problems were relevant to this case."

"Relevant?" Billy T. roared and leaped from his seat. "Relevant?" he screamed again, leaning closer to the Public Prosecutor with his enormous fists on the desk. "And you're supposed to be top of the hotshots in the prosecution service? Are you . . . are you an *idiot,* or what?"

Karen Borg was on her feet in a flash, holding an arm out in front of her client, as if anxious to prevent Billy T. from launching a physical attack on the man. "Honestly. Neither Halvorsrud nor I need to put up with this sort of thing. Either you calm yourself and sit down, or I'll strongly recommend that my client doesn't answer any further questions."

"'Put up with'?" Billy T. snarled through gritted teeth. "In this folder here . . ." He slammed his fingers down on the unopened folder. ". . . I have circumstantial evidence that something was really rotten in the house of Halvorsrud. And you should be aware of one thing, Halvorsrud . . ." Billy T. abruptly sat down again, scratching his skull with both hands before pointing an insistent finger at the Public Prosecutor. ". . . in this building you have at the present moment only one friend. In the whole world you have only one friend. And that's *me*. Karen, for instance . . ." He turned his finger on the lawyer. ". . . is a brilliant attorney. An extremely decent person. Nice woman. But she can't help you one iota. Not one iota, do you understand? On the other hand, I can tell you that I find your story about Salvesen so incredible that I'm interested in studying it more closely. Every day that passes without his body washing up somewhere or other strengthens your defense. If I want it to. If you cooperate. If you *answer* the questions I ask you and what's more, use that damn big brain of yours to *realize that you need to tell me what I don't ask as well!* Do you get it?"

The room went quiet. The faint hum of the computer only intensified the impression of total silence.

"Sorry," Halvorsrud said eventually, a minute or so later. "I'm truly sorry. Of course I should have mentioned that. But it seemed so remote. Just now, I mean. It's true that we've been going through a difficult period. Doris has been talking about separation. But I had no idea she had filled out a form. On Thursday, before Salvesen turned up . . ."

He is at least admirably consistent in this Salvesen story of his, Billy T. thought.

". . . we were getting on well. I had taken the Friday off, and we were going to spend the whole weekend together. On our own. The kids were away."

When he mentioned the children, something resembling physical pain again passed over his features: a muscle contraction around the eyes and a rippling below his cheekbones.

"I have to do some writing before we move on," Billy T. remarked.

He swiveled his chair nearer to the keyboard. Despite using only three fingers, he was fast, and the sound of his hammering caused Karen Borg and Sigurd Halvorsrud to shut up. Karen Borg closed her eyes, sensing that the worst was still to come. Hanne Wilhelmsen had promised her all the documents after today's interview, an offer she had accepted. For a start, it was unheard of to come to an important interview without having sight of a single document. On the other hand, she knew that Hanne would never trick her. Not directly. Now Karen Borg was sitting with an unpleasant sense of foreboding, because she knew Billy T. She was well aware of the significance of those red patches on the side of his neck.

"Okay," Billy T. said suddenly as he turned to face Halvorsrud again. "So you knew nothing about the separation application. But can you tell me why 100,000 kroner, nicely packed into an old medicine cabinet, was lying in your basement?"

The Chief Public Prosecutor did not blush. He did not show any sign of surprise. No shame. His mouth did not drop open, and he did not throw out his arms in alarm. Instead he gave Billy T. a vacant and vapid stare, with eyes that had returned to the state they had been in that morning: red and empty.

"Hello," Billy T. said, waving five fingers in the air. "Are you there? What's the meaning of this money?"

Without making a sound, Halvorsrud passed out.

First, his eyes slid shut, as though he thought it a good idea to take a nap. After that, his stiff frame slowly slipped to one side. It did not come to a stop until his head hit the wall beside the window with a little thump. Then his lower jaw sank quite discreetly. Halvorsrud resembled a passenger on an aircraft who had grown tired of the in-flight movie. His breathing was barely noticeable.

"Damn it!" Billy T. said. "Is he dead?"

Karen Borg grabbed hold of the lapels on Halvorsrud's jacket.

"Help me then," she hissed, and together they managed to maneuver Halvorsrud down into some kind of stable position, lying on the floor. Billy T. phoned for an ambulance and two officers to accompany the ailing man to hospital.

"Do you have anything more?" The stain on Karen Borg's taupe-colored skirt had magnified. She tried to cover it with her hand but gave up. She slipped off her shoes and rubbed the soles of her feet. They were alone in Billy T.'s office. He did not respond.

"Hanne promised me the documents today," Karen continued. "I expect that's still the deal."

Billy T. drew out a sheaf of copies from a gray file cabinet. He thumbed swiftly through the papers before removing two sheets fastened with a paper clip.

"You can have this," he said, yawning again as he handed her the papers. "The rest will have to wait until I've had the chance to talk to your client again. That information about the money seemed to have quite an effect."

He stared pensively through the window. It had started to rain, and huge, heavy raindrops were chasing one another in stripes down the dirty windowpane.

"Can I call in some time?" Billy T. asked out of the blue. "Some evening, preferably. I need to talk to you about something. Both you and Håkon, I mean."

"Of course. Can you give me a hint? About what it's to do with? Anything important?"

They exchanged a look so long drawn out that Karen eventually made a face and glanced down at her aching foot.

"I think so," Billy T. said softly. "I'll drop in on Monday evening if that suits? If this place doesn't burn to the ground in the meantime, that is."

"This place will still be standing even if the sky falls in," Karen muttered as she slipped her shoe back on. "You don't want to come tonight, then? We'll be at home and don't have any plans."

Billy T. considered the proposition.

"No," he said finally. "I'll see you on Monday, about eight o'clock."

11

When Eivind Torsvik was thirteen years old, he sliced off both his ears.

He had no intention of dying from blood loss or an infection. The previous day he had been to the pharmacy and bought sterile compresses and three rolls of sterile bandages with money he had stolen. He placed the detached ears in a box padded with wool, then trooped to school, wearing blood-soaked earmuffs, to show his teacher what he had done.

That was what it had taken.

In many ways, even then he had felt it was too late. At the same time he knew there was nevertheless something left. He was ruined for life, that was true, but there was still something inside him worth cherishing. If only someone would take him in hand.

It cost him his ears to get help.

Now, at the age of twenty-seven, he felt that the sacrifice had not been too great. Admittedly, it was difficult to get glasses to sit properly—he had to buy frames so tight they pinched his scalp. And people looked at him oddly. However, he didn't run into very many of them. In summer, there were swarms of people around the cottage where he lived, but the regular summer visitors had become accustomed to the earless young man who always smiled despite speaking only rarely. They respected his boundaries—those around his acre of property as well as his personal space.

Days like today were pleasant.

It was Saturday, March 6. The drizzle colored the morning gray, and the wind painted white crests of foam across the fjord. Eivind Torsvik had stayed up until 4:00 a.m. the previous night, but he felt fresh and fit all the same. He would soon complete his fourth novel.

Which was excellent. During the final spurt, normally around this time every year, the writing consumed him totally. It did not leave him much time for his real mission in life. His sophisticated computer equipment, which dominated half his living room and emitted an odor reminiscent of stuffy industrial facilities, was reduced to a simple word-processing machine.

Eivind Torsvik padded barefoot along the shore. The rocks were cold and jagged beneath his feet, and he felt omnipotent. The saltwater stung his skin as he plunged into the sea. The temperature could not have been more than 45 degrees or so. Freezing and short of breath, he put 10 yards between himself and the shore before turning around abruptly and swimming back at breakneck speed with his head underwater.

It was time for lunch.

Then he would make himself as ready as possible.

12

"Why does this keep happening, over and over again?"

Hanne Wilhelmsen banged the copies of *Dagbladet* and *Verdens Gang* down on the table. Erik Henriksen's food stuck in his throat, and he sprayed a hail of half-chewed bread crumbs over the newspapers.

"What is it?" Karl Sommarøy asked as he took a big gulp from a glass of milk.

"Why do these journalists know more than we do? Why did nobody call to wake me?"

No one felt impelled to answer. Hanne Wilhelmsen, seated in a chair at the end of the table in the spartanly furnished conference room, started to leaf through the copy of *VG*, growing increasingly infuriated.

"You've got a milk moustache," she said suddenly, looking at Sommarøy and drawing a line across her own top lip. "Is it true that Halvorsrud was once fined for a violent crime?"

"Almost exactly thirty years ago," Karl Sommarøy said stiffly, wiping his mouth. "When he was sixteen he was fined fifty kroner for slapping a friend during the annual May 17 celebrations. A drunk and silly sixteen-year-old, Hanne. It wasn't serious enough to stop him from getting his attorney's license. Or making a career in the prosecution service. The incident was deleted from every archive a long time ago. Doubtful that it has much to do with this case here."

"Let me be the judge of that," Hanne said pointedly. "I'm sick of reading news about my cases in the papers. How do people *know* these things?"

She lobbed the newspaper away with a grimace, and grabbed a cup from the tray in the center of the oblong table.

"Tips," Erik Henriksen volunteered, having got his breath back. "For a thousand tax-free kroner, there's no limit to what the average Norwegian is prepared to sell."

"I have some news about those computer disks," Karianne Holbeck said with a smile.

Hanne had not even noticed her sitting there.

"From the medicine cabinet?"

Karianne Holbeck nodded.

"And what have you come up with?" Hanne sat up straight and pulled her chair up to the table.

"They contain information about four different cases. Financial crimes handled by Økokrim. Fairly major lawsuits, as far as I can tell. Anyway, I recognized three of the names. Influential people. The strange thing is that the disks don't contain actual copies of the case documents. More like summaries. They're detailed, but in form and content they don't really look like police reports."

The atmosphere in the windowless conference room was stuffy and smelled of stale packed lunches. Hanne Wilhelmsen knew she was already coming down with a headache. She massaged her temples with her forefingers and closed her eyes.

"Can you tell anything about who wrote them?"

"Not yet. We're studying them more closely now, of course."

Hanne opened her eyes and gazed at Erik Henriksen. She gave a faint smile and ruffled his bright red hair. At one time, he had been in love with her: a puppy dog scampering around her legs, delighted by every tiny sign of her confidence and trust. When he had finally come to appreciate the hopelessness of the entire enterprise, the Chief Inspector's continual references to his inferiority and youth had begun to irritate him.

"Help her, Erik," Hanne Wilhelmsen said. "And . . ." She looked at Karianne Holbeck again. There was something about this newcomer she found attractive. The Police Sergeant could not be more than twenty-seven or twenty-eight years old. Robust without being plump, she was forever giving odd little tosses of her head to throw her mid-length blond hair back over her shoulders. Her eyes reminded Hanne of a dog she used to walk when she was a young girl: golden-brown eyes speckled with green, alert but reserved, direct but not very easy to read. "Is there an update on the computer?"

"Yes." Karianne Holbeck nodded. "The hard disk was new, it turns out."

The door crashed open and Billy T. burst in, filling the room with his presence, which made Karianne Holbeck fall silent.

"Go on," Hanne Wilhelmsen encouraged, without looking in Billy T.'s direction. Offended, he sat down beside Karl Sommarøy and drew the sensational newspaper headlines toward him.

"The hard disk had been replaced," Karianne Holbeck explained. "It was probably done quite recently. We've checked the production number. The computer was old, as we thought. Old and well used. But the innards were—"

"New," Hanne said pensively, squeezing her eyes shut.

Ever since one evening before Christmas in 1992, when she had been struck down outside her own office, she had been plagued with recurring headaches. In the past six months, they had worsened.

"Do we know who used the computer?"

"Not at the moment," Karianne said, struggling to adjust the stopper on a thermos that was making a complaining, squeaking sound. "But from the surroundings, I'd say it was the wife. Doris Flo Halvorsrud. There were notes and memos around the computer about shopping and furnishings and that sort of thing. And the place was so . . . I don't quite know how to describe it. Feminine? Potted plants and a little teddy bear on top of the computer. Things like that. Someone should ask Halvorsrud. And the children, maybe. They're coming back tomorrow."

"How did the interview go?"

Hanne Wilhelmsen clasped her hands behind her neck and looked directly at Billy T. He spat on his fingers to moisten them as he riffled testily through the pages of *VG*.

"He fainted, for God's sake."

"What?"

"He fainted. In the middle of the interview. I'd just asked him about the money in the basement and the guy simply passed out. Collapsed calmly and with barely a sound."

"Have you written up the interview?"

"Yes, but it's not been signed, of course. Halvorsrud's at Ullevål Hospital. It's nothing serious, apparently. He'll be back here tomorrow."

"So long as someone in a white coat doesn't come to the conclusion that the air in here's no good for him." Erik Henriksen jammed a cigarette behind his ear and continued. "Which would be par for the course. Ordinary prisoners have to put up with the unpleasantness of our back yard for weeks on end. But when we haul in someone wearing an expensive suit, then it's detrimental to their health to stay there for more than three hours."

"Shall we go for a walk?" Billy T. said out of the blue, looking at Hanne.

"A walk?" she said incredulously. "Now?"

"Yes. You and me. A professional stroll. We can talk about the case as we walk. I need a breath of fresh air."

Standing up so suddenly that his chair threatened to topple over, he headed for the door as if the matter had already been decided.

"Come on," he commanded, slapping her on the shoulder. Hanne twisted around but remained seated.

"Get in touch with Økokrim, Karianne. Have a look at those cases described on the disks. Find out . . ." She held up her hands and counted on her fingers. ". . . if they are under investigation, whether they've been prosecuted, whether they've been dropped, and . . ." Hanne stopped short. "And who might have made the decision to dismiss them," she said slowly. "If it's Halvorsrud, then get one of the other public prosecutors to look more closely at the cases. To see if the grounds for dismissal were reasonable. And you, Karl . . ."

She stared at Sommarøy. She always found it difficult to meet his eyes. Her gaze usually slid down his face: she was fascinated by his near chinlessness. The first time she met him, she thought the strange lower half of his face might have been the result of an accident. The man was well built and athletic, with unruly curly hair. His green eyes were large, with short, masculine lashes. The curvature of his prominent nose would have lent his profile an almost authoritative expression, had it not been for the almost invisible chin beneath his tiny, narrow mouth. It was as if God had played a prank on Karl Sommarøy by giving him the chin of a four-year-old child.

". . . you collect all the witness statements we have at this point, write a summary, and have it on my desk by nine o'clock tomorrow morning. Together with copies of all the interviews."

"We're already talking about almost twenty interviews," Karl Sommarøy complained, drumming on the table with his left hand. "And there's not much of significance in any of them."

"That should be simple and straightforward, then. Nine o'clock tomorrow morning."

Hanne Wilhelmsen got to her feet.

"I'm going out for a short walk," she explained, smiling so broadly that the newcomers in the conference room looked at her in amazement.

She wheeled round abruptly in the doorway and nodded in the direction of Karianne Holbeck.

"You understand where I'm going with those cases on the disks?"

"I've already been thinking along the same lines myself," Karianne said, with a heavy sigh. "If we're right, Halvorsrud will be in a tight spot."

"He is already," Erik Henriksen muttered. "I'm willing to bet a thousand kroner they'll throw the book at him."

No one took the bet.

13

Evald Bromo had never used the Internet for that kind of thing. He knew how much existed out there. He had simply never dared.

Apathetic, he stared at the absurd pattern on the screensaver: a cube dividing into balls that grew larger, transformed into flowers, and then shriveled into triangles composed of four colors. Over and over again. Slowly, he removed his glasses and used his shirttail to polish them thoroughly before putting them on again. The triangle became a cube. The cube turned into balls that grew larger.

"The Åsgard development," he said to himself in an undertone, and grasped the computer mouse.

The screensaver vanished. A blank page appeared before him, untouched for the past two hours.

It seemed probable that Statoil had suffered a catastrophic budget failure in what was perhaps the most significant prestige project in the state-owned company's almost thirty-year history. The gigantic Åsgard project—development of the site at Halten Bank, the gas pipeline to Kårstø in Rogaland, the expansion of the processing plant at Kårstø, and the gas pipeline Europipe II—should, as stated in the plans, have cost around twenty-five billion. According to the tip Evald Bromo had received, the actual sum could be somewhere in the region of ten to fifteen billion more than the original figure. If correct, it was impossible to predict who would still be standing on the battlefield in a couple of months' time. The managing director of the group probably wouldn't survive. Nor the board of directors.

Evald Bromo had not managed to write a single word.

He thought of everything out there. A few keystrokes away. The physical tension caused his knees to knock, unconsciously and with increasing force, until the pain brought him to a halt.

Evald Bromo knew what that tension meant.

He knew what he had to do, but he did not want to do it. Not this time. Two emails had dropped into his life and made everything impossible. A spell on the Internet might have helped. At least for a short time.

He could not.

Electronic traces were stored everywhere.

Evald Bromo decided to run home. Perhaps he would run all evening. He stood up, stripped off his jacket, shirt, and trousers, and put on his yellow-and-black Adidas running gear. When he tied the laces on his running shoes, he noticed he was already perspiring. His hands were moist, and he was aware of a pungent odor from his body as he headed for the door.

He forgot to tell the duty editor that his story was not finished. When it dawned on him—three miles of sprinting later—he slowed down momentarily before pushing off again at full speed.

Evald Bromo could not even be bothered to phone.

14

The raw air stung her cheeks, and Hanne Wilhelmsen stopped. She threw her head back and closed her eyes as she felt the dampness from the ground creep through the flimsy soles of her shoes and up through her legs like a chilly caress. As she breathed deeply through her nose, it struck her that this was the first time in ages that she had felt no compulsion to smoke. The trees, bleak and winter-gray, lined the forest track, with the occasional coltsfoot flower poking its head up through the rotting leaves. Though Hanne was cold, she felt fit.

"Good idea," she said, linking her arm through Billy T.'s. "I really needed to get outside for a bit."

Billy T. had told her about the interview. About Halvorsrud's insistence on his story regarding Ståle Salvesen. About his own reluctant belief in the Chief Public Prosecutor. About his growing fascination with this case that, at the outset, had merely repelled him.

"*If* Halvorsrud is telling the truth," he reasoned, "then I can see only two possibilities. Either he is in fact mistaken. He *believes* the murderer was Salvesen, but it was actually someone else. Someone who looks like him."

Hanne wrinkled her nose.

"Agreed," Billy T. said bluntly. "It sounds unlikely. Especially since he was there for such a long time, and since Halvorsrud is so adamant that it was him. The alternative, of course, is that Salvesen is actually not dead at all."

"It's possible," Hanne concurred. "He arranges a suicide on Monday, goes into hiding in order to strike on Thursday, and then takes off for another part of the world."

They exchanged doubtful looks.

"I've read about that kind of thing," Billy T. said, pausing. "Seen it in films and suchlike, I mean. But to be perfectly honest, I've never heard of a case like that in real life."

"Which doesn't mean that it can't have happened," Hanne said. "He might have seen those movies too."

They turned off the forest track and onto a path that, only a few yards later, brought them to a picnic area beside Skarselva. The river, deep and swollen with rain, flowed toward the lake at Maridalsvannet; a chill, damp cloud hung over the riverbank. Without wiping off the winter dirt from the weathered wooden bench, Hanne and Billy T. sat down facing the water.

"They ought to make this smell into a perfume," Hanne commented with a smile, sniffing the air. "We have to find a motive. Within the realm of possibility."

"Within the realm of possibility," Billy T. repeated. "If we just . . . for fun . . . Let's imagine for a moment that Halvorsrud is telling the truth. And is right. Why the fuck would Salvesen kill a public prosecutor's wife? They haven't even met!"

"No. But Ståle Salvesen was almost entirely ruined by that investigation you were talking about. At the start of the nineties. The one Halvorsrud initiated and led."

"True enough," Billy T. said, pivoting around so he was almost facing Hanne. "Obviously Salvesen's life took a dramatic turn for the worse when Økokrim came after him. That's indisputable. But why *now?* If he was so filled with hate for Halvorsrud that he wanted to kill the guy's wife, why on earth did he put it on the back burner for seven or eight years?"

Hanne did not answer.

The Salvesen story did not hold water. Hanne Wilhelmsen's guiding principle had always been that the simplest solution represented the truth. What was self-evident was also what was right. Crimes were most often impulsive, seldom complicated, and almost never conspiratorial.

Admittedly, there were exceptions to these rules. Over the years, she had solved a not inconsiderable number of cases exactly because she was aware that all suppositions have their exceptions.

"Arranges his own fake suicide . . ." She snapped a twig off a small birch tree and stuck it in her mouth. It tasted bitter. The sap felt like glue on her lips. "With no motive other than that the man was investigated a number of years ago. And without a prosecution even being brought."

Hanne spat out the birch sap, discarded the twig, and moved down to the water's edge. The river's roar thundered in her eardrums and she laughed out loud without knowing why.

"Now you're going to hear a different theory," she shouted at Billy T. "What if Halvorsrud sold information from Økokrim to people under investigation?"

The riverbank was slippery. Hanne stepped carefully from one stone to another. Suddenly her foot slid from under her. The ice-cold water came up to her knee as she struggled to regain her balance.

"Perhaps his wife had found out," she continued, shaking her dripping leg vigorously. "Even wrote about it on her computer. Since she wants to be married to a hero rather than a villain, she demands a divorce. We should really make a run for it back to the car. I'll end up with pneumonia."

They raced each other, pushing and shoving and trying to trip each other up as they ran as fast as they could to the car.

"But Halvorsrud didn't want a divorce," Hanne panted as she raised her hand in a victory gesture. "Doris had become a threat. A serious one. He kills her, cooks up a story so fantastic that people are compelled to believe it, and sticks to it, come hell or high water."

"But damn it, Hanne," Billy T. said as he struggled to squeeze himself into their banged-up unmarked police car. "Why doesn't he arrange an accident instead? A car crash? A house fire? A samurai sword, Hanne. A downright decapitation!"

The vehicle spluttered its way down Maridalsveien. The traffic was light, despite it being a Saturday afternoon in one of the most popular walking areas in the entire Oslo region. The engine died on the bend beside the ruins of Mariakirken, St. Mary's Church.

"Fucking shit car!" Billy T. thumped his fist on the steering wheel.

Hanne laughed. "This car's like a small child. I know it well. Eager to start with, but then once its legs get tired, it refuses outright. Maybe we need to carry it home?"

She whooped with laughter when, in an eruption of rage, Billy T. got himself entangled somehow so that he could neither get in nor out of the cramped driving seat.

"Call the station," he snarled. "Phone the fucking fire service, if necessary. Get me out of here!"

Hanne Wilhelmsen stepped out of the car and tugged her jacket more snugly around herself as she sauntered down toward Maridalsvannet lake, taking her cell phone from her pocket. Two minutes later, she received confirmation that help was on the way.

The ice had not yet melted. It lay like a dirty gray lid on Oslo's primary source of drinking water. Hanne paused when she spotted a fully grown elk standing beside the lake, drinking from the surface water. It must have caught her scent; the huge beast jerked its head up vigilantly, then trotted over to a grove of trees and disappeared among the branches.

Hanne Wilhelmsen immediately felt an inexplicable sense of certainty. Ståle Salvesen was dead. Of course she could not be sure of that. But she knew it all the same.

"Get a grip," she told herself crossly.

Then she shook off the idea and went to help Billy T., who was still completely wedged inside the ancient Ford Fiesta, swearing so loudly his voice must have echoed throughout the surrounding valley.

15

Typing the final period was always accompanied by a little ceremony. Eivind Torsvik had opened a bottle of Vigne de L'Enfant
Jésus that morning. The red wine had now been breathing for ten
hours. Holding his glass up to the light from the computer screen, he
let the liquid roll around the sides. He relished the prospect of soon
being able to tap the period key for the last time.

He had never been a good student. He had hardly attended elementary school. After he had sliced off his ears and his life had at long
last improved a little bit during his teenage years, he had quickly realized that he lacked basic knowledge. And so he had more or less given
up. He could cope without it.

Eivind Torsvik knew little about the history of democracy. Of
course he had heard of the American Civil War and the Russian
Revolution, but he had only a vague notion of when they'd happened
and what they'd really been about. As far as literature was concerned,
he confined himself to three books: *Moby Dick*; Knut Hamsun's dark
psychological novel *Hunger*; and Jens Bjørneboe's fictionalized biogra-
phy of troubled author Ragnhild Jølsen, *The Dream and the Wheel*.
Never anything else. He'd read them during his first weeks in jail when
he could not sleep. Since then, he had read each of them again three
times. The sleep deprivation had resulted in a week in the hospital.
When he decided to start writing, he made the decision never to read
what others had written. It only distracted him. When he was given an
IQ test as part of his forensic psychiatric assessment, he astonished
everyone apart from himself by scoring considerably higher than average. Eivind Torsvik had used his excellent brain to write books that no
one could open without reading to the very end. Besides, he was good
at English, a language he had learned from watching American B movies on video while all the other children were at school.

Since he seldom read newspapers, the publishing company had
mailed him the reviews after his first book was released. For the first
time in his life, Eivind Torsvik had felt really satisfied. Not because he
was flattered by the acclaim—which he was to some degree—but
because he felt appreciated and understood. His debut book was a
doorstop of more than seven hundred pages about a happy hooker

who reigned over the rundown backstreets of Amsterdam. Eivind Torsvik had never set foot in Amsterdam. When, one year later, he learned that the book had nevertheless become a bestseller in the Netherlands, he sent a friendly thank-you note to the warden at Ullersmo Prison; the man had set down a computer that was almost ready to be thrown out, saying, "Here you are, Eivind. Here's your ticket to the outside world."

Eivind Torsvik rarely thought about the years he had spent in jail. Not that it was particularly painful to look back to his time behind bars. In the course of the four years he did for the homicide he had committed on his eighteenth birthday, he learned everything he needed to live a good life. As well as writing, he learned about computing. The guards never caused trouble for Eivind Torsvik; they treated him with respect and sometimes even with something approaching kindness. The other prisoners mostly left him in peace. They called him "Angel Boy." Although the name was probably meant as a jibe at his fair curls and eternal, impenetrable smile, he never felt insulted. "Angel Boy" was okay. Since he had been jailed for murder, even newcomers let Angel Boy live his life without too much interference. After a couple of months, no one commented on his missing ears.

When he now, for the first time in ages, cast his mind back to the cell where he had lived for four years, it was because he was going to type his final period. He closed his eyes and took stock. Five days before he was due to be released, he had experienced for the very first time the joy of declaring a manuscript finished. Since he had not had access to red wine in prison, he had bought a bottle of sparkling apple juice some time in advance. A guard had smiled at his request but had provided a fancy stemmed glass all the same. When Eivind Torsvik had toasted himself and his very first novel, he had felt the tingle of carbon dioxide on the roof of his mouth as the closest he had ever come to a genuine sexual experience.

He took a gulp of the wine. It was warm inside the cottage: cozy, almost hot. Eivind Torsvik sat in T-shirt and jeans, and as he finally swallowed the red wine, he let his finger touch the period key.

If he was not exactly looking forward to the next four months, he nevertheless felt a profound satisfaction at the thought of setting to work on something different.

16

Hanne Wilhelmsen had no desire to sleep. She blinked her eyes, shook her head roughly, and tried her best to stay awake. There had been food on the table, again, when she arrived home. Cecilie had lit candles, again, and put on exquisite music that had filled the living room with something demanding attention. And for the umpteenth evening, week, perhaps month in a row, Hanne was suffused with something that most resembled irritation. Obviously it was her conscience. She caught hold of that, hugging the feeling of inadequacy to herself and attempting to force it to keep her eyes open.

"I'm giving in," she said at last. "Sorry, Cecilie, but I simply *must* sleep. I'm on the point of collapse, I—"

The music stopped. The silence was so overpowering that it made Hanne weigh up whether she might manage another half hour or so. For the sake of peace in the household. For Cecilie's sake.

"I'm going to bed," she said softly. "Thanks for dinner. It was really delicious."

Cecilie Vibe said nothing. She sat with her fork raised in front of her mouth. A tiny piece of fish was about to break off, and she stared at it until it finally dropped into the lemon sauce that had partially, quite unappetizingly, congealed on her plate. When she heard Hanne close the bedroom door behind her, she could not even muster the strength to cry.

Instead, she sat up all night reading a book.

It was Sunday, March 7. The pearly dawn light crept into the apartment. In the end, Cecilie fell asleep in her chair. When Hanne rose around eight o'clock, she spread a blanket over her partner without waking her, forgot about breakfast, and disappeared.

17

Preben Halvorsrud was too young to understand his own sorrow and bewilderment. His face was marked with defiance and denial. The acne around the bridge of his nose was fiery red, and his eyelashes, long and curling like a girl's, had become matted with tears. His mouth was set in an unsympathetic grimace, its corners moist with spit he did not dare to lick dry. The boy had hardly glanced at Billy T. when the policeman had taken him to his aunt's house. And they had barely exchanged a look since.

"Great that you can stay at your aunt's house, don't you think?"

Billy T. was about to give up. He could not bear interviewing youngsters. Youngsters did not belong in a police headquarters. Anyone under twenty was a youngster as far as Billy T. was concerned. He had driven and wrecked a stolen car himself when he was nineteen. His gratitude to his friend's father was boundless. He'd made the culprits paint the house as their punishment. The police never got to hear about the incident. When, three years later, Billy T. had applied to police college, he was able to slap his mandatory spotless record down on the table. The episode had taught him two things: first, that there were no limits to the idiocies teenagers could devise. Second, that most things could be forgiven.

Preben Halvorsrud was nineteen and hadn't even stolen a bottle of soda. He had not done anything whatsoever. Nevertheless, he was sitting in an uncomfortable office in the police headquarters biting his fingers to the quick because he had no nails left to nibble. He twisted in his seat and spread his legs with no inkling that this made him appear childish rather than manly.

"When do I get to see my dad, then?"

He was speaking to his own trouser leg.

"Not easy to say," Billy T. replied. "When we've managed to get our heads slightly higher above water and can work out what actually happened."

As he spoke, he realized how absurd his answer was. It did not tell the boy anything at all. Preben Halvorsrud wanted to see his father now. Straightaway.

"Soon," Billy T. corrected himself. "As soon as possible."

He had used up all his questions. Treading warily, he had tried to discover what the boy knew about his parents' relationship. Preben had answered for the most part in monosyllables. However, the boy displayed a sulky, reluctant concern for his siblings. He was especially anxious about his sixteen-year-old sister.

"When's the funeral?" he said all of a sudden, staring out the window.

Billy T. did not respond. He did not know. It was only three days since Preben Halvorsrud's mother had been beheaded. So far, Billy T. and the rest of the eleven police investigators working on the case had concentrated on gathering all the threads into a single weave that, at the end of the day, would show them who had murdered Doris Flo Halvorsrud. But of course the woman had to be buried. For one ludicrous moment Billy T. envisaged two separate coffins: a large one for her body and a small, pretty one for her head. He suppressed an extremely inappropriate smile.

"Can Dad go?"

The boy looked at him for a brief instant. He was the spitting image of his mother, despite his late, ongoing puberty and being saddled with an overlarge nose and a complexion that must cause him serious problems with girls.

"Go from here? No. He has to stay here for a while. As I said, it—"

"I didn't mean from here. I realize that's not on. I meant to the funeral. My mother's funeral. Can Dad go to that?"

Rubbing his face, Billy T. sniffed long and hard. "I'm really not sure about that, Preben. I'll do my best."

"It would be good for my sister, you see. She's . . . a daddy's girl, you might say."

"And what about you, then?" Billy T. asked. "How do you feel about it?"

The boy shrugged. "Nah—"

"Do you think it's important for your father? To go to the funeral, I mean?"

Preben Halvorsrud made a face that was impossible to interpret. Maybe he was just exhausted. "Mmm." He nodded gently.

"Why?"

"They really *loved* each other, you know!"

For the first time, fury broke through his unsympathetic defiance. The nineteen-year-old straightened up in his chair and took his hand away from his mouth.

"My parents have been married for over twenty years. Of course, I understand that things haven't been fucking easy all the time. I don't think it is for anybody. You, for example . . ." A grubby, blood-tipped finger pointed at Billy T. "Are you married?"

"No," Billy T. said. "But I'm getting married this summer."

"Do you have children?"

"Four. Soon five."

"Wow," Preben Halvorsrud exclaimed, withdrawing his finger. "With the same woman?"

"No. But it's not me we're talking about right now." Billy T. banged a desk drawer with unnecessary force.

"Yes," Preben said. "It is you we're talking about. If your children have different mothers, then you do know what I'm talking about. Things aren't that fucking easy all the time. You haven't made such a good job of it yourself, have you? Staying with one person the whole time, I mean. If the mother of one of your children died, it would be important for you to go to her funeral, wouldn't it? Don't you think?"

The pitch of his voice rose to a falsetto, as if he was actually only fifteen. That was the age he looked as well. His eyes were about to spill over into tears. The fragile shield of indifference was about to shatter. Billy T. sighed loudly as he got to his feet. The feeling of being a scumbag almost paralyzed him as he towered over the boy. Preben Halvorsrud crumpled beneath him.

"So they *did* have problems, then."

The boy nodded imperceptibly.

"In what way?"

Preben sniffed noisily and used the back of his hand to rub his eyes. Then he lifted his chin and made eye contact with Billy T. The tears, hanging heavily on his eyelashes, threatening to fall at any second, glittered in the pale gray daylight.

"What do you really know about your own parents?" he said softly. "About that kind of thing, I mean."

Billy T. shuddered. Without thinking about it, he stroked Preben's hair. The youth stiffened at his touch but did not pull away.

"You're right," Billy T. said. "We don't actually know much. I'll drive you home. To your aunt's house, I mean. But before we go, I'd like to know about—"

Billy T. opened a desk drawer and removed a large black flashlight wrapped inside a transparent plastic bag.

"Do you recognize this? Does it belong to you, perhaps?"

Preben reached out his hand to take the flashlight, but changed his mind.

"It belongs to Marius. At least he has one like that. Identical, I'd say."

"That's fine," Billy T. said with a smile, replacing the flashlight in the drawer. "Now let's go."

Outside the police headquarters, as they made their way through the drizzle to the car, Preben Halvorsrud halted.

"Do you have to talk to Thea and Marius as well?"

Billy T. gave a quick, slight shrug, then slapped the young man on the shoulder. He was thinner than his baggy clothes made him appear.

"No," he said finally. "I promise I won't bother your brother and sister."

"Good," Preben Halvorsrud answered. "Thea should be left in peace."

His smile, the first Billy T. had seen, made the nineteen-year-old seem five years younger again. His lank, fashionably cut hair fell across his forehead, and Billy T. hoped he hadn't made a promise that might prove impossible to keep.

18

Police Chief Hans Christian Mykland of Oslo Police District had been in his job for exactly two years, two months, two weeks, and two days. These four totals had greeted him from the fridge door that morning. They were written elegantly in felt pen on a sheet of paper held in place by two magnets: a pig dressed as a clown and a miniature version of the astronomical clock in the Old Town Square in Prague. Though Mykland had been visibly annoyed, he'd left the sheet where it was. He had never told his employers in the Justice Department about the agreement he had entered into with his family when he had applied for the job as head honcho of the Oslo police force.

Three years, max.

His sons, at that time twelve and fifteen, had wholeheartedly supported their mother. To cap it all, the youngest had produced a kind of contract for his father to sign before he had been allowed to accept the position. He had obeyed the boy because the twelve-year-old had for a split second become his eldest brother, Mykland's eldest son. Simen had been only twenty when he had taken his own life. Alone at their summer cottage, he had inflicted eleven brutal wounds on himself with a rusty old sheath knife. The doctor had looked away when Mykland had asked him how long it had taken for his son to die.

Shortly after Hans Christian Mykland was appointed Chief of Police, on April 4, 1997, Prime Minister Birgitte Volter had been found dead in her office. Shot in the head. The case had caused a stir throughout the Western world, and Hans Christian Mykland subsequently proved to his family what they had suspected all along—that the job of police chief was no nine-to-five existence.

He enjoyed it, though.

Admittedly, he sometimes felt like Sisyphus. Crime in Oslo could not be staunched. The police force was awarded more and more resources, but it was never enough. The police district was reorganized and made more efficient, but criminality was like a malignant tumor that could only be slowed, not wiped out.

All the same, it was worth it.

Norway was still a law-abiding country. Its citizens, even in the capital, could still feel reasonably safe. At least if they knew which areas to avoid, and at which times of day they should stay at home.

Hans Christian Mykland was becoming popular. It was true that the start had been rather hesitant. Making the transition from the administrative position as head of CID to the more general and far more outgoing business of being police chief had not been easy. But he'd gotten used to it. Slowly but surely. Now there were daily signs that the staff not only respected him but were also beginning to value him as a human being as well as a boss. The Police Chief thanked God for that every single night before he fell asleep.

The job was more satisfying than he had imagined. He liked the work. He loved the contact with the general public. He enjoyed the approbation of his subordinates. Hans Christian Mykland was on top of his job and had absolutely no desire to call it a day. All the same, he had barely ten months left. A promise was a promise, even if he had been heavily pressurized into making it.

If Hanne Wilhelmsen had known how the Police Chief's morning had started, she would possibly have understood the man's ill humor. She could not fathom the reason for his long face and curt, barked responses.

"Why on earth wasn't this case submitted on Friday?" Police Chief

Mykland scratched his blue-black stubble in irritation as he stared at the Chief Inspector.

"We just didn't have the chance to gather—" Hanne Wilhelmsen began.

"Saturday then? We always do custody hearings on Saturdays if necessary!" Shaking his head, the Police Chief gave a sudden smile. "Sorry, Hanne," he said in a completely different tone of voice. "I've had a bad morning. My family isn't too happy about me working on a Sunday. But I . . ." He clawed at his neck before tugging distractedly at the collar of his uniform shirt. "Three and a half days without a court order . . ."

He left that hanging. Hanne Wilhelmsen was well aware that whichever police prosecutor turned up at the District Court tomorrow could expect criticism from the judge. The court had to sanction holding Sigurd Halvorsrud behind bars. Going by the book, that should have been done within twenty-four hours of his arrest. It was one thing that far too much time had elapsed. Even worse was that the documents would clearly state that as early as Friday, Chief Public Prosecutor Halvorsrud had agreed to being kept in custody for two weeks. The police could have brought the case then.

However, Hanne Wilhelmsen had been hoping for more than two weeks. She could not stand working with short deadlines. As a rule it led to everyone becoming unnecessarily stressed, and stress spoiled their work. People became sloppy. The investigation suffered. Nonetheless, Hanne Wilhelmsen could appreciate to some degree why the defense lawyers made such a fuss about the need to impose strict time limits on the police in order to increase efficiency and decrease custody times; she never took it personally. When she was in charge of an investigation, she made sure the custody period was used for its true purpose.

"We'll have to put up with the criticism," she said, twisting her head from side to side. "Anyway, they won't set him free. We've got more than enough on him."

Tilting his head to one side, the Police Chief stared at her. A frown appeared above the bridge of his nose. He picked up a pewter paper knife and sat fiddling with the cold metal.

"If I knew you better, I'd invite you to dinner," he said so unexpectedly that Hanne Wilhelmsen did not quite know where to look. "But I'll have to leave it. How do you feel about it?"

"Feel? Well . . . it might be nice."

The Police Chief laughed loudly.

"I didn't mean dinner. The case! What do you think? Did he do it?"

Hanne felt a tingling sensation behind one temple. She tried to conceal the rapid breathing caused by her embarrassment, and launched into the report she had come to deliver.

"There are eleven of us working on the case. Plus technicians, of course. So far, the witness statements from neighbors haven't gotten us anywhere. They're all shocked and upset and so on. Nobody can think who might have any interest in seeing Mrs. Halvorsrud dead. Door-to-door inquiries told us nothing. No one saw anything, no one heard anything. In total we've held twenty-six interviews, including a fairly short one with Halvorsrud's eldest son. Didn't get anywhere much with that either. Other than that he seems to have realized that things weren't entirely rosy between his parents."

She stopped. Cecilie. Hanne had forgotten to phone. She glanced at her wristwatch and swore inwardly.

"What we have is quite ample, as far as it goes. The man's fingerprints on the weapon. No one else's, in fact, not even the prints of one of the itchy-fingered youngsters. No one can tell me that the sword has hung on the wall for years without one of the children touching it."

"Which might mean that the sword was wiped clean before Halvorsrud touched it," the Police Chief said, indicating for Hanne to continue.

"Of course. But that's only speculation. His fingerprints are also on the flashlight that to all appearances was used to knock his wife unconscious. His, and no one else's. He totally denies having ever seen the flashlight, even less having picked it up. The pathologist's preliminary findings indicate that she was killed between ten and eleven. The phone call from Halvorsrud did not come until ten past twelve. Midnight, that is."

Hanne Wilhelmsen leafed through the papers on her lap, more in agitation than because she actually needed to refer to them.

"So, Halvorsrud sat with his dead wife for one to two hours before calling the police. His clothes were spattered with blood. As if that wasn't enough . . ." She closed the green folder and pushed it across the massive desk in front of the Police Chief. "We found 100,000 kroner in used notes hidden in his basement. Together with computer disks dealing with cases he has worked on at Økokrim. He flatly denies having any knowledge whatsoever of all that."

"But," the Police Chief interrupted, taking hold of the papers she had offered him, "yesterday I was informed that the interview with Halvorsrud hadn't been completed. He fainted, I was told, and was admitted to the hospital."

"Just temporarily," Hanne Wilhelmsen said tersely. "He's fit as a fiddle today. Stubborn as a mule into the bargain. We authorized another twenty-four hours in the hospital, but the guy refused. He wanted to go back to the cell again. 'Just like all the others,' as he put it. I interviewed him for several hours this afternoon."

She got to her feet and stood observing the magnificent view from the sixth floor of the police headquarters building. The leaden afternoon was toiling its way toward evening. Gray-black clouds were racing southward. It would be a cold night. The imposing, shapeless mass of Ekebergåsen hill lay to the east. Oslo Fjord was churning white, and a dilapidated Danish ferry was heaving laboriously to its usual berth at Vippetangen.

"I used to love this city."

Hanne was not sure whether she actually said this or whether the thought just passed through her head. She used to feel at home there. Oslo was Hanne Wilhelmsen's city. Admittedly she was nineteen when she'd first moved to the capital, but that was when her life had begun. Childhood was a partially erased memory of something that though not exactly unpleasant had been totally insignificant. Hanne Wilhelmsen's life had taken off with Cecilie and their tiny apartment in Jens Bjelkes gate. Two years later they had moved from the 325 square feet with its toilet on the landing and an acrid smell of dead rats in the walls. Three apartments had come and gone since. Bigger and better each time, as it should be.

Hanne was aware of a gnawing sensation in her diaphragm. She longed to go back to Jens Bjelkes gate. To the beginning, and the way everything had once been.

Now I live here, Hanne Wilhelmsen thought, realizing that the police headquarters at Grønlandsleiret 44 was the only place in the world where she felt truly at home.

"How's he taking it all?" she heard the Police Chief say, and turned to face him again.

"Quite strangely," she answered in a laconic tone.

Resuming her seat, she asked for a cup of coffee. The Police Chief went off into the outer office himself and returned with two white cups and an ashtray. Hanne Wilhelmsen took one cup and left the ashtray unused even though she had a pack of cigarettes in her pocket.

"Until today, he was up and down. Changeable. One minute distant and almost in shock. The next resolute and lucid. The fluctuations were so sudden that . . . that I found them convincing. But today . . ." Her fingers played with the contours of the cigarette packet through the material of her right trouser pocket. Then she capitulated. "Today, you would think he had decided to conduct his own case. Honestly."

Savoring the cigarette smoke, she suddenly wondered why the Police Chief was wearing a uniform on a Sunday in his office. On the other hand, when she thought about it, she could not recall ever having seen him in plain clothes.

"He was exactly as we have always known him. Precise. Insistent. Persistent. Quite arrogant. Logical too, for that matter. Why would he remain sitting beside the body, pick up the sword, be spattered with his wife's blood if he really had killed her? And so on. Why didn't he arrange an accident instead if he'd wanted to get rid of her? He raised all the questions a competent member of the prosecution would ask in such a case. Not to mention a defense lawyer. As far as the money and computer disks were concerned, he was rock solid. He had no idea about them, he said, with his eyes fixed on mine. Didn't even blink. To cap it all, he claimed he hadn't been inside that messy storeroom for at least two years."

"Any fingerprints on the money?"

The Police Chief's chair needed oiling. A grinding noise accompanied his monotonous swiveling.

"Don't know yet. We'll have the results tonight or tomorrow."

"What about the children? Was the boy asked about the money?"

"I don't think so. We've decided to keep that particular card as close to our chests as we can. Fortunately the newspapers haven't heard about it."

"So far." The Police Chief had started to clean his nails with the letter opener. His hands were rough, more like those of someone who did

manual labor than someone who shuffled paper and went to pro-
tracted meetings.

"He was like a new man today," Hanne said, stubbing out her half-
smoked cigarette. "Or should I say, back to his old self. He did not
budge an inch. On Friday, he seemed a little hesitant about the Ståle
Salvesen story. For a while I thought he had lied and understood that
it was all over when he learned that Salvesen is probably no longer
alive. But today—"

"Dead certain," Mykland mumbled.

"Absolutely."

"What about you?"

"Very . . ." Hanne Wilhelmsen faltered. Stroking the scar on her
forehead, she pinned her gaze on the ashtray. The cigarette was still
smoking slightly, and she stubbed it out again with an expression of
distaste. "Extremely uncertain."

Putting the letter opener aside, the Police Chief folded his hands
over his stomach. The grinding noise from the chair grew louder.

"Do you remember the case of the boy from the children's foster
home?" Hanne said softly. "You were head of CID then, weren't you?
Was it in '93?"

"'94," the Police Chief replied.

The case of the murdered foster home director had made a greater
impression on him than most other cases. Perhaps especially because
it culminated in a patrol car knocking down and killing a twelve-year-
old runaway boy. The driver had been shattered and resigned three
months later. Nerves.

"I've never felt entirely certain about that," Hanne said.

"Maren . . . Kvalseid? Kvalvik? She confessed."

"Kalsvik. Maren Kalsvik. Yes, she confessed. And was sentenced to
fourteen years in jail. It bothered me for a long time afterward. Still
bothers me, in fact. I'm not at all sure she was guilty."

"Let's not waste our worries on that kind of thing, Hanne," the Police
Chief said wearily. "She confessed, and as far as I'm aware, she's never
gone back on that. There are enough prisoners sitting in Norwegian
jails protesting their innocence year after year. A couple of them have
even turned out to be right."

He rubbed the bridge of his nose, looking slightly irritated, before
taking a gulp of coffee.

"But what about Prime Minister Volter, then!" An insistent tone had crept into Hanne Wilhelmsen's voice and she ignored the Police Chief's skeptical expression. "If her husband hadn't come to us with those ancient letters, we'd have easily gained a conviction against that neo-Nazi upstart for her murder."

"Where are you going with this?" Mykland asked.

"Going?"

She flung her hands wide, half in resignation, half in annoyance. "I'm not really going anywhere with it. I just think it's becoming increasingly important to realize that we can make mistakes. That innocent people can be found guilty because we jump to conclusions far too hastily. That we . . . that some of us can get lost in the details of circumstantial evidence and close our eyes to the fact that sometimes strange and remarkable incidents *do* occur. Sometimes incidents *are* incidental."

"You're getting old, Hanne." His smile was friendly now, almost comradely. "Your youthful eagerness has subsided. That's a good thing. Your capacity for doubt and reflection has grown. That's also a good thing. It makes you an even better policewoman. If that's possible."

Now the expression on his face was almost flirtatious. "You're the best we have, Hanne. Don't take off now and go all soft. We've got defense lawyers for those kinds of scruples."

"Scruples," she repeated slowly. "Is that what we call it?"

Silence fell. Even the irritating sound of the unoiled office chair ceased.

"The point is, though, that I believe him. I have a feeling that Halvorsrud might be telling the truth."

The Police Chief nodded. His cheeks were even darker now, as if his beard had grown even as they sat there. There was a knock at the door. Mykland barked a response, and Karl Sommarøy entered the room.

"I think you'll be interested in this," he said, smiling as broadly as he could with his babyish mouth.

Hanne Wilhelmsen took the sheet of paper he offered her. Her eyes ran over the short text. Then she looked up, and let her eyes meet the Police Chief's for a moment before she announced, "Halvorsrud's fingerprints are on the bag of money."

She stood up and returned to her own office to prepare the case documents for the next day's remand hearing.

"Police Prosecutor Skar can at least take a brighter view of tomorrow's hearing after this," she said sardonically to Karl Sommarøy before she closed her door.

It was now seven o'clock on Sunday evening, and she was unlikely to make it home before eleven. There was really little point in phoning Cecilie. She certainly would not be expecting her home before night in all probability.

Hanne lit her seventh cigarette of the day, feeling dreadful.

19

"Fucking bitch!"

The stones were slippery with green algae. The gulls squealed in disdain as they tossed wildly in the gusty wind. The boy spat out his wad of snuff and wiped the black saliva with his jacket sleeve.

He had hardly been able to believe it when Terese had phoned the day after the party. It was one thing that she had made out with him; there had been hardly anyone else left there, apart from him. But then she had been on the phone. The next day. He hadn't understood shit.

He didn't now, either. He had been ready for Terese for ages. They all were. And then it was his turn. For three weeks she had made the boy believe that the world was rosy. But he was only seventeen. He had no money, and he didn't drive a car.

Terese had been sitting in Anders Skog's car yesterday. A new Volkswagen Beetle.

"If I jump across to that little rock and don't fall flat on my face, she'll realize that pansy coach is an idiot."

The boy shouted into the wind, and his tears mixed with sea spray to form a viscous mask over his face.

He fell, injuring himself badly.

He thought the red object floating among the clumps of seaweed between the reefs and the shore might be blood from his own leg. Then he understood what it actually was.

"What an idiot you can be," he muttered as he dragged the water-logged windbreaker ashore.

There was something in the breast pocket. The zipper was tricky to open, but the struggle at least gave him something else to think about.

"Oh, fuck! More than thirteen hundred smackers!"

The banknotes were soaking wet, but whole and genuine, as far as he could tell. "Ståle Salvesen" was written underneath the blurred photograph on the driver's license.

There wasn't another soul in sight out there in that weather. Only him. Two five-hundred-kroner notes, three hundred notes, and a fifty-kroner note went straight into his pocket. He lay on his stomach and shoved the windbreaker into a cavity the sea had spent thousands of years carving out under the rock. Then he placed three large stones on top. He put the driver's license back into the wallet, glanced down at his torn trouser leg covered in bloodstains and green algae, straightened his back, strained his rib cage, and hurled the wallet belonging to some Ståle guy all the way out to sea.

"Fuck you, Terese!" roared the boyish voice as he jumped from the rocks on to dry land.

20

"She got a real scolding," Billy T. said, helping himself to the lasagna. "But it would probably have been worse if you had made more of a fuss. Anyway, the guy was remanded in custody for four weeks. If he'd been anyone other than the Chief Public Prosecutor, we'd have gotten eight. Agreed?"

He passed the flameproof casserole to Karen Borg.

"She's quite smart," Karen said, unperturbed. "Is she completely new?"

"She's been with us for three months now. Great girl. Annmari Skar. Started at police college and then went on to study law. That's what makes a good police prosecutor."

Tone-Marit Steen shook her head and touched her belly when Karen offered her food. Her face contracted into a grimace.

"When are you actually due?"

Håkon Sand put more wood onto the fire in the soapstone fireplace and swore under his breath when he burned his fingers on the fireguard.

"In one week's time," Tone-Marit groaned, her face suddenly becoming red and moist. "But I think she might arrive early."

"He," Billy T. said so quickly that tomato sauce sprayed from his mouth across the white tablecloth. "Oh, fuck. Sorry. The boy'll come when he's good and ready. Don't believe for one second in all that due-date stuff."

"Oh!" Tone-Marit said.

A puddle spread rapidly between her legs, the liquid making a dark stain on her red maternity tunic.

"Oops," Karen responded.

"Doctor!" Billy T. bellowed. "Hospital! Håkon!"

"What do you want *me* to do about it?" Håkon screamed, a log of wood in one hand and a poker in the other. Stretched across his now quite substantial stomach, he wore a green apron with "Chef Sand" in childish felt letters across the chest. On his head he wore an old-fashioned chef's hat that made him look like a chubby candlestick.

"She's on her way," Tone-Marit moaned.

"He'll have to wait, for God's sake," Billy T. wailed, crashing out into the hallway to fetch his jacket and car keys.

"Karen. She's coming." Tone-Marit had lain down on the floor. She opened her thighs and let Karen pull off her tights and underpants.

"Heavens above," Håkon said.

"No!" Billy T. countered.

"Boil some water," Håkon suggested.

"Why?" was Billy T.'s whining response.

"Get some bed linen," Karen requested. "And yes, boil some water. Not too much, it takes too long. Put the poultry shears into the water."

"Poultry shears," Håkon muttered, grateful for having finally landed in his own sphere of competence. "Bed linen."

"Phone the hospital, Billy T." Karen Borg got up from her knees and gave him a push. The enormous figure was standing there bewildered, rattling his car keys. "Get an ambulance here. We can still make it, I think."

"Nooo," Tone-Marit hissed through gritted teeth. "Can't you hear me? She's coming! *Now!*"

"You've already got four children," Håkon yelled at Billy T., who had turned visibly pale. "You need to pull yourself together!"

What none of them knew was that Billy T. had never been present at any of his children's births. The youngest, Truls, he hadn't even known about until the boy was three months old. He was—like his three elder brothers, Nicolay, Alexander, and Peter—the result of a short fling that was over long before nine months had passed. Billy T. had quite simply not heard word of the births until they were done. As far as he was concerned, a newborn baby was a sweet-smelling, freshly washed charmer in white clothes and a woolen blanket.

"The head's on its way," he said softly, feeling the blood slowly returning to his brain.

"Sit down here," Karen said irritably as she dashed into the kitchen to make the phone call herself.

Billy T. knelt down beside Tone-Marit and held her hand tightly.

"It's a girl, Billy T.," she moaned, her breath making a grunting noise. "Tell me it doesn't matter that it's a girl."

He leaned across and put his mouth to her ear.

"I've wanted a girl all my life," he whispered. "But don't tell anyone that. It kind of doesn't suit me."

She began to break into a strained smile that disappeared in a violent contraction. The baby's head was fully out now, and Billy T. moved to place his hands carefully around it. Håkon Sand had stepped closer, still holding the log and poker in his hands.

"Are you planning to kill the child, or what?" Billy T. said in a fury. "Put them down and *boil those fucking shears*!"

"They'll come as fast as they can," Karen said, entering with a pillow and two large white sheets. "I've put the water on. Here!"

She tucked the pillow under Tone-Marit's head and helped her find a more comfortable position.

"Shit," Håkon Sand said.

His five-year-old son was standing in the doorway.

"Billitee," the boy said, sounding delighted. "Can you put me to bed again?"

"Come here, young man," Håkon said, trying to shield the boy from what was taking place on the floor in front of the fireplace. "You'll have to make do with Daddy tonight."

"Let the boy come," Billy T. said with a smile, and before either of his parents managed to intervene, Hans Wilhelm was kneeling down, staring wide-eyed at the baby that was now halfway out.

"This is my little girl," Billy T. said. "This baby is mine and Tone-Marit's."

The baby was born.

Billy T. had become father to a big, healthy girl. Tone-Marit wept and laughed and tried to find the face of the baby who was wrapped in an enormous sheet and had the rubber band from a jar of jam around the stump of her umbilical cord. Karen was sitting with Hans Wilhelm on her knee; the boy was sucking his thumb and agitating to hold the new baby. Håkon stared in consternation at the log and poker he held in his hands, and finally put them down.

Since no one apart from his mother had ever seen him cry, Billy T. excused himself meekly before locking himself in the toilet.

He stayed there until the paramedics rang the doorbell.

21

It was nine o'clock on Monday evening, and the apartment was clean and tidy. Since Billy T. had taken care of the custody hearing together with Police Prosecutor Annmari Skar, Hanne Wilhelmsen had headed home from the office early, at two o'clock. There were flowers in a ceramic vase on the dining table, and a cheese quiche on the point of collapse in the oven.

Cecilie had still not arrived home. Hanne felt a touch of anxiety but brushed it off. If some experiment or other had gone awry, things could take some time. Cecilie was hoping to complete her postgrad thesis by the autumn and Hanne had grown accustomed to the possibility of late evenings. In fact it suited her down to the ground.

Suddenly she was standing there. Hanne must have dropped off in front of the TV. Cecilie stood in the center of the living room, pale and drawn and still wearing her outdoor clothes.

"I'm ill," she said.

"You're not well?" Hanne got slowly to her feet. "Lie down here, then." She pointed at the sofa. "Would you like some food all the same?"

"I'm really ill, Hanne. Seriously."

Hanne Wilhelmsen blinked, attempting to swallow the sense of dread that threatened to rob her of her breath. "Seriously," she repeated hoarsely. "How serious is it?"

"Cancer. I've got cancer. I'm being operated on this Wednesday. Tomorrow. The day after tomorrow, I mean. Wednesday."

She continued to stand there, motionless, without showing any sign of taking off her bulky winter coat or sitting down. Hanne wanted to approach her, wanted to put her arms round Cecilie, smile and say that it was all nonsense, of course it was; no one was sick, just lie down and you can have something to eat. But Hanne was about to keel over. She had to stand totally, totally still or she would fall down.

"Where are you having the operation?" she whispered.

"At Ullevål."

"I mean where on your body? Your head? Stomach?"

"You haven't wanted to listen to me." There was no hint of reproach in her voice. Cecilie was simply stating the fact. The way they both knew things had been, for a long time.

"I'm sorry."

The phrase was meaningless, and Hanne wanted to eat her words. Instead she repeated them, still without moving anything other than her lips. "I'm sorry, Cecilie. I'm sorry."

Then she lifted her hands to her face and burst into tears, behavior so foreign to her that it scared them both. Her body shook violently and she dropped to her knees.

Cecilie stood observing her. She wanted to make physical contact with the imploring, begging figure. For a second she tried to raise her hand; Hanne was so close that she could have stroked her head—some kind of blessing. But her arm was too heavy. Instead she turned around, walked back to the hallway, pulled off her coat, and left it lying on the floor.

"Cecilie," she heard Hanne sob.

It was impossible to answer. Not now, and perhaps never. As a matter of routine, she crossed to the kitchen and switched off the oven before going to bed. When Hanne followed her at some point during the night, Cecilie withdrew so far over to her own side of the double bed that she nearly toppled onto the floor.

If only she would touch me, Hanne thought. *If only she would snuggle into my back*.

When the first light of daybreak appeared, Hanne Wilhelmsen and Cecilie Vibe had listened to each other's breathing all night long, but they had not so much as brushed against each other.

22

Exhaustion sat like barbed wire around her head, stabbing and aching, and Hanne Wilhelmsen felt as if she would never get to sleep again. She massaged her forehead and must have swayed because Karl Sommarøy made a grab for her.

"Hey," he said. "Are you feeling poorly?"

"Just tired." Smiling feebly, she raised her hand to reassure her colleague. "Slightly dizzy. It's gone now."

The apartment looked like a shell encasing a life that had barely existed. The beige sofa was old but not shabby. The coffee table was bare; only a fine layer of dust indicated the passage of time. The walls were blank and white. No pictures, no bookshelves. Not even an old newspaper visible anywhere. Even the noise of the city sounded distant and unreal through the closed windows, as if someone had switched on a half-hearted sound effect.

"I'm beginning to think that all this Ståle Salvesen business is just bloody hogwash," Karl Sommarøy muttered. He had rubber gloves on his hands and was at a loss about what to do. "Halvorsrud has demonstrably lied about so much. About the separation. About the packet of money. He's probably lying about this as well. Besides, the guy's dead. Very likely."

Hanne did not reply. Instead she entered the bedroom.

Ståle Salvesen had obviously not envisaged entertaining many female visitors. The bed was twin size. The bed linen appeared clean. A pair of navy-blue pajamas, neatly folded, came to light when she lifted the quilt. There was no bedside table, nor were there any books or magazines. Ståle Salvesen did not even possess an alarm clock. Then again, perhaps he had not had very much to get up for in recent years.

The walls were deep yellow, but there were no decorative items hanging on them. She took her time opening the three drawers, one by one. The top drawer contained socks, neatly folded into four pairs, all black. The next one was empty, and the third was full to the brim with underwear.

"Are there any other drawers in the apartment?" she asked in an undertone.

"Only in the kitchen," she heard Sommarøy answer from the living room. "Two of them are full of flatware and utensils, and the rest are empty."

"How many drawers do you have at home?" Hanne Wilhelmsen asked almost absent-mindedly.

"What?" Sommarøy stood leaning on the door frame.

"Drawers," Hanne repeated. "How many do you have?"

"Well . . . Five in the bedroom. Six in the unit in the living room. A few more in a sideboard the wife inherited, I don't know exactly how many. And then the kids have lots. Yes, and there are a couple in the bathroom. That's about it."

"How many of them are empty?"

"Empty? None!" Sommarøy laughed. His laughter was in keeping with his microscopic lower jaw: shrill and high-pitched, like a child trying to pretend something was funny when they hadn't quite understood the joke. "My wife's not too damn happy about it," he added.

"Exactly," Hanne mumbled as she opened the bedroom closet.

It had double doors: one side was divided into shelves, and the other was open, with a bar for coat hangers. Both sides were half-filled with neatly organized clothes that smelled faintly of tobacco. She pulled two suits aside to check if anything was hidden behind them, but found nothing.

"Don't you see what this is?" she asked. She pushed past him to get back to the hallway where a solitary bare light bulb was suspended from the ceiling, shining a bluish-white light on a single winter overcoat hanging on a peg beside the front door.

"What it is? It's an apartment that hasn't exactly been a very bright or cheery place to live—"

"There's something missing here." She was standing in the kitchen now. The units were from the fifties, with lopsided sliding doors and greasy shelf paper stuck down with old-fashioned thumbtacks. The countertops were worn and covered with scratches, but there was a faint odor of detergent, and the immaculate dishcloth draped over the faucet smelled of bleach. Hanne opened one drawer after another.

"What are you looking for, actually?"

Like everyone else in the division, Karl Sommarøy had become used to Hanne Wilhelmsen participating far more actively in an investigation than was usual for a chief inspector. Rumors circulated that she had even come to an agreement with the Chief of Police. Apparently she had threatened to resign when there had been terrible grumbles from the lower ranks. Karl Sommarøy was one of those who thought Hanne's approach entirely acceptable. However, recently she had become increasingly grumpy and at times annoyingly taciturn.

"I'm looking for something that isn't here," she replied, leaning down into an empty drawer. "Look here."

She ran her right forefinger around the curved edges of the drawer insert. When she lifted her finger to show him, he saw specks of dust and crumbs on the tip.

"So?" he said, wrinkling his brow.

"There was something here. This apartment is too empty to be true. Ståle Salvesen has lived here for more than three years."

"A helpless bum," Sommarøy muttered.

"No. A bankrupt hotshot. A man who obviously has intelligence, and who once ran a business that carried him some distance. He hasn't lived four years in a vacuum. He must have had interests. Something or other. Something to kill time at least. The point is that he has taken the trouble to remove absolutely every trace of the life he lived. When all is said and done, this apartment looks like a crummy hotel room. With no identity."

"But," Sommarøy objected, "it's quite usual for suicidal people to clean up after themselves. First, I mean. Before they—"

"Clean up, yes. But this place is more than that—it's virtually autoclaved."

Karl Sommarøy kept his mouth shut.

"Disinfected," Hanne explained. "Sterilized."

"There are some items in the fridge," Sommarøy mumbled, slightly disgruntled.

Hanne Wilhelmsen opened it. A smell of stale food hit her, and she screwed up her nose.

"Why hasn't this stuff been removed?" she said irritably.

"Who would have done that?" he answered, indignant.

Hanne Wilhelmsen gave a faint smile. "Not you in any case. We'll take it with us. And you're right. It's odd that he didn't empty the fridge before he jumped."

For a moment or two she stood peering into the milk carton and staring at moldy unwrapped yellow cheese, a yogurt long past its sell-by date, withered lettuce, and two tomatoes that had gone soft. Suddenly something crossed her face, a twitch Karl Sommarøy could not interpret.

"Of course," she said under her breath.

"Of course what?"

"Nothing. I'm not sure. Let's take a look in the bathroom."

It was minuscule. It would have been perfectly possible to sit on the toilet and shower and brush your teeth all at the same time. The lino-leum on the floor was loose around the drain, and even the strong aroma of bleach could not disguise the smell of mold from the con-crete underneath. The basin was cracked. The empty cabinet beside the mirror was askew. Only a lone frayed toothbrush in a glass sug-gested that anyone had actually lived there.

"Let's go," Hanne finally said.

The phone was located in the hallway, on a rickety little table. Hanne Wilhelmsen lifted the receiver and pressed the redial button before putting the phone to her ear.

"Hello, Directory Assistance here," she heard after three rings. She replaced the receiver without speaking.

"Directory Assistance," she said softly. "The last thing he did was to call Directory Assistance. Find out if the conversation can be traced. If we can discover what he asked about. What number he wanted."

"A number he then didn't actually call," Karl Sommarøy said impa-tiently.

"At least not from here," Hanne replied.

She caught sight of a bundle of papers that had fallen to the floor as she lifted the receiver. They must have been caught between the table and the wall. She crouched down to retrieve them. Four or five bills held together with a large paper clip. She produced a plastic bag from her pocket and inserted the bundle of receipts.

Beside the phone there was a small blank notepad, with a ballpoint pen lying obliquely on top; it almost seemed staged. Hanne removed the pen and took the notepad through to the living room. She held the top sheet up to the light. Something had been written on the sheet that had been torn off. A faint impression became visible when she held the paper at a certain angle.

"01.09.99," she read out slowly. "The first of September 1999?"

"The first of September," Karl Sommarøy repeated, intrigued. "What the hell's happening then?"

"That's what I would like to know," Hanne said. "Now we're leaving."

She folded the sheet of paper neatly, pushing it inside another plastic bag before tucking everything inside her pocket. Her headache was really plaguing her, but she no longer felt so tired.

23

"A girl!"

Billy T. crashed through the door, and before Hanne had gotten as far as looking up, he had yanked her from her chair.

"A beautiful, black-haired girl who's the spitting image of me!"

He screwed up his eyes and gave her a smacker of a kiss before returning her to her seat. Then he produced two enormous cigars and offered her one.

"She was born at Karen and Håkon's house," he roared, puffing energetically to get the cigar properly alight before sitting down himself. "I was the midwife, Hanne! It was . . ." The smoke poured out of his mouth in a gust of satisfaction. "It was the damned loveliest thing I've ever experienced. Ever. But—"

He stared at Hanne.

"Congratulations," she said dully. "Brilliant. The girl, I mean."

"What on earth is wrong with you?"

He stubbed out the cigar with vigorous movements before leaning closer to her.

"Are you—" He leaned back without warning. "You've spoken to Cecilie," he said slowly.

"I speak to Cecilie every day," she said in a dismissive tone. "How is Tone-Marit?"

"Nothing is certain yet, Hanne."

"Certain? Isn't she well?"

"I'm not talking about Tone-Marit. I mean Cecilie. The cancer."

Hanne Wilhelmsen fiddled with the cigar.

"So you knew about it," she said sharply. "That's great. That you and Cecilie can share secrets, I mean. Fantastic. Maybe you could start sharing some secrets with me as well. For instance, you could begin by telling me where you were. You should have been here five hours ago."

The cigar broke in two. She took one-half in each hand and crushed both of them. There was a dry crunch of tobacco leaves.

"Hanne Wilhelmsen!" Billy T. rolled his eyes and tried to grasp one of her hands. She pulled it away brusquely and demonstratively as shreds of tobacco scattered in every direction. "Hanne," he said again, trying to make eye contact with her. "I really want to talk to you about this. Please!"

If she had returned his gaze, she would have caught sight of something she had never seen in his eyes before: a desperation bordering on fury. His eyes had turned gray, and his mouth was hanging half open, seemingly discouraged, as if he did not know whether he should speak or remain silent.

"Please," he repeated in earnest.

Hanne rubbed her hands together. "I understand you have good reasons for being late. Forget it. All the same, I'd like you to . . ." Handing him a sheet of paper, she stared out the window. "I'd like an overview of every grotesque murder in the past decade. In the whole of Norway. By that I mean mutilation, severed extremities . . . that sort of thing. I want details, perpetrators, motives, the outcome of the cases, and so on. ASAP. Which means immediately."

The room fell totally silent for several seconds before Billy T. stood up abruptly and hammered both fists on the table. The ashtray jumped and tumbled onto the floor.

"It's broken," Hanne said tersely. "I'll expect you to get me a new one."

Billy T. drew himself up to his full height. White blotches appeared around his flared nostrils. His cheeks were red and mottled, and his eyes welled up with tears.

"You're pathetic," he spat. "You're fucking *pathetic*, Hanne Wilhelmsen."

"Right now I can't waste much time on what you think of me," she replied, pushing her hair away from her forehead. "I'm particularly interested in decapitations. If there are any, that is. Go further back in time if necessary. And you can ask Karl to investigate Ståle Salvesen. I want to know all there is to know about that guy. And by that I mean more than you've managed to gather for that . . ."

She snapped her fingers at the two sheets containing sparse information from the Population Register.

". . . that *pathetic* report there. And one more thing . . ." She looked him in the eye. He was trembling with rage, and she felt a stab of satisfaction when she noted that the tears in his eyes were threatening to spill over. "From now on I suggest we keep our private lives to ourselves. At least during office hours."

She smiled briefly and made a peremptory hand signal to indicate that he could leave. "Dismissed," she said insistently when he made no move to obey.

"You fucking need help," he finally spluttered as he approached the door.

"Lovely news about your daughter," Hanne said. "I really mean that. Say hi to Tone-Marit for me and tell her I said that."

The noise of the slamming door sang in her ears.

It was Tuesday afternoon, March 9, and Hanne Wilhelmsen swore a silent oath. She would solve the mystery of Sigurd Halvorsrud's beheaded wife within three weeks. Four at most.

24

The girl had been both cheap and willing. It had all been accomplished quickly. Evald Bromo now stood on the quayside, staring intently into the black waters.

He was not brave enough.

The craving had been too intense. Margaret thought he was at a seminar. He had walked the streets for twenty-four hours, and although he had tried to avoid the city center for as long as possible, he had finally ended up there. Afterward he had gone to the harbor. A narrow strip of light was beginning to appear in the east, and Evald Bromo had started to get the days mixed up. He wheeled around and raised his eyes. The City Hall towered above him: dark gray contours against a black, starless sky. What he wanted to do most of all was turn back. He tried to work up the courage to retrace the required steps along the quayside and down the fjord.

He could not do it.

There were five months and twenty-two days left until the first of September, and he still could not keep away from little girls.

25

She wondered why hospitals always had that hospital odor. Perhaps it was like garbage. Regardless of what was placed in a trash can liner, whether it be meat or vegetables, diapers or fish, strong cheese or empty milk cartons, after a few hours it always smelled the same.

Hanne Wilhelmsen had called in sick. As she replaced the receiver after delivering the message to Beate in the front office, she swallowed down something resembling shame. She had not said a word about Cecilie.

Cecilie had protested. It was not necessary for Hanne to be present. There wasn't really anything she could do. It was a waste of time. Hanne had sat on the edge of her bed late last night; the nurse had rather brusquely tried to prevent her from entering the room where Cecilie lay almost merging into the white bedcovers.

"Just be here when I wake," she had requested, stroking her fingers along the back of Hanne's left hand. "That won't be until late in the afternoon. Why don't you leave it until then?"

All the same, she smiled when Hanne turned up at seven o'clock on Wednesday morning. Her face showed something of its old cheerfulness; one eye closed more than the other because her smile was slightly crooked.

"You came," was all she managed to say before an aide arrived to transport her for the operation. "You came after all."

Hanne Wilhelmsen shut her eyes on the chaotic thoughts that had already made her feel exhausted even though it was not yet ten o'clock. She had made an effort to read a crime novel for half an hour, but it was unrealistic and boring. Then she tried to concentrate on Doris Flo Halvorsrud's murder, but all she could summon up was an image of the headless woman surrounded by a vast black darkness.

She must have slept in spite of her uncomfortable position, because the voice startled her.

"So this is where you are."

Police Chief Hans Mykland was wearing a red checked flannel shirt and blue trousers that must have been from the seventies. The crease line was stitched, and across the thigh, where the fabric stretched as he sat down in the chair beside her, the material was threadbare and pilled. She hardly recognized him.

"I don't always wear my uniform," he said with a smile. "I thought I couldn't really come here without changing."

Hanne Wilhelmsen stared at his shoes without uttering a word. They were brown and must have been bought at the same time as the trousers. She felt faint and could not fathom how he had discovered where she was.

"When do they reckon it'll be over?" he said, looking around. "Is there a coffee machine anywhere near here?"

Hanne remained silent. The Police Chief put his hand on her thigh. Hanne Wilhelmsen, who hated being touched by anyone she did not know well, shook her head faintly at the reassurance that his hand conveyed. It warmed her, and she felt an overwhelming urge to slip back into sleep.

"Here," he said, offering her a candy. "You'd probably prefer a smoke, but you'll have to make do with this. Have they said anything about when they'll be finished?"

"About two o'clock," Hanne Wilhelmsen mumbled, rubbing her face, still confused about why the Police Chief was there. "Approximately, if everything goes to plan."

"How are you doing?"

He pulled back his hand, and wriggled in his seat in an effort to make eye contact. She would not cooperate, and covered her face with her hands.

"All right," she said into her palms, sounding muffled.

The Police Chief chuckled, a soft laugh that echoed faintly off the concrete walls.

"Have you ever admitted that you're *not* doing fine?" he asked. "Have you ever answered, for example, 'No, at this point I'm feeling really awful'?"

Hanne did not reply, but she did at least remove her hands and force some kind of smile. They sat in prolonged silence.

"My boy died," Hans Christian Mykland said suddenly. "My eldest son. He died four years ago. I thought I would die too. Quite literally. I didn't sleep. I didn't eat. When I cast my mind back to the months after Simen's death, I don't really think I *felt* so very much, either. I spent most of my time concentrating on . . ." He laughed softly again, and Hanne looked at him at last. "I focused on my skin," he said.

"Your kin?" Hanne asked, clearing her throat.

"No. My *skin*. I went around trying to touch the limits of my own being. Take *hold* of it, I mean. It was quite fascinating. I could lie all night long, probing it piece by piece, inch by inch. I expect I had some kind of need to—"

Hanne Wilhelmsen shuddered, and he stopped.

"Strange, you saying that," she murmured. "I know what you mean."

The hospital aide parked a bed directly in front of them. An old woman was lying asleep in the midst of all the snowy whiteness, a cannula firmly taped to her skinny hand with its large, prominent veins. Saline fluid dripped from a transparent plastic bag down into the woman's arm. Her eyes fluttered open when the bed came to a halt. Hanne thought for an instant that she could detect a smile meant only for her.

She was so beautiful.

Hanne Wilhelmsen could not take her eyes off her. The woman's hair was brilliant white and pulled back from her narrow face. She had high cheekbones, and in the almost imperceptible moment when she may have smiled and had certainly opened her eyes, Hanne noted that her eyes were a paler blue than any she had seen before. The skin that stretched across her facial features seemed so soft that Hanne felt an urge to stand up and stroke her cheek.

She did so.

The woman opened her eyes again, properly this time, before raising her free hand and placing it carefully on top of Hanne's. The aide returned and wheeled the woman away.

"And then there were the two of us," Mykland said, mostly to himself.

Hanne remained on her feet, watching the bed until it disappeared around a corner down the corridor.

"How did you know I was here?" she asked in an undertone, without resuming her seat. "Why are you here?"

"Sit down," Mykland said.

She ignored his instruction.

"Sit down," he repeated, this time in a harsher voice.

He was her superior officer. She sat down, still without looking at him.

"You can take compassionate leave," he said. "It is hereby granted. For as long as you want. You—"

He checked himself, and Hanne completed the sentence for him.

"Deserve it," she spat out. "I *deserve* it. Do you have any idea how bloody sick I am of always hearing that I *deserve* some time off? Isn't that just a pretty euphemism for *you all* deserving some time off from *me*?"

"Now you're being paranoid, Hanne."

His voice sounded dejected as he continued. "Can't you simply accept that people think you're smart? And that's the sum total. And that people in the police station—"

"The district," she interrupted crossly.

". . . that people think it's only right that you take a few days off in this situation?"

Hanne inhaled sharply, as if she wanted to say something. But she held her breath, shaking her head.

"You have a gigantic communication problem," he said quietly. "You should know that you're the very first colleague I've mentioned my son's death to. You gave me no response whatsoever. I can live with that. Can you?"

"Sorry," Hanne mumbled. "I'm really sorry. But I'd really prefer to be left alone."

"No."

He put his hand on her thigh again. Now, feeling nothing but disgust at his touch, she stiffened.

"That's not what you want," Mykland continued. "What you want most of all is for someone to talk to you. Listen to you. *Get you to talk.* That's what I'm trying to do. I haven't had much success."

The hospital smell suddenly became overwhelming. Hanne Wilhelmsen's body tensed even further; there was a pain in her thigh, and she did her utmost to stretch it to make the man remove his hand. A wave of nausea coursed through her, and she swallowed only with difficulty.

"I want to work," she said through gritted teeth. "All I want is to be left in peace and allowed to get on with my job. I have . . ." She stood up abruptly, and faced him as she counted on her fingers and hissed, ". . . a knife killing. A bar fight. A racially motivated attack. And on top of all that, the case of a decapitated woman that I don't have a clue about. Have you *any idea* how much we have to do in the department? Have you any idea about me and what is best for Hanne Wilhelmsen personally at this very minute?" When she spoke her name, she tapped her right forefinger on her chest so hard that it hurt. "No. You've no idea. *I* on the other hand, *I* know that all I can do as things stand just now is *get on with my job! Cope with my job. Can you understand that?*"

The words reverberated off the walls. A Pakistani couple sitting along the corridor turned inquisitively in their direction. A nurse slowed down and looked as if he intended to stop and ask if he could be of assistance. When he met Hanne Wilhelmsen's gaze, he decided to mind his own business and picked up speed again.

"Do you believe in God, Hanne?"

"Really!" She slapped herself on the forehead in an exaggerated, mocking gesture. "That's why you came! A little missionary expedition to Ullevål to save Hanne Wilhelmsen's lost soul. No. I don't believe in God. And he doesn't particularly believe in me either."

For lack of anything better to do, she began to walk. The Police Chief stood up slowly and followed her.

"You're wrong," he said almost inaudibly behind her back. "I was just interested."

She increased her pace but did not really know where she was headed. When she finally reached the end of the corridor, she turned on her heel and made an attempt to retrace her steps. Mykland stopped her.

"I won't bother you any longer. I only came to talk to you. To show you that I care. I imagined, wrongly, perhaps"—a self-conscious smile spread over his face—"that I know something about how you're feeling. But you don't know me. This was an effort to put that right. For what it's worth, I'm all ears if you should change your mind. You should at least talk to Billy T."

Hanne made another attempt to walk past him, but did not succeed.

"That guy is as fond of you as it's possible for someone who's not a relative to be," Mykland commented. "You must see that. And value it. Maybe even make use of it. Now I'll be on my way."

His hand just brushed her shoulder as he let her go. He stood there, following her with his eyes.

"Billy T.," Hanne muttered contemptuously, rummaging furiously in her bag for the second-rate crime novel.

When she looked up, the Police Chief was gone. The Pakistani couple had been joined by a small child, who was clambering on two vacant beds placed against the wall opposite. Hanne Wilhelmsen struggled to make sense of the emotion she experienced when she realized that Mykland had not actually pursued her. Most of all, it felt like disappointment.

26

The Chief Editor of *Aftenposten* was one of those people who rejoiced in the myriad opportunities made possible by technology. As early as 1984, she had invested in her first computer—a so-called portable machine from Toshiba. It would be more accurate to call it transportable than actually portable, and it had cost more than sixty thousand kroner. As soon as something called the Internet came into existence, she had arranged to get connected. She was so early on the scene that there was hardly anyone to send emails to.

Now she received over a hundred emails a day. She had repeatedly tried to persuade her contacts—and not least her staff—to rank their communications according to how urgent they were. A flag or an exclamation mark, it was all the same to her, but the workday would be considerably improved if people were more disciplined about clarifying the contents of their emails.

Almost in a dream, she sat going through that morning's inbox. She had just discovered a run in the left leg of her tights, but the third desk drawer from the top, where she usually had several spare pairs, was empty. She tugged distractedly at the hem of her skirt, making rapid keystrokes as she worked her way through the list without really doing any more than skimming the majority of them.

One message made her stop in her tracks. The subject box stated, "You should be concerned." The email was short: "You ought to investigate what is wrong with Evald Bromo. He has been upset about something lately. As his Chief Editor, you should ask him whether something is bothering him."

She read the message twice before shrugging and clicking the inbox closed. Then she looked at the clock. She was ten minutes late for a meeting.

On her way out of the office, she twisted around to check her tights. The nail varnish had not succeeded in stopping the run, and now it had widened and run all the way down to her high-heeled black shoes. She suppressed a colorful oath.

As far as she was aware, there was nothing the matter with Evald Bromo.

27

"IKEA," Billy T. said derisively, scanning the room. "This is quite different from your old office at Aker Brygge!"

He sat down warily in the vacant chair, as if not entirely sure whether it would bear his weight. Then he produced a half-liter plastic bottle of soda from the pocket of his voluminous jacket.

"But very comfortable," he said as he slurped, holding out the bottle to Karen Borg. "Do you want some?"

"No thanks."

She swiveled from side to side in her wide office chair as she sipped a cup of tea. Since she had resigned from a renowned commercial-law practice with a fashionable address and expensive furnishings from Expo-Nova in order to start out on her own without any help other than a secretary obtained through a public agency, she had not touched coffee. There was a certain symbolism about it all. At Aker Brygge, everyone drank cappuccinos. Here, in this bright, personal room with green potted plants and a portfolio as diverse as a general store, it had to be tea.

"Sad about Cecilie," she said, shaking her head slowly. "Really dreadful. I just wish I had known about this earlier."

"It wouldn't have been any use," Billy T. replied, yawning. "It's totally impossible to speak to Hanne. Besides, she didn't know about it herself until Monday. I spoke to Cecilie by phone yesterday. She is having surgery . . ." He fished out a pocket watch and squinted at the hands on the dial. ". . . right now."

They fell silent. Billy T. noticed a faint scent of vanilla and leaned over to the cup Karen Borg was holding between her hands. He smiled feebly and glanced out the window, where a man was standing on scaffolding and wiping a dirty cloth over the glass. He waved his squeegee cheerfully at Billy T. and dropped his cleaning rag in his haste. It did not faze him, and he pulled out a new cloth from a bucket of water that should have been replenished three stories earlier.

"How serious is it really?" Karen eventually asked, putting her cup aside.

"They'll know that today, as far as I understand. But don't phone Hanne. She should be locked in a cage. Dangerous to approach right now. She'll more than likely bite your ear off."

The window cleaner was finished and waved goodbye politely as he was hoisted up to the next floor. His work had hardly been worth the effort, since he'd left streaks of dirt like prison bars across the glass.

"Muffin bag," Billy T. said suddenly, placing a folder with a pink cover on Karen's desk.

"What?"

"The money was wrapped in a muffin bag from Hansen the baker's. Five fingerprints. Two are unidentified. The three others belong to Halvorsrud. So it wasn't very smart of the guy to deny any knowledge of the cash."

"Having his hands on a bag of muffins hardly proves anything," Karen Borg said tersely. "Did you find any prints on the money?"

"Yes. Lots of different ones. None identified. But they were all used notes, so that in itself isn't so strange."

He spent some time rubbing his scalp vigorously with his knuckles. A cloud of dry skin flakes momentarily encircled his head like a halo in the light from outside.

"It's not my job to give advice to your client," he said, picking up the soda bottle again. "But wouldn't it be an idea to provide an explanation that's a little more credible? Everything, *absolutely* everything, points to him having killed his wife. Couldn't he mention something about sudden madness, say that something snapped in him when she wanted a divorce or something like that? Then he'll get ten years in jail, out after six. More or less. And make it to his daughter's wedding, at least."

"But he didn't do it," Karen Borg remarked, yet again turning down the offer of some lukewarm soda. "It's as simple as that. That's the way he sees it. And that's what I must respond to. And there's one thing I don't know if you've considered."

Billy T.'s eyes opened wide in a shocked grimace, as if the mere idea that something in this case had not been carefully mulled over and analyzed by the police was outrageous.

"Let's assume that Ståle Salvesen *did* take his own life last Monday. Perhaps Halvorsrud was mistaken. He believed . . . he *believes* that Ståle Salvesen is the murderer, but actually it was someone else. Someone who looks like him. Either by some odd, ill-fated coincidence, or because—"

"Or because the murderer *wanted* to look like Salvesen," Billy T. finished for her, draining the remains of the soda. "Of course we've considered that. We still are, for that matter. But *why*?"

"You spend too much time with Hanne," Karen said drily. "Besides, you're the ones who need to find the motive. That's not my job. Fortunately."

"How are the children doing, anyway?" Billy T. asked. "It wasn't exactly much fun hauling the boy in for an interview, with his mother dead and his father behind bars for God knows how long."

"The boys are doing fine," Karen said, wrinkling her brow as if something was needling her. "Thea not so good. According to my brother, who's an old friend of the family, she's completely inconsolable. The strange thing is that she seems far more upset about her father being in prison than about her mother's death. She's stopped eating. Refuses to go to school. Hardly says a word. Floods of tears and wild rages, and demands to see her father. Wants her father home. Barely mentions her mother."

"Impossible to predict people's reactions in such situations," Billy T.

said with a yawn. "Especially youngsters. I have to go. I'll make sure the folder is supplemented in the fullness of time."

As he placed his fist on the door knob, Karen said in an undertone, obviously mainly to herself, "Maybe Håkon—"

Billy T. turned round and gave her a long look.

"Yes," he said finally. "Maybe Håkon is the one to speak to Hanne. In any case, it's certainly not me."

"What is it we really see in her?" Karen Borg asked, still speaking into thin air. "Why are we so fond of Hanne? She's sulky and . . . grumpy. Frequently, at least. Introverted and reserved. We're all at her beck and call. Why is that?"

Billy T. ran his hand over the door knob.

"Because she's not always like that. Perhaps we . . . When she suddenly opens up and . . . I don't know. I just know that she's my best friend."

"You admire her. Unreservedly. We all do. Her cleverness. That obstinate intellect of hers. But . . . Why are we so damned vulnerable as far as she is concerned? Why—"

"I care about her. You do too. There isn't an explanation for everything in this world of ours."

His voice was suddenly dismissive and brusque, like an echo of Hanne herself. Then he raised his fingers abruptly to his brow and headed off.

28

The time was twenty-five minutes past twelve on March 10, 1999. Karianne Holbeck already had a seven-hour workday behind her and was attempting to massage the back of her neck. When she flexed her arm, she realized that she must have put on more weight. She also noticed it with her jeans; they strained so much that she could no longer sit with her top fly button fastened. It annoyed her no end. On the fourth of January, she had shown great optimism and determination by purchasing a six-month subscription to the local gym, but to date she had been there only once.

The phone rang again.

"Holbeck," she barked into the receiver.

"Good afternoon. My name is—"

Police Sergeant Karianne Holbeck did not catch the name. Not even part of it. All she picked up was that it had something to do with a foreigner.

"What's this about?" she said indifferently as she took out the fitness center brochure, making an effort to find out how late in the evening it stayed open.

"I'm phoning about that attorney," the voice continued. "The one they're writing about in the newspapers. That guy called Halvorsrud."

"Halvorsrud," Holbeck murmured, looking at the clock. "He's not an attorney. He's the Chief Public Prosecutor."

"I'm from Turkey, you understand."

The man persevered. "I have a vegetable shop in Grünerløkka."

The gym stayed open until eight. So there was at least some hope of doing a session there that evening.

"You understand," the voice on the phone insisted. "Last year, I was reported to the police. Just a piece of nonsense, you know, but they said that I hadn't paid my tax properly. Something wrong with the accounts as well, they said. Then I got a phone call from Halvorsrud. He could help me, he said. He would meet me one evening. He would talk to me about how much it would cost to put . . . to put my affairs in order, he said. I didn't completely understand. My wife, she said no."

Karianne Holbeck's interest had increased dramatically. She hunted desperately for a pen, without success.

"Did he *say* that he was the person on the phone? Did he *introduce* himself as Sigurd Halvorsrud?"

"Yes, that was what he said. He didn't say what he was, an attorney or anything, but I wrote down the name. I have the piece of paper here."

Karianne Holbeck cleared her throat, angrily pulling out drawer after drawer to find something to write with. No luck.

"I don't know if this is something for the police, but I thought I—"

"Can you come here?" Holbeck interrupted him. "I'd like to speak to you in person."

She glanced at the Donald Duck clock that was threatening to fall off the desk. "Two o'clock?"

"No, I'm really, really busy now. I can come on Monday. Monday at ten, for instance. I can come and ask for—"

"Holbeck," Karianne said too distinctly, as if speaking to someone hard of hearing. "Ka-ri-anne Hol-beck. But wait a moment . . ."

She put down the receiver and stormed out to the front office in search of a writing implement.

"Hello," she said breathlessly into the phone when she returned. "Are you there?"

He was not. All she could hear was a nerve-racking, monotonous engaged signal. She pressed the button desperately, but the line was still completely dead.

"Bloody foreigner," she spluttered, dangling the handset.

Then she slapped her hand over her mouth, hoping to God that no one had heard her through the open door on to the corridor.

All she could do was hope that the man would in fact turn up on Monday, which was far from certain. Karianne Holbeck had considerable experience with foreigners, who were thoroughly unreliable. She was in no way racist. As far as she was concerned, all people were equal. The problem was simply that Turks and Iranians, Pakistanis and North Africans, Vietnamese and Latin Americans could not be depended upon. Monday or Tuesday, at one o'clock or five, it was impossible to say whether the guy would make contact at all.

Karianne Holbeck could not even remember what sort of shop the guy ran. She thought she had heard the name Grünerløkka, but she was not sure. He was definitely Turkish. As if that was any help.

"This is what happens when my workday begins at half past six," she muttered in irritation, realizing that she had committed a blunder of enormous proportions.

29

It suddenly dawned on Eivind Torsvik that he had not used his voice for a couple weeks. It was almost as if he had forgotten what it sounded like. He stretched out on the sofa and tried to concentrate on remembering what tone it had. He knew he sounded younger than his years. His intonation was clear and melodious, with a touch of something outlandish that could give the false impression he was not actually Norwegian. A teacher at elementary school had once come across him when as a young boy he had broken into the gymnasium to spend the night there. Eivind was singing old Eagles songs in an effort to stave off his fear. The teacher had been dumbstruck, and Eivind suspected he had stood there listening for some time before he finally stepped out of the shadows. The man had said something about Eivind being exceptionally musical. He was probably just trying to be friendly. But Eivind had stood up and taken to his heels. Now, when he cast his mind back and tried to recall what he had done afterward, he could not remember. Since that night, he hadn't sung a single note.

It was pleasant lying there like that.

He dozed off into a peculiar state somewhere between sleep and wakefulness. Of course, he could have just gone ahead and said something. But that would be too easy. The motes dancing behind his eyelids gathered slowly into a central red point. There. That was it. He spoke slowly and distinctly. "Now it's coming together nicely. Soon we'll have them."

His voice was exactly as he remembered it. Clear and a tad childish, it fitted the nickname he had been given in prison very well.

"I am the Angel," Eivind Torsvik said with satisfaction, before falling fast asleep.

30

"My goodness," Håkon Sand said, "you're here?"

He found himself looking at his watch. It was almost midnight. He could not understand what Police Chief Hans Christian Mykland was doing outside the low-rise brick apartment block in Lille Tøyen where Hanne and Cecilie lived. Even less so at this time of night.

"You're looking good," the Police Chief said cheerfully, clapping Public Prosecutor Håkon Sand affably on the shoulder. "Are you being well looked after over there in Hambros plass?"

Håkon mumbled dismissively. He really had no idea why the Police Chief was there. He stuck a finger in his ear and scratched frantically.

"I thought I should pay a visit to our mutual friend," Mykland said, tossing his head in the direction of the second-floor window. "Just wondering how she's getting on."

The joviality suddenly vanished. In the dim light from a streetlamp in the driveway, Håkon Sand noticed a concern on the Police Chief's face that he could not interpret. The man looked older than Håkon thought he was. It could have been because of the grayish-yellow semidarkness, or even the shabby beige parka.

"Do you know each other?" he blurted out. "I mean . . . Do you know Hanne socially?"

The Police Chief smiled, shaking his head only slightly.

"That would be something of an exaggeration. I'm just concerned. She isn't having an easy time at the moment. But . . ." He shrugged and gave a broad smile. ". . . now that you're here, Hanne's in capable hands. I'll go. Good night."

Håkon murmured some kind of goodbye and stood watching the Police Chief as he jogged the 20 or 30 yards across to an old yellow Saab. The car protested noisily, but after two explosive bangs from the exhaust, it moved reluctantly uphill, leaving a trail of coal-black smoke. Håkon gave a deep sigh as he pressed the entry buzzer.

No one answered.

He pressed again, for so long that he began to feel impolite. So he took his finger off the button, stepped back three paces, and peered up at the kitchen window on the second floor. Behind the curtains the ceiling light was on. Apart from that, the apartment block was in total darkness, except for a light someone had forgotten to switch off in the basement. A rectangular window shed a cold-blue light on his feet.

She was at home. Håkon was sure of that. He had called the hospital. A friendly nurse had confirmed that Hanne Wilhelmsen had left a sleeping Cecilie Vibe around eleven o'clock.

"For fuck's sake, Hanne."

Angrily, he pressed the buzzer, this time going beyond what could be considered good manners. He kept his finger on the button for what seemed an eternity, and was just about to concede defeat when the lock suddenly buzzed. He tugged at the door and found it open.

He didn't really understand why he was feeling so anxious. His heart was pounding in a way he had not experienced since he had prosecuted his first case in the Supreme Court. When he opened his palms, he could see the perspiration glistening on the lines on them. Håkon Sand did not know what it was he feared.

Hanne Wilhelmsen was an old, good friend. He could not quite grasp why he felt terrified as he approached the door with its brass plaque: "HW & CV."

Matters did not improve when she opened the door.

Her face was so tear-stained she was unrecognizable. Her eyes were two narrow lines in all the puffiness, and her lower lip was trembling so ferociously that Håkon could not focus on anything else. He stared at a drop of spit that quivered on a painful-looking crack in the middle of Hanne's lip; now it let go and ran down the dimple in her chin. Her cheeks were flushed, and it looked as though her entire frame had shrunk. Her hands were hanging lifelessly by her thighs, and her shoulders disappeared altogether inside her far too large college sweater.

He could not think of anything to say. Instead he sat down on the stairs. The concrete step was icy cold through the seat of his trousers. He rubbed his hands together, no longer able to face looking at Hanne.

"Come in," she said finally, in a voice he had never heard before.

He stood up clumsily, breathless, and lingered in the hallway without removing his jacket, even though Hanne had disappeared into the living room.

The apartment smelled of Cecilie. The scent of Boss Woman filled the air. He sniffed the room. The fragrance was unmistakable. Conspicuous, too. Then he spotted an almost empty bottle on the hall table. He stepped hesitantly in the direction of the living room. The perfume was even stronger in there.

"You've emptied the bottle," he said, biting his lip.

Hanne did not reply. She sat erect in an armchair, without reclining against the back. Her hands were on her lap, open, as if expecting a gift. She was staring at something so intently that Håkon peered to see what it was. A blank, white wall.

At last he wriggled out of his heavy jacket and left it lying at his feet. Then he crossed the room slowly and sat down on the sofa. Absentmindedly he picked up an orange from the fruit bowl and sat juggling it from one hand to the other.

"How did it go?" he finally managed to say.

"Game over," Hanne said unequivocally. "Metastasis in the liver. Nothing can be done."

The orange split open. Lukewarm juice ran down Håkon's hands and dripped huge stains onto his trouser leg. Setting aside the abused piece of fruit, he held his sticky hands helplessly above his knees and burst into tears.

At long last Hanne shifted her gaze.

She looked at him. When he straightened his back to take a breath, he turned his face to hers.

"You'll have to leave," she said. "I want you to go."

He made an unrestrained effort to laugh, and struggled to catch his breath as snot and tears ran down his face.

"I'm crying," he sniffed as he wiped his face with his sleeve. "I'm crying for Cecilie. But most of all I'm crying for you. You must be feeling bloody worse than I can even imagine. You're being an idiot, Hanne, and I can't understand—"

The rest was lost in a coughing fit.

"You need to go home to your family," Hanne said, brushing the hair from her forehead with a stiff, slow movement of her right hand. "It's late."

He momentarily gazed at her in disbelief, before getting resolutely to his feet. He bumped his knee on the edge of the table and swore vehemently.

"Yes, I should," he screamed in a falsetto. "Yes, I should go home now. You just sit there. Just refuse to speak to me. Do whatever the *fuck you want!* But I'm not going. I'm staying here."

For want of something better to do, he pulled the sleeves of his sweater up and down in a rage. He sobbed like an overgrown child, and got stinging juice in his eyes when he attempted to literally hold back his tears.

"*Goddamn it, Hanne!* What is it that's happened to you?"

Later he had difficulty explaining what came next. He certainly didn't understand it at the time. It all came as such a surprise that whenever he tried to talk about it over the next few days, he struggled to describe how she had actually behaved. It was all so illogical, so unexpected, and so unlike Hanne Wilhelmsen that he kept thinking he must have dreamed it. Only when he later touched his tender breastbone did he acknowledge that she had in fact attacked him.

She rose from her chair, stepped nearer to him, and delivered a forceful slap to his ear. Then she punched him in the belly with a clenched fist and, sinking onto her knees, hammered away at his legs. Finally, she lay down with her head between her knees and her hands folded around her neck.

"Hanne," he whispered, crouching down. "Hanne. Let me help you a little."

Unresisting, she let him pull her up. She allowed his arms to hold her. Her head fell onto his shoulder. He was aware of a powerful whiff of Cecilie and suddenly realized she had emptied the perfume bottle over herself.

Håkon had no idea how long they stood there. All he could do was hold her. Gradually she grew heavier. Eventually he realized that she had fallen asleep. Carefully he let one arm slide around her waist. Like a sleepwalker, she accompanied him to the bedroom, where she lay on her stomach, fully clothed. He stayed listening to her breathing while struggling to make his own follow the same rhythm. Then he lay down quietly beside her, tucked a quilt around each of them, and closed his eyes.

"I'm scared for myself."

Håkon Sand woke with a start and felt a stab of alarm before recalling where he was. Hanne was lying in the same position as when she had gone to bed, on her stomach with her arms by her sides and her face averted. The quilt was lying on the floor beside her.

"I feel trapped inside what was once myself. Inside everything I have done. Inside everything I regret."

Håkon coughed feebly, propping himself up with his left arm and resting his face on his hand. His right hand was lying on the small of her back. He made tentative circling caresses.

"It's as if I want to escape from myself. It's as if I'm trying to run from . . ." She sighed and gasped for breath. ". . . run from my own shadow. It's impossible. I want to erase everything and start all over again. Now it's too late. It's been too late for years."

She sniffed faintly and turned on her side, with her back to him. He was unsure whether it was an attempt to move his hand away. Still he said nothing. The room was stuffy and stale, and in the crack of light from underneath the door, he saw the specks of dust dancing. In the far distance he heard a motorcycle double-shift. Then everything was quiet again, and he closed his eyes. All of a sudden, Hanne continued.

"Now I'm on my own, I can only think about everything that's fallen apart. Friendship. Love. Life. Everything."

"But—" Håkon began gently.

"Don't say anything," she said softly. "Don't say a word, please. Just be here."

She curled up into a fetal position, and he could not resist stroking her hair.

"You're right," she whispered. "I am an idiot. A . . . a destroyer. Someone who destroys things. The only thing I can do in life is be a police officer. That helps right now. It's a great help. Cecilie is probably pleased about that."

Gingerly, he leaned over her and retrieved the quilt from the floor, before creeping closer to her curled body. He felt her spine against his belly and was struck by how skinny she had become. He pressed her close and whispered meaningless words into her hair. Her hand clasped his, and only when the grip was released did he realize she had fallen asleep again. He could barely hear her breathing.

31

For more than half an hour she had lain there staring at the ceiling. She counted the seconds to see how long she could avoid blinking. Her reflexes won out over her willpower each and every time. Cautiously, she turned over in the bed. Håkon's thinning hair, sweaty, was plastered to his forehead. He was sleeping deeply and awkwardly, still fully clothed. The quilt was rolled like a sausage over his hips, and Hanne noticed that he had not even taken off his shoes. His mouth was open and he was snoring. Probably that was what had woken her. She had remembered nothing. The first flicker of wakefulness had been like every other morning: vacant—neither good nor bad. Then yesterday had come tumbling over her, and she had struggled to breathe. Devastated, she had tried to keep her eyes open forever. She could not even manage to do that.

She glanced at the clock.

Half past six.

She did not want to shower. It was as if the pungent odor of sweat and stale perfume that did not belong to her—though it pierced her heart every time she drew breath—was a suitable punishment. At least the start of it. She hesitated briefly before deciding not to write a note. Instead she placed the spare key in plain sight on the hall table. Still in the clothes she'd not only worn for the past twenty-four hours but had also slept in, she jogged the short distance to Grønlandsleiret 44.

The police headquarters was there, its curved gray edifice immutable as ever.

As she swiped her pass through the reader, causing the metal door across the staff entrance on the west side to open, it felt like scrambling aboard a ramshackle lifeboat. She moved through the corridors, finally emerging at the gigantic foyer that soared all the way up to the sixth story, but instead of heading straight for the elevator, she stepped out into the middle of the floor. The vast space was deserted, apart from an elderly dark-skinned man in a blue-and-yellow tracksuit who was washing the floor behind the counter in the southeast corner of the building. He sent a nod and a smile in Hanne's direction, but received no response.

The police headquarters was not yet really ready to face the day. Now and again a door was flung open on one of the upper floors, and from the crime desk at the main entrance, muffled cries could be heard through the bulletproof glass walls. But for the most part, silence reigned in the building, a silence Hanne usually loved.

She did not even feel tired. Worn out, perhaps; her body was stiff, but her mind felt clear and cold and focused.

Four piles of documents lay on her desk, neatly stacked side by side, green and pink folders alternating. She placed her cup of black coffee at the far end of the table and lit a cigarette. The first drag made her extremely dizzy. In a strange way, it felt pleasant, like an anesthetizing high.

She selected the bulkiest folder first.

Karianne Holbeck had collected the most important witness statements into one bundle. At the front of the folder was an overview listing the people who had been interviewed and the main points of what they had said. Hanne Wilhelmsen flicked slowly through the sheaf of papers and stopped at interview number three.

Witness Sigrid Riis considers herself the deceased's best friend. They had known each other since they were fourteen, and they were bridesmaids at each other's weddings.

The sentence reminded Hanne that there were less than three months left until she herself would be best woman at Billy T.'s nuptials. She was uncertain about what that said about the depth of a friendship. She stubbed out her cigarette. It struck her that Cecilie would soon be waking up after her sedated night. She rubbed her thumb and forefinger over the corners of her mouth and licked her lips before continuing to read.

The witness states that the deceased, Doris Flo Halvorsrud, was an outgoing and happy person. The witness cannot imagine that anyone would set out to harm the deceased. The witness thinks that the deceased had a normal number of friends and a relatively large circle of acquaintances, especially on account of her husband's profession. The deceased could be temperamental and sometimes obstinate in arguments, but she always had an amusing comment to rescue the situation if anyone felt offended by some pithy remark or other.

The witness says that, on the whole, the deceased seemed content with her marriage. Recently—for the past six months or so—the deceased and the witness had not had as much to do with each other as before. This was mainly because the witness had been living in Copenhagen for five months because she was working at the Steiner School there. When they did meet, the witness was left with the impression that the marriage was "not at its best." Among other things, the deceased had once asked how the witness had coped financially after her divorce (the witness was divorced from her husband eighteen months ago). The topic was not discussed in detail, and the witness does not recall particularly well what was said subsequent to this. On another occasion, the deceased suddenly became annoyed and called her husband "hypocritical." This happened at a dinner the witness and the deceased shared two months ago, during which the witness made a complimentary remark about an in-depth interview with the accused, Halvorsrud. The witness did not think much about the outburst at the time.

The witness says that the deceased was a good mother. She always had time for her children, and had probably sacrificed a great deal of her own career because of them. Her relationship with her two sons, Marius and Preben, was especially good. Thea, her daughter, had "always been a real daddy's girl." The witness says that there was nothing out of the ordinary about that, since it's not unusual for bright girls to be preoccupied with their fathers.

Looking up from the papers, Hanne took a swig of her coffee and thought about her own father. She could barely see the details of his face in her mind's eye any more. Hanne Wilhelmsen was an afterthought and had never felt any connection with her two siblings. She had felt like an outsider since the day she was old enough to think independently. Probably earlier, in fact. When she was eight, she spent the spring building a house in a tree at the foot of the extensive apple orchard. She found planks of wood at building sites and other places nearby. Her neighbor—an old craftsman who was over seventy years old and who made fried pork every Saturday and shared it with the little girl in the blue dungarees—gave her nails and a helping hand now and again. The tree house was beautiful, with real windows that had once been part of a bus. Hanne had placed old rag rugs on the floor and hung a picture of King Olav on the wall. Having something that belonged only to her—something the others in the family hardly bothered to come down and examine closely—had made her realize that she was at her strongest when she was entirely on her own. From then on, she pretty much withdrew from the dusty, academic family home, where, to cap it all, her parents even refused to install a TV set, "because there are so many good books, Hanne."

The witness is shocked by the brutal murder of her friend, but she cannot bring herself to believe that the accused could possibly have done this. In the witness's experience, he has been a considerate husband and father in the main, even if he of course has "had his faults," something the witness does not feel it reasonable to go into in any detail. The witness cannot think of any information other than what is expressed here that might have any relevance to the case.

The interview was signed on every sheet and at the foot of the final page, as required by the regulations.

"An ordinary life," Hanne said to herself in an undertone as she set the statement aside. "Nice man, lovely children, an occasional quarrel."

The coffee had started to go cold and she drained the rest of the cup in a single gulp. The bitter aftertaste lingered on her tongue, and she could feel the sour progress of the liquid down her gullet to a stomach that, if the hidden pain behind her breastbone was anything to go by, craved a better breakfast than smoke and black coffee.

Hanne should have been at the hospital. She should go. Soon.

The bundle from Karl Sommarøy was also tidy and rational. The name "Ståle Salvesen" had been written on the cover with a felt pen in a perpendicular, left-handed script. At the top were the old papers, printouts from the municipal treasurer, and the Population Register. The tax information stretched back a decade and showed that as recently as 1990 Salvesen had earned a personal income of more than eight million kroner. This was followed by an uninteresting, sparse list of current assets and fixtures and fittings. After that, a number of newspaper articles from *Aftenposten*'s digital archive had been taped in, old reports from the time when the world had begun to turn against Ståle Salvesen. Hanne skimmed through them without finding anything that she didn't already know. It struck her that the headlines were larger, more numerous, and far more dramatic than the case warranted, given it was later dropped. "So what else is new?" she said with a sigh.

A photograph from 1989 caught her interest.

Ståle Salvesen was not exactly handsome, but the picture showed a man with a direct gaze and a cocky, crooked smile. His eyes looked straight at the photographer and Hanne shuddered at how alive his face seemed. Salvesen had a high forehead and his thinning hair was combed back; you could discern the shadow of a cleft in his broad chin. The photograph was cropped at chest height but still gave the impression of expensive, understated attire. His suit jacket was dark, and even in a black-and-white newspaper photograph, you could see that his shirt was brilliant white against the striped tie.

There then followed a special report.

As far as Ståle Salvesen's financial background is concerned, you are referred to the enclosed newspaper cuttings and tax assessment printouts. It is obvious that he has seen a great deal of money pass through his hands, and that, after having to leave

Aurora Data because of the investigation into him and the company, he faced huge losses. It will probably take a considerable amount of effort to discover what actually became of the money. This is on hold, pending further instructions. Nowadays he owns little of any worth. His apartment is rented. His car, a 1984 Honda Civic, is hardly worth its scrap value.

Salvesen has evidently lived an extremely reclusive life in recent years. He was divorced from his wife in 1994, after having been separated for a year. It has not proved possible to talk to her as yet. She emigrated to Australia in the spring of 1995, but inquiries at the Norwegian Embassy in Canberra suggest that she may no longer be living there. I am continuing my efforts to get hold of her. She may have changed her name, and there are also some indications that she has obtained Australian citizenship. Their son, Frede Parr (he has adopted his American wife's surname!!!), lives in Houston, Texas, where he works as an IT consultant with an oil company. I spoke to him by phone on Monday, March 8, 1999, at 5:30 p.m. Norwegian time. He seemed annoyed at being disturbed and remarkably unconcerned about his father's possible suicide. He claimed not to have spoken to his father for some considerable time, possibly since 1993, though he couldn't say for certain. Nor had he heard from his mother for a couple of years. He was more definite about the timing of that, since he called her on March 23, 1997, to tell her about the birth of his second son. At that time, Mrs. Salvesen was living in Alice, Australia. Frede Parr has lost her phone number and has no idea whether his mother still goes by the name of Salvesen.

At a question from me about whether he thought his father might have committed suicide, he replied, "The odd thing is that he didn't do it years ago. He lived a wasted life. He was a wasted person."

Further investigations indicate that Salvesen had no social circle whatsoever, with one exception (see below). None of the neighbors on his floor knew him, even though he moved into the block in December 1995. At the social security office they tell me that he hardly said a word on the few occasions he was there in connection with his disability pension. A kind of general amnesia has grown up around Salvesen with regard to his social security claim, and they state that he was almost always on his own. He did not cultivate any hobbies as far as anyone knows, nor is there anything to suggest that he abused alcohol or any other intoxicant.

The apartment block in Vogts gate has a caretaker. Ole Monrad Karlsen is over seventy years old and has remained in the job because no one seems to have the heart to throw him out of the tied apartment. Two of the neighbors informed me that they'd seen Salvesen going in and out of the caretaker's residence on a number of occasions. I spoke to Karlsen on Tuesday, March 9, 1999, at 6:00 p.m.

Karlsen was very dismissive, almost angry. He did not want to talk to me. He slammed the door when I told him I was from the police, and it was only after having a discussion with him for ten minutes through the closed door that he agreed to a short conversation. Nothing came of it. All the same, I would say that there is reason to believe that Karlsen and Salvesen had some sort of friendship. As far as I could judge, there were tears in his eyes and a faint tremble at the corner of his mouth when I told him that to all appearances, Salvesen was dead. He shut his mouth then, too, after having yelled at me nonstop for several minutes.

Hanne reclined in her chair and closed her eyes.

There was something there.

There was a pattern, or perhaps more of a thread. It was fragile and difficult to catch sight of. The noises on the other side of the office door had gotten louder since the time was now approaching nine. They disturbed her and she lost the overall picture.

"Australia," she whispered. "Texas. Vogts gate. A daddy's girl. A hypocritical chief public prosecutor."

The headache struck suddenly and fiercely. She pressed her fingers on her temples; the ringing in her ears was intense and she groaned, "Ullevål."

There was a knock at the door. Hanne did not answer. The knocking was repeated. When the door opened despite the lack of an invitation, Hanne had already put on her jacket.

"Haven't time," she said swiftly to Karianne Holbeck as she slipped past her. "I'll be back in two or three hours."

"But wait," Karianne said. "I've got some—"

Hanne did not listen. She dashed to the elevator, leaving behind only a whiff of perspiration and sour perfume. Karianne Holbeck wrinkled her nose. Hanne Wilhelmsen usually smelled so pleasant.

32

Ole Monrad Karlsen, the caretaker, was upset. He had never liked the police. No more than he liked authorities of any kind. At the age of twenty-three, in 1947, he had come home to Norway having been at sea since he was fifteen, only to be called up for compulsory military service. That could not be right, he'd thought; he'd been torpedoed in 1943 and January 1945 and in his eyes had fulfilled his duty to his fatherland long since. The military authorities took a different view. Ole Monrad Karlsen had to report to the army camp and lost out on a good job ashore that the shipping company had arranged for him.

The police officer thought Ståle was dead.

Although Ole Monrad Karlsen had difficulty believing that the only friend he possessed was no longer alive, he could see the logic in it. So much fell into place. As he sat now at the kitchen table drinking strong black coffee with a dash of eau de vie, he wiped away a tear and mouthed a silent prayer for Ståle Salvesen.

He had been a good man.

Ståle had listened to him. Ståle had persuaded Ole Monrad Karlsen to talk about the war. He had never done that before. Not to anyone, not even to Klara, whom Karlsen had married in 1952 and shared a bed with until one winter's morning in 1979 when she could not be woken. They had not been blessed with children, but with Klara he had come to enjoy a gentle contentment not to be spoiled by futile chat about the catastrophes he had survived so many years ago.

However, the war had crept up on him. It was as if the strength to keep everything at bay had begun to ebb away, and increasingly he was woken suddenly in the middle of the night by terrible dreams about water: an icy-cold ocean of drowning, screaming sailor comrades.

Ståle had listened. Ståle had slipped him a bottle of liquor now and again; not that Karlsen was a drinker, but he had always enjoyed a drop or two in his coffee. Ståle's life had been destroyed by officialdom, just as Karlsen himself had lost the chance of a great shore job because the damned bureaucrats could not understand what it was like to have been a sailor during the war.

Karlsen was pleased that he had not let the policeman into his apartment. He had no business there. Ole Monrad Karlsen had not done anything illegal in his entire life, and ran his life according to his own lights. In a while he would go down to the basement to check that everything was in order. He owed that much to his good friend Ståle Salvesen.

He wiped yet another tear with the back of his weather-beaten hand and poured a generous dram into his coffee cup.

"Peace be with you," he whispered and drank a toast to the empty chair opposite him at the kitchen table. "I hope you're having a good time wherever you are. Yes, indeed, I really do."

33

A glue sniffer crawled along Akersgata. His knees had been ruined by fifteen years of solvent abuse and he had acquired a rocking, seesaw gait. Evald Bromo was aware of the stench of paint thinners before he caught sight of the guy, and he averted his gaze in a sudden wave of nausea.

"Give me a ten," the man slurred, holding out a skinny, grimy hand. "Only ten kroner!"

Evald Bromo had no desire to stop. But from experience he knew that the best way to get rid of the guy was to pay up. He slowed down and used his right hand to rummage for small change in his trouser pocket. He found a twenty kroner piece and stared at it for a second before shaking his head faintly as he handed it to the foul-smelling man. The gift obviously took the beggar by surprise. He dropped the coin and stood swaying irresolutely from side to side, as if he did not quite know what had become of the money. Annoyed, Evald Bromo hunkered down to help. Perhaps he gave the impression that he was going to take the donation back; anyway, the beggar hurriedly made a grab for it. The two men's heads clashed and Evald Bromo fell to the ground. The man made a fuss and insisted on helping Bromo back onto his feet. Bromo preferred to manage by himself. It ended with both men lying in floundering confusion directly outside *Aftenposten*'s main entrance.

Aftenposten's Chief Editor rounded the corner beside the Apotek Kronen pharmacy and dashed recklessly across Akersgata, past three vehicles waiting for a green light. When she passed the main entrance of the *Dagbladet* newspaper office, she saw that it was Evald Bromo who was spreadeagled on the sidewalk with the most troublesome of all the local beggars on top of him. She immediately assumed that the journalist was being attacked. In a fury, she thumped the glue sniffer on the back with her umbrella, then stormed into her own newspaper's reception and ordered someone to phone the police right away. After that she darted out again.

Evald Bromo was now alone, leaning on a pillar, brushing dirt and grit from his clothes. He mumbled something incomprehensible that it would be difficult to interpret as anything other than a refusal when the Chief Editor insisted on taking him to see a doctor.

"It wasn't an assault," he finally managed to enunciate. "It was just an accident. I'm not injured. Thanks."

The Chief Editor peered at him suspiciously. In a sudden glimmer, she thought of the peculiar, anonymous email.

"Is everything okay, Evald?"

She placed her hand on his lower arm and he stared as though bewitched at the long, red-lacquered talons sinking into the rough tweed of his jacket sleeve. He wanted to shake himself free, but swallowed and forced a smile and a reassurance. "Everything's fine. Honestly."

"Everything else as well? Nothing bothering you at the moment?"

"No," he said, aware that he sounded rather brusque. "I'm absolutely fine, thanks."

"Well, well," the editor said with an encouraging smile, "we have a newspaper to produce, Evald. See you later."

She disappeared into the building, majestic and poised, hugging her satisfaction to her chest like a hot-water bottle. She prided herself on taking her colleagues' welfare seriously. No one could say that she had not done her best as far as Evald Bromo was concerned. She did not even notice whether he followed her into the vast newspaper building. But then she encountered the Finance Minister on her way to the elevator.

34

It was nearly half past four when Hanne Wilhelmsen returned from the hospital. It had taken her fifteen minutes in front of the mirror in the restroom to make her face presentable, so that the redness around her eyes could be taken as the symptom of a heavy spring cold. She spread pale-brown foundation over her cheeks to disguise the worst of the blemishes and drew a dark red lipstick over her lips. She *had* to get her hair cut soon. When she would have the time and energy was impossible to predict.

"That was a long two or three hours," Karianne Holbeck said, with a mixture of reproach and curiosity, as her eyes took the measure of Hanne.

Nine detectives with CID Chief Jan Sørlie in tow quietly left the cramped conference room. The stale smell of confined humans that enveloped them hit Hanne like a brick wall as she entered the room to take a soda from the refrigerator.

"Sorry," Hanne mumbled to her boss as they passed each other. "Pressing engagement of a personal nature."

He did not say a word, but shot her a look that told her Billy T.—or perhaps that damned persistent Police Chief—had spilled the beans. Sørlie's eyes were filled with impotent sympathy, and Hanne averted her gaze as she needlessly closed the door behind her.

Billy T. tore it open again.

"Now I've got you."

He smiled faintly and sat on the chair at the end of the table. Hanne took forever to find the soda she had put there three days earlier. Finally, she could string it out no longer. She had found it ages ago.

"Would you like a summary?" Billy T. asked when Hanne finally drew back and closed the fridge door. "Some kind of picture is beginning to emerge now."

He let his finger outline an invisible pattern on the tabletop, as if he meant what he said quite literally.

"You can also have a chat," he continued in an undertone. "Or a hug."

He spread his palms in front of him and examined the backs of his hands while chewing his bottom lip. When Hanne still said nothing, but instead simply stood there indolently with the bottle in her hand and her gaze fixed on a spot a foot and a half above Billy T.'s head, he pressed on. "We could go for another walk. The air in here must be hazardous to our teeth. It feels caustic."

He ventured a smile.

"A walk would be a good idea," she answered surprisingly fast. "I'd quite like to take a closer look at Staure Bridge. How long does it take to get there?"

"No idea," Billy T. said and got to his feet. "But I've all the time in the world. Half an hour, perhaps? Let's go!"

He extended his hand as she edged round the table and passed him. She did not take it. Outside the door, Karianne Holbeck stood waiting.

"I've something I must—"

"It'll have to wait," Hanne interrupted. "Can we talk about it tomorrow?"

"No, I'm afraid I've made a mistake and—"

Hanne glanced at the clock before sighing heavily, at the same time aware she was stinking worse than ever. With her arms clamped against her body in embarrassment and the forlorn hope that she could contain some of the foul odor, she gestured to Karianne to follow her.

"We'll meet up in half an hour," she said to Billy T.

Despite the outside temperature having dropped to 45 degrees, Hanne threw her office window wide before offering Karianne Holbeck a chocolate banana from the enamel dish she had received from Cecilie on their twentieth anniversary.

"What's it about?" she asked, reclining as far back in her chair as possible.

Karianne Holbeck told her about her conversation with the man whose name she did not know but who she thought was Turkish and might own a shop in Grünerløkka. She cast her eyes down self-consciously as she summarized her potentially catastrophic error: the man might have information regarding Halvorsrud's corruption, but Karianne Holbeck had neglected to note the guy's name and address. Unfortunately. Apologies.

Hanne Wilhelmsen did not utter a word for ages. It started to feel very cold in the room, and she reluctantly closed the window and resumed her seat. Then she urged another chocolate banana on her colleague. Karianne Holbeck accepted, but sat fiddling with it until the chocolate melted and, obviously embarrassed, she had to lick her fingers.

"I must give you credit for reporting this," Hanne began; her voice was strangely monotone, as though forcing out a sentence learned by heart. "It probably doesn't matter. He's coming on Monday, isn't he? Are you sure *he* caught *your* name?"

"Fairly sure," Karianne Holbeck said, relieved. "But God only knows whether he'll turn up. He didn't sound terribly reliable."

"Oh no?" Hanne said, raising her eyebrows almost imperceptibly. "What do you mean by that? Can you tell from someone's voice whether they're reliable?"

"Well . . . ," Karianne said, squirming slightly.

Hanne noticed that her colleague had an odd habit of tossing her hair over her shoulder. The gesture was attractively feminine, but also brought to mind a little girl disclaiming all responsibility.

"I don't quite know now," Karianne continued. "In my experience, people from those parts don't have the same notion of what constitutes an appointment as we do. It's as if time doesn't mean the same to them."

Hanne Wilhelmsen could not care less that she smelled like a down-and-out. She interlaced her fingers at the nape of her neck, projecting her elbows out in the air like wings, and studied her colleague through her long bangs. Then she pursed and smacked her lips before saying, "And who do you mean by 'we'?"

"What?"

"Who are 'we'? We who do understand the principles of a specific time of day?"

"Nooo—"

"And what are 'those parts'? Turkey? Asia Minor? The Third World?"

"I didn't mean it like that," Karianne said, rubbing a red mark on her cheek that was growing dangerously fast. "I just meant . . ."

She did not continue. Hanne Wilhelmsen waited.

"It was a stupid thing to say," Karianne said, tossing her hair. "Sorry. It wasn't meant nastily."

Hanne let go of her neck and leaned forward. Picking up a pen, she began to draw circles and trapezoids on an invitation to a union meeting. She took her time. The circles were big and small, and they intersected the trapezoids in a number of small, enclosed spaces that she neatly colored with blue and red felt-tip pens.

"I don't believe it was either," Hanne said so suddenly that Karianne literally jumped in her seat. "I don't believe you *meant* anything nasty by what you said. Nevertheless, I think . . ." She tapped a brisk drumroll with the two felt-tip pens on her blotter. ". . . you should consider what you stand for. What kind of prejudices you're struggling against. Have you noticed the man who cleans downstairs in the foyer every morning? The guy who always wears a track suit in Swedish colors?"

Karianne shook her head gently. By now the redness had spread into a belt across the bridge of her nose, and she resembled a quite defenseless human raccoon.

"Maybe not. You should take the time some day. Come in early and talk to the guy. He's from Eritrea. He's a veterinarian. His Norwegian's not bad. But after four years in an Ethiopian prison, his nerves are not so good."

"I've said I'm sorry," Karianne Holbeck said, now almost defiant.

"We'll take the risk that our friend from Grünerløkka will turn up. In fact I think I'd like to talk to him myself. Did he phone the central switchboard or the operations center?"

"What?"

"112," Hanne said, rubbing her eyes without any thought for her newly applied mascara. "If he called the emergency number, then the conversation is on tape. If not, we'll have to hope that he knows what an appointment means. Check that out, please. And let me know when he arrives."

Karianne Holbeck nodded and stood up.

"Here, have another chocolate!"

Hanne held out the dish to her colleague, but Karianne did not even say "no thanks." Instead she gave the door a rather hard and quite unnecessary slam.

35

They drove in Hanne Wilhelmsen's own car. The seven-year-old white BMW had one red fender. Cecilie had crashed it the previous autumn, four days after Hanne had cancelled the comprehensive insurance policy.

"Can't we just agree not to talk about Cecilie?" Hanne said quietly, switching the windshield wipers to the fastest setting. "It would be great if you could accept that I don't want . . . Not yet, at least. Visit her yourself, please do. She'd be delighted."

Billy T. struggled to push the passenger seat farther back. The lever at the front of the seat was awkward, and suddenly he was left holding the entire thing in his hand.

"Shit!"

He stared from the lever to Hanne and back again. She looked quickly at the damage, shrugged, and used her thumb to point at the rear seat. Billy T. chucked the metal lever over his shoulder, then fastened his seat belt.

It was late afternoon, and the last of the daylight was being snuffed out by the rain-soaked asphalt. The road had narrowed, and there were no streetlamps any more. Hanne reduced her speed when she sensed the car almost aquaplaning on one of the curves.

They drove in silence.

Billy T. tracked the bluish-gray landscape with his eyes. The fields were plowed for spring, and a pungent odor of manure tickled his nostrils and made him think of his sons. He had arranged to take them on a farm vacation this year. The boys and Billy T., Tone-Marit, and their new baby girl were all going to western Norway to his cousin's farm. For two weeks. Only after it was all settled did it strike Billy T. that a vacation with relatives and four lively stepchildren might not fulfill Tone-Marit's dreams of a romantic honeymoon. But she had merely smiled when, filled with regret, he had asked if she would rather do something else. She was looking forward to it, she claimed. He had chosen to believe her.

The thought of their newborn child made him smile.

A fox scurried across the road.

Hanne immediately applied the brakes, but took her foot off the pedal just in time to avoid losing control of the vehicle. Then she slowed down some more, and they swung round the bend, where the fields suddenly opened out to the sea. The span of Staure Bridge towered majestically between the mainland and the peninsula a half mile across the fjord.

They parked on a gravel area one minute's walk from the bridge-head. Hanne glanced briefly at the papers she had stuffed down between the seat and the center console. This was where they had found Ståle Salvesen's old Honda. Now the place was deserted. A garbage can had been knocked over by the wind. A badger or perhaps just a roaming dog had hauled out the garbage; she could detect a hint of decay even in the fresh tang of the sea air.

"Strange that they don't clean up that sort of thing," she said absent-mindedly as she locked the car.

"Thirty-five minutes," Billy T. roared. He had walked ahead of her, and his voice was almost drowned out by the racket the sea made as it beat against the large pebbles.

"What?" she shouted back.

"It took us thirty-five minutes from the police station," he explained when she caught up with him. "Marvelous that something like this can be found so close to the city."

Staure Bridge was pretty narrow. Two cars could pass easily in the middle, but it would be tight if one was a truck. On the southern side, facing the sea, ran a narrow corridor-like path for pedestrians, separate from the vehicle lanes. Probably it had been added later. Hanne began to jog across the bridge. It was steep, and she came to a breathless halt after a couple of hundred yards. Billy T. ambled along after her.

"What are we looking for?" he asked, resisting the temptation to brush her hair back from her face; the breeze from the fjord was strong, and he felt a faint movement in the actual structure of the bridge below his feet.

"Nothing and everything," she said, continuing on up.

They had reached the top.

Billy T. felt uncomfortable.

"Damn it," he muttered, only just daring to peep out over the railings. "Things would have to be fucking awful to think of jumping off here."

Hanne nodded faintly. She leaned over as far as possible. The water was nothing but a gray-white churning in a black void down below. If she had not already known that it was a 20-yard drop, it would have been impossible to estimate. There was nothing to measure it against—nothing to create a realistic impression of height and distance.

"Hold me," Hanne said, beginning to clamber over the railings.

"Are you out of your mind?" Billy T. tugged at Hanne's upper arms in an effort to drag her back again.

"Ouch!" Hanne yelled. "That's sore! It's dangerous! Hold me by the shoulders, but not so hard!"

Billy T. reluctantly loosened his grasp, then took hold of her again, this time by the roomy shoulders of her pilot jacket. He felt his pulse hammering in his eardrums and found it difficult to draw breath. Hanne was hanging onto the railing, but he could not see what she was searching for with her feet.

"What the fuck are you trying to *do*?" he snarled, feeling a surge of adrenaline through his limbs when he thought for a moment he had lost his grip.

"I want . . ." Hanne groaned, bending so far down that he had to let go to avoid causing a calamity. "I want to find out if there's a way back to the mainland."

The rest was lost. Hanne was gone. Billy T.'s fear of heights was superseded by an even greater anxiety: Hanne had fallen into the sea. She had totally vanished. In desperation, he leaned over the railing, trying in vain to catch sight of something other than the gray crests of foam far, far below.

"Hanne! Hanne!"

He screamed her name time after time as he searched desperately through his pockets for his cell phone.

"Damn and blast!"

He had left it behind in the car.

"It's possible," he heard someone say.

Hanne's head appeared above the railings. She put her hands on the iron ledge and rolled herself over the edge. Then she smiled as she looked him in the eye.

"It's possible," she repeated. "The substructure of the bridge allows you to climb over the railings and give the impression that you're throwing yourself into the water. Then you can walk along the corridor underneath, all the way back to dry land. It would be difficult, I think, but far from impossible."

"Bitch," Billy T. hissed.

"I told you that's what I was doing," Hanne ventured.

"You *know* I'm not very fond of heights," he exploded, forcing his way past her.

The massive expanse of his back swayed in front of her all the way down to the shore again. Billy T. did not say a word, nor did he allow her to walk by his side for the short distance from the bridgehead across to the car. Every time she tried, he accelerated his pace. But she was the one who had the car keys.

"Sorry," she said, placing her hand on his arm when he stopped like a sulky toddler, waiting for her to open the door.

The sincerity in her voice obviously had an effect. He gave her a smile and shrugged.

"You scared me," he said curtly and quite superfluously.

"Sorry," she said again, tilting her head. "You promised me a summary. What if we . . ."

Hanne surveyed the scene. It had stopped raining, and although the air was bitter and the sea white with froth, there was a freshness about the landscape she found attractive; it made her want to linger. On the lee side of Staure Bridge, directly north of the bridgehead they had just left behind, a beach of coarse sand curved into a grove of trees.

"What if we . . ."

Hanne hesitated for a second before continuing. "Do you think we could light a bonfire and . . . stay here for a while?"

"No. It's too cold and damp. We won't find enough dry wood."

Billy T. shivered as he opened the car door. Hanne skirted the vehicle and opened the trunk. When she slammed it shut again, she was clutching a black can of gasoline in her hands.

"Here you are," she said, holding the can with her arms outstretched. "Now we can set fire to whatever we want."

Billy T. pulled a disapproving face but sloped along after her. Down on the beach, he stood with his hands thrust deep into his pockets, watching as Hanne wandered this way and that. She bent down every so often, picking up a broken branch here and a piece of driftwood there. Eventually she collected everything into a hollow surrounded by largeish stones; the place had obviously been used for the same purpose before. Finally she poured gasoline over the whole caboodle.

"Are you going to blow the place up, or what?"

Billy T. took a step back.

The bonfire flared up vigorously when Hanne lobbed four matches between the pieces of wood. Puffs of acrid, black smoke formed low clouds, choking Hanne and making her cough; tears began to run down her cheeks.

"It worked really well," she mumbled softly, making room for Billy T. on a log conveniently situated just six feet away from the raging fire.

It was a lot more pleasant there in the cove than up at the parking spot. A side wind blew across the fire, wafting the smoke away from the two police officers.

"Let me hear it," Hanne Wilhelmsen said, wiping soot off her face.

"The most important thing is probably the computer disks," Billy T. said. "The ones that were in the medicine cabinet in the basement. It turns out they contained information about cases that were dropped."

"By Halvorsrud personally?" Hanne asked dispassionately.

"Yes."

"Have they been closely scrutinized?"

"To some extent."

Billy T. wriggled his bottom to find a more comfortable position.

"In two of the cases it was fairly obvious there weren't sufficient grounds for prosecution. From an evidential point of view. Of course, that doesn't mean that the villains . . ."

". . . weren't guilty," they chorused.

"Exactly," Billy T. commented. "But it was reasonable. Whereas the other two . . ."

". . . are more dubious," Hanne said.

Billy T. nodded.

"We've been allocated someone else from the Økokrim financial crimes section to go through the cases. A woman, as it happens. She doesn't think either case should have been dropped. That in itself is not particularly noteworthy. We know how it goes. What's more important is that Halvorsrud had a huge argument with the others over there about one of them. Used all his authority in order to—"

"—make sure the case was dropped," Hanne interjected.

"That's quite annoying, you know," Billy T. said angrily, flinging a twig on the fire.

"Pardon me?"

"Finishing my sentences for me."

"Sorry."

She got to her feet to pour more gasoline on the flames. Restraining her, Billy T. took the can from her and put it behind the log they were sitting on.

"You're in the suicidal corner today, I have to say. How often do you say 'sorry' these days too?"

Not often enough, Hanne thought, though she said nothing.

"Erik Henriksen has spoken to the four people whose cases were on the disks. All of them flatly deny having had anything to do with Halvorsrud. We've run some checks on each of them. Looking for large sums of money taken out of their bank accounts that they can't fully explain. That sort of thing. Of course, we've also checked the Halvorsrud family's finances. Nothing to report so far. But we're doing more searches. There's also that story from the maybe-Turkish guy of Karianne's. That doesn't sound too good for Halvorsrud."

"And to think that a talented lawyer would have been so *stupid* as to introduce himself when offering to do something corrupt."

"That's a point," Billy T. said with a nod. "A good point."

The wind suddenly changed direction and smoke swirled into their eyes. Billy T. stood up and tried to waft it away. Hanne let out a burst of laughter and coughed as the wind turned again.

"The computer belonged to his wife," Billy T. said, sitting down again. "At least that's what we've ascertained. I got the aunt to ask the children. None of them could explain why there was nothing on it. Their mother was always sitting at it, writing, according to the children."

"Why didn't you ask them yourself?"

"I sort of promised the eldest that I wouldn't bother his siblings. Thea has apparently broken down completely, poor girl. And the flashlight *did* belong to Marius. The aunt checked that as well. He claims he lost it a while ago. Recognized it from a dent on the battery cover."

The fire had started to die down. When Hanne threw on another piece of driftwood, the last of the flames crackled noisily before drowning in smoke.

"I've been wondering about the door," she said, flailing her arms to keep warm. "How could this alleged Ståle Salvesen—or someone dressed to look like him—get inside Halvorsrud's house at all? As far as I'm aware, there was no sign of forced entry. Yet Sigurd Halvorsrud claims that the door was always locked in the evening."

"That's amazingly stupid of him as well," Billy T. murmured. "His story would have made more sense if he'd claimed that the door was open."

"They have children," Hanne said. "Shall we go?"

"What about the children?"

Billy T. remained seated, watching Hanne, who had stood up and was dancing a jig in the increasingly biting wind.

"Children lose keys at the drop of a hat. Come on."

Without waiting for him, she made a dash for the car.

"I don't really know what we're waiting for," Billy T. said once he had plopped down into the broken passenger seat. "The case seems completely cut and dried to me. It's actually very seldom that we have *such* a strong chain of circumstantial evidence as we do in this case. Halvorsrud is guilty. It's obvious."

"So what is making us hesitate, then?" Hanne said softly. She sat with her hands on her lap, toying distractedly with the car keys. "Why are we so fixated on this Ståle Salvesen?"

"You are," Billy T. corrected her. "*You* are fixated on Ståle Salvesen. I have to admit that for a while I doubted Halvorsrud's guilt. But now I'm inclined to—"

"It's all far too clean-cut," Hanne interrupted, inserting the key into the ignition. "Can't you see that? The case is absurd, but at the same time obvious. It's unthinkable that Halvorsrud would behead his wife, but at the same time everything points to him being the culprit. Don't you see what sort of picture this paints?"

Billy T., struggling with his seat belt, did not respond.

"A setup," Hanne Wilhelmsen whispered. "A *perfect* setup."

"Or more simply a fucking clumsy murder trying to *look like* a setup," Billy T. said tartly as he searched for the news channel on the radio.

"Until I see Ståle Salvesen's dead body with my own eyes, I'm keeping my mind open to the possibility that Halvorsrud might in fact be telling the truth," Hanne said.

She shot a final look in the direction of Staure Bridge before turning out of the parking spot and setting off on the return journey. They drove for twenty minutes without saying anything at all. When they passed Høvik Church on the E18, Hanne said, "There was something about Ståle Salvesen's apartment. I noticed something that bothered me. But I can't for the life of me think what it was."

She scratched her nose and squinted at the gas gauge. There was probably enough fuel to see them home.

"If it's important, it'll come back to you. You've a lot of other things on your mind at present."

Billy T. smiled and looked at Hanne. He wanted to put his hand on her thigh, as he definitely would have done under other circumstances. If everything had been the way it was before.

But nothing was the way it had been. Admittedly, on this outing Hanne had shown something of her former self. She had been physically close to him several times, and the atmosphere between them had had something of the old familiarity he so valued and was so afraid of losing. All the same, something was different. Hanne was always focused. She was always consumed by her cases. Always reflective, testing out the opinions of others. But now there was an intensity to her single-mindedness that bordered on fanaticism. Her maneuver on Staure Bridge had been risky and totally unnecessary. They could have investigated Hanne's theory without her risking her life. And he'd noticed that she had started to speak more slowly than before, and that she often seemed to be talking to herself rather than other people.

"That's where you're all mistaken," Hanne Wilhelmsen said suddenly as they drove away from the Bjørvika interchange.

"What?"

Billy T. had forgotten what he had said a few minutes earlier.

"You all think I've so much else to think about," Hanne said. "The fact is that this case is the *only* thing I'm thinking about. I don't think about anything else at all. At least not while I'm at work. Say hi to Tone-Marit for me."

She drew up outside the main entrance of the police headquarters. Billy T. hesitated. Then he unfastened his seat belt and opened the door.

"Just one thing, Hanne," he said slowly. "You stink to bloody high heaven. Go home and take a shower. Phew, how you stink!"

When he slammed the door behind him, the automatic toll-recording chip fell down from the windshield, and Hanne's ears were ringing for the rest of the evening.

36

It was Friday, March 12, and the threatening clouds that hung over the Swedish capital were making it difficult to see very far. Lars Erik Larsson produced a plastic bag from the tattered folder. He slid it out and placed it on a wooden bench. There were few people at Skansen's zoo that day. Larsson had just walked through the new Bear Mountain without so much as glimpsing a bear. Maybe they were still hibernating.

He had intended to spend longer at Djurgården, the wonderful cultural and recreational island haven in the middle of Stockholm. Perhaps going all the way out to the western tip of the island, to Plommonbacken, from where he could take the bus back to the city center if he lacked the energy to walk any farther. But there was rain in the air. When he passed Djurgården's Nordic Museum, the dark-gray clouds over Södermalm had made him change his mind. So he paid the sixty kronor to get into Skansen, the open-air museum and zoo, and took a walk around that instead.

Feeling content, he sat down and took out a neatly wrapped cheese-and-red-pepper sandwich. The coffee in his thermos flask was piping hot and the steam felt pleasant on his face. He gazed pensively across the bay. He could just make out the Kaknäs TV and radio transmission tower; its antenna struggled bravely to hold the clouds aloft.

Lars Erik Larsson was a contented man. Admittedly, he lived a quiet life, and he had not had a woman since his wife left him in 1985. But he would soon be sixty-five, and had enough on his hands with his work and his two grandchildren. When he retired in the not too distant future, he would move out to the little farm in Östhammar, where he would cultivate his flower garden and entertain a few old friends now and again.

He ate his picnic in seclusion. Only a foreign couple—if he wasn't mistaken, they were American—disturbed him as they walked past with three adolescent children, all talking vociferously. When he was

finished, he wiped his mouth with a napkin he had brought, then produced that morning's copy of the *Expressen* newspaper.

Lars Erik Larsson worked at the SE Bank in Gamla Stan, Stockholm's
Old Town. His career had been at a standstill for the past twenty years,
but that did not bother him much. He was a man with no ambition
other than to do useful work in return for his hard-earned wages. He
lived simply in a two-room apartment in Södermalm. He had inherited the farm, located 85 miles north of Stockholm and five minutes'
walk from the sea. His car was ten years old and fully paid off. Lars
Erik Larsson needed no more than he possessed. Moreover, through
his job he had seen so much money come and go, seen how easily
financial good fortune changed to tragedy, that he had never yearned
for riches.

A Norwegian woman had been beheaded, possibly by her husband.
His eyes ran down the page. The report described a "public prosecutor" who had killed his wife with a samurai sword. Typical *Expressen*.
Why in the world would they write about a case like this? If it had happened in Norway, it would hardly be of interest to anyone outside that
country. It was probably the spicy detail about the murder weapon
that had induced the tabloid newspaper to jump on the bandwagon.

Sigurd Halvorsrud.

Lars Erik Larsson looked up from his newspaper. It had started to
rain over Östermalm, and he began to pack up his belongings. There
was something familiar about that name.

Sigurd Halvorsrud.

Suddenly it came to him. It must have been several months ago, but
the incident had been so extraordinary that he still remembered it. A
man had come into the bank with a suitcase containing two hundred
thousand Swedish kronor in cash. He had opened an account and paid
all the money in the name of Sigurd Halvorsrud. The man had spoken
Norwegian.

Two hundred thousand kronor in cash was unusual, even nowadays. Perhaps especially nowadays. Money these days was mainly fig-
ures on a computer screen.

He headed for the Bergmann funicular railway.

He glanced at his watch.

Perhaps he should report it. To whom? The newspaper? Out of the
question. The police?

He thought about Lena, his nine-year-old granddaughter, who was coming to spend the whole weekend with him. They would have a lovely time, and tomorrow they were going to the opera. He was so pleased that the little girl had started to take an interest in real music.

It was best not to make a fuss. He stuffed the newspaper into a trash can as he left Skansen and decided to walk all the way home despite the threatening rain clouds. It would take just over an hour, but he had an umbrella anyway.

37

The hospital never completely settled down, it seemed. Even though a buxom nurse had completed the night rounds some considerable time ago, and all unnecessary lights had been switched off, the old buildings at Ullevål still reverberated with distant noises and movements that could be picked up all the way inside the room where Hanne Wilhelmsen sat silently in a chair trying to read.

Cecilie whimpered and attempted to turn over in her sleep.

Hanne placed her hand carefully on her arm to prevent her from moving.

The busty nurse was standing in the doorway again. Hanne was startled as she had not heard anyone approach.

"Are you sure you don't want me to wheel a bed in here for you?" the woman whispered. "You need to get some sleep."

Hanne Wilhelmsen shook her head.

The nurse came all the way over to the chair where Hanne was sitting. She laid her hand diffidently on her shoulder.

"There may be many long nights here ahead for you. I do think you should get some sleep. It's really no bother to bring in a bed."

Hanne still did not reply, but shook her head again.

"Have you taken sick leave?" the nurse whispered. "Dr. Flåbakk can certainly help you with that, in this transition period, if we can call it that."

Hanne laughed softly in resignation.

"That's not really possible," she said, trying not to yawn. "I've far too much to do at work."

"What work do you do?" the nurse asked quietly in a friendly tone, still with her hand on Hanne's shoulder. "No, let me guess!"

She cocked her head and studied Hanne Wilhelmsen.

"Lawyer," she said finally. "You're probably an attorney or something of that kind."

Hanne smiled and rubbed her left eye with her knuckle.

"Close enough. Police. I'm a chief inspector."

"How interesting!"

The woman actually sounded as if she meant it. Her hand patted Hanne's arm a couple of times. Then she checked the tubes and the IV stand and padded over to the door.

"Let me know if you change your mind about that bed," she whispered. "You can just pull that cord there, and I'll be here in a flash. Good night!"

"Good night," Hanne murmured.

She heard footsteps coming and going in the corridor. Some hurrying, others shuffling as if there was all the time in the world. Now and again muffled calls were heard between the aides, and in the far distance the faint echo of a police siren sounded.

"Hanne," Cecilie whispered, trying to move her head from side to side.

"I'm here," she answered, leaning forward. "Here."

"I'm so pleased about that."

Hanne took hold of the slender hand, trying to avoid the cannula.

"How are you feeling?"

"Okay," Cecilie said with a groan. "Can you straighten me up a bit? I'd prefer to sit up."

Hanne hesitated for a second, looking helplessly at the alarm cord that would summon the kindly nurse back. She was scared to touch anything other than Cecilie's hand.

"Help me then," Cecilie said, struggling to raise her head.

Hanne took the two extra pillows lying by the footboard and managed to tuck them behind Cecilie's back. Then she switched on the lamp on the bedside table and directed the light at the gray wall in order to dim its bright beam.

"How are *you* feeling?" Cecilie said, looking at her.

Hanne was not sure whether her eyes expressed something completely new, or whether they showed the remains of what had once been there.

"I'm feeling terrible," she said.

"I can see that. Come here."

"I am here, Cecilie."

"Come up here. Come closer."

Hanne lifted the chair underneath her and moved a couple of inches closer. Cecilie raised her hand as far as she could.

"Even closer. I want to see you properly."

Their faces were less than a foot apart. Hanne was aware of the smell of sickness as it wafted around her nostrils. She laid the palm of her hand on Cecilie's face.

"What are we going to do now?" she whispered.

"That's really up to you to decide," Cecilie said, almost inaudibly.

"What do you mean?"

Hanne let her thumb glide smoothly over Cecilie's cheek, over and over again. It struck her how soft her complexion was: soft and slightly damp, as if she had been outside walking in the rain.

"You have to make a decision," Cecilie said, clearing her throat. "You need to decide. If I have to go down this road on my own, I need to know that now."

Hanne swallowed repeatedly.

"Of course you're not going to be on your own."

She so wanted to say something more. She wanted to say she was sorry. She wanted to tell her how sorry she was that everything was no longer the way it ought to be, that everything was too late and that she had perhaps never been willing to pay the price for what she wanted more than anything in this life. Hanne wanted to crawl into bed beside Cecilie. She wanted to hold her the way she remembered they had once held each other. She wanted to run her hands over Cecilie's damaged body and promise that from now on and for as long as they were able to live together, everything would be different. Not like before, like long ago, but far better, more fitting. More truthful. Everything would be true.

Instead she kept her mouth closed. In the glimmer of light from the lamp facing the wall she saw the suggestion of a smile on Cecilie's pinched face.

"You've never been good at talking, Hanne. This has been the most difficult time, I think. It's often impossible to know what you're thinking."

She laughed impulsively, a dry, husky laughter.

"I know that," Hanne said. "I'm sorry."

"You've said that so often."

"I know that. I'm so—"

Now they both smiled.

"I do want to be with you in any case," Hanne said, leaning even closer. "I want to stay with you all the—"

She laid her cheek softly on Cecilie's. Her earlobe tickled Cecilie's lips.

"This is not about you," she said. "It has never been about you." She hid her face in Cecilie's hair and continued. "I've never been good enough. I've never made myself deserving of you. You should have found somebody stronger. Someone who dared to choose you, absolutely and completely."

"But you have done that," Cecilie said, trying to push Hanne up so that she could look into her eyes.

Hanne resisted. "No," she murmured into the hollow of Cecilie's neck. "I've been riding two horses all my life. Or three. Or four, when it suited. None of them have sort of . . . matched. I have worked so hard to keep it like that. To convince myself that it was right. But this last while—"

"You're suffocating me," Cecilie moaned. "I can't breathe."

Hanne slowly lifted her head, then rose from the chair and crossed to the window. The fog had thickened, and it was now barely possible to see across to the parking lot where a solitary BMW with a red fender was sitting.

"In everything I've done, in everything I've been, I've prided myself on the fact that I'm smart. *Smart.*"

She put her right hand on her forehead and massaged her eye socket vigorously with her thumb and index finger.

"But lately . . . The past six months, perhaps, I've begun to have doubts."

"About us," Cecilie said, more as a statement of fact than a question.

"No!"

Hanne turned round, throwing out her arms.

"Not about us. Never about us! About me!"

She pounded her chest, then reined herself in.

"It's *me* I doubt," she hissed. "I . . . I've become so scared of getting things wrong. I look back and bury myself in all the times I've done the wrong thing. On all levels. With friends. With you. I've let everyone down. The truth is, I let people down all the time."

She inhaled deeply and turned to face the window again. She saw her own reflection in the glass. When she continued, she was gazing into her own eyes.

"I've even got scared about my old cases. That I might have contributed to a major injustice. At night I lie and . . . at night I'm scared . . . I'm even afraid of being sued. That's how far it's gone. It's as if all the people I've put in prison have conspired together and . . . I try to avoid people I've hurt, and even . . . people I can't possibly have done anything to. It's as if I . . . well. The only way I can keep going is to concentrate all my attention on fresh cases. A continual stream of fresh cases."

"So you avoid relating to people."

"Yes. Maybe. Or—"

"And me."

Hanne suddenly sat down. The chair scraped against the freshly polished linoleum floor. She grabbed Cecilie's hand in both of hers.

"But don't you understand that I don't *want* it to be like this," she said. "There's never been anyone but you. Ever. It's just that when I look at you, I see my own . . . my own cowardice."

Cecilie tried to reach across to the lamp. It was too dark. It was as if Hanne was aging as she sat there; the shadows made her features sharper and her eyes more deeply set.

"Don't touch it," Hanne said under her breath. "Please."

"It's been *my* choice as well," Cecilie said.

"What has?"

"You. I could have been tougher. I could have protested about those two telephones. About the initials on the door. About you never wanting me to attend parties at your work. I could have said something."

"You did say something." Hanne smiled faintly, rubbing the small of her back.

"Do you want a cushion?" Cecilie asked.

"You've objected constantly."

"Not seriously. I've been too scared as well."

"You've never been scared."

Hanne sat up straight and took a deep breath. A half bottle of lukewarm mineral water on the bedside table threatened to topple over when she tried to adjust her chair.

"I've always been scared, Hanne. Scared of losing you. Scared of making such big demands that you would choose to leave me."

The door opened and the footboard of a bed was thrust inside the room.

"Now you're going to sleep whether you want to or not," the nurse announced when she came into view. "You can't stay awake all night long, you know. Those chairs are really useless."

Swift, experienced hands maneuvered the new bed into place beside Cecilie's. Hanne stood up and hovered listlessly, wedged in by the window.

"Are you okay?" The nurse caressed Cecilie's head and once again checked that the IV drip was correctly regulated. She hummed softly and without waiting for an answer disappeared out the door.

"Lie down."

Cecilie gestured at the newly made bed. Hanne sat gingerly on the edge. Without removing anything other than her shoes, she stretched out carefully on the quilt.

I wish I knew how long you have left, Hanne Wilhelmsen thought. *I would really like to know how much time we have before you die.*

But she did not say that aloud, and would never dare to ask.

38

Eivind Torsvik's fingers raced furiously over the keyboard. In the course of half an hour, he had sent five emails to different addresses, all abroad.

They did not understand this. They did not know enough. They were not all as competent as he was, or as patient. But he was totally dependent on them. Only by cooperating across borders could they have any hope of prevailing. Of winning. Because that was what this was: a battle. A war.

Wait, he wrote. We are close to our goal, but we must wait.

Wait for further orders.

God only knew whether they would obey.

39

Thea Flo Halvorsrud was only sixteen years old. Since she had not taken any nourishment for a week, she was in a pretty poor state. Now and then she took a sip of water from the glass kept constantly filled on her bedside table. However, she refused to touch the food that was carried in to her four times a day. Her dead mother's sister, Aunt Vera, was on the verge of a nervous breakdown. Twice she had tried to obtain psychiatric help for her niece. The first time, she was asked to come in and see the emergency psychiatric doctor. Since her niece refused to get up, that advice was worthless. The second time—when she had moved heaven and earth and refused to hang up until she had been given promises of assistance—a young doctor with acne and skinny, nervous hands had turned up. Thea had not given him so much as a glance, far less a meaningful conversation. In the end the doctor had flung out his arms apologetically and said something about compulsory treatment.

That was out of the question.

Aunt Vera had phoned Karen Borg.

"I've really no idea what to do," Thea's aunt said as she ushered Karen Borg into the guest room, where the sixteen-year-old was lying in a sea of pink cushions on a white-lacquered, large single bed.

"It would probably be best if I talked to her on my own," Karen said softly, making a sign for the agitated, well-meaning aunt to leave the room.

Dabbing her eyes, Aunt Vera backed out through the doorway.

The room was spacious, airy, and pink. The chest of drawers was antique rose, the carpet patterned with tiny flowers, and even the curtains had a pale-pink valance. Five bright-pink soft toys were sitting on the window ledge—three rabbits, a teddy bear, and something that looked like a hippopotamus—staring vacantly into the room. Karen Borg sent a silent thank-you to Håkon for having persuaded her to paint their daughter's bedroom green and blue.

"Hi," she said quietly as she sat down in a chair beside the bed. "I'm Karen Borg. I'm your dad's attorney."

This information did not make any notable impression. The girl curled up into a fetal position and pulled the quilt over her head.

"Your dad asked me to send you his love. I talked to him earlier today. He's worried about you."

A faint movement under the quilt perhaps indicated that the girl had at least heard what she'd said.

"Is there anything . . . is there anything at all I can do for you, Thea?"

There was no response. Now the girl lay stock-still, as if in addition to everything else, she had also stopped breathing.

"Thea," Karen said. "Thea! Are you sleeping? Do you hear what I'm saying?"

Suddenly the girl turned around in the bed, and a head came into view. Blond, greasy hair sticking out in every direction.

"If you're Dad's attorney, you'd do better getting him out of jail instead of bothering me!"

Then she threw herself onto her back and buried herself in the quilt and cushions once more. Karen Borg caught herself smiling. There were distinct similarities between this teenage girl and Karen's own barely two-year-old daughter. But there were very obvious differences. At two, Liv was usually smiling again after five minutes. Sixteen-year-old Thea had gone on a hunger strike for a week, which was worrying, bordering on life-threatening.

"If you were to take the time to talk to me, it would perhaps be easier for me to do that job of mine," Karen said, hoping at the same time that she was not promising too much.

A faint smell of hot chocolate crept into the room. Thea's aunt Vera had explained that she regularly tried to stimulate her niece's appetite by putting food that smelled appealing near the door. Karen Borg did not have much faith that she would manage to tempt the daughter of a recently beheaded woman with chocolate and cream.

"Would you prefer me to leave?" she said despondently, making a move to stand up.

Something made her hesitate. A light breeze from the half-open window caused the curtains to flutter, and the ears of the smallest rabbit flapped in the draft. Underneath the quilt, the movements became calmer again. The girl sat up reluctantly with her back to the headboard. The face was that of a child, but the eyes had sunk so far into her head that she could have passed for ten years older than she was. Her narrow mouth trembled, and she fingered the corner of the quilt cover incessantly.

"You believe Dad," she said in an undertone. "Since you're his lawyer, you must believe he's innocent."

Karen Borg did not consider the occasion appropriate for a lecture on legal ethics.

"Yes," she said tersely. "I believe him."

The girl gave a faint smile.

"Aunt Vera doesn't."

Karen thought she could hear a noise outside the door. After some rapid deliberation, she let the eavesdropper remain.

"Maybe so. But she doesn't know your father as well as you do, and there are quite a lot of things to indicate that he has in fact done something wrong. You mustn't forget that."

Thea muttered something inaudible.

"Your father has to prepare himself to remain in custody for a good while yet. You can't really stop eating until he comes out again. That would mean you'd starve to death."

"Then that's just what I'll do," Thea said harshly. "I'm not touching anything until Dad comes back. So that we can move home again."

"Now you're being a bit childish."

"I am a child! According to the Convention on the Rights of the Child, I'm a child until I'm eighteen! That's not for two years yet."

Karen Borg laughed softly.

"The problem is that you won't ever *be* grown-up unless you eat some food."

The girl did not answer. She fidgeted repeatedly with the corner of the quilt. A thread had loosened, and she put it into her mouth.

"As I said, your dad is really worried. After all this . . . all this with your mother and—"

"Don't talk about Mum!"

Her features contracted into a face that was difficult to read.

Karen Borg had no idea which she would have thought was worse: that her mother had been murdered or that her father was suspected of the homicide. Probably she would not have been in any condition to understand either of those things. At least not at sixteen. She smoothed her skirt and ran her hand over her hair without really understanding why she was sitting there. This girl needed help, not advice from a lawyer.

"Your father will come to the funeral on Monday at least," she said after a lengthy pause. The girl had calmed down slightly again. "You'll see him then. It would probably be sensible to have something to eat over the weekend, so that you'll be fit to go."

"Mum," Thea said feebly. "Dad. Dad!"

Then she lay quietly on her back and pulled the quilt over her head once more. Her sobs were muffled by down and cotton, but nevertheless carried far enough for Aunt Vera to open the door. At a loss, she stopped in the center of the room, where she stood wringing her hands.

"What shall we do?" she said desperately. "What on earth shall we do?"

"We'll find a doctor for Thea," Karen Borg said resolutely. "And we'll do it today."

As she turned to go, she saw Preben Halvorsrud leaning against the door frame. He stared past her and out of the window. The little rabbit had fallen soundlessly to the floor. It was impossible to read anything at all in the young man's gaze. At the same time, there was something in his eyes that made Karen Borg shiver and wish herself far away from there.

"I've been saying that all week," he said dully. "Thea needs help. She also needs Dad. Have you thought about getting him home soon? So that Thea can stop living in this pink cave, I mean."

Now he made eye contact with her. It was like staring into the eyes of an old man, out of place in the boy's immature face.

"We'll see," Karen Borg said curtly, avoiding Preben's gaze as best she could.

40

Her head felt empty and light.

Hanne Wilhelmsen tried to hold on to one thought at a time. Her eyes flickered, and everything merged into a hallucinatory color chart. She poured bitter coffee from a thermos and drank most of the contents in one gulp.

It was now Saturday evening. Since she had stayed at the hospital until late morning, she did not figure on leaving police headquarters before close to midnight. Tonight she would sleep at home.

She took out a little glass box with a plastic lid from a desk drawer. Royal jelly from China. The pills were supposed to have a miraculously reviving effect. She read the label: "For rheumatism, weight loss, hair loss, pneumonia, compromised immune system, and depression." Depression sounded right at least. Hanne poured the brown pills out onto her hand and looked at them for a couple of seconds before placing three of them on her tongue and swallowing them with the last few drops of coffee. They slid down her gullet.

She looked despairingly at the three bundles in front of her.

One had to do with the Halvorsrud case. That was far from being the worst. She had kept herself acceptably up to date all week and felt a certain degree of satisfaction at the thought that she probably knew as much about the case as anyone else. It was the two other bundles that really bothered her. The other cases. The robberies. The bar fights. The rest of the world had not stood still during this past week.

"Eeny, meeny . . ." She began to giggle foolishly as she let her finger tap one bundle and then the next.

She stopped at the Halvorsrud papers all the same. Billy T.'s slapdash handwriting on the pink folder was illegible. The following text, thank God, was typewritten.

I have done as you asked and searched for particularly grotesque murders. Fortunately, there are not very many of them. You will recall a couple of cases: among others, the father and/ or daughter Håverstad's knife through Cato Iversen's balls obviously qualifies as grotesque . . .

Worst of all is probably the "gay murder" in Frogner Park a few years ago. You probably don't want a detailed description, but there is a report attached here. The problem in this context is that the killer took his own life in prison. No question about it, I believe. He is pushing up daisies. So unless he has risen from the dead, he is definitely not the person who beheaded Mrs. Halvorsrud.

Four other cases are enclosed in summary. The most interesting one is from 1990. An eighteen-year-old (it all actually happened on his birthday) kidnapped his own foster father. He subjected him to extreme violence (for example, by slashing his nipples) and chopped off his penis. The man did not die immediately of his wounds, and was presumably still alive when his testicles were also cut away. He bled to death, in all likelihood. The killer, Eivind Torsvik, had been sexually abused by his foster father for a number of years. When he finally worked up the courage to tell the authorities about the abuse (which he did in quite a dramatic fashion—by slicing off his ears and bringing them with him to school to show his teacher!), the case took an incredibly long time to get through the courts (typically enough). The foster father was sentenced to eighteen months' imprisonment, and was let out after barely a year. Eivind Torsvik was obviously not particularly happy with the punishment meted out to his abuser. After he killed him, he gave himself up to the police, and confessed. Strange boy. I remember him well. A sharp guy, and friendly too (not to his foster father, of course . . .); in short, a young man it was impossible not to feel a certain sympathy for. During the trial he said that he had waited until his eighteenth birthday to kill his foster father because he wanted to accept his punishment as a grown man. Since then he's achieved success as an author. You've perhaps read some of his writing. Red Light in Amsterdam was a huge bestseller both here and abroad.

Well, Eivind Torsvik and two of the other killers in the enclosed reports are at large. Nonetheless, I feel you're on the wrong track here. All these homicides have some sort of sexual aspect to them. Abuse, provocation, hatred for gays, rape. That kind of thing.

Do you really believe that Doris Halvorsrud was a sexual offender? Surely not . . . If you insist, I'll widen the search to include the whole of Scandinavia. There have been a couple of grisly cases, including the notorious "body-parts murder" in which a prostitute was murdered and dismembered. Waste of time, if you ask me. But then you're not!

Have as good a weekend as possible, and I'll see you on Monday. Before that, if you like. Tone-Marit is coming home

from the hospital today with our wee baby girl. But I can always
pop out for a couple of hours. Phone me.

There was a knock at the door.

"Come in," Hanne mumbled.

They knocked again.

"Come in, then!"

A trainee officer opened the door. Hanne Wilhelmsen had seen him
before but did not know his name.

"Yes?"

"The Custody Sergeant said to say hi," the trainee began.

"Thanks. Say hi back from me."

"It's about Halvorsrud."

"Yes," Hanne replied. "What about him?"

"He's making a fuss about wanting to talk to you. I didn't know you
were here, so I've left a message on your answering machine at home.
You can just forget about that now since—"

"What does he want?"

The young man looked doubtful, as if not quite sure whether it was
worth disturbing her so late on a Saturday evening.

"They're saying something about him wanting to confess," he said,
tilting his head as he tugged at his earlobe. "He wants to speak to you,
he says, and it's urgent. He says of course . . ." His earlobe grew increasingly red. "Oddly enough he wants to confess. I thought the guy was
denying everything! At least that's what I heard."

The boy smiled self-consciously and made a move to leave.

"Have you called his attorney?" Hanne asked indelicately.

The trainee stopped in his tracks.

"Nooo," he replied. "Should I have?"

"Yes. Do it now. Karen Borg. Holmenveien 12. Phone her home."

All of a sudden she felt remarkably wide awake. Hot blood rushed
to her cheeks, and she jogged down to the custody cells. Halvorsrud
could not confess.

The trip out to Staure Bridge had reinforced Hanne Wilhelmsen's
belief in Sigurd Halvorsrud's innocence. Naturally she could not
explain why. Perhaps it was the design of the bridge: it *was* possible to
stage a suicide by clambering back ashore along the substructure
beneath the road. Or perhaps it was simply a feeling, a clarity that had

struck her out there in the open, far away from everything hanging over her here in the city. She did not know. But she now felt it even more strongly: Halvorsrud must not confess.

Once before, Hanne Wilhelmsen had let a person be convicted of murder when she was probably innocent. Maren Kalsvik had been sentenced to fourteen years. Because she had confessed. Because she *could* have murdered her boss. Because the simplest solution for them all—the police, the newspapers, the court, all of them—was to let Maren Kalsvik go to prison. Hanne had tried to drown her doubts with the comprehensive, unqualified confession, never subsequently withdrawn. But she had never quite managed to assuage her sense of having been wrong.

The murder of foster-home director Agnes Vestavik in 1994 had been too grotesque to be left unsolved. Maren Kalsvik had been willing to atone for it, maybe on behalf of them all.

Something like that must not be allowed to happen again.

41

Evald Bromo had gone to bed. It was a Saturday night and not yet eleven o'clock. He had run 10 miles while Margaret was watching TV. When he came home, she offered him an open shrimp sandwich and a cold beer. She did not say very much when she set out the food. She had become increasingly quiet over the past week or so. Evald Bromo drank the beer but left the sandwich. Margaret did not even try to persuade him.

He had deliberately left the bathroom door slightly ajar. The light was still switched on in there, bathing the bedroom in a soft darkness, and from the street outside Evald could hear the noise made by a bunch of teenagers unable to find a party. He closed his eyes and listened for the television. Perhaps Margaret had switched it off. She might even have gone out. He did not approve of her going for a walk so late at night. It was only two weeks since a woman of nearly fifty had been raped in the park beside the children's playground.

He had to change his email address. The daily messages about how many days were left until the first of September were driving him crazy. He did not want any more of them. The problem was finding a plausible reason for the change. All of the email addresses belonging to *Aftenposten* journalists followed a logical system: his own was evald.bromo@aftenposten.no. Of course he could complain about unsolicited mail, but that would risk the IT technician wanting to see examples.

He almost could not be bothered to do his job. Since he was a hard-working, conscientious journalist, he could keep things going with excuses and pretexts for a while longer. But not for very long. He had stopped looking at the unsolicited messages when they arrived, but the mere knowledge that they were there before he deleted them was like having a list of deadlines for his own doom forced upon him.

He could hand in his resignation.

Then his address would be deleted.

He could start work at another newspaper, *Dagens Næringsliv*. The offer he received from them last year was probably still on the table.

On the other hand, the first of September would come around there too.

Evald heard a door slam.

When Margaret crept into the bedroom a few minutes later, he feigned sleep. He lay wide awake with his back to his wife until four o'clock on Sunday morning, when he slipped into a state of semiconsciousness. Three hours later he woke, wheezing into the quilt cover that was plastered to his body. He could not recollect what he had dreamed about.

42

Karen Borg waved her right finger in the air. It was dramatically wrapped in three blue Band-Aids adorned with smiling Mickey Mouse faces.

"Cut myself with the bread knife," she said by way of apology, and neglected to take Sigurd Halvorsrud's proffered hand.

The Chief Public Prosecutor had been sitting in Hanne Wilhelmsen's office for just short of half an hour. The Custody Sergeant had been annoyed when Hanne asked to have him brought up to her office instead of using the lawyer's room beside the cells.

Halvorsrud and the Chief Inspector had barely exchanged a word.

"What's this about?" Karen Borg asked as she sat down in the vacant chair. "An odd time to be summoned, it has to be said."

She glanced far from discreetly at her black-and-gold Rado wristwatch. It showed twenty minutes to midnight.

"Halvorsrud wanted to talk to me," Hanne Wilhelmsen said slowly, with emphasis. "I didn't think it right to comply with that request without you being present. As the case stands, I mean."

She let her gaze slide from the attorney to her client.

Sigurd Halvorsrud had undergone a striking transformation in the past few weeks. He had lost a great deal of weight. He still insisted on wearing a suit, shirt, and tie. Although the intention was obviously to maintain some kind of dignity, his attire seemed defiant and forlorn. His jacket hung pitifully loose across his shoulders and had started to get grubby. When the man stood up, his trousers threatened to fall down. In addition, a wan, injured expression had appeared around his mouth, an awkward moroseness that made his entire appearance seem pathetic. The furrows around his eyes had deepened, and his gaze flicked from side to side.

"I would like to consider the possibility of a confession," he said lamely.

He then cleared his throat and repeated with greater conviction, "I'll confess if the police will agree to an alternative to custody."

He still did not make eye contact with either of them. Hanne gave Karen a cursory glance. The lawyer appeared confused and closed her mouth with a bump when she realized she was sitting with it open.

"Perhaps you two ought to have a chat on your own first," Hanne suggested, rising from her seat. "I can go out for a while."

"No," snapped the Chief Public Prosecutor. "Please stay."

Hanne remained on her feet.

"This can't be a secret meeting, Halvorsrud. You know that very well. At the very least I have to write a special report. You will also be aware that I don't have the authority to deal with anything like that. That's not how we do things. Not in Norway, and certainly not in this case. You've already said enough to ensure it won't be easy for us to avoid using it against you later. Let's not make things even worse."

Finally Halvorsrud met her eye. His eyes reminded her momentarily of Cecilie's. It was as though the man knew it was all over. There was nothing anyone could do. At least not Hanne Wilhelmsen.

"At least not me," Hanne whispered.

"Pardon?" Halvorsrud said.

"Nothing."

She shook her head and crossed to the door.

"Please," Halvorsrud begged meekly. "Don't go!"

She stopped and looked at Karen Borg.

Karen shrugged, still seemingly bewildered. "Perhaps we could have a word in the corridor?" she suggested, looking directly at Hanne.

Hanne Wilhelmsen nodded faintly. Karen Borg followed her out through the yellow door. Hanne stood with her hand on the doorknob.

"What on earth's all this?" Karen whispered.

"He wants out."

"I realize that," Karen Borg said, slightly irritated. "What the hell have all of you done to the guy?"

"We haven't done anything at all. Apart from keeping him locked up for a couple of weeks." Rubbing her eyes, Hanne continued tersely, "It has a tendency to do things to people. That's part of the point, you might say."

Two uniformed officers came walking through the yellow zone. Hanne Wilhelmsen and Karen Borg remained silent as they passed. One of them raised his hand in greeting. When they were out of earshot, Karen whispered, "I spoke to him this morning. He's brokenhearted about his daughter. She won't eat and she can't sleep. I've arranged medical help, but you know how reluctant they are to resort to compulsory treatment."

"Fortunately," Hanne murmured, barely audible.

"You should have seen her, Hanne."

"I haven't. Luckily."

They looked at each other. Karen scrutinized her face so closely that Hanne averted her eyes after a few seconds.

"Besides, I'm afraid he's starting to get seriously ill himself," Karen said. "Not that he complains, but you can see it in him, of course. We both know that being held in custody can be a tremendous strain, but have you honestly seen anyone take it *so* badly?"

Hanne let go of the door knob and covered her face with both hands, massaging vigorously and sniffing loudly. When she removed her hands, her cheeks were flushed.

"I can name a few," she said tartly.

"But you understand that this *confession* . . ." Karen Borg spat the word out, so literally that Hanne felt a light spray on her face. "It's just a piece of nonsense!"

"Maybe," Hanne said, blinking. "Maybe so."

Karen Borg began to walk along the corridor. After four paces, she turned on her heel and walked back.

"We can't let him do this," she said, flinging out her arms in despair. "You know as well as I do how difficult it is to talk your way out of a confession later!"

"Well," Hanne said, staring at the attorney's feet, "there are examples of that as well. As awful as we police officers are, people can talk their way out of most things. We virtually resort to torture, you know. To force out false confessions. At least that's how you lawyers would have it." She gave a crooked smile and crossed her arms.

"I visited Cecilie this morning," Karen said.

"When I asked you to come here, it was precisely because I understand all the points you're making," Hanne said. "I'm not out to make things worse for Halvorsrud either."

"It was good to see her. Good and really distressing at the same time. Strange." Karen laid her hand on Hanne's arm. "It's so great that things are better between you," she said softly. "It's obviously done Cecilie good."

"If I were you," Hanne said, "I would talk him out of it."

She took a step back, almost imperceptible, and continued. "I'll see what I can do about that special report. Dress it up a little. Insofar as I can. I can say something about him just being at the end of his tether and wanting to talk to someone. And so on and so forth."

Karen Borg drew her hand away. "How will it go on Monday?" she asked, clearly discouraged. "At the funeral, I mean."

"I'll see what I can do." Hanne retreated even farther, and blew her hair out of her eyes.

"No repeat of the Rashool case," Karen Borg pleaded. "Forget the handcuffs and all that stuff, please. They look so awful at a funeral."

Hanne gestured to indicate they should return to her office. Karen stopped her with a movement of her right hand. Staring fixedly at the Mickey Mouse Band-Aids, Hanne smiled faintly.

"Are you managing to sleep?" Karen asked.

"If I were you . . ." Hanne began, glancing conspiratorially over her shoulder. "If I were Halvorsrud's attorney, I would demand a new custody hearing. Apply for a reversal! The guy wants some kind of alternative to custody. Go for it, then! Get him to report in instead—a couple of times a day or something. Try. Arrange bail for the guy!"

"Bail? A surety bond?"

"Yes! We have the option to do that in Norway as well. The fact that it's never used doesn't mean it's not permissible. Check paragraph 188, if you would. His daughter is seriously ill. The man has friends in the system. He looks terrible. You said so yourself. Show some guts, then, and try!"

"'The guy wants' . . . 'Friends in the system' . . ." Karen Borg shook her head slowly. She positioned herself in front of the door, her legs as wide as her tight skirt would allow. "What's going on with you?" She wrinkled her brow in disbelief.

"Listen up," Hanne said in a low, eager voice, her face only five inches from Karen's. "When it comes to reasonable grounds for suspicion, we've got Halvorsrud by the balls. But strictly speaking, there's little risk of the man tampering with the evidence now. We've gone through his house with a fine-tooth comb. We've interviewed umpteen witnesses. We've bagged everything of interest at the family home and at his office. Plus a lot more besides, to be honest. Danger of a repeat offense? Hardly!"

She tapped her forefinger on her temple as she continued. "Will the girl succumb before her dad is able to help her?"

Karen Borg did not answer. She studied Hanne's eyes. They were a darker shade of blue than she remembered. The prominent black circles around the irises seemed to have grown in size. There was something new in Hanne's eyes. The pupils were large, and for a second Karen could see a wide-angled reflection of herself inside all the darkness.

"But what about paragraph 172?" she whispered, attempting to push Hanne farther away from the door. "I'd rather he couldn't hear us."

"Imprisonment on the grounds of the crime being particularly serious?"

Karen nodded.

Hanne gave a theatrical sigh and refused to budge. "Do you know how many days on average people are remanded in custody for now?"

"Sixty-something." Karen Borg placed both palms on Hanne's shoulders and did not stop until a couple of yards had opened up between the Chief Inspector and the door.

"Sixty-seven days," Hanne Wilhelmsen stated accurately. "Norwegian citizens are kept behind lock and key for sixty-seven days *without* trial. On average. It's ridiculous. No . . ." Once again, she looked over her shoulder. "Run with disproportionate response. Make use of the girl. Try, anyway. Don't be so bloody spineless."

Karen could restrain her no longer. Hanne forced her way past and opened the door into her office. Sigurd Halvorsrud was still sitting with his spine rigid and his hands on his lap. He glanced up only briefly, then went back to studying something on the exterior of the dark windowpane.

"Are you ready to discuss the matter now?" he asked.

"No," Hanne Wilhelmsen said. "I'm ready to let you have an in-depth discussion with your attorney. As for me, I was thinking of going home to sleep."

She leaned over an intercom and asked to have two wardens sent up from the cells.

"Now you can sit here in privacy," she told Halvorsrud. "Then we can talk again tomorrow if you still have something to say. Okay?"

"You're treating me like a child," he said quietly, still without looking in her direction.

"No," Hanne Wilhelmsen said, clicking the fingers of her left hand.

He flinched, and turned his head.

"I'm treating you as I'm duty-bound to," she said. "I'm trying to discover the truth about this case. My job is not to make you confess. My task is to obtain a confession if it's the truth."

"You believe me," he said impassively. "You realize I'm innocent."

"I haven't said that," Hanne said, trying to soften the harshness in her own voice. "I've certainly not said that."

Two uniformed officers stood at the door. One blew a bubble with his gum. Hanne chose to overlook it.

"Let Karen Borg sit here and talk to her client for as long as she wishes. You can stand outside the door. Don't forget to make sure you get home to your family soon."

The final remark was directed at Karen.

"My mother's visiting," Karen said casually. "She's looking after the children. Håkon's . . . Håkon's out tonight." Her fleeting smile was impossible to interpret.

Hanne gave a lengthy yawn. "See you later, then," she said, putting on a leather jacket with fringes and beaded Native American embroidery on the front. "Just call me tomorrow if there is anything. My cell phone is switched on."

As she closed the door behind her, she could no longer restrain herself.

"Bubble gum is *damned* unsuitable with that uniform," she said sharply to one of the officers. "It looks really dreadful."

He swallowed the pink lump on the spot.

43

The door was unlocked.

For a start, the alarm light was switched off. In other words, the security lock was open. When she peered through the crack between the door and its frame, she saw that the Yale lock was not engaged either.

It could not possibly be Cecilie. Her physician had said that the earliest she could come home was the middle of next week. Hanne Wilhelmsen stared tensely at the door, aware that her pulse was racing, as if she expected someone to suddenly burst out of the apartment.

Her eyes lingered on the door plate. "HW & CV."

She had never thought about how hurtful it might be. When she bought the brass plate, the anonymous initials had seemed like a good idea. It was simply sensible not to announce that two women were living there. Women who could be raped. Cecilie had listened to Hanne's principled police arguments and quietly stated that "Wilhelmsen & Vibe" would also not have given away too much. Sullen and slightly annoyed, Hanne had screwed on the plate, and since then the subject had never been mentioned.

Tentatively, she put her hand on the door knob.

She could hear someone inside. When she put her ear to the door, she thought she could identify noises in the kitchen. Saucepans and running water. She opened the door wide and stormed into the hallway.

"Hello," she said loudly, aware that her voice was shaking.

No one answered. She could smell food: ginger and coriander.

"Hi," Håkon Sand said, putting his head round the kitchen door, smiling broadly. "You're late."

"You scared me to death," Hanne muttered, quickly scratching her ear. "You damn near scared me to death."

"Sorry," Håkon said without much conviction. "I had the keys, of course. Thought you wouldn't be getting much to eat as things stand. Hadn't really planned on such a late supper, but then Karen called me on my cell phone and said you'd be late."

"I would have been anyway," Hanne said.

She was not really sure how she felt. Her pulse was still thumping at breakneck speed because of the surprise, and that irritated her. She was not easily frightened. Not usually, anyway. Besides, she had behaved like an amateur. If there really had been a burglar in the apartment, she could have come to grief. The right thing would have been to beat a hasty retreat, call for reinforcements, and wait.

She was hungry. Ravenous.

Not that it had bothered her very much; she couldn't remember when she had last felt hungry. Now, however, she was aware of a painful gnawing in her stomach, and it dawned on her that she had eaten nothing but two slices of dry bread with hospital cheese that morning.

"What have you made?" she asked, venturing a smile.

"Something delicious."

"You always make something delicious."

Hanne sat at the kitchen table. A shiver of cramp in her neck made her turn her head from side to side. The table was set beautifully, with the silver cutlery Cecilie had inherited from her grandmother and two candlesticks Hanne could scarcely recall ever having seen. The napkin in front of her was artfully folded.

"It looks like a swan," she said softly, making a face at the headache she felt coming on. "You're so kind, Håkon."

"I'm not kind," he said, putting down the wooden ladle. "I'm fond of you. That's something quite different. Now you're going to eat something, and then I'll massage your neck."

He pointed at her with a whisk before swiftly, skillfully, whipping the sauce in the pan.

"Then you're going to sleep. *Without* an alarm clock. How's the Halvorsrud case going?"

Hanne was breathing heavily. An unfamiliar warmth spread through her body. She wriggled out of her jacket and sat in silence wondering how she was actually feeling. She grabbed the pitcher of water and poured herself a glass. Her arm was trembling slightly and she spilled some but didn't bother to wipe it away. Then it struck her that she was pleased about his visit. She was hungry and was going to have some food. She had a headache and was going to have a massage. She was dead tired and perhaps would not have to sleep alone.

"Are you going to stay the night?" she asked distractedly.

"If you want me to," Håkon answered laconically. "I can at least stay until you fall asleep."

They ate in silence.

Hanne ate four helpings of baked halibut with ginger sauce without uttering a word. When she finally laid down her knife and fork and reluctantly opened out the swan to wipe her mouth, she gazed at Håkon and said, "Something's bothering me about this Ståle Salvesen."

Håkon did not reply. Instead he removed her plate, then dried his hands on a grubby towel and stood behind her chair.

"Take off your blouse," he said.

His hands felt burning hot on her bare shoulders. She shivered and closed her eyes. His thumbs pressed on two tender spots under her shoulder blades, and made the hairs on her neck quite literally stand on end. She gave a soft, prolonged moan.

"There's something about his apartment," she whispered, persevering. "Something I saw. Maybe something I found. Or didn't find. I just can't think what it was."

"Forget it," he said in an undertone. "Forget it for tonight."

44

It was Sunday evening, March 21, and Karlsen the caretaker was feeling somewhat under the weather. There had been a bit too much

brandy the night before. Karlsen was not used to more than an occasional nip in his coffee. Pure spirits were too potent. After all, he was
no longer young. During the war, on shore leave in the States, he had
sometimes gone on a bender. But not now. No more than a tiny drop
to slake his thirst when his dreams became crowded with wolves in
German helmets and he could not get back to sleep.

Karlsen mourned his friend Ståle Salvesen.

Truth to tell, he felt slightly wounded as well. If his friend had been
planning to leave this world's vale of tears—something Karlsen could
well understand after the treatment Ståle had been subjected to by the
damned authorities—then he might have given a sign of some sort.
Some kind of goodbye. Karlsen understood of course that the man
couldn't very well have told him about his gloomy intentions, for then
the old wartime sailor would have done his utmost to talk his friend
out of it. Life still had a few pleasures to offer. The pleasant evenings
in the tiny living room with quiet conversation and some jazz on the
gramophone had cheered Karlsen up at least.

He sighed deeply and impatiently stirred the aspirin that was taking
its time to dissolve in the glass of water. Then he lifted his gaze and let
it linger on the photograph of Klara. The frame still bore the narrow
black ribbon he had bought the day she was buried. Tears filled his
eyes at the sight of the strapping woman with permed hair and that
beautiful brooch on her chest. He had inherited it from his mother
and given it to Klara as an engagement present. Annoyed, he shook his
head and downed the medication in one gulp. The bitter taste made
him shudder, and he was tempted to drink the last swig from the
liquor bottle.

He let it be.

Then it dawned on him: Ståle Salvesen *had* given him a sign. An
advance warning, a kind of farewell. Of course he had!

Karlsen stood up and finally put on a percolator of coffee. He felt
better now. Ståle had no one but him. There was only him. Ståle could
rely on Ole Monrad Karlsen. That was why he had been asked to do
him one last favor. Naturally Karlsen had wondered about it when he
was asked, but now he understood everything.

Ståle Salvesen *had* said goodbye.

In his own way.

45

Mustafa Özdemir was a man of his word. As early as half past nine, he had reported to the information desk in the spacious foyer of police headquarters and asked to speak to Karianne Holbeck. It was Monday morning, and he had an important appointment. He was dressed for the occasion in brown trousers and shoes and a pale-blue shirt. His tie was old and perhaps a touch too wide, but he did not keep up to date with that sort of thing. The police lady would just have to accept that; a tie was a tie, after all. His jacket had loud checks and was on the tight side. Mustafa Özdemir felt fine nevertheless; he was freshly showered and had even spent almost a quarter of an hour carefully trimming his bushy, coal-black beard.

Karianne Holbeck felt a stab of relief when she clapped eyes on him. Admittedly, he looked exactly as she had anticipated: she had never understood why all the men from those parts wore beards. Perhaps it was like people from the Trøndelag district of Norway, who, it seemed, always liked to have something underneath their noses. At least this man did not smell sweaty, and his clothes were well cared for, if somewhat old-fashioned.

"Take a seat," she said, pointing at a chair. "It's great that you came."

"We had an appointment, didn't we?"

He appeared offended, as if there had been an insinuation of unreliability in what she said. That was true enough, and she tried to improve the atmosphere by offering him some coffee.

"No, thanks very much," he said deprecatingly, waving his right hand. "If I drink coffee, I get problems with my stomach, you see."

Özdemir made an eloquent gesture before smiling broadly.

Hanne Wilhelmsen entered Karianne Holbeck's office without knocking.

"Mustafa," she said in amazement, offering her hand. "Is it you?"

"Hanna," he said, beaming, and leapt to his feet. "Hanna!"

"Hanne," Karianne Holbeck whispered, blushing faintly on the man's behalf. "She's called Hanne. With an 'e.'"

"Hanna, my friend!" He was reluctant to let go of her hand. "Why are you here, Hanna? Do you know this lady?"

He waved his hand in Karianne Holbeck's direction as if he found the thought of a friendship between these two women totally out of the question. Finally he resumed his seat. Hanne Wilhelmsen remained on her feet, holding the door open with her hip, since there was no third chair.

"I work here," she said, smiling at his histrionically wide eyes. "I work in the police force."

"You've never mentioned that," he complained. "For heaven's sake! My Hanna's a policewoman!"

He leaned across the table to Karianne Holbeck, who obviously felt disturbed by the witness's familiar tone with the Chief Inspector.

"Hanna's my favorite customer," he said, waving his finger with its sprouting black hairs at Hanne. "So many people go to Sultan in Thorvald Meyers gate . . ." He made a sorrowful face as he smacked his lips. "Everybody wants to go to Sultan, you know. But not Hanna. She comes to Özdemir Import. Always, you know."

"I can fetch a chair," Karianne said, trying to squeeze past Hanne Wilhelmsen.

"No, I can do that myself. Take his personal details in the meantime." It was less than a minute before she returned.

"I hear you received an exciting phone call last autumn," she said once she had sat down. "Tell me about it, won't you?"

Karianne Holbeck felt crushed. She felt harassed. It was one thing for the Chief Inspector to enter her office without even having the courtesy to give a tiny little knock on the door first. Worse was that she now obviously intended to take over the interview, but without taking overall responsibility for it: it was quite clear that Hanne Wilhelmsen had no intention of writing down a single syllable of the report that would necessarily result from such an interview. In that case she would have moved the interview into her own office and used her own computer. Most of all Karianne Holbeck wanted to tell the Chief Inspector to get lost. Instead, she found an extra cup and filled it with coffee before placing it in front of Hanne Wilhelmsen.

Mustafa Özdemir began to tell his story.

His voice was calmer now. Following his polite opening comments about the merits of Hanne Wilhelmsen, Karianne Holbeck had pigeon-holed him as a linguistically challenged, tiresome Turk. Now he was completely different. The brown eyes beneath the thick eyebrows kept unwavering eye contact with one of the two police officers at all times.

The story about his tax problems flowed easily, clearly, and credibly. Having had his books inspected, Mustafa Özdemir was to be prosecuted for defective accounting and tax evasion. According to him, it was all an unfortunate misunderstanding. He promptly sought legal assistance, and five months later the case was dropped. The problem was that he had been mentioned in a related case reported in the *Verdens Gang* newspaper. The article had been about sleaze in the shops run by immigrants that had become so popular, and Özdemir Import had been referred to by name. It had of course affected his trade. At present it looked as though the compensation claim he had raised against the newspaper would not succeed.

"But before that . . ." he eventually said, producing a box of candy and offering it to the others. "Before my case was dropped, this Sigurd Halvorsrud phoned me. One evening. It was actually my wife who took the call. She had to search for me for a while. I was in the storeroom, you see. He said that he could sort it all out."

"And he introduced himself?" Hanne Wilhelmsen asked explicitly, glancing across at her colleague. "With his full name?"

"Yes, yes," Özdemir insisted, taking out a folded sheet of paper from his back pocket. "You can see here. I wrote down the name."

"Sigor Halvorsrod" was written on the paper. Hanne held it between her forefinger and thumb, noisily sucking the candy.

"And then?" she asked, sniffing slightly. "What happened then?"

Özdemir shifted in his seat and crossed his legs. Then he put his fingertips together, into a steeple formation, and for the first time did not look at either of them. Instead he squinted at a point somewhere between the two policewomen and paused for several seconds before continuing.

"The first phone call came on the tenth of November," he said slowly. "That must have been a . . . Tuesday, isn't that right?"

Karianne Holbeck turned to check a calendar for the previous year that was hanging on the wall behind her.

"Mhmm." She nodded. "Tuesday, November 10, 1998."

"I didn't understand very much about it, you know."

He spoke considerably more slowly now, as if examining his own memory and unwilling to say too much.

"So I said a little of yes and mhmm and so on, and I said I'd have to think about it. I . . ."

He cocked his head, and Hanne could swear she saw a hint of red under his dark skin.

"I was quite devastated about that case, you see. Norwegian police and us foreigners . . ."

Shrugging, he peered meaningfully at Hanne Wilhelmsen. She gave a faint smile in return without looking at her colleague.

"I understand," she said tersely. "You were a little tempted, in other words."

"But I also wasn't sure what the man really meant," Özdemir said, shaking his head. "He wasn't . . . wasn't very clear. Do you know what I mean?"

Hanne Wilhelmsen nodded again. "Did he say anything at all about money? About you having to pay anything?"

"No . . . not really. It was just as if I *understood* that, you see. No." Mustafa Özdemir looked dejectedly from one to the other. "It would be better if I could tell you exactly what the man said. But it's so long ago, you know. I don't remember exactly, but I realized afterward that if I could pay him some money, then my case would disappear. Dismitted. No . . . dismissed, I mean."

Özdemir scratched his neck.

"My wife, she asked me what it was about, you see. She didn't like the man's voice. She gave me a terrible argument when I told her he might be able to help us."

"But did you make any arrangement?" Karianne Holbeck asked; this was the first time she had spoken in the entire interview. "Did you get a number to phone?"

"No, he said he'd call me."

"Did he do that?" Hanne Wilhelmsen asked him.

"Yes. He phoned two days later. In the evening again. He probably knew the shop was open late. My wife and I, you know, we're nearly always in the shop. My daughter too. You know Sophia, Hanna. She's qualified in business studies, you know."

A soft expression crossed his face when he talked about his daughter. Hanne knew Mustafa had only one child, a daughter aged twenty. Why Sophia was an only child, she had no idea, but the young woman was all the more loved and unfortunately also quite overprotected by her parents. Hanne knew the girl wanted to study medicine, but her father had said she had to wait until she was twenty-five. Sophia attended evening classes to take the science subjects she needed to begin medical studies. Her father met her faithfully outside Bjørknes private high school three times a week in order to see her safely home.

"What did he say then?"

"Not very much. The same as the first time. But now I was very strong and clear. Out of the question, I said. He was . . . polite? Didn't get angry or anything. He just said goodbye. Since then, I haven't heard anything. Then . . ."

He smiled broadly and his even, white teeth came into sight underneath his moustache.

"Then I had a good lawyer, you see. He sorted it all out and everything was fine."

Hanne Wilhelmsen closed her eyes. "I'd like to ask you a big favor, Mustafa. If you don't want to . . . If you think it's disagreeable or anything, just say so. You're in no way compelled to say yes."

She opened her eyes suddenly and stared at the man in the shoddy checked jacket.

"For my Hanna, I'll do anything at all!"

"Well," Hanne said. "This isn't exactly for me, but for the police. Can we have your permission to ask Telenor for a printout of all incoming calls to your phone on the days in question? I'm not entirely sure whether it's possible, from a purely technical point of view, but in any case we need your permission."

Mustafa Özdemir hesitated for barely a second, then gave a sudden burst of laughter.

"That's fine," he said. "I don't have anything to hide, you know."

"Then you write this down," Hanne said, speaking to Karianne as she got to her feet. "And write out a warrant we can show to Telenor into the bargain."

She held out her hand to Mustafa Özdemir, who sprang out of his seat and clasped both hands around hers.

"Thanks for getting in touch," Hanne Wilhelmsen said.

"You must come to me soon," he answered earnestly. "Bring that beautiful friend of yours with you, and you'll get the excellent tomatoes my wife has been growing in our bath!"

"And thank *you* very much," Hanne said to Karianne Holbeck as she was about to leave the room. "It's so good of you to take care of the paperwork!"

"A modicum of thanks helps a little, at least," Karianne whispered under her breath and nodded as the door closed. "But not much."

And then she started to write.

46

At first Hanne Wilhelmsen thought she had run into Billy T. The man was massive, and when he used one arm to lift her up off her knees again, while gathering the papers she had dropped with the other, he employed a strength she thought she recognized. However, when she raised her eyes, she saw she was mistaken.

"Sorry," the man said unhappily, reluctant to let her go.

"It was my fault." Hanne tried to brush him aside. "Long time no see."

He smiled as he slapped a business card on top of the papers she had at last managed to collect into a bundle. "Iver K. Feirand, Chief Inspector."

"Congratulations," she said deferentially. "I should have said that to you ages ago."

"It was only two months ago."

Iver Feirand was a newly appointed chief inspector with responsibility for sexual assaults on children, one of the foremost experts in the country. At the beginning of the eighties, after the eyes of the Ministry of Justice, the prosecution authorities, and the police had been opened to the fact that sexual abuse of children was not simply a foreign phenomenon, several investigators had been allowed to specialize in that area. They themselves were of the opinion that there ought to be three times as many of them, but a few was at least better than none at all. Over the years, Iver Feirand had served at Interpol in Lyon and Scotland Yard in London and had also followed an advanced course with the American FBI. He shared Hanne's fascination with everything the United States had to offer.

"What've you been up to?" He smiled and held out his hands, ready to carry her papers. Hanne shook her head.

"The Halvorsrud murder. Plus a ton of other cases." She glanced eloquently at the five thick folders she was carrying.

"Hell, what a case," he said, accompanying her along the corridor. "When are you going to break the guy?"

"Don't know. Don't even know if he did it."

Iver Feirand gave a loud and hearty laugh. "You *never* know for sure whether anyone has done anything!"

"Strictly speaking, that should always be our attitude until sentence is passed. Don't you agree?"

He shrugged, and at once became serious. "The problem for us is exactly the opposite," he said, thrusting his hands deep into his pockets. "The people we arrest are so guilty it's spilling out of them. Yet it's so rare for us to achieve a conviction. But you . . ."

He stopped and placed his hand on her shoulder. Unwillingly, she slowed down and turned to face him.

"I hear rumors that you're going to sell your bike," he said doubtfully, scratching his forehead. "Is that true?"

"Where did you hear that?"

Hanne could not for the life of her think whether she had mentioned her plans to get rid of her Harley to anyone other than Cecilie.

"Not sure. But is it true?"

"I'm thinking about it."

"Why?"

Hanne sighed and set off again. "I'd prefer to keep that to myself."

"Is there anything wrong with it?"

"No."

"What do you want for it?"

They had reached Hanne's office door. Iver Feirand, legs straddled, blocked her path.

"I don't know," Hanne said resignedly. "I haven't even decided to sell it yet."

That was not true. She knew the motorbike had to go. She had tried not to think about it; she still had not made up her mind why it was so important for her to be rid of it.

"How many times has it been painted?" Iver Feirand asked. "I mean, it wasn't actually pink when you bought it, was it?

"Oh yes. I ordered it specially from the factory."

"Listen . . ."

He scratched his throat.

"If you're going to sell it, you must let me know. I'm really damn interested, if the price is right. My old woman'll be annoyed, of course, but now it's my turn in this life. So I'd like to get it repainted. Give me a call, would you?"

He took his leave of her by putting two fingers to his forehead, before jogging back to the blue zone. Hanne remained there for a few more seconds, watching him go. He looked so like Billy T. from the back, though Iver Feirand's backside was much more attractive.

"A hundred and twenty thousand perhaps," she murmured. "At least."

47

A young boy of around twelve stood on his own in front of the congregation, wearing a white ankle-length gown that seemed too big for him. His hands were folded neatly over his middle. Perhaps he had received strict instructions to stand like that, but the constant twiddling of his thumbs could indicate the boy was simply nervous and did not quite know where to put his pale fingers. A shock of blond, curly hair wreathed his head like a halo, and his high-pitched, angelic voice crept along the bare walls of pale terracotta.

The boy sang two verses of the Norwegian psalm "Å leva det er å elska" (To Live Is to Love), and the funeral service was over.

Billy T. opened his eyes.

He had been sitting in an uncomfortable position and now hurried out of the church ahead of the rest of the packed congregation.

Everyone was there. The Director of Public Prosecution, tall, slim, and obviously just as ill at ease on the hard pews as Billy T., was seated in the second row. At least six renowned lawyers had chosen to pay Doris Flo Halvorsrud their last respects, as far as Billy T. could count. In addition, there was a huge throng of public prosecutors, from the Økokrim police department as well as the appellate courts. None of them were in a hurry to step out into the center aisle; they sat stretching their backs and craning their necks in an effort to be seen. Both by Halvorsrud himself, who was sitting in the front row and was clearly struggling to free himself from his daughter, and by the rest of the congregation.

Only the police tried to be discreet.

At the end of the two front pews sat four police officers, dressed in dark civilian clothes. A trained eye would have identified them as soon as they arrived. They appeared self-conscious in their suits; their constant shoulder shrugging and repeated snatching at their trouser legs implied that they were used to more practical attire. The four men kept their eyes fixed unwaveringly on Sigurd Halvorsrud for an hour and a half. While everyone else tried to avoid staring—it was difficult, since most people were intensely curious about how Halvorsrud would look after more than three weeks in custody—the police officers sat unabashedly gazing at the funeral's real central character.

"This is a strange demonstration," Billy T. said tersely to Karen Borg as she approached him on the gravel path outside the church, greeting him with an affable nod of the head.

"Demonstration?" she repeated in a monotone, glancing up at the church steps, where Halvorsrud was the object of whispered but nonetheless heartfelt condolences from a gathering of the prosecuting authorities, in a manner of speaking. "What do you mean by that?"

"O. J. Simpson," Billy T. continued. "White Americans thought he was guilty. Black Americans refused to believe it."

"Okay," Karen Borg replied, uninterested.

"Can't you see it? The police believe Halvorsrud is guilty. The prosecution authorities can't believe it. No, damn it; not one of their own. Lawyers versus police officers. The same old story."

He tugged at his earlobe, where the usual inverted cross had been swapped for a little diamond stud in honor of the occasion.

"Quite provocative," he went on. "On the other hand, it's almost touching to see that even you lawyers can stand together now and again. Normally you're at each other's throats."

He took the measure of Karen Borg, from head to toe, as if he had only just seen her, and gave a low whistle. She was wearing a simply cut charcoal suit with a black, collarless blouse. She was carrying her coat over her arm; a chink in the cloud cover had suddenly given the sun some warmth as people began to stream out of the church.

"You look stunning," Billy T. said, stroking the sleeve of her jacket.

"You too," she answered, smiling subtly. "I'm pleased to see you've got the sense to take off that awful devil's cross at times like this."

"It's not a cross." Billy T. sighed resignedly. "It's a stylized representation of Thor's hammer! I'm so tired of—"

He restrained himself. The Director of Public Prosecution passed them with a slow nod and the merest hint of a reticent smile at Karen Borg. He was flanked on either side by two men dressed in dark clothing. They resembled bodyguards in the way they stayed one step behind their boss, continually keeping in time. However, since one was extremely overweight and the other barely five foot seven, it was more likely that the Director would have to fend for himself if anything unforeseen or threatening occurred.

"O. J. Simpson was guilty," Karen Borg said.

"What?"

"He killed his ex-wife and her lover. Obviously."

She began walking to the parking lot. Billy T. followed with shuffling steps across the gravel.

"That's not what he says!" He gave a perfunctory laugh. "The man was freed eventually, if I might dare to remind the lady of such an inconsequential fact."

Karen Borg wheeled around suddenly. "Have you decided on a name?"

Canting his head to one side, Billy T. squinted at the shifting clouds, which had obscured the sun once more.

"No. The baby's going to remain nameless if we don't get our act together. Tone-Marit goes for all these modern ones—Julie, Amalie, Matilde, names like that. I want something decent and traditional. Ragnhild or Ingeborg. Something along those lines."

"How's O. J. Simpson getting on now, do you think?" Karen opened the driver's door of her ancient blue Audi.

"Bloody terrible, by all accounts," Billy T. replied.

"Exactly. Because everyone really *knows* that he did it. It's different with Halvorsrud. Since the prosecution authorities . . ." Karen Borg nodded in the direction of the dark-suited men clambering into their cars in the crowded parking lot. The muffled reports from the car doors as they slammed around them sounded like a halting, truncated funeral march. ". . . Since these people obviously believe in Halvorsrud's innocence, this doesn't have anything to do with social opposites. Black America didn't believe in O. J. Simpson's innocence. *Poor*, black America did. Or I should say, they didn't give a damn whether he was guilty. Their point was that the man was above guilt or innocence. He became a victim of white power. They couldn't convict him. It would have been like convicting themselves. So don't come here drawing hopeless comparisons. Halvorsrud *is* innocent. He has quite simply not done what you're accusing him of."

"Heavens, that was quite a flare-up," Billy T. said, running his hand over his skull.

Karen Borg had been standing for so long with the car door held open, and had raised her voice so much, that people were beginning to look in their direction. Now she stepped into the car and closed the door. Billy T. knocked on the window with his knuckles. He saw her sigh resignedly before she wound the window halfway down.

"You're wrong," he said, resting his arms on the car roof. "Your rather lightweight analysis of the O. J. Simpson case is probably okay. But if you can't see that the cases have some things in common, then you've got lost in the details of your own defense."

Karen Borg began to wind up the window again with agitated gestures.

"Wait!" Billy T. barked, grabbing the edge of the glass. "Don't you see it's all a matter of identification? If Halvorsrud is guilty, then it's a setback for every member of the prosecution authorities. That's why they're all here. They want to show solidarity, that they can't believe one of their own, someone from their own social class, with the same background, the same education, financially well off, with a wife and children and an impressive home . . . That would be too much. Halvorsrud's possible guilt would strike at every single one of them. They're asking themselves: 'Could I have done this?' The answer is obviously no, and so they take the most dangerous course of action in the world as far as we who have to enforce the law and distinguish truth from untruth are concerned: they identify with the bad guy."

He slapped the roof with the palm of his hand.

"Don't you see that, Karen?"

She looked at him for some time.

"For a while I thought that you attached some credence to his explanation," she said finally. "I certainly let myself be fooled that was the situation. So did Halvorsrud. I seem to recall a tirade about you being his only friend and a lot of stuff along those lines. Stupid of us both, of course. Believing that sort of thing, I mean."

She turned the key in the ignition.

Shaking his head, Billy T. leaned away from the vehicle. Karen struggled to find first gear, and the engine produced a grinding noise before it died. She made a fresh attempt to start the car, but obviously did not have the clutch depressed. The car jumped forward six feet and the engine stalled.

"Should I take over?" Billy T. mouthed with his face only ten centimeters from the windshield.

She did not even glance in his direction. At the third attempt she managed to start the car and rolled slowly out to the road without even asking Billy T. if he needed a lift.

He turned on his heel and crossed to the lower parking lot, normally reserved for vehicles belonging to the disabled. The police vehicle was waiting there. Halvorsrud was already ensconced in the back seat. Billy T. could hear Thea Halvorsrud sobbing inconsolably from the church steps, while her two clumsy brothers and almost hysterical aunt tried in vain to comfort her.

48

When he closed his eyes, it was not his wife's coffin he saw, but that was what he wanted to remember. He had not wanted it to be brown. No one had asked him, but for some reason he had thought that it would be white. Shiny white, with a simple wreath of red roses on the lid. When he'd caught sight of the brown wood overloaded with multicolored flowers that completely obliterated the wreath from him and the children, he was filled with an impotent rage. At the end of the funeral service, the coffin looked black, and he wanted to remember it all differently.

It was his daughter's face he saw.

He opened his eyes.

It was so bright in there. The harsh, bluish-white light that told him nothing about the time of day was driving him mad. He wished he had a window, even just a tiny crack. Something impossible to escape through, but that would at least give him a little blink to indicate the passage of time. They had taken away his watch. He had no idea why.

How it might be possible to injure oneself with a plain leather strap was beyond Sigurd Halvorsrud's comprehension.

He let his eyelids slide shut once again.

He saw Thea's face. He saw her big, tear-stained eyes. He saw her mouth soundlessly forming words he did not want to see. He felt her hand in his, on his thigh; her entire body pressing so close to him that he had almost lacked the strength to remain seated. He saw her arms stretching out to him as he was firmly led away and down to the waiting police car. He felt her eyes on his back: two rays burning through his suit jacket, making it difficult to stay upright.

Chief Public Prosecutor Sigurd Halvorsrud was incarcerated in the back yard of the police headquarters for a third week. The cells were not designed to accommodate anyone for more than twenty-four hours. They had offered to move him to a better place, a prison outside the city. They had suggested several institutions he knew were far more modern than this, but he did not want to go. He did not trust them. Everything else they did was hostile. Eventually he had gotten used to the room. He wanted to remain at the police headquarters, and they had allowed him to do so.

Suddenly he sat up. The nausea came from down below, all the way from his feet, flooding through his body in violent waves, and it was pointless trying to resist. The vomit came so unexpectedly that he was unable even to turn away from the hard plank bed on which he was lying. His white shirt was sprayed with the remains of the two slices of bread he had eaten for breakfast.

He could not remember what he had eaten with the bread. It must have been mackerel in tomato sauce, but it did not taste like that. This had the bittersweet taste of iron.

Sigurd Halvorsrud continued to throw up blood for nearly a quarter of an hour before he could drag himself to the door to call for help.

49

Hanne Wilhelmsen was sitting with the Yellow Pages directory open in front of her. It seemed as if her hands had quite automatically retrieved the thick book from underneath an old copy of

Verdens Gang at the far end of the desk. She could swear it wasn't her who had leafed through it to the "Psychologists" category. She certainly did not need a psychologist and already knew far too many of them.

The book shut with a hollow thud when Billy T. popped his head round the half-open door.

"It'll soon be half past five," he said. "You're coming with me."

He held out his hand as if to haul off a stubborn child.

"Come on, let's go." He used his hands to coax her, with a broad grin on his face.

"Where are we going?" she asked, half rising from her chair and stifling a yawn.

Cecilie was coming home from the hospital the following day. Hanne was not sure whether she was really looking forward to it. Of course she longed to see her. On the few nights she had chosen to sleep at home instead of at the hospital in the hope of getting more than a couple of hours' doze out of the night, she had cried herself to sleep from a sense of loss so great it was only surpassed by the forlorn yearning she felt when she sat at Cecilie's bedside. Hanne wanted Cecilie to come home. At the same time, it felt safer having her at the hospital. Being at work all day did not feel quite as disloyal as it was sure to do when she knew she had left Cecilie on her own.

"As a matter of fact, I can't. I've got things to do at home tonight. How did the funeral go?"

"Well enough. But you have to come with me."

"I can't, I said. I have to do some housework."

She tried to persuade her hair to sit in a kind of side parting she had fashioned because she never found time to go to the hairdresser's. Her bangs were resistant, and she spat lightly on her fingers before running her hand through her hair.

"What's this all about anyway?"

"You'll see. If you don't come, I'll carry you off by force. You might call this a sort of kidnapping."

Hanne Wilhelmsen capitulated and followed him without taking hold of his outstretched hand.

50

The sea was white with foam, even all the way up there. He stood on the terrace, squinting at the wind and the island of Østerøya in the distance as he clasped his hands around the wrought-iron railings. The islet of Natholmen did not provide much shelter when the wind blew from the south, so he shook off the idea of taking the boat out onto the fjord in search of fish. An hour earlier, when he'd been at the convenience store in Solløkka buying essentials to see him through the next few days, he'd had the foresight to purchase two packs of frozen cod.

It was all a fantastic and unexpected breakthrough.

Nothing less.

When the name had appeared on the screen, he had begun to tremble. He imagined it was like winning the lottery. Like making a full recovery from an incurable, lethal illness, unexpectedly and quite inexplicably. Like finding a dearly loved family member after presuming the person dead for a number of years. A warm wave surged from his belly and he literally gasped.

He had worked on this for three years now.

In April 1996 he had taken the compensation Oslo City Council had been ordered to pay him for his lost, despoiled childhood, added to it the money that had flooded in from the sale of *Red Light in Amsterdam* to an ever-increasing number of countries, and bought the cottage. Twenty years ago he had spent a summer here, the only warm memory he had from the time before he was sent to prison. His own flesh and blood, his aunt, had sold the place long ago. Eivind Torsvik had turned up at the new owner's house and offered the man one and a half times what the property was worth. The guy had been given two hours to make up his mind. The sight of five million kroner in a suitcase was too persuasive. Three weeks later, Eivind Torsvik had moved in, with four hundred fifty pounds of electronic equipment, a duffel bag full of clothes, and an old sofa. As time went by and the work advanced, he had treated himself to new furniture and stereo equipment. The cottage at Hamburgkilen, all of five miles from Sandefjord town center, had become Eivind Torsvik's first real home. He had done everything himself. He enjoyed living alone, and knew that this was how it would always be.

The name had seared into him.

Eivind Torsvik sat on the timber bench outside the living-room window. The wind had to be close to gale force. He listened to the noise of the sea and the sound of his hair being whipped against his cheeks. He glanced up at two terns unable to ride the violent gusts of wind as they veered back through the air with hoarse, high-pitched screams. He breathed the sea air deep into his lungs and reveled in his freedom.

Now it was just a question of time.

51

In truth, the baby was unusually beautiful. Her head was well formed and the back of the skull elongated, suggesting she would not bear any particular resemblance to her father. The black, soft hair at her forehead was remarkably thick, and curved around her ears in something reminiscent of curls. Hanne Wilhelmsen had never seen a baby of Norwegian descent with such long eyelashes. They curled over the big, slightly crooked eyes that became round as saucers when the infant blinked at the bright light. The irises were of indefinable color, and would probably turn brown in the fullness of time. Her red lips were sharply outlined against her white skin. The milk button on her upper lip trembled reflexively as Hanne carefully stroked her little finger across the baby's chin.

"She really *is* good enough to eat," she whispered. "And she doesn't look like you at all."

"Thank goodness," Billy T. whispered back. "I just rush around saying these things because it's expected of me. I was delighted when I saw she hadn't inherited anything from my side of the family."

"Apart from her length," Hanne said, laughing softly as she tucked the baby's feet under the pink blanket. "She must be much longer than normal, don't you think?"

"Long and slim," Billy T. replied. "Twenty-three and a half inches at birth! And only just over eight pounds in weight."

Hanne settled the baby, who was falling asleep, into the crook of her arm. Her right hand was loosely clutching a pacifier. Hanne tried to push it into place in her tiny mouth, but she spat it out at once and it landed on the floor.

"Doesn't want it," Billy T. said with a smile, sitting down beside Hanne on the sofa. "She likes to hold the pacifier, but absolutely refuses to suck it. Smart kid. Can't be fooled."

The baby brought up some wind, and a little trickle of milk mixed with saliva ran down from the corner of her mouth. Hanne inhaled deeply through her nose, absorbing the sweet scent of the baby's breath, which felt like a punch in the abdomen. She blinked rapidly to force back the tears.

"You should have had a child yourselves," Billy T. said, putting his arm around Hanne's shoulder. "You should have done it long ago."

"Shouldn't I hold her over my shoulder when she's got wind?" Hanne murmured.

"No, it's okay. She's fast asleep now, and her breathing is fine. Why didn't you both do that?"

Hanne's eyes scanned Billy T.'s apartment. It was only two years since she had stayed there for more than a month, when she and Cecilie had been living in the United States for a year and the murder of Norway's Prime Minister, Birgitte Volter, had drawn Hanne back to her homeland for what was actually supposed to be a kind of vacation. Everything was different now. After Tone-Marit had moved in, pictures had appeared on the walls and the shelves had been stocked with books. The colossal stereo system had been banished into a closet, and only the loudspeakers still loomed under the ceiling on either side of the door leading into the hallway. Hanne was stung as she noticed for the first time that the curtains she had sewn and hung during that time had been replaced.

"Everything's so different," she whispered to the baby.

Billy T. got to his feet and lifted the infant carefully from Hanne's lap.

"Now you're going for an evening nap with Mum," he mumbled, creeping toward the bedroom.

When he returned a second later, he did not sit on the chair opposite Hanne. Instead he plopped himself down on the sofa beside her, where he had been sitting while the baby was awake. Then it had been logical for him to sit there, since he had to sit like that in order for them to share in their contemplation and admiration of the newborn. He put his arm around her shoulders once more—loosely, with his fingertips gently and evenly stroking her upper arm.

"I don't think this is so fucking easy," he said so softly that she wondered briefly whether she had heard him correctly.

"What's that?"

"This . . ."

With his free hand, he made a vague sweep of the room.

"The apartment. It's as if it isn't mine any longer. Tone-Marit . . ."

He was whispering now, barely audibly, as if afraid Tone-Marit had woken up, despite having checked so recently that she was sound asleep.

"I do want to have her here, of course," he said slowly. "I love . . . I love what she does for me. A lot of it, at least. And the baby's beautiful. I'm insanely fond of that baby. I've been really happy about every single child I've acquired."

Hanne gave a muffled laugh.

"Acquired," she repeated. "That makes it sound as if you've got five investments."

Billy T. hoisted his feet onto the table and sank down even closer to her on the deep cushions of the sofa. She could feel his chin against her ear, and simultaneously felt herself relax. She could not recall when she had last felt like this.

"But sometimes I'm climbing the walls," he continued. "I feel as if I can't breathe in here. There are baby things all over the place. There's a feminine smell in the bathroom. Tone-Marit is kind and patient and doesn't fuss the way other women do. About the toilet seat and toothpaste and so on. It's as if I do . . . I've started to do man stuff just to annoy her."

He sat up straight and turned to face her. His face was only a few inches away from hers. She stared into his ice-blue eyes but, unable to bear it for long, she let her gaze slide down to his mouth. It looked so enormous at close range. All she could see was his mouth: the cracked dry lips below the huge moustache that came and went faster than anyone could keep track of it. Right now it was gigantic, and she studied the bristling hairs one by one, aware that her thoughts were jumbled.

"And this summer we're getting *married*," he said through clenched teeth. "I can't get bloody married as long as I don't . . . When I feel like this even when the baby's only . . . Fucking hell!"

"I have to go," she said stiffly, clasping her hands around her knee.

"Go?"

He withdrew his arm abruptly, struggling with a disappointed expression that was proving difficult to conceal.

"Do you have to go? Now?"

"I told you I'd lots to do, remember? Cecilie. She's coming home tomorrow. I have to clean and tidy up the apartment."

Hanne stood up and headed for the front door.

"You didn't answer when I asked why you never had any children," she heard him say behind her back.

Slowly, as if she had not quite decided whether to respond, she turned around and looked at him. He was still seated on the sofa, still scratching the stubble on his chin like a madman.

"I don't know," she lied. "But now we can all be glad it never came to pass, can't we?"

Not until she was down on the street did she discover she had left her cell phone and a bag of groceries in Billy T.'s apartment. She hailed a taxi and was home before *Dagsrevyen*, the evening news roundup, had started on TV. There would probably be something edible in the fridge.

52

"You've become so skinny," Margaret Kleiven complained. "You've always been slim, of course, but now you're just skin and bones!"

Evald Bromo had begun to despise his wife. He had never loved her, but there had always been something positive in his feelings for her scrawny figure; a kind of fond dependence bordering on gratitude. Now he found her repulsive. On days like this, when she had hurried home from work to clean the house for the weekend, greeting him with a shabby apron over her stomach and bright-pink hands from all the scrubbing, he could hardly endure the dry touch of her lips on his cheek as he hung up his coat.

"You need to stop that running. It's not healthy. By the way, a parcel arrived for you."

"A parcel," he repeated distantly.

An odor of detergent and fried pollock wafted toward him as he entered the kitchen. Sitting down heavily in a Windsor chair, he rested his elbows on the table.

"Exhausted," he said.

"Food?"

"Yes, please."

She picked up the plate in front of him and crossed to the stove. He stared at her apathetically, trying to conjure up an appetite he had not felt for more than three weeks. The more he ran, the less he ate. The more he sprinted, the worse he slept. He had stopped taking the bus to work. He ran instead. There and back. But he was never hungry.

"Here. Eat."

She set the plate before him. Fried fish with onions and potatoes and a watery cucumber salad that had been stored too long. He prodded at the fish with his fork, with no idea how he was going to get any of it down.

"Here," Margaret said again. "This came for you in the mail. Aren't you going to unwrap it, then?"

He put down his fork. The parcel was not large, about seven inches square and fairly flat. The name and address were written in plain block capitals. No sender's name.

He grabbed the package and turned it over. No sender's address either. Then he felt a powerful jolt in his stomach, an explosion of adrenaline that spread through his limbs and made him put the parcel on his lap to avoid dropping it.

"Just a heart-rate monitor," he said tersely.

"A heart-rate monitor?" She smiled as she began to eat. "Open it, then!"

"No."

He forced down three slices of cucumber. They expanded inside his mouth, and he had difficulty breathing.

"What's *wrong* with you?" she said, irritated. "Can't you open it, so I can see what you've bought?"

"No, I can't. It's just something for my jogging, and you've no interest in that."

The fried onions tasted of rubber and grill spices.

"But honestly, Evald. Can't I just have a look at this . . . this heart-rate monitor of yours?"

She stood up and leaned across his lap. As she was about to lift the parcel, he grabbed her wrist in a flash and gripped it tightly.

"*Didn't you hear me say no?*"

He had never screamed at her like that before. Never so violently. He had never done her any physical harm either. Now he was squeezing her arm with all his might and did not release her until the tears began to run down her cheeks, which were shiny with steam from cooking.

"Sorry," he pleaded in desperation. "I'm just so worn out right now. It *is* just a heart-rate monitor. It's of *no* interest to you whatsoever."

She refused to answer. Instead she took her plate out into the living room and sat there at their grand dining table, where no guests had sat for many, many years.

Leaving his food, Evald Bromo took the package with him and disappeared out the door without a word about where he was going.

53

It was Friday, March 26, 1999, and Sigurd Halvorsrud was due to appear at the Oslo Courthouse. He had been held in custody for exactly three weeks, the result of a court order that had allowed the police a maximum of four weeks. It was unusual—quite astounding, actually—that the case was being called before the deadline expired. Admittedly, the police quite frequently released prisoners before it was strictly necessary, and there was rarely anything dramatic in that. In fact, they were duty-bound to do so if the grounds on which the court would make its judgment were no longer valid. However, the police had no desire to release Chief Public Prosecutor Halvorsrud.

Quite the opposite. Annmari Skar, the Police Prosecutor, had already started work on a petition for prolonging the custody order, which she had planned to raise the following week. On Thursday afternoon, when she received the papers from Karen Borg stating that the accused intended to petition for release and that the case would be heard on Friday morning, she had swallowed a juicy oath, at the same time thanking heaven that she had already made thorough inroads into the case.

"One week to go," she muttered to Billy T. as they hurried up the stairs in front of Oslo Courthouse and zigzagged their way through a wedding party defying the little cardboard sign requesting them not to throw grains of rice out of consideration for the little birds. "And they just couldn't wait. *One week!*"

For some reason that no one other than the administration of the courthouse could fathom, the case had been allocated courtroom 130. Annmari Skar and Billy T. passed through the almost fourteen-foot-high double wooden doors and then through the gigantic swing door into the impressive foyer of the courthouse. They were immediately plunged into an intense popping of flashbulbs. Billy T. had to stop the petite Police Prosecutor from falling when an overeager reporter from a minor TV station got it into his head to be the boldest and best and quite literally crept between Billy T.'s enormous legs in order to thrust the microphone into Annmari Skar's face. The two police officers plowed their way forward to the glass wall on the western side of the hall. They arrived at the door to the correct room without any further misfortune, but with a gaggle of journalists bringing up the rear.

"One thirty," Annmari Skar said with a sigh. "There's hardly room to breathe in here. How can all these—" She cast a despairing glance over her shoulder.

"Closed hearing," Billy T. reassured her. "We'll have a closed hearing and privacy."

"Do you think so?" Annmari Skar said bitterly. "We'll only get that if Karen Borg requests it. We haven't—"

"Shhh," Billy T. interrupted her. "Keep that in reserve."

He pushed a persistent young woman away. She was aged about twenty, with long, blond hair and a Dictaphone, and she was chewing gum.

"You're getting bloody younger by the day, you crime reporters," he said in a loud, gruff voice. "And cheekier too. The one probably goes with the other."

He used his elbows against a stripling from TV2, and eventually had to resort to using his backside as a shield so that Annmari Skar could enter the courtroom at all. Karen Borg was already installed there. She greeted them quietly, and Billy T. assumed she had accompanied her client up from the basement. Karen Borg had made barely any public comment about the case. Despite the major leaks from the police themselves—Billy T. had long ago given up speculating who had such a casual relationship with the press—she had kept resolutely silent. Admirably enough. Now she had chosen to avoid the press entirely.

The police *were* granted their petition regarding a closed hearing.

Annmari Skar knew she could not take credit for that. She had dutifully presented her phrases about how press coverage would be "harmful to the investigation" but without much confidence. Admittedly, she was convinced of Sigurd Halvorsrud's guilt, and she had more than once torn through the corridors of police headquarters in futile pursuit of the many police sources to whom the press obviously had more than liberal access. However, given that the case had already been splashed across one newspaper page after another in all its blood-dripping detail, it would be an achievement to unearth anything new that could be genuinely damaging. Now that she was nevertheless arguing the case behind closed doors, she realized it was just as much for herself that she had wanted it this way. She could not stand journalists. They were presumptuous and submissive at the same time, ignorant know-it-alls, impudent, and yet damned clever. Annmari Skar had no understanding of journalists and despised them with all her heart.

Even Karen Borg—to Annmari Skar's enormous relief—had supported the police's petition, on the grounds of needing to respect the privacy of her client's personal life, though it was probably not even this that had led to the doors being closed. The journalists had themselves to thank for that. During the hearing about whether the case should be held in private, which naturally was open to the public, they had fought over seats like seagulls squabbling over a discarded bag of shrimp. The judge, Birger Bugge, a stocky, mean-tempered guy who would soon retire on full pension and who had long since realized he would never be made an Appellate Court judge, did not share Annmari Skar's contempt for journalists. Rather, he *hated* them so vehemently that he had stopped reading every newspaper other than the *Herald Tribune*, which he bought at the Narvesen kiosk in Oslo railway station every afternoon on the way home to dinner with his wife in Ski.

"Today the court will hear case number 99-02376F/42," he intoned once the tumult had finally abated, the journalists had been chased off by a fiery court usher, and calm had been restored to Judge Birger Bugge's little kingdom. "The defense counsel is Karen Borg, the prosecutor Annmari Skar, and I, Birger Bugge, am the judge. I know of no circumstances that would disqualify me. Are there any objections?"

Billy T. caught himself shaking his head in concert with attorneys

Skar and Borg. It was rare for him to find anyone intimidating, but Judge Bugge's bulldog head could strike fear into anyone. With his pronounced underbite, conspicuous double chins, and tiny gimlet eyes under gray eyebrows that bobbed up and down like two horns on his temples, he didn't need to say much in order to command respect.

"Harumph," Judge Bugge grunted, gesturing with his hand in the direction of the witness box.

Karen Borg shot up from her seat.

"Your Honor, I request that my client be allowed to remain seated, on health grounds."

She placed her left hand gently on Halvorsrud's shoulder, as if to emphasize the man's extreme need for care and attention.

"Harumph," Judge Bugge reiterated, and Karen Borg chose to interpret that as assent. "And so you are Sigurd Harald Halvorsrud. Date of birth?"

Billy T. leafed through the documents while the personal details were attended to. Then he reclined in his chair, glancing obliquely at Annmari Skar. She was good-looking rather than actually pretty. Her body was short and quite thick-set, but she had a femininity that more than once had made him steal a secret look at her. Her face was strong and open, with large brown eyes and dark-brown hair that was beginning to be streaked with gray even though she was still a few years shy of forty. Billy T. felt a sudden drag in his gut, and had to stop himself from putting his hand on her back as she sat there drumming a pencil on the bench, to Judge Bugge's great irritation.

"Would the Police Prosecutor stop that racket immediately," he barked.

Annmari Skar stiffened and a faint blush suffused her cheeks.

And I need to fucking sharpen up, Billy T. thought, taking control of his hand as it reached halfway toward the Police Prosecutor's back.

Someone opened the door. Hanne Wilhelmsen slowly entered the almost square courtroom and conferred in a low voice with the court usher. He knew her well and let her pass before diligently closing the door behind her. A brief glance allowed Billy T. to ascertain that the journalists had not conceded defeat.

"Sorry," she said out loud to the judicial bench. "I have important information for the prosecutor."

"Harumph," Judge Bugge said yet again. "Be quick about it."

Hanne Wilhelmsen opened the low wooden swing doors separating the spectators' seats from the rest of the courtroom. She passed the witness box without glancing at Karen Borg and Halvorsrud, and leaned over the counter with her hands on the wooden surface.

"I've been called as a witness by Karen Borg," she whispered to Annmari Skar. "The document was lying on my desk when I came back from . . . Half an hour ago."

"Witness summons," Billy T. spluttered. He had leaned forward and heard what Hanne had said. "It's not bloody usual practice to call *witnesses* at a preliminary hearing!"

"Hush!" Annmari Skar put her hand on his arm. "Because it's not usual doesn't mean it's not permissible. I learned about it myself a few minutes ago."

She was holding her hand in front of her mouth, as if afraid to say what was on her mind.

"Do you know anything about why you've been asked to come?" she eventually asked, so softly that Billy T. was almost unable to catch it.

Hanne Wilhelmsen did not reply, but her gaze dropped from the Police Prosecutor's face to the copious documentation in front of her.

"Have you already discussed this with Karen Borg?" Annmari Skar continued angrily; by now she had forgotten to keep her voice down.

"Not directly," Hanne said in a hurried whisper. "I haven't spoken to her about being a witness. I really haven't."

"But why—"

"I think we'll draw a line under that now," the judge growled irascibly from the bench. "I presume all the vital information from the police has been dealt with and we can continue."

Hanne Wilhelmsen left the courtroom. As she mounted the stairs to the first floor of the courthouse to get a cup of coffee in the canteen, it struck her that she should have sent someone else with the message. Since she in all probability would be called as a witness—it was up to Judge Bugge whether in fact he wanted to hear her evidence—then strictly speaking she should not have been in the courtroom during the proceedings at all. She shrugged it off. In the first place, she was not a lawyer. And second, she had not heard anything of what was going on.

Neither had Billy T. for that matter.

His ears were buzzing with rage.

Hanne Wilhelmsen must have known something. If Karen Borg wanted to produce her as a witness, it was obviously because the defense lawyer thought Hanne had something to say to Halvorsrud's advantage. Until now, Hanne's doubt about the Chief Public Prosecutor's guilt had been professionally conditional. At least as Billy T. saw it. Damn it all, he had been puzzled too; *he* was not unused to having doubts either. That was how it should be. The police should always keep all possibilities open. Guilty or not guilty. That's what they had to find out. The police had to remain impartial. However, if Karen Borg's belief that Hanne's testimony could benefit Halvorsrud's case was based on something Hanne herself had given her, then the Chief Inspector's conduct was approaching betrayal.

He let his eyes wander around the room.

At each corner, immediately in front of the hip-height partition wall dividing the public benches, two police officers sat twiddling their thumbs. One, a female officer with very short, bleached hair and a face plastered in makeup, looked as if she was nodding off.

Halvorsrud, on the other hand, looked as though he had not slept in weeks.

Karen Borg must have gotten hold of a new suit for him. It hung better than the old dark one had at the funeral on Monday. His shirt was snowy-white and freshly ironed. It would not have surprised Billy T. if Karen had wielded the iron herself that morning. The diamond on his tie had gone; something like that could easily provoke a foul-tempered, irate judge.

His immaculate, discreet clothing made a stark contrast with the head that protruded above the tightly knotted tie. Halvorsrud's neck had become jowly, like a turkey's, because of his rapid weight loss. The lower part of his face was slack and sallow, with deep lines on either side of his formerly strong chin. His eyes were covered in a bloodshot film, like a mask someone had hastily painted on. His lips hardly moved when he spoke. His words were indistinct, his voice monotonous. Now and then he pressed a handkerchief to his mouth.

The questioning of Halvorsrud commenced.

Judge Bugge himself did not pose very many questions. Instead he gave the floor to the two sides, waving his hands in exasperation. From time to time it even appeared as if he wasn't following what was being said particularly carefully. Billy T. was well aware this was a sham;

there was hardly a sharper judge in the entire court service than Birger
Bugge. His lack of promotion through the ranks was entirely due to his
difficult manner and unfriendly tone.

Eventually Halvorsrud had said his piece. Nothing unexpected had
emerged from this. He held firm as a rock to his own innocence. He
was concerned about his daughter. He had bleeding stomach ulcers.
Nothing the police had not previously known.

"I would like to beg your indulgence and produce medical certifi-
cates for father and daughter," Karen Borg said.

Judge Bugge nodded faintly, with a heavy sigh, and extended a huge
fist for the documents that were handed to him. His eyes raced rapidly
over the papers before he passed them to the court reporter, who sat
aloof and silent on his right-hand side.

"In addition I would like to call Chief Inspector Hanne Wilhelmsen
as a witness," Karen Borg added, remaining on her feet in front of her
chair. "It is of—"

"Rather irregular," Judge Bugge grumbled. "What then is—"

"Your Honor," Annmari Skar interjected, realizing too late that she
had interrupted him.

"Would the Police Prosecutor please refrain from interrupting the
court?" Judge Bugge snarled.

Annmari Skar dropped back down into her seat.

"What then is this Wilhelmsen going to tell us?" the judge continued, directing his question at Karen Borg, who had lowered her eyes
in embarrassment on behalf of the Police Prosecutor.

"She's in charge of the police investigation, Your Honor, and I think
she can throw light on—"

"Throw light on?" Judge Bugge croaked. "We have here a prosecutor
who I would presuppose intends to *throw light on* the case from the
police point of view. Is that not so, Prosecutor?"

Annmari Skar stood up hesitantly. "Yes, Your Honor, absolutely.
Besides, matters are such that . . ."

She hesitated slightly, and thought it safest to wait for permission to
continue. This came in the shape of a forceful nod that caused the
judge's double chins to wobble in waves of flesh.

"As I see it, Ms. Borg has no authority to call Chief Inspector
Wilhelmsen as a witness in the ordinary way of things. If Wilhelmsen
is to give evidence in court, then that evidence must consist of either

an account of the investigation itself or a statement about the progress of the investigation. I cannot see why these can't be covered in my own account, potentially with the aid of my advisory assistant."

She pointed at Billy T.

"Moreover, I'd like to say that I take a dim view of the way Ms. Borg has handled this matter, Your Honor. If she considered it necessary for the case to listen to the Chief Inspector, she could have simply asked me. A witness summons is highly irregular and smacks of undue gamesmanship. Besides, I have not had the opportunity to confer with Chief Inspector Wilhelmsen in advance of—"

"Confer?" Judge Bugge repeated. "And why would it be necessary for you to confer with your own colleague? What she knows, you are sure to know also, is that not so, Ms. Skar?"

Annmari Skar was all at sea. She riffled aimlessly through the papers in front of her before concluding that she had nothing more to say and sat down without a word.

"The court does not entirely see the point of this witness statement," Judge Bugge said lugubriously. "However, in light of the grave charges made against the accused, I will permit a short interview. Is Chief Inspector Wilhelmsen available at present?"

"I expect she is standing outside waiting," Karen Borg said, clearing her throat nervously.

The court usher opened the door discreetly, and a few seconds later Hanne Wilhelmsen was standing in the witness box giving her personal details. She tried to catch Billy T.'s eye, but her colleague was studying his own hands and turned subtly away from Hanne by inclining his right shoulder toward her in a frosty gesture.

"I'll come straight to the point, Hanne Wilhelmsen." Karen Borg tugged at the lapels of her jacket, studiously avoiding looking in the direction of the Chief Inspector. Karen Borg knew what she was doing. She was shuffling her cards. Emphatically, and probably unpardonably. They had spoken so many times about this: she and Håkon, Hanne and Cecilie, and Billy T. The close friendship among legal opponents brought enormous challenges. It was self-evident that she and Håkon could not oppose each other in court. Their relationship with Hanne and Billy T. was far more ambiguous— if not legally, then at least morally. After lengthy discussion, they had arrived at the conclusion that they should all watch their step and see how far that took them. Since much of

Karen's portfolio consisted of criminal cases, she would have suffered substantially if she could never touch a Hanne Wilhelmsen case.

Things had gone well. Until now. By calling Hanne as a witness, Karen Borg had put a strain on the trust she owed Hanne as a friend. Not as a lawyer. Nevertheless, as far as Karen Borg was concerned, loyalty to her client was always of paramount importance. Always.

Hanne Wilhelmsen believed in Halvorsrud's innocence. She had expressed her doubts about the value of continued custody. She had even challenged Karen to try and petition for his release. Karen Borg could not let something like that lie. At least not when her client was about to go under.

"Do you really believe there is still a danger of evidence being destroyed in this case?"

"I *hate* you for doing this," was what Hanne Wilhelmsen wanted to yell. Instead, she coughed quietly into a tightly closed fist and answered, "The police are of that opinion. I would simply refer you to what I expect Annmari Skar has already stated."

"I'm not asking about that, Wilhelmsen. I'm asking about *your own* opinion. You are in charge of this investigation and ought to have an independent point of view about whether there are sufficient grounds for imprisonment."

Something had happened to Judge Bugge. His slack, ill-tempered face had suddenly become alert and attentive. His little eyes gleamed as he sat leaning forward marginally, his head canted to one side. It was possible to discern a malicious smile on his wet lips.

"I work for the police," Hanne Wilhelmsen said curtly. "We are of the opinion that continued custody is required."

Karen Borg sighed theatrically, looking at the judge for help. "Your Honor," she complained. "Can I have some assistance in persuading this witness to answer the questions I ask?"

"It seems to me that the Chief Inspector is answering rather well," Judge Bugge said tartly. "There might possibly be something wrong with the questions the defense counsel is asking. Continue."

"Your Honor," Annmari Skar said, sounding discouraged. "Ms. Borg is questioning the Chief Inspector on the subject of an assessment it is up to me as the Police Prosecutor to answer for. This is quite simply not proper!"

Silence descended. There was only the faint susurration from the ventilation system and the sound of sheets of paper being turned over on the table in front of Karen Borg.

"Are you aware that Halvorsrud is suffering from bleeding stomach ulcers?" Karen Borg asked in the end.

"Yes."

Silence again.

"Are you aware that his daughter has been admitted to a psychiatric ward as a result of her father's imprisonment?"

"Your Honor!" Annmari Skar flung out her arms and rolled her eyes. Judge Bugge thrust a pencil into his mouth and chewed vigorously, but did not utter a word.

Hanne shifted her weight from her left foot to her right, and folded her arms. "I know his daughter is ill. I don't know the cause. You've told me she is missing her father, but I haven't personally spoken to a doctor. I presume it hasn't been exactly easy for a sixteen-year-old to cope with her mother's murder either."

"But if I tell you that a doctor's statement exists, linking Thea's serious condition directly to the fact of her father's imprisonment, how would you then assess the importance of continuing to keep him in custody?"

"That is fortunately not up to me to decide. It is the task of the court."

"But if I ask you for your personal opinion?"

Hanne Wilhelmsen was finally aware that Billy T. had turned to face her, and she could make out a smile below his red moustache. She saw him place a hand on Annmari Skar's arm; he knew now that Hanne would pull through.

"That's hardly of interest to the court," Hanne said slowly, gazing at Judge Bugge. "I assume I'm here in my capacity as a police chief inspector. Not as a private citizen."

Karen Borg sighed histrionically, throwing out her hand in a gesture of resignation. "I give up," she murmured. "Thank you."

Cheating and skullduggery, Hanne thought, turning to leave the witness box.

She was stopped by Annmari Skar.

"I have a couple of questions for the Chief Inspector myself," she said to the judge. "It won't take long."

When he nodded, it seemed as if the Police Prosecutor hesitated. She took a deep breath and jiggled her pencil between her fingers for a moment or two before withdrawing a sheet of paper from the sheaf of documents, studying it carefully, and finally saying, "Last Saturday, Chief Inspector Wilhelmsen . . . is it true that the accused was on the brink of making a confession?"

Hanne felt hot. They had agreed to leave this matter alone. Halvorsrud's desire to bargain his way to a temporary release was a desperate attempt to be allowed to see his daughter. Annmari Skar had given her word. For the time being, the matter should be forgotten. The special report Hanne had felt duty-bound to write was comprehensive and innocuous and had not even been officially recorded yet.

"I wouldn't put it as strongly as that," she replied in an undertone.

"As strongly?"

"I would certainly not call it a confession."

"But is it not the case . . ." Annmari Skar leaned forward, waving the document as if it might contain an unqualified admission of guilt. ". . . that the accused asked to speak to you late on Saturday evening with the intention of confessing? And that you actually had a meeting with him and Ms. Borg in your office?"

Billy T. had been restless in his chair. Now he grabbed a ballpoint pen and scribbled a message on the notepad. He pushed it in front of the Police Prosecutor. She read it swiftly and turned halfway toward him as she whispered sharply, "It was Karen Borg who started this."

Then she waved the special report again, and went on. "Was he lying, perhaps? Did he not want to confess?"

Hanne Wilhelmsen swallowed. Her throat was stinging and her ears buzzed. Again she felt the numbness that came with being trapped. She was hog-tied. She was not in control. Her fingertips prickled, and she realized she was scrutinizing them without giving an answer. She caught a glimpse of her old father, that distant male figure who, when Hanne was little, had entertained his eldest children after dinner with extracts from Supreme Court reports and since then had never forgiven Hanne for not studying law. She saw his eyes behind the fine layer of steam rising from his coffee cup: blue, steely, and brimming with disappointment at the young girl sitting with her feet up on the sofa who did not want to listen. Hanne studied her fingers, contemplating that she would soon be forty and had hardly spent a single minute of the last twenty years thinking about the first twenty.

"He was desperate," she said in the end, straightening up. "He wanted to investigate possible alternatives to custody. In no way did he confess. He was checking the lay of the land, you might say. As I understood him, he was simply proposing a hypothesis. If he confessed, would he then be eligible for release on bail? Something of that nature."

"THAT'S ENOUGH NOW!!!" The note written in large block capitals was smacked down on the bench in front of Annmari Skar. Billy T. grabbed her by the arm and squeezed tightly.

It worked.

"Thank you," Annmari Skar said, sending the judge a rigid smile.

Hanne Wilhelmsen lifted her jacket from the row of wrought-iron hooks and exited the courtroom. As she heard the door slam behind her, she did not know whom she despised more: Karen Borg, Annmari Skar, or just lawyers in general.

Billy T. was similarly rattled.

He had believed it was Hanne who had been disloyal. But it was Karen. In league with a police prosecutor who had suddenly turned on him only an hour ago. He was trembling, and he felt sick.

Lawyers were a waste of space. He had always known that. Usually he laughed at them, these gowned, snotty-nosed, self-important, and omniscient knights at the court of Lady Justice. They could never control themselves. As soon as they got a whiff of something resembling a setback, they pounced. Rather than lose face. Whatever the cost. Get even. Fire away. Show off.

And now it had harmed Hanne.

With the best will in the world, Billy T. could not see what had been gained by Hanne's testimony. Not for either side. Nothing gained, but nothing lost either. For anyone.

Except Hanne. He was feeling fucking awful.

He clasped his hands, mainly to keep them occupied. When Annmari Skar had asked him to be her advisory assistant and help her with the bulky bundle of documents, he had naturally agreed.

"Never again," he muttered under his breath.

The legal summing-up contained little that was new, and nothing of surprise to anyone.

"The court finds there are reasonable grounds to suspect Sigurd Harald Halvorsrud of violating the Criminal Code, paragraph 233, subsection 2, as stated in the charge."

Judge Bugge dictated slowly, and the court reporter's fingers responded rhythmically on the keyboard. The judge was keeping pace with a screen set into the table before him, and continued. "The court refers to police documents 2-2 to 2-9, in which it is stated that the accused was arrested at his residence where his wife, Doris Flo Halvorsrud, was killed by her head being severed from her body or by a blow to the back of her head. It has been ascertained that the finger-prints of the accused were left on the sword it is assumed was used to commit the crime. Furthermore, the court lays some—though not conclusive—weight on the finding that the accused did not alert the police immediately after the crime had taken place. The court also finds reason to point out that the accused and deceased's three chil-dren were away at the time of the murder, an absence that in all prob-ability, at least in the case of two of the children in question, had been initiated by the accused."

Annmari Skar leaned back discreetly in her chair. Billy T. heard a faint sigh. She had won. He looked across at Halvorsrud, who had been sitting unmoved ever since he had been questioned.

"The court nevertheless wishes to emphasize that it does not find the case against the accused particularly convincing," Judge Bugge continued. "In particular, the court places considerable weight on the inability of the police to pinpoint an adequate motive. With reference to police documents . . ." He paused temporarily to leaf through his papers. ". . . 7-1 to 7-7, in which a number of disconnected facts emerge purporting to support a theory that the accused had allowed himself to be paid for unlawful acts in the course of discharging his duties as Chief Public Prosecutor. The court wishes to observe that these facts are barely coherent enough for any significance to be attached to them. The court points especially to the police having until now been unable to find anything irregular in the accused's finances, apart from the hundred thousand kroner found in the medicine cabinet in the base-ment of the house belonging to the accused and the deceased. The accused denies any knowledge of this money, and his fingerprints have not been found on the banknotes. The presence of his fingerprints on the bag containing the money could be accounted for by a chance occurrence and is not accorded any significance by the court."

Annmari Skar began to wiggle her foot. She cast a glance at Billy T. as two thin lines became etched on her face.

"The court further points out that no irregularities were discovered in the cases of the four people referred to on the computer disks found with the above-mentioned sum of money. The court is surprised that the police have not conducted a more comprehensive investigation into this point. It has only been submitted to the court that . . . No, strike that last sentence."

Judge Bugge poked his finger into his ear and scratched vigorously. The court reporter complied, and the judge pressed on. "The court is only aware of the existence of interviews with each of the people who, according to the police's theory, are thought to have paid the accused to have their cases dropped. All the persons involved deny any dealings with the accused beyond what would naturally happen in such cases. The police have not as yet given the court grounds to doubt the assertions of the witnesses. Furthermore, the court does not find any reason to attach particular significance to the statement by the witness of Turkish origin that he was telephoned by the accused last autumn with an offer of assistance in getting a criminal case shelved. The court does not call the witness's reliability into question, but cannot see that a well-educated, experienced lawyer would have given his own name when making such an approach. The court cannot discount the possibility that others may have been motivated to discredit the accused by making the phone call. As far as the police allegations that the deceased's computer had been . . ." Searching for the right word, he smacked his lips loudly. ". . . manipulated by the accused, the court considers this to be sheer speculation."

Judge Bugge coughed noisily and grabbed a plastic cup filled with water. He drained it in one gulp, cleared his throat again, and continued, while intently following the words that appeared on the screen only seconds after he had spoken them.

"The court notes that the police are also unable to dismiss the idea that the accused may be telling the truth when he claims that a certain Ståle Salvesen was responsible for the murder of his wife. The court would be pleased to have this claim investigated further, especially since Ståle Salvesen's body has still not been found."

Billy T. noticed Halvorsrud's hand covering his eyes. His shoulders were quivering slightly, as though he was weeping. Karen Borg looked tense and made constant rabbit-like movements with her nose that made Billy T. crack a smile despite the court's gross criticism of the work undertaken by the police.

"At least he finds reasonable grounds for suspicion," Annmari Skar whispered. "Thank God for that."

"Don't be so hasty with your thanks," Billy T. muttered.

"The court seriously doubts there is any danger of contamination of evidence if the accused is now released from custody," Judge Bugge continued in a hoarse, monotonous voice. "Particular emphasis is placed on the investigation that still remains to be conducted into the allegations of corruption. As far as the technical circumstances surrounding the actual killing are concerned, the court presumes that all evidence has now been secured against influence or manipulation."

"Yes," Annmari Skar mouthed, before placing her lips against Billy T.'s ear to whisper, "We've got him!"

Billy T. pulled away.

"The conditions for the continuation of custody in accordance with Criminal Code paragraph 171 are therefore fulfilled. However . . ." For the first time, the judge looked up from his screen. He let his eyes dart from Karen Borg to Annmari Skar, before letting them settle on Halvorsrud, who was still shielding his face with his right hand.

"Delete 'however,'" Judge Bugge said. "Write: the accused has presented a subsidiary petition with reference to Criminal Code paragraph 184, subsection 5, cf. paragraph 174. The court makes the following comments. It is established that the accused's daughter, Thea Flo Halvorsrud, d.o.b. 10.02.83, is seriously ill. According to the medical certificate signed by the Chief Psychiatric Consultant at Ullevål Hospital, Professor Øystein Glück, on 22.03.99, it is evident that Thea has not eaten for almost three weeks. She has this week suffered a psychotic collapse, and is now receiving involuntary treatment. The illness is believed to have been provoked by the trauma of her mother's death and her father's imprisonment. Professor Glück emphasizes that the best thing for the child would undoubtedly be . . ." The judge tapped the screen with a stubby finger. "Underline 'undoubtedly.'" He swallowed and smacked his lips, before continuing. ". . . to be reunited with her father. Otherwise there is grave risk to the girl's psychological and physical health."

Halvorsrud had raised his head. Now he was staring at the judge with his mouth half open. He had placed his hands flat on the table in front of him. Billy T. could see that the little finger on his left hand was vibrating on the desk pad.

"The accused has pleaded the case that his own physical condition also justifies release conditional on a duty to report at regular intervals or some other alternative to custody. The court cannot conclude that the accused's stomach ulcers, at least partly caused by his imprisonment, place the accused in a situation different from anyone else who has to tolerate being held in custody. The court bases this on the fact that the accused is receiving appropriate medical treatment while held on remand. However, the concern for the accused's daughter is so considerable that this, in addition to the other circumstances of the case, indicates a justification for release. Following this the court does not see any reason to go into any further detail with regard to the police's subsidiary reference to Criminal Code paragraph 172."

"What?" Annmari Skar ran her right hand through her hair and pinched her neck with the left. She stared at Billy T. for a second or two before closing her mouth with a snap.

Judge Bugge sneeringly disregarded her outburst, and continued while making a move to tidy the sheaf of papers facing him. "The alternatives to imprisonment according to Criminal Code paragraph 188 are considered satisfactory. Conclusion: Sigurd Harald Halvorsrud is released, with the condition that he report on a daily basis to the nearest police station. The police are also requested to seize the accused's passport. Ms. Skar?"

Judge Bugge smiled at the Police Prosecutor. His smile was as absurd as the remainder of his figure: a contraction at the corner of his mouth exposed his canines and made his tiny eyes disappear completely under the rolls of fat on his forehead.

"The police wish to appeal," Annmari Skar said firmly. "We also request that the release be delayed."

The judge's smile vanished. He remained seated as if frozen to the spot, with his hands full of papers and his gaze fixed unwaveringly on the Police Prosecutor.

"Do you know, madam," he said suddenly, as the silence became conspicuous, "I do not believe I'm in the mood to grant that. If you had been listening while I dictated the verdict, you would have understood that the accused's daughter is in an extremely grave condition. The appeal will presumably be dealt with by the Appellate Court this coming Monday. I would prefer that young Miss Halvorsrud has the weekend at home with her father. Will a written application be submitted?"

"I . . ." Annmari Skar was a competent prosecutor. Unlike most police officers who studied for a law degree at her age, she had passed her final examination with flying colors. She was thorough and quick-witted. Never before had she been denied a request for delayed implementation. She had not even heard of such a thing happening before. Delayed implementation was strictly routine: if the police did not get their petition for custody approved, the accused always remained in custody until the Appellate Court had given its verdict.

However at this very moment, on this Friday afternoon at the end of March, as the time was approaching half past two, Annmari Skar could not for the life of her remember what provisions she might use to support her plea. Could she appeal the decision on delayed implementation?

She leafed frantically through the codex, her hands trembling; the flimsy paper tore when she arrived at the Criminal Code. She felt a lump in her throat, and her breathing became labored. Her fingers raced up and down the pages, but the print was tiny and malevolent; she found nothing.

"The court is adjourned."

The judge's gavel banged on the table, and Judge Bugge limped out through the back door.

"He did it," Billy T. heard Halvorsrud say. "He let me go." The Chief Public Prosecutor stared in disbelief at his defense counsel.

"That's right," Karen Borg said quietly. "You can go home now. Together with Thea."

PART 2

54

Norway was at war for the first time since the spring of 1945. NATO had carried out its threats, and Slobodan Milošević's Serbian troops were to be forcibly expelled from Kosovo. The ethnic cleansing that had to date cost several thousand Kosovan Albanians their lives and made a quarter of a million of them homeless, was to be stopped. And Norway was involved in the attack.

You would not have known it. It was the night before Sunday March 28, 1999, and Evald Bromo could see no unusual signs of unrest anywhere. He wandered through the streets of Oslo carrying a small package measuring about six square inches in a bag under his arm.

Some jostling in front of the entrance to the restaurant at Stortorvets Gjæstgiveri was the closest thing there was to any violence. The streets were full of people who obviously could not care less about the war. They already had enough on their plates and were mostly obsessed with trying to get into some place or other before closing time.

He still had not opened the package.

It might be something entirely innocuous.

But he was sure of one thing: the package was from Pokerface. The email terrorist. He had no idea how he knew that. It had something to do with the plain script. Something about the grayish-brown, anonymous paper. Something or other about the way the postage stamp was affixed in the corner—at right angles and the exact same distance from the top of the envelope as the side—told him that the person who had wrapped the parcel had taken great pains with it. Nevertheless there were no details about the sender.

It must be Pokerface.

As long as he did not open it, he could continue hoping that the package contained something completely innocent. Perhaps it was an advertising promotion. The neutral wrapper could be a way of tricking him into opening it instead of throwing the whole shebang into the trash, where all the other gaudy missives ended up, unopened and unread.

An unregistered taxi containing two dark-skinned teenagers drove slowly past him in Grensen. He picked up his pace to demonstrate lack of interest. A young woman looked him up and down when he dropped the parcel and bent over quick as a flash to retrieve it. He did not meet her gaze but pulled his jacket more snugly around him as he stared at the ground and hurried onward.

There was too much activity at the *Aftenposten* offices on this Saturday night. Of course it was because of the Kosovo crisis. People everywhere. Earlier in the day he had written a report about the impact of the war on the world's stock exchanges. The article was slipshod and lightweight, and his editor had shaken his head, unimpressed, as he made clear it could not be used.

Bloody war.

Evald Bromo left the office ten minutes after he arrived. The plan had been to open the parcel in peace and quiet, but there was no peace and quiet to be found anywhere.

Bloody war.

He could grab a coffee. A pub, where he could sit down quietly in a corner and be on his own.

There were no quiet pubs. Not at two o'clock on a Saturday night.

He walked aimlessly along Akersgata.

Pale-green light spilled out from the sixth and top floors of the government tower block. The Minister of Justice and the Prime Minister were obviously at work.

Damned war.

Evald Bromo cut to the right after the ramp leading down into the Ibsen Tunnel. When he passed the Deichman Library, he could not muster the energy to go any farther. He felt his pulse race alarmingly, despite the fact he had not been running. On the contrary, he had been walking increasingly slowly since he'd left the newspaper offices. Without coming to any real decision, he sat down on the stone steps. The cold traveled along his spine, and he shivered. Then he ripped open the package.

It contained a CD.

Music?

Evald Bromo felt a ferocious sense of relief, as if he was intoxicated; his head felt light and hot, his sight was blurred and his breathing shallow. Someone had sent him a CD. Admittedly, the cover was totally white, but when he opened it, he saw a compact disc. Exactly as he had anticipated.

And a folded sheet of paper.

He held it in his hand for a few seconds before opening the paper with leaden fingers. It was covered in microscopic lettering. He blinked energetically in order to read what was written on the cramped lines.

When he had read the long letter twice over, he folded it carefully. He fumbled slightly in his attempts to return the letter to the constricted space inside the CD cover, but eventually succeeded. He remained seated on the steps of Oslo's old central library for more than half an hour. He was the only one there and was left alone. Even four boys in their twenties did not give him more than a cursory glance and a slurred comment as they staggered past, yelling. The contents of the letter were so astonishing, so sensational, and so catastrophic that in many ways they felt like a relief.

He slowly got to his feet, pushing the CD case deep into the inside pocket of his leather jacket, and took a deep breath as he was overcome by a sense of having reached the end of the road. A strange, empty sense of peace overwhelmed him. He knew what he had to do. He would pull himself together, perhaps in a couple of days, and then he would speak to Kai.

Kai would be able to help him.

Kai had helped him before, and Kai would know how Evald should handle the information he had just received.

55

"The door plate is lovely," Cecilie said with a smile.

Hanne shrugged her shoulders in embarrassment. "It looks a bit stupid with the faded woodwork around it," she said. "The old one was bigger than the new one. I should have taken measurements when I placed the order."

"Cecilie Vibe & Hanne Wilhelmsen" announced the brass plate that was now screwed onto the front door. Hanne was afraid Cecilie had not noticed it. She had not said anything since she'd gotten home from the hospital. That was four days ago now.

"What are you thinking about?" Cecilie asked.

They had been for a short stroll around the neighborhood at the crack of dawn. Cecilie felt tired and did not say very much. She leaned against Hanne as they walked, and accepted her hand when they returned after twenty minutes and began to climb the difficult stairs. Now she was lying on the sofa with a blanket over her legs and a cup of tea in her hands. Hanne sat in the chair opposite, fingering an apple.

"The door plate," Hanne replied.

"It's lovely. Elegant, really. Beautiful lettering."

"Not ours. The one we had at home. At my mother and father's house."

"Oh, I see."

Cecilie tried to replace her cup on the coffee table. Her hand was shaking and she spilled it all over the carpet. Hanne shuffled off to the kitchen for paper towels. When she returned, she stood with the towels in her hand and squinted at the sunlight slicing through the awnings pulled down over the terrace.

"I wasn't included. My mother and father and my two siblings had their names on the door plate. Father's at the top. Then mother. Inger and Kaare at the bottom, in smaller script. I wasn't mentioned at all."

"But . . . you did live there?"

"I was an afterthought, of course. The door plate was already there, you see. When I came along, I mean. There was no room to add another name. And it didn't occur to anybody that they should really get another one made. The odd thing is . . ." She kneeled down and wiped the tea with rough, hurried movements. ". . . I've actually never thought about it. I can't recall being affected by it. Then, I mean. It didn't strike me until now, when I bought a new one for us, that it was actually . . . it was rather odd."

She moaned softly as she stood up, and remained there with the wet towel in her hands. Tea was dripping onto her jeans, but she was oblivious.

"Why didn't it bother me?" she said quietly. "Can you explain to me why it didn't affect me that I was never listed on our door plate?"

"Sit down."

Cecilie patted her thigh and drew closer to the back of the sofa.

Staring at the paper towel, Hanne put it down in the fruit bowl in the center of the table and sat down in the narrow space beside Cecilie's hips.

"You'd just forgotten about it," Cecilie said. "You'd forgotten you were hurt by it."

She placed her right hand on Hanne's. Cecilie's skin was dry and warm, and Hanne intertwined her fingers in Cecilie's.

"I don't think so," she said, shaking her head. "I don't think they meant it badly. Just as . . . when I started at police college, my mother and father were so disappointed. That didn't matter to me either. All the same . . ."

Cecilie laughed softly. "With parents who were professors of law and zoology, it's perhaps not so strange that they found it worrying that their daughter was going to play cops and robbers for the rest of her life. They got over it eventually."

"Not really. At the beginning it was probably a bit exciting. I always had such amusing stories to tell at the family dinner table. In a way I was the one that kept the family in touch with reality. But now . . . lately . . ."

"You no longer sit at the family dinner table. Not ever. When did you actually last see them?"

Hanne withdrew her hands. "Let's not talk about that any more," she said, making a move to stand up.

Cecilie held her back. "It doesn't bother me any longer," she whispered. "It doesn't matter to me that I've never met them. It's you I want. You I chose. Not them."

"Let's just drop it," Hanne said.

"Karen phoned yesterday," Cecilie said, reaching out for the empty teacup.

"Bitch!" Hanne spluttered. "I'm never going to speak to that woman again!"

She headed for the kitchen and returned with a bowl of cornflakes and milk. "Do you want some?"

"No, thanks. We're invited to the cottage at Ula for the Easter weekend. Friday 'til Monday. I said yes."

Cornflakes and milk sprayed from Hanne's mouth across the table. "*YES?* You said *yes*? When you know how furious I am with Karen?"

She put down the bowl with a thump and tapped the spoon against her knee as she continued.

"In the first place I don't want to be with Karen at Easter. Perhaps never. Second, it's far too exhausting for you to travel out to Ula. There'll be all that noise and fuss with the children. Out of the question."

Cecilie fell silent. She straightened the blanket as it began to slide off her. She sank back against the cushions, as if she suddenly felt extremely tired. Her complexion was almost transparent, and Hanne could see her pulse beating in the slender veins above her temple.

"I didn't mean it like that," Hanne said, pushing her half-eaten bowl of cereal away. "I didn't mean to get angry."

"I would really like to go," Cecilie said, with her hand over her eyes to shield herself from the strong sunlight flooding through the window. "And you need to come with me. It won't be too exhausting. I can't just sit here and rest for what's left of . . . Please. Please come with me."

Hanne crossed to the veranda door and closed the curtains. "Better?" she asked.

"Much better. Will you come?"

"I'll think about it."

She refused to promise any more than that.

56

Ståle Salvesen would have been unrecognizable to almost anyone, no matter how well they had known him while he was alive. His facial features had disappeared into a grayish-blue, swollen mask. Whole sheets of skin and subcutaneous fat had begun to loosen, and his nose was about to disintegrate.

He had been lying at a depth of 350 feet for several weeks, still caught fast on a forgotten hook in the pilot house of the old fishing boat that had gone down with all hands one winter's night in 1952.

Ståle Salvesen's boots had been bought at a rummage sale four years earlier. They had more than fit their purpose: sturdy green seaman's boots. He had used them often; as long as the weather was neither too cold nor too warm, the shabby old boots had offered good protection against slush and other damp conditions.

Now the shaft of the left boot was about to tear.

The hook on the pilot house wall ate its way though the last of the rubber as a powerful current caught hold of the partly decomposed corpse.

Ståle Salvesen's body slowly floated up to the surface.

57

Sigurd Halvorsrud could not settle. He had felt it as he stepped inside the house: he needed to get away. Not now, not in the immediate future, but soon. If he was freed. If he was not convicted.

The entire place reminded him of Doris. The furniture, carpets, curtains, even the antiques they had purchased together, at auctions, in narrow backstreets in foreign countries and snobbish outlets in Frogner, every object, large and small, bore the unmistakable signature of Doris. It was intolerable. An accusation suffused the walls, and a threat lay in everything around him. He sat in an armchair staring out across the Oslo Fjord and felt something resembling a longing to return to the yellow painted walls of the cell. At least he had been on his own there. Entirely alone. Here, Doris was everywhere.

"Daddy," he heard behind him, and turned his head.

"Yes, my sweetheart?"

"Can I sleep in your bed tonight too?"

Thea's legs were bare underneath a gigantic T-shirt. Standing there in the doorway scratching her leg with one foot, without makeup and with her hair falling loosely over her shoulders, she looked younger than her years. It was a relief to see that. Yesterday, when they'd been reunited and she had barely taken her eyes off him for hours on end, her eyes had seemed really old. Today, at the breakfast table, she had smiled. Not broadly and there'd certainly been no warmth in it, but the faint expansion of her mouth had been a sign that things were improving. Sigurd Halvorsrud had been terrified by the conversation he'd had with Professor Glück before he was allowed to see Thea. She was seriously ill, worse than he had imagined. The boys had agreed to stay at their Aunt Vera's for another couple of days. Until Thea had settled down. Until they saw how things were with her.

"Of course you can," he said gently. "I'll come quite soon. Have you taken your pills?"

"Mhmm. Night night."

He stood up and crossed the floor with his arms extended. His daughter snuggled up to him, burying her face in the large woolen sweater he was wearing; it was chilly in the living room. He had kept the windows open since he'd come home, to air the room.

"Go to sleep now," he said, kissing her head. "I'll come to bed soon."

"Are you going to work tomorrow?"

"No. We'll stay at home, both of us. Then we can really relax and enjoy ourselves."

Naturally she did not know that he had been suspended. She would probably miss the remainder of the school year herself. She had no idea about that either.

"Good night, then."

He kissed her again.

When, half an hour later, Sigurd Halvorsrud crept upstairs and gingerly opened the door to his own bedroom, he heard the regular, heavy breathing of a sixteen-year-old who was fast asleep. It was the medication that had knocked her out. He had been doubtful about taking her home at all after his discussion with Professor Glück, but the psychiatrist had been convinced that the very best course for Thea was to return home. Together with her dad.

He closed the door without a sound.

Then he padded down to the ground floor, took an old oilskin jacket out of the cloakroom closet, pulled a woolen hat onto his head, and opened the front door, clutching the bunch of keys tightly to prevent them rattling.

The light from the wrought-iron lamps lining the driveway illuminated the space beside the garage and extended all the way to the massive oak trees bordering his neighbor's garden. That was how Doris had wanted it. She did not like the dark. Sigurd Halvorsrud lingered for several minutes. All he could see was a brindled cat strutting across the lawn and observing him arrogantly with its shining eyes. In the far distance he could hear the drone of the city, but there was not a soul to be seen. Closing the door behind him, he turned the key in the lock and headed down to the road. There were two cars parked three hundred feet down the gentle slope, but he recognized them both. They belonged to Pettersen, who was remodeling his garage and so had to leave the cars outside.

Turning around, he clambered into his own Opel Omega, switched on the ignition, and rolled slowly out of the driveway.

He was not going back to prison.

He would make sure he was never convicted.

Only half a mile along the road, he drew to a halt. A police car was parked in the Ruud family's driveway. It might be a coincidence. He could not see anyone in the car. Nevertheless, he reduced his speed, stopped, turned around, and drove back to his own garage, where he locked the car and the garage door, and went back inside his own house.

He could afford to wait.

58

At last, something that might generously be called an interrogation room. The lack of offices at police headquarters was annoying, and Hanne Wilhelmsen had felt they could do without one for the time being. Now they were in a situation of having the accused freed on bail, with strange clues pointing in every conceivable direction, and they were obviously further from securing a conviction than they had been at any point since Doris Flo Halvorsrud was executed. The court had given its judgment. Halvorsrud was a free man until further notice.

The Chief of Police was newly shaved and sported an unflattering piece of toilet paper glued to his chin with blood.

"Went for a short run at lunchtime," he said apologetically. "Had a shave afterward. A bit too rushed."

Hanne Wilhelmsen sat at the head of the table in the rectangular, windowless room. Behind her hung a blank sheet on the flip chart. She was toying with two felt pens while she waited for them all to sit.

"The newspapers went to town over the weekend," Erik Henriksen said loudly. "Mockery all over the place. *Verdens Gang* and *Dagbladet* are riding two horses. In the first place, we've now got what's turned out to be one of the numerous 'police scandals'—"

"And what's more, it's a scandal that the Chief Public Prosecutor was released," Karianne Holbeck completed, drinking diet soda from a plastic cup. "They should really make up their minds. Either we're the

ones who are doing a dreadful job, or else it's the difference between
the devil and the deep blue sea."

"That lot'll scream bloody murder anyway," Karl Sommarøy said,
yawning.

The Superintendent arrived last. The deep cleft in his forehead
appeared to have become permanent. He looked at Hanne and rested
his hands on the table.

"We now have a total of twelve investigators," she began. "The purpose of this meeting is to summarize where we stand at present, as
well as dividing the tasks required in the next few days. I had—"

She picked at the unflattering headband she had been forced to
resort to in order to see anything at all.

Unabashed, Billy T. chuckled. "Dainty little thing, that!"

Hanne ignored him and continued. "As I see it, we've a great deal to
learn from the court's decision."

A murmur of discontent rippled through the room. Hanne raised
her voice.

"Judge Bugge indicated a number of weaknesses in the investigation
to date. We must concentrate on three main lines of inquiry."

Standing up, she removed the lid from the blue marker pen and
began to write on the flip chart.

"A: the corruption lead. Where are we with that, Erik?"

Erik Henriksen leaned forward and studied a mark on the table.
"Økokrim's computer team has helped us by going through Halvorsrud's
office computer. Nothing there of any interest. They've been damn
thorough, looking for deleted documents and that sort of thing. Nada."

He raised his eyes. "What's more, I've called in the four people
mentioned on the computer disks for supplementary interviews. But
I honestly don't think . . ."

He scratched his fiery-red hair irascibly.

"The prospect doesn't look particularly bright. I did the previous
interviews, and either all four of them are damned good at play-acting,
or else they're all telling the truth. Besides, it turns out that the phone
call to that pal of yours—that Turkish guy—it came from a phone box
in Olav Ryes plass. Both of them, for that matter. Whoever it was who
phoned, in other words, was standing only a stone's throw away from
the Özdemir Import store when he called. I'm beginning to think that
this whole corruption—"

"We're trying not to jump to any conclusions as yet," Hanne interrupted. "You and Petter and Karianne are to keep digging."

"It's not that fucking easy," Erik muttered so quietly that only Karianne Holbeck, sitting next to him, heard.

Smiling, she raised her eyebrows resignedly without looking at the Chief Inspector farther along the table.

Hanne sighed demonstratively. "Has the money in the medicine cabinet been traced? Do we know anything at all about it?"

"No," Erik replied in a sullen tone. "Nothing other than that it's all in used notes, none of which are from later than 1993. Old and well used, in other words. With a zillion insignificant fingerprints."

"B: Ståle Salvesen," Hanne Wilhelmsen said, writing on the flip chart again. "Anything new?"

Karl Sommarøy cleared his throat. "A total blank. I've had another conversation with his son, but nothing more emerged from that than at the first interview. He was just even more bad-tempered. I've also checked with the phone company to see if it's possible to find out which number he asked for when he made his very last phone call to Directory Assistance. If he asked for the 'connect to number' service, it might be possible. Otherwise not. It's a bit difficult to initiate that kind of trace anyway, since we're going to need a court order. Is it so important?"

"And of course the body hasn't turned up," Hanne said, without answering.

"No."

Silence descended on the room. The Chief of Police picked the toilet paper off his chin, rolled it into a little pea-sized ball, and tucked it into his pocket. The Superintendent's eyes were fixed on Hanne, who stood there silently, a faraway expression on her face, as if she found the entire proceedings uninteresting. Karl Sommarøy offered candies to everyone gathered around the table.

"C," Hanne said all of a sudden. "C is a smokescreen. The motive for killing Doris Halvorsrud might lie in a completely different direction from the lines we've been working on up 'til now."

"What about a combination?" the Superintendent suggested softly.

They all stared down the table. The Superintendent's dark-brown eyes under his thick black brows were still nailed to Hanne.

"A combination," Hanne said thoughtfully as she replaced the lid on the marker.

"Yes. Let's assume that Halvorsrud did *not* kill his wife. Until now we haven't identified anyone who might have a motive for hurting him. Apart from Salvesen. Perhaps."

"That case of his was nearly *ten years* ago," Billy T. said, shaking his head. "Everyone who works for the police or the prosecution authorities ends up with so-called enemies. Louts and thugs who really hate us because we put them behind lock and key. They almost never take revenge. At least not ten years later!"

"True," the Superintendent said patiently. "But if we agree that these different corruption leads—"

He got to his feet and edged behind the backs of the five detectives sitting on Billy T.'s side of the long table. He reached out his hand to Hanne and was handed a marker. He then turned the page on the flip chart and began to write.

"(1) Phone call to Özdemir," he said as he wrote. "(2) Money in a medicine cabinet in the basement. (3) Computer disks with documents concerning four dropped cases that are detailed, but nevertheless not of great interest to the police."

He turned to face the others.

"Of which at least two had highly doubtful grounds for being dropped, but all the same . . ."

The frown line between his eyes grew even deeper, before he turned around again.

"(4)," he wrote, continuing. "An inexplicably new hard disk in the wife's computer."

As he fumbled with the marker, his thumb became stained with blue ink.

"What's this?" he said, shooting a challenging look at Hanne, who had remained seated with her arms folded and a blank expression on her face while the Superintendent was speaking.

"Completely amateurish," she said softly. "It stinks of a setup."

She inhaled, and indicated the points on the paper, one by one.

"The phone call: entirely unlikely that it actually came from Halvorsrud. The money in the basement?"

She hesitated as her finger rested on the second point listed.

"Halvorsrud is smart. When he phoned us, he must have known that the house was going to be turned upside down. The computer disks . . ."

Holding her breath again, she rubbed her cheek. "I can't work that out. Strictly speaking, Doris's computer doesn't have to mean anything at all."

"But what about the divorce papers?" Karianne asked, blushing, which Hanne had come to realize she did at the drop of a hat. "Why didn't he tell us anything about those?"

Hanne nodded slowly.

"You have a point. But isn't that quite common? Haven't we all had to struggle unnecessarily because witnesses and suspects think it's a good idea to tell little white lies about things they consider unpleasant?"

Karianne shrugged one shoulder and looked down.

"But," Billy T. began, "what did you actually mean when you said we might be talking about a combination?"

The Superintendent picked out a match from a box in the pocket of his tight jeans and put it into his mouth. "That Ståle Salvesen might not be dead. That he's the one who has set up all of this. And that there are other factors involved that we don't know about. In other words . . ." He flipped back to Hanne's original list. ". . . A, B, and not least C," he said. "A smokescreen. There are things we don't know."

"Obviously," Billy T. replied. "But we could of course stretch this hypothesis even further . . ." He grinned as he tugged at his moustache. "What if the *intention* was for this to look like a setup? What if there's a killer sitting somewhere worrying himself sick because the police haven't discovered it yet? He must be happy, then, that Halvorsrud's been set free at last!"

"And your point is?" Hanne asked tersely. "If the murderer isn't Ståle Salvesen or Sigurd Halvorsrud, the whole idea must have been for one of them to get the blame?"

"Well," the Superintendent said, spitting matchstick splinters, "unfortunately I have to go to another meeting."

The chair legs scraped on the floor as the assembled company made room for the Superintendent to make his exit. When he reached the door, he turned to stare intently at the flip chart. Then he snapped the matchstick he was chewing, spitting half onto the floor, and said pensively, "For Halvorsrud's sake, we'll have to hope Ståle Salvesen's body never turns up. For the sake of the Chief Public Prosecutor, we'll have to hope there quite simply is no corpse. As far as I'm concerned, I don't know what I'm hoping for. Good day."

It was Monday, March 29, 1999, and almost three o'clock. Hanne Wilhelmsen suddenly thought of a promise she had made to herself three weeks earlier. This case was going to be solved. Today.

59

Evald Bromo had heard about the kebab rats in the shrubbery beside the fountain at Spikersuppa but had never actually seen them. Now he was standing on the sidewalk in front of the National Theater watching the huge beasts fighting over the discarded scraps of food tossed under the bushes by late-night drunks. The gray rodents were as large as half-grown cats, and Evald shuddered. Eventually the taxi rank in Roald Amundsens gate filled up and cabs blocked his view. He looked at his watch.

Kai was late.

Evald was aware that he ought to visit his mother. He used to stop at the nursing home virtually every day. Now it was Tuesday afternoon and he had not visited the old woman since Friday.

Evald Bromo felt better now than he could remember.

The sense of calm that had suffused him when he sat on the steps outside the Deichman Library on Saturday night had persisted. Even though he continually wavered about the decision he had taken, he managed to return to it at regular intervals. That helped. Admittedly, the decision would have catastrophic consequences. Everything would be over. However, it would be better than waiting. These past weeks had almost killed him. There were still five months to go until September 1. It was too long. He knew that now; after sleepless nights and unproductive, anxiety-filled days, it would be better than continuing like this.

However much he turned it over in his mind, he knew it was the right thing to do. Evald Bromo turned hurriedly toward the City Hall, aware of an aroma of coffee from the quayside. He sniffed deeply and tried to recall whether he had ever felt proud of himself. Pleased, perhaps; he had been pleased when he had got his job at *Dagbladet*, and even happier when *Aftenposten* had in effect headhunted him. The offer from *Dagens Næringsliv*, the financial and business newspaper, had flattered him; and when he woke the day after his doomed wedding, with Margaret sleeping beside him in her pink nightdress, he had felt a sort of contentment about the choice he had made. Pride, on the other hand, was something he could not remember having felt since the onset of puberty, when his lust for little girls had come upon him like a lead weight he had never managed to throw off. When he had completed his marathon run and had won a place in the national top ten or fifteen, he had been satisfied, but nothing more. Never proud.

Now he knew what that was like.

It made him excited, and allowed him to take a trip down memory lane to the time when he was a young child and had no need to feel ashamed about anything.

The decision had been made, and he hugged the knowledge to himself. At the same time, he knew he was too weak. He would never dare do it without assistance. He needed someone. Someone who would understand without condemning.

Kai could help him. Kai had helped him before: the one time when Evald Bromo had been in danger of being exposed. Seven years ago. Evald Bromo had escaped, thanks to Kai. He had no idea why Kai had bothered with him. As the years passed, he'd gotten an inkling, but he'd let it lie. Instead, he had steadily shown his gratitude. Gifts and money initially, small tokens to nurture loyalty. Favors for a friend, eventually, never anything really major, but sufficiently often to blur the lines as to who was actually in debt to whom.

Evald Bromo waved a friendly greeting when the headlights of Kai's white Ford Escort blinked twice as he pulled into the curb. Kai leaned over and opened the passenger door.

"Hi," he said cheerfully as Evald settled into the passenger seat. "Long time no see."

Evald nodded and fastened his seat belt.

"Where shall we go?" Evald asked as they approached Storo and the ring road.

"Maridalen, I thought. Or somewhere up there, where we can get some privacy?"

"No," Evald answered doubtfully. "What about Sognsvann?"

"As you wish," Kai said with a smile, taking a left turn at the intersection.

By the time they drove into the gigantic parking lot at the Sognsvann lake and recreation area, Evald Bromo had related his story. He'd told Kai about the emails, about what was going to happen on September 1, about the package containing a CD and a closely written letter, about the decision he had now made, and why he needed help.

Kai parked at the far end of the parking lot, where joggers and walkers seldom strayed. They sheltered behind a delivery truck with its license plates removed, and Kai switched on the radio. Evald turned it off again.

"Pokerface," Kai said, stroking his forefinger in a circular motion on his trousered thigh. "Are you sure you can't connect that name with anything?"

"Quite sure," Evald said. "I don't even play poker."

Kai fingered the leather steering-wheel cover. It was worn, and the leather strap holding the cover in place had become slack.

"What have you done with the CD?"

"Here," Evald Bromo said, producing the case from his inside pocket.

Kai studied it for a long time before opening it. He took out the CD and held it between his thumb and middle finger. It was shiny like a mirror on one side, grooved and dull on the other. He scrutinized the iridescence on the recorded side as he turned it slowly from side to side.

"Have you listened to it?"

He replaced the disk inside the case.

"No. I know what it contains. It's described in there."

Evald pointed at the letter that had now slid down between Kai's thighs. The man in the driving seat picked it up, unfolded the sheet of paper, and skimmed it.

"Or so he says," he said curtly, handing everything back to his companion. "I think you're right. You're doing the right thing, and of course I'll help you as much as I can. I'll think about it, and then I'll contact you in . . ."

He scratched his forehead before adjusting the automatic toll-recording chip that had slipped out of its holder behind the rearview mirror on the windshield.

"I'll phone you on Monday."

"That's Easter Monday," Evald reminded him, shoving the CD case back into his pocket. "What about tomorrow?"

"I can't," Kai said. "I'm going away for Easter with the whole family early tomorrow morning. Tuesday, then. Tuesday of next week. I'll call you then."

An old man came sauntering out of the woods just thirty feet in front of them. He struggled to negotiate his way around an uprooted tree, then disappeared along the course of a stream without looking at the two men in the car.

"You should hide those things," Kai advised him. "Hide the CD case somewhere no one can find it. Not your wife, not anyone. Not at home, not at the office. Preferably somewhere outside. Far away. Leave it there until we meet. Bring it with you then."

Evald nodded absent-mindedly, touching his breast pocket where the CD was concealed.

"Just one more thing," Kai said as he turned the ignition. "You've heard that Sigurd Halvorsrud's been released from custody?"

He turned and looked at Evald before shifting into reverse gear and backing out of the space between the delivery truck and the woods.

"Yes," Evald Bromo replied.

"Doesn't that change things?"

"No. I'm not going to change my mind."

"Good," Kai answered. "You're doing the right thing."

Smiling, he patted his companion lightly and reassuringly on the thigh.

"Good," he repeated.

60

The night before Maundy Thursday, 1999, Sigurd Halvorsrud made a fresh attempt to leave his home without being spotted. He had hardly been out the door since he was released from custody, apart from his obligatory daily trip to the police headquarters to report in. Both boys had moved home again. They did any shopping that was required. Only in the evening did Halvorsrud dare to venture out for a short walk, usually in the company of his daughter. Thea was better. She was sleeping well at night, and that morning she had managed to concentrate on reading a book for several hours. Halvorsrud enjoyed his evening walks with his daughter. Father and daughter exchanged barely a word, but she sometimes held his hand. When he was in danger of walking too fast, she tugged at the sleeve of his jacket to keep him by her side. Then he would put his arm around her shoulders and, with a timid smile, she would walk even more slowly.

This evening she had not accompanied him.

She had gone to bed early, and he had taken his evening stroll extremely late. It was almost a quarter past midnight when he shook the dirt and gravel off his shoes and closed the door behind him, having been out walking for more than half an hour. The house was silent. Only the massive grandfather clock in the hallway was ticking sluggishly; the beats, combined with the sound of his own pulse in his eardrums, caused him to hold his breath momentarily before twisting out of his jacket and heading for the living room.

The polar-bear-skin rug had been removed long ago.

The parquet flooring was paler where the rug had been; it had left an outline, a bulky blob with arms, legs, and head. In the faint glimmer from the floor lamp beside the sofa, the impression was reminiscent of a dead body. Halvorsrud dimmed the light and turned away. He sat down in an armchair beside the window and remained there, not entirely sure whether he had nodded off, until he was satisfied that all the children were asleep, at about half past one.

Then he let himself out again.

He had not noticed any police presence earlier that night. He had been extra cautious, keeping his eyes peeled. The Easter holidays had begun, and the police force might be short of staff too. In any case, the street was totally deserted. Pettersen's garage was still out of commission and his vehicles were parked on the road. Apart from that, there was not a single car in the vicinity. Sigurd Halvorsrud sat behind the wheel and began to drive in the direction of Oslo city center.

He thought himself unseen, but he was mistaken.

61

Cecilie was a lot better. In the car on Route E18 she had sung along loudly to a CD of old Cat Stevens songs and in between had talked nonstop. They had taken a break to fill up with gasoline at the strange new roundabout directly south of Holmestrand, and Cecilie had bought ice cream and managed to eat it without feeling sick. When Hanne turned onto the final stretch leading down to Karen Borg's cottage—built on the ruins of the original one, following a fierce fire at the beginning of the nineties that had almost cost Karen her life—Cecilie could hardly wait.

"I'm so looking forward to it," she said aloud. "It'll be so lovely to start spring beside the sea!"

She laughed as Hanne had forgotten she could laugh. Hanne swallowed the last remnants of her reluctance and felt happy she had agreed to come. She was still furious at Karen, but she decided to let it drop when she saw her waving frantically from the terrace. Hanne drove in underneath an old pine tree and parked.

"Silie, Siiiilie!" Hans Wilhelm yelled. He stormed over toward Cecilie as she stepped out of the vehicle, then came to a sudden halt five feet away and held out a grubby hand.

"You're very sick, Silie. You can't put up with much. Daddy has a big secret."

He bowed. Cecilie laughed and rumpled his hair. Hanne lifted up Liv, who had come toddling after her brother with what looked like a dead cat tucked under her arm.

"Pussycat," the two-year-old said proudly, holding the limp soft toy up to Hanne. "Hanne cuddle Pussycat."

Hanne gave Pussycat a hug. Håkon came down to the parking area to help with their luggage. Hans Wilhelm forgot all the admonitions and hung onto Cecilie like a horsefly, making a fuss about a secret he was not allowed to talk about but that was big and red and really cool. The sky was only lightly overcast and looked promising, and the temperature had climbed sufficiently for them to sit outside by the south-facing wall to have coffee and waffles. Karen had understood Hanne's offer of a truce when they'd first exchanged looks. On the Skagerrak, the sea was churning white, and the wind was veering in a northeasterly direction as the afternoon drew in.

"When are you going to show it off?" Karen eventually said, nodding at Håkon over a glass of Farris mineral water.

Standing up abruptly, Håkon Sand flung out his arms demonstratively and roared at the sea. "NOW!"

"Now! Now!" Hans Wilhelm yelled, charging inside through the veranda doorway.

They could hear feet tramping down the stairs to the basement and the outside door down there slamming behind him.

"Come on," Håkon said to Hanne. "You're coming to see something."

"I'll stay here," Cecilie said with a smile, drawing the blanket more snugly around her when Hanne looked at her quizzically. "I'm fine right here."

There was a motorcycle inside the garage.

A Yamaha Diversion 900 cc, bright red with a half fairing.

"Eh?"

As far as Hanne was aware, Håkon had sat on a motorbike only once before in all his life. That was as a pillion passenger on a bike she had stolen and ridden because they had had to reach the cottage that had stood here previously that same evening, before it burned to the ground. The trip had been extremely dangerous, wet and freezing cold, and Håkon had later sworn that nothing would persuade him onto anything with two wheels and an engine ever again.

"That can't be yours," she said doubtfully, gazing at Håkon.

"Yeees!" Hans Wilhelm screamed, climbing quick as a flash onto the seat.

"Ooops," Hanne said, lifting him down again. "We need to put it onto the center stand first. Never leave it resting on the side stand, Håkon. It might topple."

With well-practiced movements, she heaved the motorbike onto the two-legged stand in front of the rear wheel. Then she placed Hans Wilhelm on the seat and pulled the helmet hanging on the handlebars onto his head.

"Like so," she said, knocking on the helmet. "Now you look fantastic."

"The bike, then," Håkon mumbled, scratching himself on the belly. "What do you think of it?"

Hanne did not answer. She circled the crimson machine twice, patted the gasoline tank, hunkered down and studied the engine, and ran her fingers lightly over the leather seat behind the little boy who was broom-brooming and roaring, obviously taking part in an important race.

"Beautiful color." She nodded and put her hands on the side. "Red. Lovely."

Håkon wrinkled his nose.

"But have you applied for . . ." Hanne went on. "Have you really got a license for such a heavy bike?"

"Yep. Four weeks ago. Then I bought this last week."

He was smiling broadly into his holiday beard. His upper lip was full of snuff, and the juice was running blackly between his front teeth.

"And you had the guts to do that," Hanne said distractedly.

Håkon removed the helmet from Hans Wilhelm, lifted the boy off the bike and slapped him fondly on the backside.

"Run up and see Mummy and tell her I said you could have some soda."

The boy tore out of the garage.

"It was just something I had to do," Håkon said slowly. "Call it a boy's toy if you like. Call it a middle-aged crisis if you want. Call it whatever you damn well like, but there was something about not daring to do it. I wanted to do it. To dare to do it. First of all it was important to get the license. Then it became important to buy the bike."

Hanne raised her leg and sat astride the motorbike.

"It must be damn easy to ride," she said tersely, rocking a little on the seat. "Low center of gravity and childlike sitting position."

"Try it out, then."

Håkon felt miffed. Hurt, even. He wanted to leave. He had looked forward to this. When he'd bought the bike, he'd done so because of other people. So that everyone around him would admire him. So that Hans Wilhelm would have something to boast about. So that Karen would shake her head and roll her eyes and call him macho-man. So that his colleagues would gaze lingeringly after him as he whizzed home in his multicolored leather suit and red helmet. And so that Hanne would be impressed. At the very beginning, before the first wobbling trips around the parking lot at the Munch Museum on the driving school's motorbike, he'd thought he was doing this for himself. But he was scared. He was scared every time he sat on the frightening, noisy monster. He was never in full control, and every single trip was a sweaty and pressured experience it took him half an hour to recover from. Håkon Sand had taken some time to admit the truth to himself and thought he would never confess it to anyone else: he had wasted more than a hundred thousand kroner in order to make an impression. But Hanne did not like the motorbike. Håkon had been looking forward to this scenario for an entire week, but she did not even like his new bike.

"Nice for a Japanese bike," she said in a conciliatory tone. "A very good bike for someone who can't tinker with it. Safe and good and easy to ride."

"Have a test ride," he repeated. "Here. You can borrow my suit. Have you got your own bike out again yet? For spring?"

She hesitatingly accepted the leather suit. Holding it up in front of herself, she shook her head.

"It's far too big for me," she said. "And no. The Harley's in storage. Waiting for a new exhaust. Anyway, I've not had a minute to spare. For the third . . ."

She held the suit up against her body and stared down at her frame. "Besides, I'm going to sell it."

"Sell it? Why on earth? You're practically attached to that Harley for the entire six months of summer!"

"Exactly," she said curtly. "Time to grow up."

Håkon spat his snuff out onto the concrete garage floor, and she rushed to add, "I don't mean that you're childish, by the way. To be honest, I think it's really impressive that you've managed it. I remember how frightened you were when . . ."

She laughed loudly and slipped off her running shoes.

"You nearly fainted from fright when we stole that motorbike to get here in time that night. But then you stormed into a burning building to rescue Karen. You're brave about the important things, Håkon. You're not like most other men. You're not the show-off type. You're kind and faithful and wise. Karen doesn't know how lucky she is."

She tenderly stroked the stubble on his face. Her hand rested on his cheek, and she stretched up on tiptoe to brush her lips gently on his forehead.

"I mean it," she said, gazing into his eyes for a few seconds before starting to step into the suit that was far too big for her. "I've never thanked you for coming that evening. And the following Sunday. I'm not going to either. You're kind, Håkon. Really, truly kind. And then you've put on such a lot of bloody weight since you've had children."

She tugged at the green-and-gray leather that puffed out around her stomach and pulled up the zipper.

"Look at me! A multicolored monster! Why didn't you buy a black suit?"

Håkon sat down on an old saw bench. The garage showed signs of having survived the fire almost seven years earlier, standing as it did a third of a mile away from the cottage. Admittedly, it had been freshly painted in the same shade of red as the cottage, but the interior stank of gasoline and oil, damp and stuffy. Someone years ago had tried to create a system for storing garden tools, implements, and bicycles on the walls. Now the nails were bent, and the outlines painted on the fiberboard to ensure that items were suspended in the right places had almost disappeared. At the farthest end, on the gable wall, an ancient hammock was hanging low, its fabric ripped.

"I have done all this to impress," he muttered. "Just to impress."

Hanne was taken aback. She sat down beside him on the saw bench with the helmet on her knee.

"What do you mean?" she asked, stroking her hair back from her forehead.

"I just wanted to make an impression. That was why I took the test. And bought this damn bike."

He kicked out in the direction of the motorcycle without saying any more.

"I'm tempted to laugh," Hanne said.

"I'm sure you are."

"I'm not laughing."

"Just go ahead and laugh. I deserve it."

Her laughter ricocheted off the walls and Håkon rubbed his face.

"I'm fucking petrified every time I ride it," he said with feeling. "You should have seen me on the trip down here. I took four hours from Oslo. Blamed it on the traffic. Actually I was sitting in every second roadside café trying to pluck up the courage to continue. Now I don't quite know how I'm going to get myself out of this."

He got to his feet. Hans Wilhelm had come back and was sucking on a straw in a half-liter bottle of soda.

"Are you going to try it?" the boy slurped.

"Yes. I think I will go for a spin. This will be the first one this year."

"Can I come with you?"

"Sorry. You'll have to wait a couple of years or so."

Hanne laced up her running shoes again before slipping the helmet over her head and lifting the visor. She switched on the ignition.

"I won't be long. An hour or so. When's dinner?"

"Late," Håkon said, patting the luggage carrier. "We'll wait until the children have gone to bed. Have a really good trip."

When he saw how she accelerated out of the garage and maneuvered the motorbike over the loose gravel in the courtyard outside, he realized he was never going to master his new Yamaha Diversion.

"I want to come with you," Hans Wilhelm whined. "I *never* get to come along."

"Come on, let's play Nintendo," his father comforted him.

In the far distance they could both hear the dwindling noise of a powerful motorbike. The temperature had started to drop. The swallows were flying low above the tops of the pine trees, and there was a scent of rain in the air.

It would be best to close the garage doors.

62

Ole Monrad Karlsen opened the door a crack without removing the security chain.

He had been sitting there at his leisure on Good Friday, reading the Monday edition of *Østlands-Posten*, the only newspaper Karlsen had any time for. The Oslo newspapers were so full of murder and sex. In the *Østlands-Posten*, which he had subscribed to since he had married and it became clear that Klara did not want to move to Larvik, he could follow all the goings-on, big and small, in his hometown. Admittedly, he'd been very young when he'd signed on as a seaman before the war and moved out of his parents' little house in Torstrand, in Reipmakergata just beside the Fram stadium, but he had always longed to return home. Continually. After Klara died, he had considered moving south again. His sister had invited him to move in with her. She had been recently widowed herself, and would appreciate the company. The nagging had continued for months. She still asked quite frequently, in her letters, which arrived monthly, and her sporadic phone calls. Karlsen's brother-in-law had been an engineer with the local council, and his sister had been left on her own in an enormous villa in Greveveien. He was given to understand it was empty and gloomy. The idea of moving was tempting, naturally, but then there was this caretaker's job. And the apartment. It was as though Klara's presence still permeated the walls: this was the apartment he and Klara had shared, and that memory belonged to them. He would stay there until he had to be carried out feet-first.

Then the doorbell had rung, several times.

Ole Monrad Karlsen was extremely vexed at being disturbed but shuffled reluctantly in his slippers to the door.

"What is it?" he asked brusquely with one eye peering through the chink.

The man outside was fairly tall, wearing a gray overcoat, and most certainly did not belong here at Vogts gate 14.

"Are you from the police again?" Karlsen asked gruffly. "I've nothing more to say about Ståle. If he's dead, then he's dead. Not much I can do about it."

"I'm not from the police," the man said. "I just have a couple of questions about something that happened here last night."

Karlsen immediately stiffened and pushed the door so that the opening measured only a few inches.

"What about it?" he grunted.

"I was walking home about two o'clock last night. I live right down the street here, you see. I'd been at a party up at . . . Could I come in?"

The stranger took a tentative step toward the door. Ole Monrad Karlsen did not react.

"Well," the man said, running a skinny finger over his bottom lip. "So I was walking past the block here, and I saw something that looked like . . ."

He placed the flat of his hand on the door frame and moved his face close to Karlsen's.

"It really would be much better if you'd let me come in," he said. "Or if you could open the door at least. It's a bit annoying to stand here making conversation without being able to see you properly."

Karlsen was of two minds. Perhaps he ought to have called the police last night, after all. God only knew what this guy might be up to if he didn't take the time to talk to him.

"Wait a minute," he said grumpily. He closed the door and removed the metal chain.

He opened up again, a wider gap this time, but did not let go of the door handle.

"That's better," the man said cheerfully.

He reminded him of someone. Karlsen thought he might have seen him before. If he was from the neighborhood as he claimed, then that could be it.

"It looked as though a man was trying to break in at the main door down here," the stranger continued, pointing down the corridor. "I called the police from my cell phone, but I didn't have time to wait. The reason I'm bothering you at the minute is just that I'd like to know if they ever turned up. The police, I mean. Did they come?"

Karlsen grudgingly let go of the door and rubbed his hand over his sore shoulder. He should have phoned the police himself. The burglar in the basement last night had come straight at him. Karlsen had been woken by strange sounds in the apartment block. With an iron rake in his hand, he had approached the basement door, noticing it was ajar and banging on its hinges. The guy had rushed headlong at Karlsen before he'd had time to collect himself, running as if the Devil himself was at his heels. He had struck Karlsen on the left side and nearly sent him flying. When the thug had disappeared and he had found nothing missing from the basement, Karlsen had thought it not worth the bother of alerting the police.

"There's nothing but trouble with the authorities," he mumbled, looking down at his feet.

"So they came, then?"

The man looked doubtful.

"No."

"But there was a break-in? Was I right about that?"

"Only in the basement. Nothing worth getting worked up about. I chased him out the door myself. Who are you, anyway?"

The man turned slowly on his heel.

"Then I apologize for disturbing you. Enjoy the rest of the Easter weekend."

He touched his hand to his forehead by way of farewell, and turned his back. Moments later he was gone. Karlsen locked the door with the double lock and security chain before returning to his newspaper. Again it struck him that he had seen that strange man before. He just could not recall where. Then he dismissed the thought with a heavy sigh.

He should have accepted his sister's invitation to spend the Easter weekend with her. It would have been pleasant to visit his old stomping grounds at this time of year, in the spring. It had become so dismal here since Ståle had gone missing. Perhaps the woods at Bøkeskogen would be green already. Although that did not usually happen until around May 17. He decided to take a trip there when that time came.

"I'll certainly do that," Karlsen said, pouring himself a small brandy.

It was Easter after all, and so, on second thought, he added a little extra.

63

The woman in the bed couldn't weigh more than 90 pounds. Her hands were skinny, and Evald Bromo felt a stab of irritation when he saw that her nails had grown too long again. He caressed the rough back of her hand as he prattled away to his sleeping mother.

At least she had a single room.

When she had finally obtained a place in a nursing home, she was already lost to this world. She never recognized him, but it used to be some consolation when she had the strength to continually mistake him for other people. One minute she would behave ingratiatingly and flirt with him, calling him Peder, presumably an old flame from long ago. The next minute she would scold him and furiously slap him with her knitting. Then he was his own father. For the past two years, she had barely spoken a word. She slept most of the time, and Evald did not honestly know whether it meant anything to her that he visited. He never stayed long but always felt a sense of disquiet if more than a couple of days went by since he had last been there.

Although the nurses were slovenly about his mother's personal hygiene—there was a strong smell of old woman and her nails were always too long—the room was kept neat. Evald himself had chosen the things she had been allowed to bring with her from her apartment in Gamlebyen. A dresser his mother had bought with money she had won on a shared lottery ticket took up most of the space. The chair he was sitting on was so old he could not remember a time when it had not existed. The cover had been replaced several times, and he had carved his initials under the seat one day when he had been ill and had to stay home from school while his mother was at work. In the corner by the window sat a little chest decorated with traditional flower painting. It was more like a large box, with his mother's first name elegantly painted in blue on the lid.

Evald crossed the room and crouched down in front of the chest. He stroked his hand across the worn lid and used his finger to trace the letters of his mother's name. He lingered on the "a" of Olga, and then let his fingers retrace the same outline. He inserted the key in the lock, the black, handcrafted key kept in the very smallest drawer of the dresser, underneath a box of four silver spoons.

The lock was sticky, but with a little force, the bolt inside the simple mechanism was coaxed undone. Evald opened the lid.

He had never seen what his mother stored in her chest. It would have been as unthinkable to open the chest as it would have been to open and read her letters. Even now, with his mother lying for a second year with no signs of life other than what her stubborn heart saddled her with, it made him uncomfortable to rummage through his mother's belongings. He caught himself glancing over his shoulder, as if expecting the old woman to sit up suddenly in the bed and rail at her son's inappropriate meddling with things that most definitely were none of his business.

On the top lay Evald Bromo's report cards from elementary school. He did not open them but placed them on the window ledge. Underneath lay a little pink box with a shabby lid and tied with string. He untied the knot and opened the box.

He didn't even know that his mother had kept it. When he had received his first paycheck the summer he turned thirteen, having delivered newspapers on rainy, foggy mornings for two months, he had spent all his money on a cameo. Fingering the brooch, Evald closed his eyes. A faint scent of lavender and perspiration crept out of his memory. That day many years ago, his mother had opened the gift and stared at the piece of jewelry, blinking her eyes before she embraced him.

There were locks of hair from when Evald was two, and old postcards. There were banknotes from China, and he wondered where she had gotten them. A broad gold wedding band with an illegible inscription was linked to an old-fashioned key with a red silk ribbon. Evald leafed rapidly through an old red passbook from the post office, filled with stamps proving that his mother had paid ten kroner into the savings bank every Friday. In Evald's name. He had never seen anything of the money. She had probably thought he did not need it.

For more than an hour, Evald Bromo searched through his mother's life. Finally, he took out a CD case from the jacket he had hung on the hook beside the door. Then he laid it at the bottom of the chest, before putting all his mother's belongings back in place, in layers, exactly as he had found them. And then he locked the large box.

When he was about to replace the key under the silver spoons in the very smallest drawer of the dresser, he hesitated. He should perhaps take it with him. But he shook his head briefly, opened the largest drawer, and thrust the black key in between his mother's modest, voluminous underpants. They would never be used. The nursing home had its own underwear that could tolerate washing in boiling water.

As Evald Bromo kissed his mother's hand in farewell, he felt a sudden glimmer of awareness that she was the only person he had ever loved.

64

Lars Erik Larsson was in a real quandary. He was about to put the final coat of paint on the little cabin in Östhammar and was annoyed because it looked as though he was going to run out of paint. The plan was for everything to be finished now, for Easter, when the summer season opened; he spent every single Easter on his own up here, getting the house and garden ready after the winter.

And he was in a quandary.

Since he had read about the Norwegian public prosecutor and recognized the name from a deposit made in his own bank, he had scoured the newspapers on a daily basis. As time passed and nothing more had been reported, he had calmed down. However, the *Expressen* had come out with fresh coverage last weekend. "Norwegian Police Scandal" was the headline. Apparently the man had been set free again. Still charged, but a free man until further notice.

He should perhaps report it. At least to his boss.

He had little inclination to talk to the police. But if he went to his boss, there would be a hell of an uproar all the same.

He shook the large paint can and swore under his breath because the south wall would not be finished. But there was still plenty to keep him busy. The rose bed, for example, did not look attractive following the depredations of winter and the deer.

He did not quite know what to do.

65

H anne Wilhelmsen was not disposed to admit it, but she liked Håkon's motorbike. It was very different from her Harley: lighter and more responsive. It was pleasant to sit leaning forward slightly, and the short fork made the curves more enjoyable to negotiate.

She had already passed Sandefjord town center and was on her way east along Route 303. As she passed the Gokstad burial mound, she briefly contemplated making a stop. She slowed down, but the long straight stretch was too tempting. The bike accelerated powerfully before rearing up; after sixty-five feet on the rear wheel, she let the front wheel hit the asphalt. This was a 60 kph zone and she had done at least 90 along the flat.

The sign indicating a right turn at the next junction called to mind a summer almost thirty years earlier. Her parents had virtually forced the twelve-year-old Hanne to enroll in the YWCA girl guides. Her tears and complaints had been entirely futile: for one whole winter she had been compelled to struggle off to meetings and camping trips with little girls she could not abide and who prayed to a God with whom she had never had any relationship. She had never understood why her parents, who otherwise did not bother particularly about their afterthought's activities, were so firm about the girl guides. Her mother's face had contorted into a worried frown, saying something about social training, but Hanne herself suspected even then that it was all a ruse to get rid of her. The only positive aspect of Hanne's ten-month-long career in the YWCA was the summer camp at Knattholmen, where there had also been boys. She remembered an endless summer of swimming, come rain or shine, and brutal soccer matches. Better still, Hanne had been in charge of building a monumental house, sixty-five square feet, in the island's largest oak tree.

She turned off the main road.

She wanted to see if her handiwork was still standing.

The spring weather encouraged her to lift her visor and feel the wind on her face. It was filled with the odor of manure and decay, growth and cultivation. There was drizzle in the air, but still not enough to make riding the bike unpleasant.

After ten minutes, the winding country road ended at a parking area. A sign welcomed her to Natholmen, where the Knattholmen campsite was situated. Hanne let the bike slide carefully toward the narrow track that sloped down to the bridge over to the island. A crooked, rickety frame supported mailboxes stuffed full of circulars that had accumulated over the winter while the summer cottage owners were absent. Only three of the boxes looked empty, obviously belonging to people who lived there all year round. Hanne halted for a second or two when she saw a single red light warning her of a car approaching from the opposite direction.

Her eyes fell on one of the empty mailboxes.

"EIVIND TORSVIK"

The name sounded familiar. She planted both feet firmly on the ground and straightened her back. Then she remembered: Billy T.'s report about the earless boy they had all let down. The writer. The murderer.

When an ancient pickup truck trundled slowly up the hill, Hanne lifted off her helmet and gestured to the driver. He pulled over and rolled down his window.

"Do you know this area?" Hanne asked.

"I live out there now," the man said, chortling as he pointed back with his thumb. "And have done for thirty years. So I suppose you could say I know the area!"

"Eivind Torsvik," Hanne said, indicating the mailbox. "Do you know where he lives?"

The man laughed again, with a hoarse splutter, and lobbed a wet cigarette butt out the window.

"Torsvik, yes. Strange guy. Murderer, you understand. Did you know that?"

Hanne nodded with some impatience.

"But he wouldn't hurt a fly, you know. I bump into him now and then, when he's out fishing. He smiles and says hello and is friendly. Doesn't say so very much, but apart from that he's fine. Lives just down there. Turn right at the bottom of the hill, before the bridge, and follow the road all the way along. The last cottage you come to. White. The very last one."

"Thanks," Hanne said, hanging her helmet on the handlebars. "Have a good day!"

Easing off the brake, the driver tipped his cap and drove on.

She had not really intended to speak to Eivind Torsvik. Hadn't even thought about it, in truth. Nevertheless, she drove cautiously down the hill, following the old man's directions, jolting along a badly constructed summer track beside the sea, until she finally caught sight of a white building a bit more than fifty feet from the end. A pennant in red, white, and blue was hanging, limp and wet and with a tattered point, from a flagpole several yards from the south-facing wall. The cottage was in a fantastic location, on a promontory only a few yards from the sea and with an open outlook to the south.

Hanne parked the motorcycle, pulled the zipper on her suit halfway down, and after a moment's hesitation, trudged up to the cottage along a paved path.

The front door was locked, and there was no sign of life other than the gulls screeching above the roof. The pennant's cord slapped softly and sadly against the flagpole in the light breeze. Hanne walked up to the door. She did not see a doorbell and knocked on the door instead.

She heard nothing. She knocked again.

As she was about to turn to leave—it would soon be evening and she had already been away from Cecilie for too long, and what was she doing here anyway—the door opened.

The man staring at her looked more like a boy. Slightly built and smooth complexioned, he wore a T-shirt, jeans, and a pair of heavy sandals. His hair was thin and curly, and although Hanne had in a way been prepared for it, she could not stop herself from staring at the spot where his left ear should have been. Eivind Torsvik was holding a pair of glasses in his hand, and Hanne caught herself wondering how he managed to get them to stay on.

"Hi," he said, sounding wary. "Hello there."

"Hello," Hanne answered, feeling idiotic as she played with the zipper and desperately tried to think of something to say. "Hello there!"

Suddenly Eivind Torsvik stretched his hand straight out into the air. "It's going to rain," he said, with a crooked smile. "Do you want to come in?"

Hanne found it remarkable that he invited her in without any fuss, but followed him all the same. When she was well inside the door, she realized why Eivind Torsvik was able to live there all year round. The hallway led into an enormous, blue-painted kitchen and Hanne spied several doors, presumably leading into bedrooms. Eivind Torsvik indicated for her to follow him down a two-stage staircase, where the man had an extensive work area in front of a south-facing picture window, with living-room furniture and a colossal stereo unit at the other end of the rectangular room.

"Sit down," Eivind Torsvik said, using his hand to indicate an armchair. "Can I offer you anything?"

"No thanks," Hanne muttered. She had begun to perspire inside the leather suit, and the room was unusually warm. "Or . . . perhaps some water."

Eivind Torsvik returned with a half liter of Farris mineral water and a glass filled with ice cubes. He opened the bottle, offered her the glass, and poured. The water sparkled vigorously, spraying Hanne's hand.

"Sorry," he said with a smile. "But it's only water."

They sat down in their respective chairs without looking at each other. Hanne found the man's behavior very odd, until it occurred to her that Eivind Torsvik must have an even greater problem understanding hers. She still had not uttered a peep about why she was there.

"I work with the police," she said in the end, taking a swig of the Farris.

He did not say anything, but she could see a worried expression, or maybe it was curiosity, cross his childlike face.

"It's not really to do with you exactly."

She drank some more, and wondered if it would be too forward to take off her suit.

"I was out riding and saw your name on the mailbox up there, and then I thought . . ."

She was aware of an embarrassing, inappropriate giggle bubbling up from her diaphragm. She hid her face in her glass yet again. What was she doing there? Why had she followed something that was not even an explicable impulse but only the stupid result of a dormant inquisitiveness that could not be controlled when she spotted his name on the mailbox? Admittedly, she was not quite herself at present, but at other times when she had called on people on more or less a split-second impulse, it had at least been because they had a distant, if not direct, connection with the case she was working on. Eivind Torsvik's name had cropped up in a document and had then disappeared. There was absolutely no reason to believe that the man had the slightest idea about the circumstances surrounding the brutal murder of Doris Flo Halvorsrud. Hanne laughed out loud and got some Farris up her nose.

"Sorry," she gasped, wiping her mouth with the back of her hand. "You must think I'm completely crazy."

"No," Eivind Torsvik said in a serious tone. "A bit strange, perhaps, but not completely crazy. Who are you, anyway?"

"Apologies," Hanne said, coughing. "My name is Hanne Wilhelmsen. I'm a chief inspector at the Oslo Police District. At present I'm working on a case concerning a woman who was beheaded. We've been thinking it was her husband—"

"Sigurd Halvorsrud," Eivind Torsvik said, nodding. "I've read about it on the Internet."

He cast a glance at the computer system at the other end of the room before smiling broadly and clasping his hands on his stomach. His fingers were long and elegant, and Hanne caught herself marveling that this man had actually committed a bestial murder.

"You had a list compiled, of course." He nodded slowly as he spoke. "A list of especially spectacular murders in the last . . . let's say the last ten years? Fifteen?"

Hanne wriggled her upper body out of the leather suit and fidgeted with one of the sleeves without looking at the young man.

"And so, naturally, my name cropped up."

He stretched out his legs and let one foot balance on top of the other.

"Did you ever suspect me? Am I still a suspect, perhaps?"

His mouth had acquired a slightly mocking expression, a teasing half-smile that caused Hanne to sit up straight in her seat.

"Of course not," she said apologetically. "We don't suspect people simply on the basis of what they've done previously."

His laughter was enchanting. It began softly and then gurgled up a scale of notes that made it sound like an improvised song.

"But that's precisely how you do operate," he said, with feigned reproach, as if he felt offended by a blatant lie. "And I find that quite natural. Why else would the police quarrel so vehemently with the Data Protection Authority and Parliament about those DNA registers? If you ask me, the protection of personal privacy has been taken too far."

Suddenly there was a glimmer of something resembling enthusiasm in the young man's eyes. Until now he had been conspicuously quiet, considering Hanne's behavior.

"You know of course what sort of crimes have the greatest percentage of recidivism," he said. "Theft and sexual crimes. Thieves are, in the strict sense of the word, not really dangerous. Whereas people who commit sexual crimes . . . They continue to do damage practically unhindered by an impotent legal system."

He suddenly stamped his feet down on the floor in front of his chair, gazing intently into Hanne Wilhelmsen's eyes as he went on. "Of course you go after repeat offenders. It's only right."

His face opened up, and he laughed again.

"But you've hardly come here to arrest me on your own. I'm probably still considered dangerous."

He studied the woman who claimed to be from the police. Something told him she was not lying. When he looked past the far-too-large leather suit and the untidy hair, the woman was attractive. Her face was almost beautiful, strong and with no makeup. Eivind Torsvik seldom felt at ease in the company of other people. There was a reason he lived out here. Even when summer brought all the cottage people and other tourists, he was on the whole left to his own devices. His property was large enough for that. But this strange woman of indeterminate age—she could be anything from thirty to forty-five—made him feel relaxed in a way that surprised him. When he heard the knock on the door, he had at first decided not to answer it. Something had nevertheless persuaded him to go to the door, and the moment he saw her, he knew he was going to ask her in. He did not understand why. Hardly anyone apart from him had been inside the walls of the cottage since he had moved in. However, there was something about the woman, a loneliness in the dark-blue eyes, that inspired some kind of solidarity he could not explain.

"What do you do out here?" Hanne said all of a sudden. "Do you just write?"

"'Just,'" he repeated, leaning across to her. "If you think being a writer's simply a matter of 'just,' then you're mistaken."

"I didn't mean it like that," she said hastily. "It's just that you've got such a phenomenal amount of equipment over there that I thought perhaps you did something else. In addition, I mean. To your writing."

"Most of it's entirely unnecessary," he said simply. "Computer, screen, and keyboard are all I need. I also have a scanner, two extra machines, a CD burner . . . I've got far too much equipment. I like that."

"Internet connection too, I suppose."

"Of course. I surf for hours. The phone bills can be sky-high at times."

Hanne Wilhelmsen suddenly stopped breathing. She cocked her head and fixed her gaze on a bronze figure on the windowsill facing west: St. George fighting the dragon. The snake-like creature curled around the horse's legs and St. George held his lance aloft, ready to strike.

"The phone bills," she repeated softly and slowly, as if afraid of losing her grip on a train of thought. "Do you have two lines? Numbers, I mean? One for the telephone and one for the computer?"

"No," Eivind Torsvik replied, squinting in amazement. "ISDN. One number. Why do you ask?"

"When someone receives two bills from the phone company," she said, in a dreamy voice, "but has only one telephone . . . how do you explain that?"

He shrugged his shoulders. "Maybe they got their Internet connection before ISDN was available?"

"Or . . ." She stood up abruptly. "I've disturbed you quite unnecessarily and for far too long," she said. "I need to head for home."

"Are you going to Oslo?" he asked, peering out through the window. "It's raining in earnest now."

"Only to Ula. Takes no more than twenty minutes."

He accompanied her across the paved terrace directly in front of the cottage door. The wind had gotten considerably stronger. A boat lay knocking against a jetty sixty feet away.

"Obviously haven't tightened the rope properly," he said, seemingly to himself. "All the best to you."

Hanne did not respond but offered him her hand.

When she rode slowly along the bumpy track, she wondered why Ståle Salvesen had paid Telenor for two phone lines.

She had inspected his apartment extremely thoroughly.

He had only one telephone installed.

66

Evald Bromo was not sure whether it was still Easter Saturday. He had been running for two hours, and it entered his head that it must be past midnight. He ran more easily tonight than for ages, as if he were running toward something, full of anticipation, and not simply sprinting away from a fate impossible to shake off. His running shoes hit the asphalt with a rhythmic swish-swish, and he felt strong.

When he arrived home, he would take a long shower before eating the food Margaret had almost certainly prepared for him. If he were really fortunate, she would already be fast asleep in bed.

One last hill lay ahead of him. He increased his speed and felt a taste of blood spread through his mouth. Faster and faster he ran: there were only 40 yards left, 30, 20, 10. He had to cross the road, and at the very top he would take the side road to the left, stealing a few yards by cutting the corner beneath an old copper beech.

The blow that struck him on the head was so savage that he barely registered being shepherded subsequently into the rear seat of a car. There, he was violently sick.

Everything went dark.

67

Margaret Kleiven had been sleeping heavily. Before Easter she had consulted a physician, as she had been having difficulty sleeping in the past few weeks. Evald had changed so much. Surly. Quick-tempered. It was true she had previously been aware of these aspects of her husband's personality, but his tirades had been infrequent and never lasted long. Now he was silent and sullen and blew his top at the slightest thing. She had never understood much about his running, but it was good, of course, that he liked to keep himself fit. Recently, however, his training regime had taken over altogether. He was out for hours at a time, and came home completely exhausted. Margaret had more than once heard the unmistakable sounds of someone retching behind the locked bathroom door. The doctor had given her something to help her sleep, and the mere knowledge that these tiny pills lay inside the cabinet seemed to be enough. She was not used to medication, and she would put off using them for as long as possible.

Yesterday evening he had been in a more subdued mood. They had watched some TV and Evald had even glanced across at her when he thought she would not notice. That made her feel calmer, and when he suggested a game of backgammon, she had smilingly accepted. At half past ten or thereabouts, he had gone out for a run. She did not like it, it was far too late, but he had now become used to these long runs before bedtime and insisted she should just go to bed. Margaret had left out two sandwiches on a plate in the kitchen. Even though he ate hardly anything these days, it was not for her lack of effort.

She yawned and raised her arms above her head. The sunlight was penetrating the dark curtains and it suddenly dawned on her that it was Easter Sunday.

She would boil eggs for breakfast.

Evald was already up and about.

Margaret Kleiven rose from the bed and padded through to the bathroom.

There was no whiff of soap or aftershave. The mirror was clear of condensation. She ran her fingers over the shower curtain. It was bone dry. She grabbed Evald's large yellow towel and pinched it between her fingers. It too was bone dry.

That was very odd. If he had showered after his night run, there would still be traces of dampness in there. It was only eight o'clock. Margaret returned to the bedroom.

She stared at the bed. Strangely enough, she had not noticed that Evald's side was still completely undisturbed. A sudden anxiety clutched at her throat. She rushed downstairs and stood in front of the kitchen door, afraid to go in. Then she pulled herself together and gingerly opened the door.

Two sandwiches, one with roast beef and one with cheese and paprika, were still sitting on a plate on the oval pine table. The plastic wrap covering them had not been touched.

Margaret wheeled around and returned to the hallway.

Three pairs of running shoes were lined up on the shoe rack. The fourth pair was missing. The new ones. The ones Evald had bought only a month ago. He wore out five pairs in the course of a year, but usually kept the old ones for a while. They were okay for wearing in heavy rain.

"Evald," she said softly, then repeated in a louder voice, "*Evald!*"

Five minutes later, Margaret Kleiven had established that Evald was nowhere to be found inside the house and that the clothes he had been wearing last night were also gone.

No doubt about it: he had not come home.

She dropped the telephone receiver when she tried to pick it up. Then she sat down on the stairs and forced herself to calm down sufficiently to dial the *Aftenposten* number.

Evald was not there. Not in his office. Not anywhere.

Margaret Kleiven burst into tears. She fiddled with the wedding ring that had become slack recently, and felt a growing sense of fear about to overwhelm her.

Evald might be at a friend's house.

Margaret could not think of anyone Evald might visit so early on Easter morning.

Evald might have come home last night, decided not to eat anything, slept beside her, made the bed again, put on yesterday's running gear, and gone out for another run.

She inhaled and exhaled deeply, slowly.

That must be what had happened.

But that was not what had happened. She knew that within herself. Something was dreadfully wrong.

If Evald was not back by ten, she would phone the police. Margaret Kleiven remained sitting on the stairs cradling the phone on her knee, staring at the wall clock directly opposite. The sunshine that had crept across the living room floor had already begun to climb up the wall. The bright reflections of Evald's old trophies on the bookshelf were projected across the room, making her eyes blink. It promised to be an extraordinarily beautiful day.

68

The two police officers walking with determined footsteps up the driveway of the Halvorsrud family home both wore sunglasses. One of them, a woman of around twenty-five, murmured that she should have been a lawyer. The Halvorsrud family's villa looked magnificent in the spring weather. The glazed Dutch roof tiles glittered in the sunshine. Even though the garden had obviously not yet been fixed up for the season, the grounds were extensive and the garage provided a generous double parking space.

The elder of the two, a dark-haired man with a thick beard, rang the doorbell. Removing his glasses, he gestured impatiently to his colleague to follow suit.

After two more prolonged rings, the door was finally opened.

Halvorsrud, in a blue-and-white-striped bathrobe, stood squinting at them.

"What's this about?" he said, half asleep, before stealing a glance at his watch. "Oh. Sorry."

"You've a duty to report to us every day at twelve o'clock," the woman said, making an attempt to look over Halvorsrud's shoulder.

A young teenage girl crept downstairs, dressed in an oversized T-shirt.

"I know that," Halvorsrud said, disconsolate. "Of course I know that. I've simply overslept. I can't do anything other than apologize."

Producing a piece of paper from his breast pocket, the uniformed man unfolded it and held it out to Sigurd Halvorsrud.

"Daddy?"

The young girl's voice sounded anxious, and Halvorsrud turned to face her.

"Everything's all right, darling. We've just slept in."

He turned around again and skimmed the document he had been handed.

"Do you have something to write with?" he muttered, placing the sheet of paper against the hallway wall.

"Here."

Halvorsrud took the ballpoint pen the man offered him and scribbled his signature.

"So," he said, tugging the belt of his bathrobe more tightly. "Apologies once again."

"Just don't let it happen again," the police officer said with a smile. "Have a nice day."

Halvorsrud stood watching them go, with his arm around his daughter's shoulders. When the two police officers resumed their seats in the patrol car parked immediately beside the driveway, the younger of them commented as she put her sunglasses back on, "If it was up to me, we'd have locked him up again. It's not every Tom, Dick, and Harry that gets that kind of treatment."

"Lawyers rule the world," her colleague replied, tucking the signed paper into the glove compartment.

69

Ole Monrad Karlsen had endured a dreadful night at Vogts gate 14. A gang of youths in the adjacent block had done their best to keep the entire neighborhood awake until almost daybreak. Karlsen had not been the only one annoyed by this: the police had turned up about 4:00 a.m., obviously following up a complaint from someone or other. The noise level had dropped considerably for half an hour or so and Karlsen had been on the verge of falling asleep when the noise thundered out again.

On the first Sunday of the month, it was time to change the light bulbs on the stairway and in the basement and the loft. It made little difference to Ole Monrad Karlsen that it was Easter Sunday. He had his routines, and it would take more than a public holiday or a sleepless night to interfere with him carrying out his duties. He swore under his breath when he discovered that all four light bulbs on Staircase A had gone. The block was large, with twenty-four apartments and two stairways.

Actually, he had intended to head for Staircase B before going down to the basement. However, as he had come shuffling downstairs from the first level, carrying four used and six new light bulbs in a plastic bag, he'd noticed that the basement door was ajar. This was not the first time. Lately he had written three stern notices with reminders that the outside doors and basement were to be kept locked.

"AT ALL TIMES," read the declaration in red felt pen at the foot of the notice.

Karlsen was infuriated. After the last uninvited guest—the thug who had given him a sore shoulder, which still caused him pain at night—he had noted that no locks had been broken open. In other words, the lout had been able to get in because someone had been slipshod about procedures. Fortunately nothing had been stolen. Karlsen had surprised the thief in the nick of time.

Now someone had damaged the door.

It was banging against the door frame in the slight draft. The timber around the lock was splintered and showed white against the old blue paint.

"It was that then . . ."

Karlsen took it all as a personal affront. This was his block. He was responsible for keeping everything in order, for people taking their turn to wash the stairs, for circulars not being left dangling from mailboxes, for the sidewalk being hosed down, and for the plumber coming when necessary. He was responsible for ensuring that everything functioned smoothly. In an apartment block such as this, where one-third of the residents were on welfare and the turnover of tenants was so rapid that Karlsen sometimes found himself puzzling over who actually belonged there, a firm hand on the tiller was essential.

Someone had broken into *his* basement.

Incensed, he stomped down the stairs.

At the bottom, he almost stumbled over something. He reached his hand out to the wall for support and managed to stay on his feet. Then he looked down.

There was a head lying there.

Farther along the narrow corridor in the basement lay the body that obviously belonged to it, arms lying by its side and legs crossed, as if the headless corpse was just taking a little nap.

Feeling the blood rush from his brain, Karlsen swallowed hard.

Karlsen had encountered worse things than this. He had watched floundering comrades drown in icy seas; once he had hauled his best friend into a crowded lifeboat, out of an ocean aflame with blazing oil, only to discover that his friend's lower body was missing.

Ole Monrad Karlsen placed his hand over his eyes, swallowed again, and concluded that this time he really should call the police.

70

"Don't answer it," Cecilie murmured.

Fluffy summer clouds drifted slowly above them. Amorphous and transparent, they made the sky look pale and the sun appear white. Hanne and Cecilie were stretched out on their backs, holding hands. It was already late morning, and they could feel the heat from the rock beneath them through their clothes. The wind had abated. The terns were screeching and for a second or two Hanne had hoped that it was them that she had heard when her cell phone rang.

"Have to," she said disconsolately, sitting up. "Wilhelmsen?" she said into the phone.

Someone spoke for a long time at the other end of the line. Hanne did not utter a word until she wound up the conversation by saying she would phone back in ten minutes. She then disconnected the call and sat gazing out across the sea. A fishing boat chugged into the harbor, and on the horizon a tanker was plying a westward course.

"Who was it?" Cecilie said softly without opening her eyes.

Hanne did not reply. She grasped Cecilie's hand and squeezed it.

Cecilie sat up. "Thanks for coming here with me," she whispered, picking a dry sea pink from a crack in the rocks. "I'm having such a lovely time. Do you have to leave?"

She leaned against Hanne, tickling her under the nose with the flower. Hanne smiled stiffly and rubbed her face.

"There's been a murder," she said quietly. "Another decapitation."

Cecilie put her arm around her and felt Hanne's hair against her cheek. "And Halvorsrud's out," she said slowly. "Does this have anything to do with him?"

Hanne shrugged.

"Who knows?" she said, sounding discouraged. "But it seems curious to have two beheadings in one month. I've no idea . . ."

Falling silent, she put her head in her hands. Cecilie haltingly raised herself up in order to kneel behind her. She embraced Hanne and rocked her slowly from side to side.

"It's Easter Sunday," she whispered with her lips on Hanne's ear. "They'll manage fine without you until tomorrow. Don't you think?"

Three children aged about twelve suddenly appeared on a rocky crag only ten yards away from them. The girls were whispering and one sniggered loudly with her hand in front of her mouth. Then they were gone, just as abruptly as they had arrived.

"I have to go," Hanne said, getting stiffly to her feet. "But if you want to stay, I can try to find some time to come for you tomorrow evening. You won't be able to travel back with Håkon and Karen. It would be too wearing with the children in the car."

Cecilie clutched Hanne's hand and began to take shaky steps toward the path beyond the coastal rocks.

"You're never going to have time to come for me," she said firmly. "I'll come back with you now."

71

It was 8:00 p.m. on Monday, April 5. Hanne Wilhelmsen had barely been home to change clothes that morning and could feel the onset of a familiar headache. Opening her eyes wide, she made an effort to focus on the document Billy T. had delivered an hour earlier. She was grateful that he had never objected to her demand for daily written reports. Most of the detectives felt that the official documents ought to be sufficient and were reluctant to take the time to write personal letters to the Chief Inspector. Hanne Wilhelmsen insisted on it nevertheless, to a chorus of mostly noisy protest. Receiving daily summaries of the countless pieces of information, steadily mounting, which lay in folders and loose-leaf binders, helped her to retain an overall picture. Also, in her experience, investigators took greater liberties when they knew what they wrote was not going to be officially recorded, so they aired personal opinions and hunches. Hanne Wilhelmsen wanted it that way, so that was what she got.

She swallowed down two aspirins with lukewarm coffee, and read as she massaged her scalp with her fingertips.

The murder victim is Evald Bromo, a journalist in Aftenposten's *financial section. He was forty-six years old, married to Margaret Kleiven, no children. Never convicted of any crime.*

Evald Bromo, like Doris Flo Halvorsrud, had injuries from a powerful blow to the back of the head. Whether that killed him, or whether he was decapitated while still alive, will become clear in the next few days. He was found by the caretaker, Ole Monrad Karlsen, at Vogts gate 14. Provisionally, Karlsen is entirely beyond suspicion. He is surly and difficult, but Sommarøy believes the guy clearly has nothing to do with the incident.

Vogts gate 14 is a block of rented apartments with twenty-four units, many of which are public housing for tenants on social security. The block itself is in private ownership, which explains why Karlsen is still caretaker long after having reached pension age. Ståle Salvesen rented from the local authority.

Evald Bromo left his home around half past ten on Saturday night to go jogging. He was apparently very fit for his age, and according to his wife there was nothing unusual about such an outing.

His wife went to bed immediately after her husband went out. When she woke the next morning around eight o'clock, there were signs in the house that Evald Bromo had not come home. The provisional time of death is estimated at between midnight and two o'clock on Sunday morning, so this seems to add up. His wife waited for a couple of hours before alerting the police to her husband's disappearance. She had not wanted to create a commotion in case it turned out that her husband had simply gone out running again. Karianne, who has spoken to the wife, says she seems totally devastated and really bewildered about what has happened. I've requested that she be interviewed again tomorrow. On Sunday afternoon it was barely possible to get any sense out of her.

The weapon used to behead Bromo has not been found. Probably a sword of some kind was used. It must have been relatively heavy and extremely sharp. It was a clean cut and the forensic experts maintain that it took no more than two or three blows to sever the head from the body.

It is evident that the door to the basement was broken open, but it is likely that the outside door had been left open. According to what we have learned, it's a fairly frequent occurrence for the residents to set the latch to the open position. The intercom system's remote opening mechanism is sometimes out of order and many residents do not want to have to go downstairs to open the door for visitors.

Bromo was in all probability decapitated in the place where his body was found. In any case, he must have been unconscious (if not dead) when it happened. As of now, we have not found any sign of a struggle. There was nothing but ordinary dirt under his nails, and his body had no other injuries apart from the blow to the back of the head and the actual decapitation.

We are keeping an open mind about whether Bromo went down into the basement under his own steam or whether he was carried down. If it was the latter, we are probably talking about a male, very strong perpetrator (or several perpetrators). Neither the staircase nor the corpse bears any sign that Bromo was dragged down to the basement (dead or unconscious). That means he either walked by himself, or was carried. Accordingly, since there were no signs of struggle, the latter seems most likely. Furthermore, it should be added that Bromo was of slim build, six feet tall and weighing only 150 pounds.

In fact, the police were sent to the area at three o'clock on Sunday morning. Complaints had been made about a party in the block opposite the crime scene. The patrol did not see or hear anything suspicious at or around Vogts gate 14.

The most remarkable aspect of this case is of course that the body was found in the basement of the apartment block where Ståle Salvesen lived. Even if the murder had been committed by means other than decapitation, such a coincidence would have been striking. When, on top of everything else, we are talking about an execution in the same manner as was inflicted on

Doris F. H., then this probably indicates some kind of connection between the killings.

Erik H. and Karl are now investigating whether there are any points of intersection between Evald Bromo and Ståle Salvesen. Bromo's wife had never heard Salvesen's name before, so there can't be any close relationship, at least. At present we do not know anything other than that Bromo covered the story about the investigation into Aurora Data and Salvesen. In other words, it is likely that the two of them met and spoke at some point many years ago.

Naturally, we are also investigating whether there is any link between Sigurd Halvorsrud and Bromo. To date there is nothing to suggest that. Since they both worked on financial crimes, it is highly probable that they at least knew of each other. We're hauling Halvorsrud in for an interview tomorrow. I'll take care of that myself.

Today, we have conducted a total of six witness interviews. (It has been difficult to get hold of people because of the Easter holidays.) Three were with Bromo's closest colleagues, who all claim to have known Bromo reasonably well. He is generally described as a relatively quiet, shy man who seldom had much social contact with others. They know little of Bromo's social circle, but assert that he mainly stayed at home with his wife when he was not out running. Apparently he used to be a very competent long-distance runner. One of the witnesses describes Bromo's attitude to running as "fanatical." None of the witnesses can think of anyone who might be out to get Bromo, although they all emphasize that as journalists, they occasionally have a strained relationship with people they write about.

In a manner of speaking, Ståle Salvesen is a "dead joker."

It's about time we initiated an organized search for him. Perhaps we should have done so earlier. The currents at Staure

Bridge are such that a body could certainly be pushed down and even become snagged on the seabed. Personally, I don't think we'll find anything. My gut feeling tells me that Ståle Salvesen is someplace or other, alive and well.

Hanne Wilhelmsen tried to identify her own gut feeling. It told her nothing apart from that she had not eaten for twelve hours.

"Damn it, Hanne!"

Karl Sommarøy charged in through the half-open door and hurled a sheet of paper with two magnified fingerprints onto the desk in front of her. Then he stood beside her with his left arm across her shoulder and his right finger stabbing at the paper.

"Can you believe that?" He laughed his girlish chuckle, slapping his whole hand down on the table.

"Fingerprints, obviously," Hanne said with a sigh.

She stifled a yawn and considered reprimanding her colleague. Although the door had been slightly open, he should have knocked.

"I see that," she said instead.

"But who do you think they belong to?"

Breathless with excitement, Karl Sommarøy continued without waiting for Hanne to guess.

"They were found beside Evald Bromo's corpse. One on a storeroom wall five feet farther along the basement corridor, and one on the wall beside the stairs."

Her headache had intensified. Something was pulsing behind her right eye, as if a nail had lodged in there and wanted to get out. Hanne pushed her knuckle into her eye socket and pressed hard.

"So who do they belong to?" she said in a disgruntled voice, trying to make him release his grip on her shoulders. "I'm a bit too tired to play games."

"They belong to Sigurd Halvorsrud!" Karl said, laughing again: high-pitched, reedy, and piercing. "Sigurd Halvorsrud has been in Ståle Salvesen's basement, where Evald Bromo's body was found. I'm really damn curious about how he's going to explain that!"

Hanne Wilhelmsen let her fingers follow the fine lines on the enlarged prints in front of her. They curved around one another like contour lines on an old orienteering map. The terrain was unique: of the nearly five billion people in the world, only Sigurd Halvorsrud could have left these marks in the basement where Evald Bromo was murdered. The Chief Public Prosecutor could not talk his way out of that.

72

It was calm as a millpond on the outer Oslo Fjord. A couple of nautical miles south of the Færder Lighthouse, an oceangoing yacht was becalmed with two crew on board. Petter Weider and Jonas Broch were both twenty-five years old and studied law when they were not out sailing. Which meant that they read a minimal amount. During the Easter holidays, which they should have spent poring over their books since exams were just over a month away, they had sailed to Copenhagen for marijuana. Not large quantities—only half a kilo each, exclusively for personal use. A little for friends too, perhaps. Just as a treat.

The return voyage had taken longer than expected. In the middle of the Skagerrak, the wind had dropped considerably. By the time the students caught sight of the Færder Lighthouse on the morning of Tuesday, April 6, the sea was unusually calm for the time of year. The sun was blazing in the eastern sky, and they were able to stow their thick lifejackets and sit in the cockpit wearing only their woolen sweaters.

It was a perfect day for a real joint. No point in using their engine when, strictly speaking, they had nothing other than a stuffy reading room awaiting them on shore.

The merchandise they had purchased through an old acquaintance at the University of Copenhagen contained what the advertisement had promised. Petter and Jonas had already forgotten that they had failed their exams twice in a row and that the student loan fund would revoke their aid if they did not pass this time. The gentle slapping of sails in search of wind, combined with the waves lapping around the boat, encouraged the young men to look on the bright side of life. If their exams went down the drain this time too, they could always sail around the world. For a couple of years anyway. To Zanzibar at least, where Jonas had been the previous year during the Christmas holidays. And certainly to the Maldives, where they could laze around, traveling from island to island, and maybe even earn some money from tourists who were bored out of their skulls parading around the same little stretch of land.

"There's a man lying in the water," Petter said lethargically. "Starboard side."

Jonas sniggered. "What's he doing?" he whispered dramatically.

"He's dead."

"Completely?"

"Fairly."

"Have we any more beer?"

Petter thrust his fist into a cooler bag and pulled out a half-liter can of Tuborg. He tossed it to Jonas before opening one for himself.

"The guy's still there," Petter mumbled.

"Cut it out." Jonas sat up straighter and locked the tiller. "Where is he?"

"There!"

"For fuck's sake! *Goddamn it, Petter!* He really *is* dead!"

"That's what I told you," Petter muttered, offended.

Jonas leaned over the gunwale and splashed saltwater on his face. He rubbed his temples vigorously and gave his head an energetic shake.

"We'll have to haul him in. Throw me the boat hook!"

Between them, the two students succeeded in grabbing hold of the corpse's clothes. They dragged the body, heavy as lead, slowly toward the gunwale. The man—for some reason they realized immediately that it was a man—was lying face down in the water.

"Turn him over," Petter said doubtfully.

"You do it!"

"No fucking way. Do you think we should take it on board?"

Jonas attempted to grab underneath the body's stomach. His grip caused an air bubble in the clothing to burst.

"For God's sake! That stinks! Let it go! Fucking hell, let it go!" Yelling, Petter propelled himself over to the port side of the boat. His back struck the cooler bag and a stream of curses ensued.

"We can't just let it go," Jonas snarled, retching over the corpse. "We'll have to alert the police, you idiot!"

Petter got to his feet, rubbing his sore back as he grimaced at the foul stench that had wafted across the entire boat.

"Can't we just tow it ashore? If we give it some slack, we'll get rid of that God-awful smell."

"Bloody idiot! The guy's whole body is falling apart. If we haul it as much as ten yards, there won't be anything left of him. Now just give me some rope and stop behaving like a damn fool. Help me here, for fuck's sake!"

A quarter of an hour later, Petter Weider and Jonas Broch had secured the corpse they had found by tying it to the gunwale. They had called the police over their VHF radio. It would not be long until they arrived.

"Fuck!"

It dawned on them both in the same split second. In the forward cabin they had stashed almost a kilo of marijuana. Even though it was unlikely that the police would thoroughly search the yacht belonging to two helpful law students, they could not take that chance. They would both be lawyers in the fullness of time, star attorneys with fat bank accounts. Petter was almost in tears as Jonas resolutely emptied two plastic bags of tobacco-like narcotics into the sea.

What he had not taken into account was the exceptional calmness of the sea.

The cannabis would not sink. Instead it attached itself to the side of the boat, drawn in by the gentle current created by the ocean yacht as it moved slowly toward land.

And that was how it came about that when the police were finally able to take over responsibility for the body they would identify twenty-four hours later as Ståle Salvesen, the dead, almost decomposed man was exquisitely peppered with narcotics.

73

"Sigurd Halvorsrud," Billy T. said slowly, tugging his earlobe as he toyed with an inverted gold cross. "Sigurd Olav Halvorsrud."

He folded his arms and fixed his gaze on the man who had been brought in, who was sitting stiff as a board on the opposite side of the desk. Beside him sat Karen Borg, wearing trousers for once. She fingered the folder she had placed on her knee ten minutes earlier but still had not opened. Subtly, she pushed her chair a few inches away from her client, as if she had long ago given up her belief in Sigurd

Halvorsrud's innocence and was desperately attempting to distance herself.

"What were you up to in that basement, then, Halvorsrud?"

Billy T. suddenly leaned across the table.

"My client has not yet admitted he was there," Karen Borg said in reproving tones. "I suggest we begin there."

Billy T. smiled and chewed at his beard.

"Until now your client hasn't said so much as a single word," he said harshly. "And he's quite entitled to do that. But as far as this interview is concerned, we'll do things exactly the way I decide."

He opened a half-liter bottle of soda and drank half of it in a long gulp. Then he slammed the bottle down on the table and rubbed his hands.

"I'm starting over," he said cheerfully. "What were you doing in the basement at Vogts gate 14 last Saturday night?"

During the three weeks Halvorsrud had been held in a holding cell, before Judge Bugge's perverse decision to send him home to his daughter, the man had hardly been out of his formal clothes. Every single day, he had dressed in his normal working attire: suit with shirt and tie. Now he was sitting in a pair of worn jeans and suspenders, and a brown-and-green flannel shirt, open at the neck, through which a few wiry gray hairs protruded. Billy T. had read the arrest report. The man had insisted on changing. He had not been allowed to, and obviously felt ill at ease in his disheveled attire, as if it was too intimate to show oneself like that in public. Halvorsrud held his hands over his crotch and coughed interminably, as if something had lodged in his throat.

"I," he began. "I . . . I . . ."

He did not get any further. Instead he leaned over to Karen Borg and whispered a short instruction. Her back stiffened and eventually she placed the folder on the floor again.

"My client wishes to take advantage of his right to silence," she said firmly.

Billy T. looked obliquely at Erik Henriksen, sitting on the only other chair in the interview room. He had not as yet spoken a word.

"Do you hear that, Erik? Our friend here thinks it best not to give a statement."

"All the same to us," his colleague answered with a nod. "Then the application to remand him in custody will go much more easily. I'm sure he'll explain himself later. 'If it be now, 'tis not to come; if it be not to come, it will be now; if it be not now, yet it will come.'"

He yawned and stretched his arms above his head.

"*Hamlet*," he added lethargically. "Act five. I'll pass the message to Annmari. And then I'll send in a couple of officers to take the Chief Public Prosecutor over to a cell."

Karen Borg followed her client out the door when Halvorsrud was led away. Billy T. laid a heavy fist on her shoulder and whispered, "Jenny."

Karen wheeled around. "What?"

"The little girl is going to be called Jenny. Suitably modern, suitably old-fashioned. Typical compromise. Nice, huh?"

Karen Borg looked at the floor and began to walk along the corridor. Billy T. strode after her.

"Don't you like it?"

"Oh yes," she said, unsmiling. "'Jenny' is just fine."

"Billy T.!"

A trainee in uniform came running up to them as they both turned around. Breathless, he thrust a yellow slip of paper into the police officer's hand.

"From Hanne Wilhelmsen," he gasped. "She also asked if you would phone her on her cell phone. As soon as possible."

Billy T. read the message before folding the note and tucking it into his pocket.

"Strange time to go to Vestfold," he muttered crossly. "What the fuck's she doing there?"

When he turned around again, Karen Borg was gone.

74

The location was even more stunning in brilliant spring weather. It struck Hanne Wilhelmsen as she jogged along the paved path leading to Eivind Torsvik's cottage: Vestfold was the most beautiful region in the country. Smooth, golden rocks crept down to the fresh, gray-blue water. The trees had burst into leaf in the past few days, and their emerald crowns reached out to the summer that as of that very moment seemed right around the corner. The grassy ridges over-flowed with wood anemones. The piercing light was painful to the eyes and Hanne put on her sunglasses. She paused to look out across the sea from the terrace in front of the cottage. The sparkle of the sun's reflections played across the flat surface of the fjord. A young boy's voice broke as he shouted to his friend on the shore from a little islet only thirty yards away. They both began to laugh. The sound carried some distance, echoing across the narrows of Hamburgkilen.

"Great that you could come! And so fast!"

Hanne Wilhelmsen was startled to hear his voice, and whirled round. Eivind Torsvik was also wearing sunglasses. The earpieces had been unbent and curved backward, where they were tied with a rubber band.

"Smart," she said without thinking, pointing to his glasses.

He laughed: an engaging, childish laugh that made her smile broadly.

"Not many people have ever commented on that," he said, laughing again.

He pointed to the sunny wall beside the picture window. Two large wooden chairs, with blue-and-white-striped cushions, had been put out there since her last visit. Hanne sat down in one and lifted her face to the sun. It was not yet half past three in the afternoon. Her cheeks were burning.

"What a wonderful spot," she said softly. "What an amazing cottage you have."

Eivind Torsvik sat beside her without responding. He drew a blanket around his narrow shoulders, and Hanne could hear his regular breathing through the sound of a boat slowly passing by. She closed her eyes behind her glasses, feeling drained and unspeakably tired.

He had been so insistent. When he phoned, she had first asked him to come to Oslo. Eivind Torsvik had expressed great understanding about Hanne Wilhelmsen's work situation, but had nevertheless rejected her request out of hand. He had not been outside the Sandefjord area for many years, he told her, and that was how it was going to continue. If she was interested in what he had to say about Evald Bromo, she would have to come to the cottage at the far end of Årø. In person and on her own. There was no question of him talking to anyone else.

Now she was sitting beside the strange boy-man, ready to fall asleep. She felt comfortable in Eivind Torsvik's presence: the pressure behind her eyes lessened, and her shoulders relaxed. Even though they had exchanged only a few words when she had highly inappropriately lumbered into the man's private space last Saturday, it was as if they had known each other for a long time.

Eivind Torsvik was a man who insulated himself and his property from the rest of the world. Being a writer made it possible to take this to extremes: he barely needed to have contact with anyone. Eivind Torsvik needed no one. Hanne found herself envying him, before she actually nodded off.

She must have dozed for several minutes because when she woke, he was standing in front of her holding a steaming cup of tea with an extra blanket over his arm.

"Here," he said, handing them both to her. "It can get chilly as the afternoon draws on. Now I'll tell you about what I really do out here."

He fetched a cup of tea for himself and sat down again while he stirred in the sugar. Hanne shook her head when he offered her the sugar bowl.

"What do you think is the worst thing about working for the police?" he asked mildly, so quietly that Hanne thought for a second that she had not quite caught what he had said. "The very worst thing about being responsible for upholding the law, I mean."

"Criminal procedure," she said without hesitation. "Having so many rules to adhere to. That there's so much we can't do, I mean. Even when we're absolutely certain of people's guilt."

"I thought so," he said, nodding in satisfaction.

The tea had a slight hint of cinnamon and apple. Hanne held the cup to her face and inhaled the fragrant steam.

"Shall I tell you why I write?"

He gazed at her, and raised his sunglasses so that they rested on his forehead. Hanne nodded calmly as she drank from her cup.

"Because I have lived a life that it's possible to write about," he said, smiling in astonishment, as if he had only just discovered the explanation for something he had been pondering for a long time. "I never write about myself. Yet I do so all the time. Books deal with lived life. I lived more than most before I turned eighteen. Then it was over. I killed a man, and since then I have reconciled myself to the one life I was given being over."

Hanne helped herself to more tea from the thermos on the paving stones between them. She opened her mouth to protest; she
looked around and raised her hand to shade herself from the strong
sunlight.

"I'm not saying that I'm worthless," he said resolutely, anticipating
her objection. "On the contrary. My books give pleasure to many people. To me too. By writing, I steal a life that's not my own. Simultaneously,
I give something to others that I thought for a long time I wouldn't be
able to. You can gain real satisfaction from writing books. You don't,
however, gain happiness. I have—"

It was the first time Hanne had heard him interrupt himself. His
voice was soft and light. The words always flowed effortlessly. Now he
cocked his head, drew his glasses back down onto his nose and reclined
in the chair.

"You're familiar with my previous history. I won't bother you with
it. But I was not particularly old when I realized I had lost the ability
to become attached to other people. 'Reduced ability to form attach-
ments.' That's what the psychologists called it in the countless reports
that exist on me." He pulled the blanket more snugly around his shoulders. "They don't even have any idea what that is!"

Hanne could discern a slight trembling as it spread down his arm.
His complexion was pale, and she could see a twitch along one side of
his nose.

"Enough of that," he said dismissively, trying to tie a knot in the
thick blanket across his chest. "That certainly wasn't why I asked you
to come. I don't just write books. I do something far more important.
Do you remember Belgium?"

"Belgium," Hanne repeated. "Dioxins and Belgian Blue cattle.
Corruption and sexual sadism. Political murder. Salmonella and
import bans. Belgium: a delightful country in the center of Europe."

She glanced across at him. He was not smiling. She shifted her gaze
self-consciously out to the fjord. The laughing boys had jumped into a
rowing boat and were amusing themselves by rowing in circles with
one oar each.

"Marc Dutroux," Eivind Torsvik said into empty space. "Do you
remember him?"

Of course she remembered Marc Dutroux, "the monster from
Charleroi." God only knew how many lives he had taken, both literally

and figuratively. The pedophile scandal that had rocked Belgium in the late summer and autumn of 1996 had sent shock waves across the world. Mass arrests followed as the bodies of children of all ages were dug up one after the other from gardens and found starved to death in specially bricked-up cellars. Eventually a picture emerged of an extensive pedophile ring, and police officers and judges and even a handful of important politicians were placed under investigation.

"The worst thing about the case was not that Marc Dutroux had obviously been protected by powerful people in the system," Eivind Torsvik said. "When it comes to pedophilia, there are no social divisions. Neither are there limits to what people will do when they feel seriously threatened. No limits at all. No, the worst thing of all . . ."

He poured the lukewarm tea out onto the paving stones. The liquid formed a dark pattern on the gray stone. The stain resembled a crab with three claws, and he sat studying the image while flicking his fingers against the empty cup.

"The really scary thing is that the system lets us down. Marc Dutroux had actually been convicted before. He had been sentenced to thirteen years' imprisonment for a series of rapes. Do you know how long he served?"

"Seven or eight years?" Hanne said with a shrug.

"Three. They let him out after three years. For good behavior. Good behavior! Huh!" He stood up abruptly. "It's a bit too cold out here now. I'm freezing. Do you have any objection to us going inside?"

Hanne had no idea how the man could be cold. The air was almost certainly about 60 degrees, and Eivind Torsvik had been sitting wrapped in a woolen blanket throughout their conversation.

"Not at all," she said all the same, and followed him into the cottage.

"I've prepared some food," she heard him say from the kitchen. "Just a salad and some bread. I assume you won't have any wine?"

"I'm driving," she said, patting her breast pocket. "Is it okay to smoke in here?"

He poked his head out from between the upper and lower units of the open-plan kitchen.

"No one's ever smoked here before. Which means that it probably won't do any harm. Go ahead."

Before Hanne had finished her cigarette, the table was set. The plates were white and the cutlery solid silver. Eivind Torsvik poured

Farris mineral water into her tall wine glass, and Alsace wine for himself.

"Did you know that the liquor store delivers to your door?" he asked as he sat down. "And that the Internet's full of excellent recipes?"

"Do you stay here all the time?"

Hanne helped herself to some caprese salad and a slice of french bread.

"No. Unfortunately I have to take a trip into town now and again. To the dentist and so on. Also, I cycle to Hasle to do some shopping sometimes. That's almost all the way into town. Solløkka nearby has more of a large convenience store. Did you know that the Dutroux case actually broke as a result of private investigations?"

Hanne tasted the salad. The mozzarella cheese was soft and flavorful, and the tomatoes unusually delicious.

"I have a small greenhouse behind here. You can have a look later, if you like. I lead such an organization. Or rather, in a manner of speaking. We're a group of twenty-two Europeans and fifteen Americans who work in collaboration. The others have accepted me as a kind of leader, even though there's never been any sort of election or formal appointment."

Hanne Wilhelmsen caught herself wondering whether it was some kind of organization to do with vegetables he was talking about. She stopped chewing and stared at him with her fork in mid-air.

"We monitor pedophiles; no more, no less."

Smiling faintly, he stared teasingly, almost challengingly, back at her, his shock of blond hair encircling his oval face, and his eyes taking on a luminosity she had not seen before. His lips appeared blood-red against his white complexion, and she suddenly noticed he had hardly any beard growth. He resembled an angel, like the scraps Hanne had long ago collected in a shoebox—ethereal, beautiful seraphim with blue eyes and glitter on their wings.

"At this very moment, you look like an angel," she blurted out.

He did not move. His gaze did not waver, and it was as if Hanne was looking at something she had nothing to do with, a life she did not want to be part of. Eivind Torsvik was not simply a man who had found a way of living with his loneliness, a way of life she was attracted to and perhaps in a sense envied. As he appeared now, sitting staring at her with the sunlight on his curls like a halo around his head, he was also something else, something she could not quite grasp, but that alarmed her and forced her to put down her knife and fork.

"I am an angel," he said. "I am the actual *Angel*. Our organization is called The Angels of Protection. TAP, in everyday parlance."

Hanne wanted to leave. This was not at all what she needed right now. She was in the middle of a murder case she could make neither head nor tail of, and did not want to be burdened by knowledge of an occult organization that might well be engaged in illegal activities in the service of good. She cleared her throat and thanked him for his hospitality while pushing her plate a couple of inches away across the table.

"Do you believe in God?"

Shaking her head, Hanne fiddled with her napkin. She wanted to go. She did not want to be there, in this cottage that was far too warm and where the buzz of the extensive IT equipment was making her headache flare up again.

"Me neither. Not at all. God's a pathetic entity human beings resort to in order to explain the inexplicable. The reason I ask is that I think there's some kind of significance in you having turned up here on Saturday. I believe your visit was one of those coincidences the like of which history has witnessed many times: sudden, unforeseen incidents that result in innovation or catastrophe. Have you had enough to eat?"

"Yes, thanks. It was delicious."

Hanne drank the rest of her mineral water and glanced at the clock.

"You mustn't go yet. I haven't given you what you need. You'll have to be more patient, Hanne Wilhelmsen. You're an impatient soul, I can see that. But don't leave."

"Okay then." She smiled wanly. "Not yet. But I really can't stay much longer."

"You must understand, I've been searching for you," he explained as he cleared the table. "Well, not you exactly, but for someone in the police force I can rely upon."

All of a sudden, he set the plates down on the table with a thud and thrust his torso forward.

"Do you know how long it took?" he asked.

His voice had taken on a different tone, a note of indignation that deepened the pitch.

"From the time I cut off my ears and reported my foster father's repeated assaults until the investigation of the case was completed?"

"No. I don't know the details of your case."

"Three years! *Three years!* Four psychologists examined me. They all came to the conclusion that I was speaking the truth. Nevertheless, I still had to stand with my backside in the air in a medical examination room surrounded by people in white coats who hadn't even said hello to me first. They fingered parts of me that should have been my private property. *Mine alone!* Something they had never been, of course. I was stolen from, time after time, for as long as I can remember. There I stood, my ass in the air, unable even to cry. I was thirteen years old, and the conclusion of the doctors was unambiguous: grievous sexual assault over many years. *I was thirteen!*"

Eivind Torsvik sank onto his chair again, rubbing his eyes gently as if he had given everything he had to give.

"And it still took three years to bring the case to court," he added sotto voce.

Hanne felt the need to say something. Eivind Torsvik's story was not new to her. She had seen it, heard it, and experienced it. Far too frequently. She searched for the right words, but could not bring herself to speak. Instead she placed her hand carefully on the table.

"And when the sentence was passed, it was absolutely ludicrous."

He inhaled deeply, holding his breath for so long that a faint flush spread over his cheeks. For the first time, Hanne could distinguish traces of a grown man in his face. The angel was gone. She was faced with a man in his mid-twenties who had lost everything he possessed before he'd even reached adulthood.

"We're all victims," he said after a lengthy pause. "All of us in The Angels of Protection. We have dedicated our lives to finding them. The molesters. The pederasts. The people who steal souls. We are not constrained by borders. Or by rules. Sex offenders do not recognize any rules, and can only be fought under similar circumstances. We watch them. We monitor them. We find them on the Internet. The majority of them are unable to keep away from the flood of child pornography found there, idiots that they are."

"But how do you do that?"

Hanne felt a curiosity she did not really want to acknowledge.

"We have our methods," Eivind Torsvik said. "We have many people working on it, and they have pursued them and conducted research over a number of years. We move like shadows in a landscape the police know nothing about. We, on the other hand, were born and brought up there. For us, it isn't particularly difficult to recognize pedophiles. We have lived with them. All of us."

He pointed at the computer beside the window.

"As for myself, I never go outside. I confine myself to the Internet. That's where my task lies. Besides, I have a system. Putting together pieces of the jigsaw. And there are lots of pieces, some of them minuscule. But eventually I'll create a picture. And when that happens—and it will happen fairly soon—we'll go to the police. Right now I have a list of . . ." He placed his hand only a few inches away from Hanne's. ". . . eleven Norwegians who have systematically abused children, and about whom the police have not even the faintest idea."

"But you must . . ." Hanne began. "Why haven't you . . . ? Are you engaged in . . . ?"

Eivind Torsvik's information was sensational.

Hanne Wilhelmsen had heard many rumors about organizations of the kind he was describing. But she had always brushed them aside as sheer nonsense. It was impossible. At least it *should* be impossible. Of course, the police struggled with chronic understaffing, institutional inertia, obstructive criminal procedure, and a great deal of incompetence in the bargain, but then they did have the law on their side. They had a system. Expertise. She was not entirely unfamiliar with the phenomenon of individuals taking matters into their own hands when the upholders of justice fell short. In the mid-nineties, she had herself investigated a rape case in which the father and daughter involved had taken forceful revenge for the wrecking of the girl's life. They were both acquitted, although the police were not suffering sleepless nights over it.

"But an entire *organization*," she said suddenly. "You must be teetering right on the edge of the law? Or else breaking it?"

"Yes," Eivind Torsvik admitted candidly. "We break it when necessary. Among other things, we engage in telephone surveillance. Not often. It's difficult to do, at least in Norway."

"You mustn't tell me that!"

She placed her hand on his. It was cool and delicate to the touch, and she could feel the knuckles against her palm.

"Don't say any more," she said in a heartfelt undertone. "I don't want to know this!"

"Calm down. The material we intend to hand over to the police when the time comes will be unassailable. Witness statements and that sort of thing. When we resort to illegality, it's only for . . . investigative purposes? Isn't that what you call it?"

Now he laughed again, that musical laughter that was impossible to hear without smiling. He seemed brighter now and withdrew his hand.

"And of course you're not going to tell any tales."

Hanne put her hands over her ears. "I don't want to hear any more. I don't want to hear another word, do you understand?"

"Evald Bromo abused little girls all his adult life."

Slowly, Hanne Wilhelmsen let her hands fall from her head. Her ears were ringing, and she swallowed repeatedly.

"What did you say?"

"Evald Bromo was a pedophile. He bought and stole sex from girls as young as ten for many years. Mostly bought, as a matter of fact. I'll give him that."

His lips narrowed, and now it looked as though a child had drawn a mouth on him with a felt-tip pen. He stood up and fetched a plastic folder, green and semitransparent, from a bookcase beside the computer.

"Here," he said. "You can have this. He can't very well be brought to justice postmortem. When I read in the online newspapers that Bromo had been found murdered, I gathered up everything we had on the guy. You can have it. But it's for your eyes only. To help you find the killer. Naturally, you can't use any of it, other than as background material for your broader investigation. I would be extremely grateful if you would destroy everything after you've read it."

Hanne stared at the green folder as if he had placed a large scorpion on the tablecloth.

"I can't," she gasped. "I certainly can't accept anything I'm not able to show to my colleagues."

"Then read it here."

He got to his feet again and picked up the dishes and silverware once more.

"I'll clear this away and make a fresh cup of tea. You liked it? That's fine. Then you can have another cigarette and read what's there."

He nodded at the folder before pushing the ashtray in her direction and heading for the kitchen.

Hanne Wilhelmsen caught herself longing for plastic gloves. The folder in front of her contained information that could be crucial to solving Evald Bromo's murder. She desperately wanted to tear off the elastic band wrapped around the folder and throw herself into reading the contents. At the same time, this ran counter to all her principles. Eivind Torsvik was the leader of a vigilante organization. Hanne Wilhelmsen was a chief inspector in the police force.

She fumbled in her breast pocket and produced a cigarette. After lighting it, she leisurely blew the smoke in the direction of the forbidden folder. Then she pulled off the elastic band.

It took slightly longer than half an hour to read the documents thoroughly, fold them neatly together again, and replace the elastic band before pushing the bundle away. As she lit a third cigarette, she barely noticed that Eivind Torsvik had returned from the kitchen and was sitting quietly in a chair in the living room, having apparently nodded off.

"Was that useful?" he asked with his eyes closed.

"How have you managed it?" she asked in a whisper.

"I already explained that to you. Surveillance. Investigation. Over many years."

"All the same. All this stuff. How on earth did you get hold of it all?"

He sat there smiling and turned his face to hers.

"Was it useful?" he repeated.

Hanne did not know how to respond. If Evald Bromo had been murdered because of his perverted sexual preferences, she could not fathom the connection with Doris Flo Halvorsrud's murder. There was nothing—not so much as a tiny speck of information—to suggest that the Chief Public Prosecutor's wife was a pedophile.

"Don't know," she said finally.

Thea.

Thea! Hanne gulped down some smoke and began coughing. She stood up so abruptly that her chair toppled backward and slammed into a glass cabinet, breaking the door.

"You must answer me one thing," she said loudly. "Who else do you have on your list?"

Eivind Torsvik raised his hands and held his palms up to Hanne in a defensive gesture.

"You got the folder on Evald Bromo because he's dead. He's beyond our reach now. As far as the others on the list are concerned, though, you're getting nothing. Not until everything is cut and dried. It won't take long."

"How long?"

Hanne heard her voice breaking.

"I can't actually answer that. One month, maybe, or six. It's too early to tell."

She picked up her chair and put it back in its place. Then she ran her fingers over the long crack that had split the glass door in two.

"But you *must* answer me one thing."

Approaching him, she crouched down in front of his chair and leaned forward with her elbows on the armrests.

"Is Sigurd Halvorsrud listed? Is Halvorsrud a pedophile too?"

His eyes were no longer the same. Hanne had felt an affinity with this young man. She had recognized him, deep down; she had seen something of herself in those blue eyes with the distinctive black edge around the iris. Now he was a stranger.

"You're getting nothing more," he said in a harsh voice.

Hanne broke eye contact as she rose stiffly.

"Then thanks for everything you've given me," she said. "The food and the tea and . . . everything."

Once she had donned the American buckskin jacket with its pearl embroidery and fringes across the chest, she produced a business card and a pen and rapidly scribbled her personal number on the back.

"Call me if you want anything," she said, handing him the card. "Any time."

"I'll certainly do that. Sooner or later."

Hanne had left a five-hundred-kroner note on the kitchen worktop without him noticing. She hoped he would understand that this was to cover the cost of replacing the glass door. As her car rolled carefully along the bumpy track, she could see him in the rearview mirror, standing at the top of the hill beside the cottage with a blanket wrapped around his shoulders, staring after her. Then she turned a corner, and Eivind Torsvik disappeared from sight.

75

"Where the hell have you been?"

Billy T.'s voice cut sharply through the cell-phone connection. Hanne had just driven on to Route E18 when it dawned on her that the phone had been switched off since she had left Oslo. On the way down she had needed peace and quiet to think, and she had not thought to switch it on again until now. She had managed to register that she had eight unanswered incoming calls when the phone rang.

"You gave me instructions to call you!" Billy T. roared. "And I've done nothing else for hours! It's nearly eight o'clock, for fuck's sake!"

"Take it easy," Hanne muttered. "Has someone died, or what?"

"Yes. Ståle Salvesen."

The steering wheel wobbled in Hanne's hands before she braked violently and turned off the road. She parked on the hard shoulder with her emergency lights flashing.

"What did you say? Ståle Salvesen?"

"Hah! And you gave me orders to phone in order to—"

"*Cut it out, Billy T.!* I'm sorry. I forgot about the phone. Is Salvesen dead?"

"We believe so. Two young fellows found a body in a pretty bad condition out in the fjord this morning. We've already located Salvesen's dentist. A preliminary identification should be available by ten o'clock tonight."

Hanne Wilhelmsen rubbed her neck. Almost three days and nights with practically no sleep meant it was totally irresponsible for her to continue driving. As her head began to swim, she gave her right cheek a hard slap.

"I'll be there in around an hour and a half."

"And one more thing, Hanne—"

"I'll be there in just over an hour, Billy T. We can talk then."

She disconnected the call.

Probably all eight messages were from Billy T. To be on the safe side, she would check. She had not spoken to Cecilie since the morning. Hanne might as well get everything over and done with while she was parked there.

The first five messages came from an increasingly angry Billy T. The sixth was from Ullevål Hospital:

"This is Dr. Flåbakk from the oncology department at Ullevål speaking. I'm trying to locate Hanne Wilhelmsen. Cecilie Vibe was admitted here this morning, and I would appreciate it if you could call me as soon as possible. My phone number is—"

Hanne felt a shock run through her entire body. A wave of heat originated in her abdomen and flooded into every one of her limbs. She immediately felt wide awake. Without returning Dr. Flåbakk's call, she switched off her phone and completed the nearly 125 miles to Oslo in fifty-five minutes.

76

Cecilie was unconscious. At least she did not wake when Hanne entered the room, accompanied by the buxom nurse who apparently was never off duty.

"The painkillers have knocked her out," the nurse said. "She probably won't wake 'til the morning. Dr. Flåbakk asked me to say hello. If you want to talk to him, he said to call him at home before eleven o'clock tonight. Do you have his number?"

Hanne shook her head. She didn't want to speak to a doctor.

"What happened?" she asked instead. "When was she admitted?"

"She phoned herself. About eleven o'clock, I think. She was so poorly that we sent an ambulance."

Hanne sobbed, trying to prevent her tears from spilling over.

"There, there."

Standing behind her, the nurse rubbed her back gently with a hand that was broad and warm.

"She might be okay again in the morning. That's how it goes with this illness. Up and down. Always up and down."

"What if she doesn't get better?" Hanne whispered, giving up entirely: the tears now flowed unhindered down her cheeks. "What if—"

"You mustn't cross your bridges until you come to them," the older woman said firmly. "Cecilie just needs to be allowed to sleep for a while. You look as if you could do with a good night's sleep yourself. I'll bring you a bed. Have you eaten?"

Leaning forward, she looked into Hanne's face.

"Not hungry," Hanne mumbled.

She was alone with Cecilie.

This morning she had seemed so well. The Easter trip to Ula had done her good. Even though they had traveled home a day early, Cecilie had seemed so contented as she shuffled around the house. Hanne had been afraid it would be impossible to leave her and go to work. But it had been Cecilie who had almost chased her out the door. She got plenty of visitors, she claimed, and anyway, she liked lying on the sofa with a good book best of all. Stubbornly, she had insisted that the medication eliminated the pain.

"I'm *not* in pain," she had said with a resigned smile that morning when Hanne had hesitated to leave her. "Tone-Marit is going to drop in with the baby this afternoon. Maybe I'll manage to finish reading the Knausgård book first. I'm absolutely fine. Off you go."

Probably Hanne had just not noticed it. Cecilie's face had become more difficult to read since she'd been ill. Her features were sharper, her mouth narrower, and her eyes more deep-set. This was a face Hanne did not really know. It left her feeling confused.

Hanne sat down gingerly on the edge of the bed.

Cecilie was sleeping with her mouth open. A gossamer trace of blood was outlined where her dehydrated lower lip had split open. Hanne took out lip balm and smeared it on her finger before running it gently over the wound. Cecilie made a faint grimace but did not wake. She had tubes in her nose and the back of her hand, as well as a cannula on the side of her throat that was more frightening than anything else in the unfamiliar gray room.

"What's that there?" Hanne whispered to the nurse, who had returned with a bed. "That tube in her neck. What's that?"

"Morphine," the nurse replied. "I brought a couple of slices of bread. Try to sleep now. Cecilie won't wake until morning."

When morning came, the visitor's bed was untouched. Hanne Wilhelmsen was sitting on a chair close to Cecilie, with her hand in hers. She had talked all night long, softly and at times completely silently. Cecilie had slept without stirring and was in the same position. Nevertheless, Hanne could swear that every so often, a convulsion had crossed her gaunt face, encouraging Hanne to continue.

When eight o'clock arrived on the morning of April 7, Hanne wrote a short note that she slipped underneath the glass of stale water on the bedside table. Then she left for police headquarters at Grønlandsleiret 44.

She had now slept for fewer than four of the past seventy-two hours.

77

"You look like something the cat dragged in!"

As Iver Feirand's gaze took the measure of Hanne Wilhelmsen, he wrinkled his nose.

"Come in," she said. "Thanks. Nice of you to say so."

"I didn't mean it like that."

He took a seat and his eyes continued to scrutinize Hanne. In the end he stood up and tried to look at her feet under the desk.

"For heaven's sake, Hanne. You used to be the best-looking cop in town. What's happened? Your hair, for instance . . ."

Gesticulating with his hands above his head, he used his tongue to make a clucking sound.

"And you've lost weight," he added. "Not so good. Is it stress, or was it deliberate?"

"Good of you to come," Hanne said wearily, fixing the clasp on her hair.

"Bloody awful," Iver Feirand said, shaking his head. "Too girlish. Take it off."

She left it there.

"Have you thought any more about the bike?" he asked eagerly.

Hanne shook her head.

"Let me know, then. I'm still interested. I thought you were busy with this Halvorsrud case."

He folded his hands behind his head and rocked back and forth in the chair. "What do you want me for?"

Though irritated by the way he was sitting, Hanne decided not to mention it.

"We're still in a rush," she said, lighting her fourth cigarette of the day, "so I'll come straight to the point. We have reason to believe that Evald Bromo abused young girls over an extended period of time. Do you know anything about that?"

"Evald Bromo?"

Iver Feirand frowned as he let the front legs of the chair drop to the floor with a thud.

"That *Aftenposten* guy who was decapitated on Sunday?"

"Mhmm."

"What do you mean by 'reason to believe'?"

Hanne fastened her hair clasp again as it had started to slide down her forehead.

"What do we usually mean by that?" she said dispiritedly. "I have a source, obviously. A damn good source. I can't say any more than that."

"Not even to me?"

He pulled down the corners of his mouth into a theatrical grin of mock disappointment.

She had quarreled furiously with Billy T. that same morning. When he heard about Eivind Torsvik and his organization, he had been ready to head off to Sandefjord with wailing sirens and a deployment of twenty officers at his back.

"Fuck, Hanne, don't you see that this earless imbecile might be sitting on information worth its weight in gold!" he had spluttered at her when she refused. "What if Halvorsrud's screwing his daughter? That's a real *stinker* of a motive, isn't it? A motive's exactly what we've been lacking, for God's sake!"

Hanne had protested that it was difficult to make a rational case for Halvorsrud beheading his wife because he was abusing their daughter, and Billy T. had calmed down somewhat. Sulky and stony-faced, he had muttered a solemn oath not to tell anyone. The concession had only been forthcoming after Hanne had cynically reminded him of the long sleepless night she had endured at the hospital.

"How is Cecilie, anyway?" Billy T. had asked submissively, and with that the matter was decided: this time they would do things Hanne's way.

"Drop it," she said to Iver Feirand. "And answer my question. Do you know this Evald Bromo?"

"Once upon a time you were an extremely pleasant lady," Feirand said, chagrined. "Beautiful, popular, admired. What's become of you?"

Closing her eyes, Hanne made an effort to count to ten. When she reached four, she opened them again, banged her fist on the table, and yelled, "Give it up, Iver! You *of all people* should understand what it's like in this job!"

She threw herself back in the chair before tearing the clasp out of her hair and flinging it at the wall.

"I asked you nicely to come here and help me," she said through gritted teeth. "All you've done up 'til now is hurl crude insults at me. According to you, I'm nasty, skinny, and my hair's a mess. That's okay. At this very moment *I've entirely different things to think about than how I look! Do you understand that?*"

She roared so loudly that she sent out a spray of spit, and she slapped the palm of her hand on the desk blotter every second word. Iver Feirand sat with his mouth open and his hands raised in surrender.

"Calm yourself. Honestly! I didn't mean it like that."

Shaking his head, he was on the point of rising to leave.

"Sit down, please."

Hanne raked her fingers through her hair and forced out a smile.

"Apologies. I'm not sleeping much these days. Stay here, please."

Iver Feirand looked doubtful, but nevertheless remained in his seat, warily, as if he intended to leap to his feet and leave the room the minute she gave the slightest sign of launching into a fresh diatribe.

"I've never encountered Evald Bromo," he said flatly. "Is there anything else you're wanting to ask?"

Hanne got up and closed the door. Then she stood with her right hand on her hip, gazing out of her grubby office window. The signs of spring that had come with the Easter weekend had turned out to be only a flicker. Rain was pouring down, and it was very dark, despite being nearly lunchtime.

"Can't we start over again?" she said in a voice she could hear was trembling. "I need to talk to you. I've been stupid and cranky, and for that I apologize."

"Fine."

Feirand looked as if he meant it now. He sat in a more businesslike fashion, with one leg crossed over the other and his hands clasped on his knees.

"I'm sorry too."

Hanne Wilhelmsen began where she had intended to begin. She told him that she had reason to investigate the possibility that Sigurd Halvorsrud had abused his daughter. Briefly, she set out the facts she was compelled to relate. It was clear that Evald Bromo was a pedophile who had abused little girls for a long time. Furthermore, there was reason to suspect that the murders of Doris Flo Halvorsrud and Bromo had been committed by the same person, or at least that the killings were somehow connected. The obstinate claims of the suspended Chief Public Prosecutor, that a man by the name of Ståle Salvesen had carried out the murder, had been called into question now that the body of the selfsame Salvesen had turned up in the Skagerrak, showing distinctive signs of having spent several weeks in the briny water. Halvorsrud was now sitting closed up like a clam in a cell in the back yard, having been sentenced to another four weeks in custody, effective from yesterday. The fingerprints in the basement at Vogts gate 14 had done the trick in court. The court hearing had lasted twenty minutes, and Halvorsrud had not even found it worth the bother of making an appearance.

"It's quite obvious that Halvorsrud has a very special relationship with his daughter," she concluded. "Of course, we're used to families being severely affected when someone is imprisoned. Especially when we're talking about well-adjusted people, if I can put it like that. But this young girl effectively became psychotic. The odd thing is that she seemed to be more upset about her father being in prison than about her mother having been murdered."

"Maybe she's just a daddy's girl," Feirand said drily. "There are enough of them."

"Yeeees . . ."

Hanne searched for an unused teabag in the top drawer. She dropped it into her cup and swore when she discovered there was no more water in the thermos flask.

"But is it not the case that the abuse of a child can have a paradoxical effect?" she asked. "That it can make the child draw unusually close to her abuser, closer than a child would normally be to a parent?"

"There's a distinction to be made here." Nodding, Iver Feirand stole a cigarette from the pack lying on the desktop.

"It's one thing to be subjected to abuse by a stranger. That happens, of course it does. It's traumatizing, dreadful, and in some cases fatal. But it's easier for the child to talk about, since he won't feel any loyalty to his abuser, and even though he may be threatened with violence or death, the truth seeps out more easily."

He sent three smoke rings up to the ceiling.

"By far the majority of abuse, however, is perpetrated by someone who knows the child. Well, or more distantly. From scout leaders through bastard priests to uncles, brothers, and fathers. Then it becomes much harder for us to find out about it."

Smiling bitterly, he took a deep drag of his cigarette before glancing around as if searching for an ashtray.

"Here. Use this."

Hanne pushed a half-full soft drink can across to him.

"The closer the abuser is to the child, the stronger the child's loyalty to that person is likely to be. Some choose to call this loyalty love. It's possible they are right. We all know we're capable of loving people even though they do us harm. Nevertheless, I would postulate that it is first and foremost other ties we are talking about here: loyalty and not least dependency. You must remember that a father, for example, will have more or less unfettered power and influence over his own child. We've dealt with cases in which the child has obstinately insisted that nothing wrong has taken place, even after the abuser has broken down and confessed. It has to do with a number of things. Shame. Fear. And perhaps a kind of love. Complicated stuff. I can lend you some books, if you like."

Hanne made a dismissive gesture with her hands.

"No time," she said. "At least not now."

The rain had intensified, and heavy drops were pounding against the glass as Hanne switched on the Anglepoise lamp at the edge of the desk.

"But you surely didn't call me here for a lecture on something you no doubt already know a great deal about," Iver Feirand commented. "What is it you really want?"

"Two things."

Hanne dropped a half-smoked cigarette into the soft drink can. It hissed angrily, and she pressed her thumb over the opening to contain the acrid smoke.

"First: Is it significant that you've never heard of Evald Bromo? I mean, you're sitting on a lot of surveillance information over there in your office."

"Well, yes and no. I don't know. Yes, as a matter of fact. It's not really so strange. If I knew a little more than you've told me, I could answer you more easily. I need to know more about his way of operating. That sort of thing."

Hanne considered this. Then she said, "Let's leave that. The other thing I wanted to ask was if you could conduct an interview with Thea. She'll need careful handling, and you're the very best."

Iver Feirand laughed loudly.

"Thanks for your confidence, but isn't this girl fifteen or sixteen years old?"

"Sixteen."

"Grown up. The police can interview her as a witness in the usual way. Then she'll have a guardian present and all that jazz. It will have to be a substitute guardian, since her mother is dead and her father is locked up in jail. Of course, I can conduct that interview for you, but it won't be a judicial examination."

Billy T. knocked on the door and entered without waiting for an answer.

"Sorry," he muttered when he caught sight of Feirand.

"Quite all right," Feirand said, glancing at his watch. "I have to run anyway. Listen . . ." Crossing to the door, he turned to face Hanne as Billy T. plopped down in the chair he'd just vacated. ". . . give me a ring if you need anything. If you want to follow the trail along the lines we've been discussing, then you'll need to construct a damn good plan. Can't we have a more formal meeting—you, me, and a couple more from management level in the investigation?"

"Okay, then," Hanne said with a smile, yawning noisily. "I'll call you."

"I've never liked that guy," Billy T. grumbled after Feirand had left, seizing a chocolate banana from the blue enamel dish. "Yuck! Old and stale!"

He spat it out into his hand and stared at the yellowish-brown goo.

"I haven't actually had time to buy candy lately," Hanne said. "Anyway, there's only one reason you don't like Iver. He's more handsome than you are. Taller, even."

"Not true. He's six foot six and I'm six foot seven. In my stocking feet."

"What is it you want?"

Billy T. wiped his hands on an old newspaper before rubbing his knuckles on his bare skull and blowing through his lips like a horse.

"I have a suggestion," he said eventually. "You're dead tired. I'm ready to drop. Jenny was screaming all night long. Tone-Marit had to get some sleep, as she bore the brunt of it yesterday. I expect you'll want to visit Cecilie this afternoon, but afterward couldn't we simply—"

"Go home to my place, make some food, talk about the case, and then catch some sleep?"

He rolled his eyes. "And to think some people are claiming you're not the same old Hanne! That's just because they don't know you. You took the words out of my mouth. Are you with me on that?"

Hanne yawned again, lingeringly. Her eyes filled with tears.

"I don't think there'll be much chat or food—mostly sleep," she said, kneading her face. "But if that's okay with you . . ."

"Okay? It's brilliant! I'll take the sofa, and you can stretch out in the double bed."

"Now I think you should give some thought to the reason why I'm alone in that bed," she said quietly, rubbing her right shoulder with her left hand.

He tilted his head to one side and leaned closer to her.

"You know perfectly well how sorry I am about all this with Cecilie," he said softly. "You know that. But we both need sleep. The baby's been screaming like mad for three nights in a row. Tone-Marit said it would be okay if I spent the night at your place, since the case is all-consuming."

"Okay, then," Hanne said. "But it's true what people say. I'm not the same old Hanne. We can meet at around five o'clock. Let's say half past five at the latest."

78

"A present? For me?"

Hanne Wilhelmsen looked quizzically up at Billy T., who had let himself into her apartment using keys she had no idea he had, nor where he had acquired them.

"Yes. Open it, then."

Hanne tore off the wrapping paper.

"An ashtray," she said in a monotone. "How lovely."

"I broke the old one in your office. That day you were so annoyed at me. Don't you remember? You ordered me to buy you a new one."

"Oh," Hanne said. "That's right, yes. Thanks. It's really lovely. Nicer than the old one."

"How was Cecilie?"

"Better."

Hanne sank onto the sofa and put her feet up on the coffee table.

"She was awake. The doctor said, if everything goes well, she can come home again tomorrow. Where did you get those keys, actually?"

He must have been in her apartment for some time. There was an aroma of old-fashioned food. The smell of something that had been simmering for some time enveloped the entire place, and she could see that the kitchen window had steamed up.

"Billy T.'s meat soup à la Puccini," Billy T. said with satisfaction, placing an enormous casserole on the dining table. "Help yourself. Healthy food for healthy boys and girls."

"Don't really feel like that right now," Hanne said skeptically as she lifted the lid. She had hauled herself off the sofa and was not entirely sure she was still hungry. "What is this?"

"Meat soup! Sit down now."

Ladling out a generous portion, he slapped it down in front of her. The pale-brown liquid overflowed the deep bowl and a piece of boiled cabbage fell into Hanne's lap. She fished it up, holding the limp, almost transparent morsel between her thumb and forefinger.

"What on earth *is* this?"

"Cabbage. Eat."

Tentatively, she dipped her spoon into the soup. It was piping hot and dripped from her lips when she slurped some of it down.

"Tasty?"

Billy T. was already halfway through his bowlful.

"Okay."

She ate half a portion. If the food wasn't exactly the best she'd ever had, it was at least warming. She washed away the taste with a glass of water and declared herself full.

"You're far too thin," Billy T. announced, eating noisily. "Have some more."

"The keys. Where did you get them?"

"Håkon. We decided it would be best if we hung on to them for a while. At least while Cecilie is in and out of the hospital."

"You might have asked."

"We *have* asked. Cecilie said it was a good idea."

Hanne was too tired to object.

"The body *was* Salvesen's," Billy T. said. "As we expected."

He was smacking his lips so rudely that Hanne clutched her hands to her ears.

"Excuse me," he slurped. "It's just impossible to eat this stuff politely."

"You could at least make an effort. What about the dentist, then?"

"Yes. Ståle Salvesen without a doubt. At the moment, they can't be very specific about the time of death, but the condition of the corpse ties in neatly with the witnessing of the suicide on Monday, March 1."

"The condition of the corpse," Hanne repeated, a note of disgust in her voice.

"You should've seen it."

"Thanks. We're eating. *You're* eating."

"Doesn't matter to me."

He gave himself a fourth helping.

"Something else of interest came in this afternoon," he said abruptly. "You've probably not heard it yet. A man deposited two hundred thousand Swedish kronor in a bank account in Gamla Stan, Stockholm, just before Christmas. You can guess in what name."

"Can't be bothered."

"Sigurd Halvorsrud."

Hanne sniggered, then laughed out loud. Then she put her head back and roared with laughter. The sound echoed off the walls, and despite having a half-chewed piece of lamb in his mouth, Billy T.'s jaw dropped.

"Halvorsrud," Hanne gasped with tears running down her cheeks. "That's all we need. Two hundred thousand!"

She could not restrain herself. Taking his time to chew, Billy T. studied her primly.

"Will you soon be finished?" he asked, showing his annoyance.

"But don't you get it! Sweden! It *has* to be a setup. Who on earth would put dirty money in a *Swedish* bank! They've got exactly the same rules as us, for heaven's sake. Sweden! If it had been Switzerland, or the Cayman Islands, or something along those lines. But Sweden!"

"Well, setup or not . . ." Billy T. said, now even more cross, putting down his spoon. "You've been going on about this setup theory of yours for ages. I was even quite taken by it myself. For a while. But now that Ståle Salvesen is demonstrably dead and has obviously been so since before that Doris-woman's murder, then the entire basis for your line of thinking has disappeared."

Hanne chortled and hiccupped, making a strenuous effort to compose herself.

"Don't they have video footage of the man who deposited the money?" she said in a conciliatory tone. "They must surely have CCTV cameras in Swedish banks, just as they do here."

"It's actually not that straightforward," Billy T. said, still nursing his grievance. "There's probably a limit on the length of time they keep the recordings. We've initiated inquiries, and may receive an answer one of these days."

They cleared the table in silence. It dawned on Hanne that she should have started the laundry. Dirty clothes were spilling out of the laundry basket in the hallway, and she swiftly picked up a pair of panties that had fallen out. Absent-mindedly, she stuffed them into her pocket. She was so tired she had stopped yawning.

"Strictly speaking, we're still high and dry," Hanne said as she sat down on the sofa.

"High and dry?" Billy T. came in carrying two cups of coffee and set one down in front of her. "Do I have to remind you that we've actually got a guy in custody?"

"And why is he there?" Hanne said, discouraged, before choosing to provide the answer herself. "Because of a host of tiny facts that are so odd and conspicuous that we obviously can't be talking about coincidences, but which at the same time form such a flimsy chain of evidence that we're miles from having Halvorsrud found guilty of murder. Of either his wife or Bromo. If Halvorsrud hadn't refused to give a statement, I really doubt whether we would have obtained a custodial remand."

"But what about the fingerprints! What the hell was Halvorsrud doing in the basement at Vogts gate 14? And if he's innocent, why is he refusing to make a statement? We're talking about a public prosecutor here, Hanne! He knows better than most that refusal to give a statement is tantamount to an admission of guilt. And the day after the murder, he failed to report to a police station. Quite significant, if you ask me."

Hanne did not reply. Her joints were aching, and Billy T.'s voice sounded distant, as if he were sitting in another room. She gently massaged the sole of her foot with her thumbs. Pain shot up her leg from the middle of her heel.

"What is actually confusing us is this pedophile business," Billy T. continued. "I still believe that we ought to devote all our resources to following the corruption lead. At least we potentially have a great deal of tangible evidence. The money in Stockholm, for example."

He dropped four sugar cubes into his coffee and stirred it with a ballpoint pen.

"No," Hanne said. "We have almost nothing to go on. As I've said until I'm blue in the face, every single element in this case that could point to Halvorsrud being corrupt is weird and illogical. Amateurish. Incomplete. There's something about this case that . . ."

She grimaced as she attempted to straighten up. Something stabbed her ferociously in the lower back.

"Like it or not, Ståle Salvesen is the only thing we have. Okay, so he committed suicide. Then he wasn't the one who killed Doris. But for a corpse, he has a surprising ability to pop up all over the place, no matter how we twist and turn. The murder of Bromo and the murder of Doris have only two features in common. Both victims were decapitated. And then there's our joker, Ståle Salvesen. If we can discover *his* role in all of this, we'll find the solution. I'm actually very confident about that. As for Evald Bromo's relations with little girls . . ." Dipping a sugar cube into her cup, she placed it on her tongue. ". . . that may not have anything to do with the case. But if . . . Let's say that Bromo and Halvorsrud are both pedophiles. What do we know about that type of person? That they have a well-known need to make contact with one another. Exchange material. Pictures. Experiences—"

"So Bromo and Halvorsrud might have been members of some kind of pedophile ring, is that what you're saying?" Billy T. wrinkled his nose as he crossed to the stereo unit. He rummaged on the CD shelf as he continued. "But how does our man Ståle fit into all this? Was he a pedophile as well, then?"

"No. Or yes. I don't know. But let's look at what we know for certain. This here is Halvorsrud."

She set down her coffee cup in the middle of the table and reached for Billy T.'s mug. "And this is Evald Bromo."

A silver dish containing the musty remains of old peanuts was placed in front of the two coffee cups to form a triangle.

"Where's Doris?"

"Doris can go to hell," Hanne said wearily.

She pointed from the Halvorsrud cup to the Bromo mug.

"Common denominators? They both worked in finance. Both had pretty successful professional careers. Neither previously found guilty of any crime."

"Both are men, and both are middle-aged," Billy T. muttered. "There's nothing but bloody middle-of-the-road stuff here, as usual." He let his fingers run impatiently over the CD spines.

"Then we'll look at the links to Salvesen," Hanne continued. "Don't put on any music, please. I can't stand it right now. In contrast to him and him . . ." Her finger smacked against the cups. ". . . Salvesen was a fallen man. Up like a lion in the eighties, down like a sheepskin rug a decade later. The only connection we're aware of between him and the other two is his bankruptcy case and the investigation directed at him. Halvorsrud was responsible for that, and Bromo wrote about it."

"Ten years ago," Billy T. said grumpily. Finally his face brightened and he inserted a CD in the player. "Schubert!"

"Turn it down, at least. But what if—"

Billy T. turned the volume even higher. He stood in the center of the room, eyes closed and smiling broadly. "*That's* what I call music."

Thrusting her fingers into her ears, Hanne stared intently at the three objects on the table in front of her.

"What if Bromo knew about Halvorsrud's abuse of his daughter or other children?" she whispered to herself. "What if he actually threatened Halvorsrud? But why . . . Turn down the music, for fuck's sake!"

Billy T. complied at last. Hanne stared up at him as she continued. "If Halvorsrud for some reason wanted to murder Bromo, why choose a place like Vogts gate 14? And why in God's name would he place his signature on the murder so emphatically by decapitating the guy? He must have realized that we would immediately look in his direction . . ."

"Copycat," Billy T. said.

"Exactly."

"Someone wanted it to look like a Halvorsrud murder."

"Precisely."

"And it happened at night. The time when most of us have no alibi other than the person sleeping beside us. If we have someone."

"For sure."

"Can it—"

"Doris and Bromo may have been killed by two different people," Hanne said slowly and distinctly. "If neither of them was Halvorsrud, then we have not one but *two* murderers on the loose out there."

"Two," Billy T. reiterated faintly. "I'm dead on my feet."

Hanne lifted the Halvorsrud cup to her mouth. The coffee had gone cold.

"I think I'll have to take a pill," she said. "I'm overtired."

Billy T. plopped himself down on the sofa beside her. Schubert's piano concerto had reached a dramatic climax, and he turned the volume up again with the remote control as he put his arm around Hanne's shoulders.

"Listen to this," he whispered. "Listen right now!"

She relaxed. Billy T. gave off a slight male odor, mixed with boiled cabbage. The woolen fibers in his sweater tickled her cheek. He sat completely still, with his head leaning back and his eyes shut. His arm lay pleasantly heavy on her, and she caressed his hand gently. Big and warm and entirely still, it was resting only inches away from Hanne's right breast. She let two fingers run along the veins outlined coarsely on the back of his hand. When she looked up again, he was smiling. She studied his familiar features: the prominent, straight nose, the pale-blue eyes that at that very moment appeared gray and more deep-set than she had seen them before, the lips he moistened with his tongue before he became totally serious, placing his free hand on her cheek and giving her a long, lingering kiss.

79

A man was hammering his fist on a tiled wall.

"Fuck. Fuck. Fuck."

The scalding water streamed over his body.

He had never imagined anyone would find out about Evald Bromo's abuse of little girls. Bromo was the most careful abuser the naked man in the shower had ever come across. Only once had Bromo been sloppy. That was many years ago, and the mistake had turned out to be rectifiable.

"Shit. Goddamn it!"

There was only one link between him and Evald Bromo. He had been 100 percent certain it could never be discovered. *One hundred percent.*

Now he had no idea what he should do.

"Daddy!" a voice yelled outside the locked door. "You're using up all the hot water! It's my turn now! Daddy!"

If he had been aware that anyone knew, it would all have been done differently.

80

When Hanne woke on Thursday morning, at first she did not know where she was. The room was in semidarkness, and the clammy air smelled unpleasant.

She was at home, lying in her own bed. The curtains were not fluttering because the window was closed. They always slept with the window open. Cecilie and Hanne.

Billy T. was lying on his stomach beside her, still in a deep sleep, with his mouth open, snoring softly. His bare arm was crushing her against the mattress. The quilt had slipped off him. Although a long time had elapsed since summer, she could see he still had a suntan stripe where his white backside met the darker skin on his back.

Hanne felt a sudden stab of anxiety, a physical pain that coursed through her entire body. Billy T. murmured something in his sleep and turned over.

Hanne made an effort to move. He was no longer holding her down. His face was averted. Unable to breathe, she shifted her back ever so slightly to lie with her arms stiffly by her side, flanking her naked body.

Cecilie was coming home today.

81

Olga Bromo was dying.

It crossed the mind of the care assistant washing her that this might be the very last time. The old woman had deteriorated very suddenly on Saturday night. Her pulse, which had steadily kept her going through two meaningless years in a virtual coma, had suddenly become irregular and weak. The assistant had read that Olga Bromo's son had been killed around the same time. During the following days, her heart had stopped beating twice. Life had nevertheless returned, as if in ill-tempered defiance of the care assistant's relief that the senile, eighty-two-year-old woman was finally allowed to slip away.

"You were so close to each other," the assistant said, in a friendly, soft voice, as he wrung out the washcloth. "He visited you nearly every day, didn't he? Not everybody's so fortunate."

Olga Bromo lay in a white flannel nightdress with a pink ribbon around the neck. The care assistant had gone to the trouble of dressing her in one of her own nightdresses instead of the practical, sexless shift they usually used on the patients.

He had hardly finished tying a bow in the ribbon at her neck when Olga Bromo died. A faint gurgling in her throat was all that could be heard before she stopped drawing breath. The assistant stood with his finger on the inside of the old woman's frail wrist for several minutes.

82

Hanne Wilhelmsen was struggling to see clearly. A film had formed over her eyes, and she blinked repeatedly in an effort to rid herself of what seemed like a sticky, gray mass adhering to the cornea, occluding her vision. Fear pricked her every time she drew breath and she inhaled with short, shallow gasps.

"Sorry," she said to Iver Feirand as she fingered the cigarette pack without removing one. "I think I might need glasses."

"Exhausted, I reckon. I understand how you're feeling."

"Do we ever feel energetic?"

"Energetic?"

Hanne Wilhelmsen pushed her thumb and forefinger into her eye sockets and rubbed her eyes vigorously.

"I think I've felt exhausted for twenty years," she said under her breath. "The more I work, the more I have to do. The more I work, the less—"

Abruptly, she sat upright and tossed the half-full pack of Marlboro Lights into the wastepaper basket.

"In any case, I should give that up."

"Wise. I should give up myself."

"You look pretty wiped out too."

Iver Feirand smiled wanly, lighting a cigarette from his own pack.

"If you think *you've* a lot to do, you should see what my office looks like. I had to send the family off for Easter by themselves because of work. Everything's piling up. Everything's become so much harder. It's as though the whole system has become more spineless. Judges, doctors, kindergarten staff . . . The Bjugn kindergarten abuse case was a catastrophe. It's one thing that the number of reported incidents of abuse dropped substantially after all those acquittals. That was probably to be expected. And they've picked up again anyway. Worse was that everybody else chickened out. It's—"

He pulled a grimace as he stubbed out his half-smoked cigarette.

"I must give up too. It's not even any bloody good. Thea will need careful handling. I've started to gather a lot of material. From her school and . . ."

Iver Feirand's voice sounded increasingly distant to Hanne—muffled and more and more monotonous. In the end it was difficult to distinguish one word from another. Feirand's face became a blur, a shimmering speck against a colorless background. She tried to take deep breaths but felt a jab in her abdomen every time she inhaled. Cecilie, she thought.

Cecilie. Cecilie.

Most of all she had wanted to get up from the bed and leave. She'd wanted to let Billy T. lie where he was and simply disappear. For good. Go away. Let everything go. She would forget the job. Sigurd Halvorsrud and Evald Bromo, Billy T. and the persistent Police Chief who understood far more than she wanted him to; the whole of Grønlandsleiret 44 and all the people there would be wiped from her memory, erased entirely. Never again would she think about Cecilie and her illness. She could travel to Rio and live with the street children there. She could forget who and what she was.

Never before had she experienced this excruciating compulsion to flee.

As the years had passed and life had become more difficult to deal with, she had retreated inside herself. That was where she got her strength, and had done ever since, one quiet night as an eleven-year-old, she had laid down on the roof of the old villa while everyone else was asleep. She could recall it now: the roof tiles cutting painfully into her shoulder blades, the cold breeze of the September night as it swept through the dense trees, the firmament above her, with its myriad stars that told her how strong she was, but only when she was alone. Only if no one actually knew what she was doing or thinking.

Hanne Wilhelmsen had coped like that for a long time. In the beginning—the beginning that gave her Cecilie and drove her away from her family and a childhood she subsequently expended a great deal of energy on trying to forget—everything had seemed so simple. They were so young. She had felt so strong. The defenses she constructed to protect herself and keep others away were obvious to everyone. When it dawned on her that people respected her for what she was—introverted and methodical, smart and hard working at school—she knew she had made the right choice. That was the way she wanted it.

Cecilie was the first person Hanne had loved, and Hanne's first lover. She suddenly pictured her in her mind's eye, behind the bike sheds where they smoked at high school; teasing and almost flirting when she finally spoke to her after Hanne had been casting surreptitious glances in her direction for nearly two years. They did not know each other. Cecilie was popular and boisterous and hung out with people Hanne could not stand. Hanne Wilhelmsen was a serious young woman who disguised her figure beneath Icelandic sweaters and an old military jacket and smoked roll-up cigarettes on her own behind the bike sheds while everyone else huddled inside. Hanne was smart in school, and perhaps that was why Cecilie had sauntered up to her one day when heavy rain made it impossible for her to stand outside.

"Hi," she said, cocking her head in a way that made Hanne bury her face deep inside her Palestinian scarf. "I hear you're damn great at math. Do you think you could help me, then?"

Hanne had loved Cecilie from that instant. She still did. Panting for breath as she sat in her office on the third floor of the police headquarters, she tried to listen to her colleague but could hear nothing but the echo of Cecilie's voice: "I'm ill. Seriously ill."

Hanne Wilhelmsen always fled inward. When she'd woken that morning with Billy T. by her side and a feeling of being completely paralyzed, she'd realized she was at the end of the road. There were no more places to run.

When she finally managed to get up, she spent fifteen minutes in the shower. Then she dressed and woke him by calling out his name. When he'd grunted and reached out for her, she'd twisted away. All she said was that the bed linen had to be changed. He struggled to make contact, talking and swearing and swinging out with his huge arms, threatening and imploring and hampering her efforts to remove the quilt cover and sheet, stuff them into the washing machine, set the program to 190 degrees, take out clean linens, make the bed, vacuum the bedroom, blast the room with ventilation, and then take another shower before heading off to work. Not a word had she uttered, except that the bed linen had to be changed. He had left the apartment with her. As they stood outside the door, she had peremptorily held out the palm of her hand to him, looking him in the eye for the first time. When she saw his confusion, she lowered her eyes and commanded, "The key."

He had taken out a small key ring and placed it in her hand.

They had gone their separate ways to Grønlandsleiret 44. His back had seemed incredibly narrow as he disappeared across the lawn behind the apartment block. Hanne had taken a circuitous route through Tøyen Park.

". . . as considerately as possible," Feirand finished.

Hanne blinked. "Hmm."

She did not have the faintest idea what Feirand had said.

"Excellent," she mumbled. "You do what you think best. What time frame are you considering?"

Feirand squinted at her in astonishment.

"So, as I said . . . I'll speak to her on Saturday. As far as I understand, she's still receiving treatment, and everything will of course be done in consultation with—"

"Fine."

Hanne forced out a smile. She had to go. She had to be alone. Bile was pressing on her larynx and she tried to swallow as her mouth filled with phlegm.

"We'll talk later, then?"

"Okay. I'll keep you posted."

As he was about to leave the room, he stood deep in thought for some time, gazing at her, before shrugging and closing the door quietly behind him.

Hanne Wilhelmsen was sick as a dog and did not even manage to grab the wastepaper basket before vomiting. Mucus and bile spewed across the desk and case folders.

"My God, are you ill?" Karl Sommarøy blurted out when he suddenly appeared in the doorway. "Can I be of assistance?"

"Leave me in peace," Hanne murmured. "Can't I just get some peace for once? And isn't it time people started knocking on doors around here?"

Karl Sommarøy backed out and let the door slam behind him.

83

"You'd better get that pal of yours to pull herself together. She's gone too bloody far this time."

Karl Sommarøy stared at Billy T., who was sitting in the canteen on the sixth floor of police headquarters with a soda and a newspaper. Sommarøy balanced an iced bun on a cup of coffee in one hand and a bowl of cornflakes on top of a glass of milk in the other.

"Haven't you heard of trays?" Billy T. said grumpily, immersing himself in his copy of *Dagbladet* in an attempt to persuade his colleague to find somewhere else to sit; there was hardly another soul in the place.

Karl Sommarøy did not take the hint.

"It's one thing that she's got a great reputation," he continued, undeterred, once he was settled on the seat directly opposite Billy T. "I understand from people who've been here longer than me that she's practically a genius. But that's no excuse for being rude. You should've seen what she—"

"Shut up," Billy T. said harshly.

"But honestly—"

"*Shut your mouth!*"

"For God's sake. You'd think it was catching!"

He lifted the bowl of cornflakes to his mouth and shoveled them down. His weak chin disappeared from sight.

"I must surely be allowed to make a damn comment," he said, munching noisily. "The way she behaves toward her subordinates, she should've been given an unconditional reprimand. But as far as I can tell, the Police Chief treats her like some kind of mascot. I've no idea why. You—"

Billy T. had already raised the newspaper to his face, and was now leafing through it angrily.

"They say she was quite a babe in her time," Karl Sommarøy said in a loud whisper. "Is that true? And that she's actually . . . bent? Lesbian, I mean? She doesn't look like one, but—"

Folding the newspaper, Billy T. leaned across the table and seized hold of his colleague's shirt front. His face was only ten inches from the other man's as he snarled, "Hanne Wilhelmsen's the best officer in the station. Do you hear? What she doesn't know about police work, nobody needs to worry about. She knows the difference between right and wrong, she knows more about the law than most of the police prosecutors here, she works about three times as hard as everyone else, including you, and what's more she's really beautiful. Right now she's overworked and has a partner who might die at any moment, so you'll just have to . . ." He banged his free hand on the table, splashing the cornflakes. ". . . *fucking put up with* her not having the longest fuse in the world right now!"

Releasing Sommarøy abruptly, he shot him a look that brimmed with contempt before downing the rest of his soda and getting to his feet.

"But listen here—" Sommarøy said, taken aback and trying to straighten his shirt.

"No," Billy T. roared, waving a massive finger in the air. "*You're* the one who should listen here. What Hanne Wilhelmsen does in her spare time is none of your business. Understood? If there's anything she wants you to know about her personal life, then you wait until she tells you yourself. In any case, you're a total *idiot* to come here making nasty comments about a person you must at least have realized is my very best friend."

"Okay, okay, okay!"

Sommarøy made a peace sign with his right hand and lowered his head.

"That wasn't really what I came over here to talk to you about," he said meekly. "Sorry. I mean that. Sit down."

Billy T. was aware he was shaking. For only the second time in his adult life, he felt the urge to weep. Since the morning, he had struggled to find the words he needed to say to Hanne, phrases that could recast last night as an incident that had not actually taken place. He had to say something that would make it possible for them to retain what they had and had always had, together. Billy T. had to keep hold of Hanne: an existence without her seemed as meaningless as a life without his children. His thoughts had ricocheted from Hanne to Tone-Marit: he needed to tell his future wife what had happened. He had to confess his betrayal and obtain her forgiveness so that they could wed without delay, tomorrow, or even better, this evening; they should get married and he would wear a ring and never do anything like that again.

Billy T. knew that he could never say anything. Tone-Marit was not going to hear about it. This evening she was going to grin at him across the dinner table, ask about news from work, and perhaps tell him that Jenny had produced her first smile. She was going to snuggle up to him tonight and sleep with her hand in his as she had started to do since the baby was born, as if the child's existence was final proof that they belonged together. Billy T. was never going to tell Tone-Marit about what had happened when he had spent the night with his best friend in order to escape from a shrieking infant and get an undisturbed night's sleep.

"What's it about?" he asked, sitting down heavily in the chair again.

"I've been thinking about Vogts gate 14," Sommarøy said in a jovial voice, trying to catch his colleague's eye as he chewed on the iced bun. "The phone company has confirmed that Salvesen had two accounts. One was for the Internet."

"Internet," Billy T. reiterated.

"Yes. Odd. We didn't get a glimpse of a computer in his apartment, and besides, what the hell would a guy like that be doing with Internet access? Then it struck me that I should go and have another look. Will you come with me?"

Billy T. wanted to go home. He felt he could never go home again.

He wanted to talk to Hanne. Hanne did not want to talk to him. He had knocked on her office door three times, and each time she had turned away when he opened the door. She had not said a word, but it had been impossible to defy those raised shoulders and the icy glance she gave him before turning her back on him.

"When were you thinking of going?" he asked in a monotone.

"Around four o'clock. Don't have time before that. Will you come?"

"We'll meet in the garage at four. You can arrange a car."

When Billy T. left the canteen, he spotted Hanne Wilhelmsen's back disappearing into the elevator. Since she had not been to the canteen, he assumed she had been in a meeting with the Chief of Police, whose office was on the same floor. Billy T. continued to stand there as the shiny metal doors slid shut. Then he shuffled down the stairs, very slowly, to allow her time to make an exit before he reached the third floor.

84

Sigurd Halvorsrud was sitting on a bunk bed with no mattress in a cell in the back yard of the police headquarters, convulsively clutching at his knees. He dug his nails through the fabric of his jeans and into his skin until his fingertips became numb. Then he relaxed briefly before repeating the exercise.

"Innocent," he whispered into the clammy air. "I'm innocent. Innocent. I'm innocent."

Chief Public Prosecutor Sigurd Halvorsrud had never killed anyone.

As far as he knew, he had never done anything worse than break the speed limit now and again. If he had still possessed the ability to reflect properly as he sat there, it would have dawned on him that he had in fact been fined for hitting one of his teenage pals when he was drunk, on May 17 of the year he had turned sixteen.

However, Sigurd Halvorsrud's brain had become overheated.

During his first period of imprisonment, while all the absurdity was still so recent that it was still possible to draw on his acumen and experience, he had been hopeful. This was Norway. In Norway innocent people were not found guilty. When that did happen, it happened only to vagrants, drunks, and semicriminal losers who may not have done what they were convicted of, but who had only themselves to blame for coming under police scrutiny anyway.

Sigurd Halvorsrud was himself part of a system he believed in, a conventional, civilized justice administration to which he had dedicated his professional life and was also woven into the very fabric of his being, his personality, his ego, everything that was him. His belief in himself and his own strength was to a large degree grounded in confidence in the *System*. In the first weeks—when the yellow walls had suffocated him and every morning he had argued with the custody officers to be allowed his usual daily shower; when he had dressed in his suit and tie as normal, combing his hair neatly with hair tonic and clipping his nails once a week as was his wont—during this period he had despite everything conducted himself with self-belief and hence a belief in the System. Being held for the murder of his wife was nothing but a temporary lapse. Justice would prevail sooner or later.

That was how the System operated.

Paradoxically, it was after he was released from custody that he realized he was wrong.

As the legal ruling was being dictated, Sigurd Halvorsrud had raised his eyes to the judge with the bulldog head, understanding that he was actually being allowed to go home. Incredulous relief mixed with an arrogant sense of victory: justice had finally been done.

That first evening at home, after Thea had finally fallen asleep, it had dawned on him that this was an illusion. His case no longer had anything to do with the law or justice. His life, his daughter's life, the entire existence of the Halvorsrud family, had been ruined by a power far stronger than the blind authority of the Goddess of Justice.

Sigurd Halvorsrud was now carrying a stigma. He might as well have had it printed on his forehead. When he sat leafing through his own notes—elegant, handwritten pages with analyses and facts about everything he had experienced from the murder of Doris to his release the day before—he realized he had to do something. He made a decision.

Karen Borg was right.

Judge Bugge was right.

The police were a considerable distance from a prosecution. Even further from securing a conviction. When Sigurd Halvorsrud responded to the bare facts in his own case, he saw it was extremely likely that he would never have to face a jury. That made him elated; the blood rushed through his veins and his cheeks burned, until he began to scan the newspapers his sister-in-law had kept for him and placed in a stack beside the kitchen table, in chronological order.

Sigurd Halvorsrud was a condemned man.

He had just been released, but he was nevertheless condemned for the rest of his life. When he was in custody and forbidden all letters and visitors, they had also denied him access to newspapers and radio broadcasts. He had read old magazines and paperbacks, fearing the worst. But this was worse still.

At times his case had even overshadowed the war in Kosovo.

His life was smeared across the newspapers like a Picasso painting: twisted and distorted, lacking proportion, and in colors he certainly did not recognize. Nevertheless, it was all about him. Unmistakably about him. The journalists had delved into every corner of his past. He was startled when he saw a full-page photograph of himself in his student cap: his naked, eighteen-year-old face with its chin thrust forward and a self-assured smile, as if nothing could prevent him from scaling the heights; his eyes betraying a vulnerable insecurity he still had not learned to hide. Anonymous schoolmates, invisible colleagues, nameless neighbors: they had all, willingly and with ill-concealed glee at having something important to say at last, made known their opinions about Sigurd Halvorsrud, the wife murderer. Strong and stubborn, sly and short-tempered, cunning and unpredictable, family friend and center of their social circle: the characterizations stung his eyes and he shut the papers, rolling them into logs that took him two hours to burn in the fireplace.

Sigurd Halvorsrud had lost everything.

He had one way of saving himself and what was left of his family. He could not simply sit still and hope he would never be convicted. He had to get rid of the stigma. Only then could he hope for full restitution. Only then would the newspapers sensibly edit everything they had written up to now and draft new articles in which only positive angles were aired. Only then would the newspapers be forced to beat their chests and say, "Look! We always kept an open mind about the possibility that the man was innocent. Look! We wrote that he was a good father to his family and a respected colleague even when he was being held in custody."

Sigurd Halvorsrud had to find whoever had murdered Doris. He knew who it was. It was Ståle Salvesen.

For that reason he had made a clumsy attempt to investigate the apartment at Vogts gate 14. He had searched for anything at all. Since the police had never believed his explanation, they could quite easily have overlooked something important. As far as they were concerned, Ståle Salvesen was a benefits claimant, presumed dead. Only in his eyes was Ståle Salvesen a murderer.

Since he had no experience breaking the law, he had behaved stupidly enough to be taken by surprise by some old man down in the basement. When he'd failed to find anything except moldy food in Salvesen's apartment, he'd wanted to check if he had a storeroom.

That was why he had left fingerprints in a place where a dead body had turned up several days later. A beheaded journalist who was known to him, of course: the guy had covered his own area of professional expertise and had done so for many years. They had probably spoken on the phone as well, though as far as he could remember, they had never met face-to-face.

Then it turned out that Salvesen was dead after all.

That news had torpedoed everything.

Salvesen should not be dead. Ståle Salvesen should be sitting on a beach in Brazil enjoying a chilled beer. He should be trekking through the Andes mountains, alone in the magnificent landscape he had always dreamed about. Perhaps he should be lying in the sweaty embrace of a prostitute in the backstreets of Manila; for that matter, he might have taken casual employment as a sheep shearer in New Zealand.

Instead, he had turned up as a decomposing corpse in the Skagerrak.

That made Halvorsrud's brain explode.

The only thing he could now do was keep hold of his innocence. He clung to it, clutching the sentence he mumbled over and over again: "I am innocent."

When the cart arrived with his dinner, he refused to take any. The custody officer shrugged indifferently and went away. When he returned several hours later to repeat his offer of something to eat, Sigurd Halvorsrud was sitting in exactly the same position as earlier that day: erect, with his hands around his knees, rocking almost imperceptibly from side to side and murmuring something the man in uniform could not catch.

It was actually quite creepy, and the officer thought it might be best to call a doctor. In the morning, anyway, if the man was no better by then.

Perhaps the Chief Public Prosecutor was in the process of losing his mind.

85

"I've talked to his pal before. Let me arrange this."

Karl Sommarøy was not quite sure why Billy T. had agreed to accompany him. He appeared totally uninterested, standing there in a well-worn leather jacket, shivering in the chilly spring breeze. Either the big guy was exhausted beyond anything Karl Sommarøy had experienced, or else some other serious problem was troubling him. Billy T. answered mainly in monosyllables. He had fiddled with a key ring throughout the entire journey from Grønlandsleiret to Vogts gate, repetitively and irritatingly. His eyes were dead and his face, which had become inflamed during his terrifying rage in the canteen, was now lifeless and lacking all expression. Every time he moved, Billy T. left a sweaty odor in his wake.

"That caretaker Karlsen's a sourpuss, but I don't think there's any malice in him."

They rang the doorbell for the second time.

"Yes?" rasped a voice over the intercom speaker.

"This is Sergeant Karl Sommarøy from the Oslo Police District. We'd like to check—" The sound of the door buzzer made him wink conspiratorially at Billy T. He grabbed the handle and pulled open the door.

"You see?" he said.

"Unnecessary," Billy T. muttered. "We have the keys."

He raised the key ring he was holding between his thumb and finger to Sommarøy's eye level.

"Goddamn it," the Sergeant said crossly. "You might have said."

"What's this about?" Karlsen stood, legs astride, in the corridor inside, wearing yellowish-brown slippers with no socks. He was dressed in beige trousers held up by suspenders, and his shirt had a large grease stain on the breast pocket. Billy T. noticed crumbs on his stubbly face.

"Everything's by the book," Billy T. said, holding up his police badge. "We just want to do a little check on Salvesen's apartment."

"Good luck. It's empty."

"Empty?"

Karl Sommarøy and Billy T. exchanged glances.

"I emptied it last week."

"What did you say you did?"

"Emptied it. The apartment. Took out all Ståle's belongings. It'll soon be taken over by another tenant, I think. Don't want anyone rummaging through Ståle's things."

Billy T. looked at the ceiling and his mouth moved without emitting a sound. Then he took a deep breath, lowered his head, and gave Karlsen a broad smile.

"Would you be so kind as to escort us up to Ståle's apartment?" he said, silkily smooth, placing his hand on the old man's back.

Karlsen was fifteen inches shorter than Billy T. He squirmed under his touch, declaring loudly that he was in the middle of eating his dinner. Billy T. changed his grip, instead taking hold of the caretaker's upper arm as he strode determinedly toward the elevator.

"What floor are we going to?"

"The fourth," Sommarøy said.

"Let me go," Karlsen protested.

"I will. When you've learned a few elementary rules about accepted practice. Here."

The elevator pinged and gave a heavy groan before shuddering to a halt. The three of them stepped out and trudged along the corridor, Karl Sommarøy leading the way and Billy T. following with Karlsen in tow.

"Look at this," Billy T. said, placing a grubby finger on the lock where only fragments of the police seal remained. "Might it have been you, for instance, who removed that little whatchamacallit there?"

Ole Monrad Karlsen again struggled to break free.

"I'm going to report this," he said angrily when the grip showed no sign of loosening. "I'm most definitely going to do that."

"That's fine," Billy T. snarled. "And I'll make sure you get a really substantial fine for this here."

He inserted the key into the lock, and it rotated easily. Carefully, he turned the door knob and opened the front door. Hit by a smell of stagnant air and decay, he stepped back and stared at the little handwritten card fastened to the door frame by two tacks. "S. Salvesen". He stood for so long, deep in his own thoughts, that Karl Sommarøy finally coughed and gave him a friendly nudge in the back.

"Shall we let the caretaker go, then?"

Billy T. glanced down obliquely at the diminutive old man and nodded calmly.

"I think we should. He can sit in his apartment and wait until we're finished. In case we have any questions for him. Okay?"

It was unclear to the two police officers whether Karlsen considered that acceptable or not. The pint-sized old man padded off along the corridor with a cheerful muttering of incomprehensible words. They stood watching his retreating back until the elevator doors closed again.

"You were a bit hard on him, don't you think? An old wartime sailor and all that."

Sommarøy did not wait for a response. Instead he entered Ståle Salvesen's apartment. When he and Hanne Wilhelmsen had been there what seemed like an eternity ago, the apartment had appeared uninhabited. Now it was quite simply abandoned. In the hallway they could discern a pale patch on the wall paneling where the telephone table had been. A dirty line was traced along the living room wallpaper where the sofa back had rested against the wall. There were very few vestiges of human occupation, apart from an air of general, rundown despondency that permeated the entire place. And the stench from the kitchen.

Karlsen had removed everything that could be said to have been Ståle Salvesen's personal belongings. The spartan furnishings, the few kitchen utensils, and the neatly folded clothes left behind in the apartment after Salvesen's own efforts at clearing things out prior to his death. The refrigerator, on the other hand, was obviously the property of the local authority. Karlsen had not felt compelled to take with him a yogurt, a carton of milk, a block of yellow cheese that had turned blue, something that might once have been a lettuce, and two tomatoes into the bargain.

"Damn and blast! Hanne and I agreed to take this lot with us when we were here. We completely forgot."

Sommarøy grimaced at the contents of the fridge: the stench had not improved by the door having been left open for some considerable time. Billy T. grabbed the milk carton and the yogurt.

"Twenty-seventh of February," he read aloud slowly. "This milk could probably walk by itself. Twenty-third of January. It might be fun to open this yogurt."

He handed it to his colleague, who pulled back, holding his nose.

"Anyway, there's no sign of a computer in here," he said nasally. "Let's look at the phone socket."

Billy T. replaced the dairy products and closed the fridge door before opening the window slightly and following Sommarøy out into the hallway. The windowless corridor was almost dark, and he ran his fingers over the light switch on the wall beside the front door. The bulb was gone.

"There's only one socket here," Karl Sommarøy groaned, crouching down and struggling to look. "A good old-fashioned phone plug with three pins."

Kneeling down, Billy T. let his hand follow the cable from the gray-brown plug along the baseboard to the front door. One cable, one plug. There was scarcely room for the two men and, losing his balance, Karl Sommarøy used his hands to steady himself.

"And here's another one," he said eagerly. "A modern socket with one of those plastic gizmos!"

Billy T. squinted to see the tiny, square plastic holder attached to the wall just above the floor. Then he pushed Karl Sommarøy aside and used his fingers to feel his way along the cable.

"The entry point seems to be the same as the other one," he said as he opened the front door and peered at the dirty green wall beside the door frame. "Yep, both cables are threaded in through this tube here. The phone company's usual stuff. But the strange thing is . . ." He peered inside the apartment again. ". . . the cable then seems to go *out* of the apartment."

Karl Sommarøy farted as he stood up.

"This does actually merit a fanfare," Billy T. commented, scratching his moustache. "Let's see if we can follow the cable."

It was obvious that someone had tried to conceal it. Although it must have been relatively new—inside the apartment, the cable shone white against the faded wall—someone had painted over it where it ran down the hallway along shabby brown baseboard. At the end of the corridor it disappeared into a hole.

The window frame was swollen, and it had obviously not been opened in ages. When Billy T. gave it a forceful push with his shoulder, one of the eight tiny panes of glass cracked into three pieces.

"Look at this," he said, leaning out as far as he dared before quickly hauling himself in again. "Can you see? It looks as if the cable runs down. How far do you think?"

"Impossible to say. It just continues until you can't see it any longer."

They closed the window.

"The basement," they suddenly chorused.

"The basement," Billy T. repeated, grinning broadly. "It looks as if we might need some help from the caretaker."

They charged down the stairs. The sound of the iron studs on Billy T.'s boots bounced off the walls, and when they reached ground level, Ole Monrad Karlsen had changed into black shoes.

86

Cecilie was possibly fit enough to be at home, but she certainly did not look it. She was stretched out on the sofa when Hanne arrived at around five o'clock: drawn, pale, and her smile no more than a tug at the corners of her mouth that never extended as far as her eyes.

"Tone-Marit drove me back," she said, reaching out her hand to Hanne without making any attempt to stand up. "Her mother looked after Jenny for an hour or so, so that Tone-Marit could drive me home."

"But why . . . why didn't you call me?" Hanne stuttered.

"I did. The receptionist or whoever it was said she had no idea where you were."

"But my cell phone, then!"

Hanne was almost shouting as she patted the pocket of the leather jacket with fringes and pearl embroidery that Cecilie had paid a fortune for while they were in the United States. She produced an almost unused Ericsson model.

"Fuck. For fuck's sake."

She hit herself on the forehead with the phone.

"Shit. Shit. Shit!"

"You forgot to switch it on," Cecilie whispered. "Come and sit down."

Hanne wriggled out of her jacket and left it lying on the floor. Then she shoved the coffee table out of the way and knelt down at the end of the sofa.

"Sorry," she said, kissing the inside of Cecilie's wrist. "I'm so dreadfully sorry. I promise I'll never switch it off again. Never. How are you feeling? A bit better?"

She studied Cecilie's features. She had dreaded this moment all day long. Hanne had suffered chest pains and a stomachache from anxiety about seeing Cecilie. She carefully followed the lines around her mouth with her finger, those gray-white lips with dried toothpaste in the corners; her finger ran along the sides of her nose and up to the bluish, almost transparent bags underneath her eyes.

"I love you, Cecilie. I don't know how I'll manage to live without you."

"You're going to have to."

Cecilie's voice was hoarse and she coughed warily before curling her hand around Hanne's head and raking her fingers through her unkempt hair.

"I don't want to!" Hanne tried to hold back the tears where they belonged, far down inside her abdomen, where they could plague her without bothering Cecilie. "I don't want to be alone."

"You'll never be alone. If you'll just grow up and realize there are lots of people who are very fond of you, then you'll never need to be alone."

Hanne pulled back abruptly. She remained on her knees, staring at Cecilie, no longer able to keep back the tears.

"When you die, I'll have no one."

Cecilie smiled again, more genuinely this time. There was a sudden twinkle in her dull eyes as she pulled Hanne close again.

"What a baby! You're the best in the world at feeling sorry for yourself. Listen to me, my darling. You're not yet forty years old. You might live twice as long. At least. There are droves of people who'll want to be part of your life."

"I don't want them. I want you. I've always wanted you."

Cecilie kissed her lingeringly on the forehead. In a way her lips already felt dead: cold and dry, with rough flakes that snagged against her skin. Hanne hiccupped through her sobs and leaned her head on Cecilie's chest.

"Am I too heavy for you?" she asked, almost smothered by the woolen blanket. "Does it hurt you when I lie like this?'

Cecilie did not smell the way she used to. Hanne inhaled the unfamiliar scent of soap and hospital. She closed her eyes at the sudden memory of Cecilie sitting in her room poring over math books, her brows knitted and a lock of her long hair in her mouth, sucking loudly and complaining repeatedly about the incomprehensibility of integral calculus. She had smelled so sweet. Her fragrance had been that of a young woman, the whiff of sweet body odor cutting through the cheap perfume, making Hanne lean against her and kiss her mouth ever so gently before quickly pulling back and uttering her very, very first, "Sorry."

Cecilie had laughed that time, almost twenty years ago. She had laughed softly, the wet lock of hair plastered in an arc above the corner of her mouth until she tucked her hair behind her ear and kissed Hanne again, longer this time, much longer and far more audaciously.

Hanne was never going to tell Cecilie what had happened last night. Before she arrived home, she had made up her mind. Cecilie deserved the truth. Hanne could not live with such a secret.

Then she'd breathed in the scent of soap and hospital.

Cecilie would never get to know. There was nothing to know.

"Can I get you anything?" she whispered as she rubbed her cheek gingerly on Cecilie's breast under the woolen blanket. "Is there anything you'd like, my dearest?"

"Yogurt. I think I'd like some yogurt. If we have any."

"Do you know what problem you were struggling with the day we got together?"

Hanne had hauled herself up.

"What?"

"That day. When you came to my house to get help with your math. Do you remember which integral you couldn't work out?"

Cecilie cautiously adjusted the blanket, as if her entire body was aching.

"No . . ."

Hanne grabbed an old newspaper and a pen from the bookshelf.

"This one," she said, holding up the newspaper to Cecilie's face.

$$\int_0^3 (x^2 + 3x + 4)\, dx$$

Cecilie laughed uproariously. She laughed for a long time, almost the way she had laughed at the time, nineteen years earlier, and when she finally stopped, she shook her head, saying, "You're so strange, Hanne. My goodness, how strange you are. Do you remember that so precisely, or are you kidding me?"

"A definite integral. The solution is 34.5."

Hanne could still hear Cecilie giggling as she opened the fridge door. She picked up a natural yogurt and checked the date stamp. Four days left of its shelf life. When she peeled off the aluminum foil lid, she suddenly fell into a reverie.

"Hanne?"

She must have stood there, lost in thought, for several minutes without making a sound.

"Hanne, what are you doing?"

"I'm coming," she said, producing a teaspoon from the silverware drawer.

She poured the yogurt into a dish, adding some strawberry jam in the middle, before setting it down on the coffee table.

"I just need to make a phone call," she said casually. "Won't take long."

Cecilie heard Hanne's most formal voice filtering through from the hallway as she tried to swallow some nourishment.

"This is Chief Inspector Hanne Wilhelmsen. I would like to check some information about a stolen car. Yes, oh yes. It concerns a—"

A sudden sharp pain caused Cecilie to drop her spoon. The yogurt and jam fell to the floor, and her hand shook as she tried to save the dish from following suit. Very carefully, she brought out the morphine pump from behind her thighs. She administered an extra dose and slowly relaxed as the pain subsided.

"You mustn't go to work now," she said when Hanne returned to the living room. "Please don't."

"No, of course not," Hanne said sympathetically, going to fetch a cloth to wipe up the mess on the floor. "I'll wait until tomorrow. But what do you think . . . shall I open the sofa out into a bed, so that we can lie side by side? I've bought three new videos. Maybe we could watch one of them tonight?"

"Lovely. I'd really like that. I'd like it if you could be here at home more often in the time ahead."

Hanne took Cecilie's face in her hands and kissed her softly on the mouth.

"If I'm the genius everyone says I am, then it won't be long before I can take time off," she whispered. "Real time off. So that we can be together all the time. Just you and me."

"That sounds terribly new and scary."

"Let me help you up. I'll make the bed."

Cecilie chose *Casablanca*. Hanne wept all through the second half. She had always thought Cecilie looked so much like Ingrid Bergman.

87

The corridor in the basement at Vogts gate was long and not particularly narrow. Billy T. discovered to his amazement that he could stand upright without difficulty in the almost fifty-foot-long corridor. When he stretched both his arms out to either side, he could only just touch the walls with his fingers. Far down at the other end, a harsh beam of light from a rectangular window hit the floor. A naked bulb hung from a light fitting just beyond the staircase, making it possible to see into that part of the basement as well.

"The storerooms are not labeled," Ole Monrad Karlsen said grimly. "But these two are mine." He slammed the flat of his hand on the doors of the first two. "And you're not rummaging around in there without a search warrant. I know what rights I've got. There's nothing in there that has anything to do with you."

"And which of these belongs to Ståle Salvesen?" Billy T. said impatiently. "I honestly don't give a shit what you've got stored down here. Show me Ståle's storeroom."

Karlsen dawdled along the dim corridor. As Billy T. passed the bare bulb, he blocked the light. Karlsen grumbled and whined noisily. Finally he reached a door made of plain wood, marked with a St. Andrew's Cross and locked with an ordinary padlock.

"Here." Karlsen thumped his fist on the timber.

Billy T. rolled his eyes and asked him politely to open the door.

"Don't have a key." The old man looked down and spat on the concrete floor. A brown gob of chewing tobacco landed beside Billy T.'s boots.

"And where did you put all Salvesen's belongings, then?"

"That's none of your business. But if you really want to know, most of it's over in my storerooms."

"You're lying," Billy T. said without looking at Karlsen. "Of course you've got a key."

He gestured to Karl, who took up a position beside him with his shoulder against the flimsy door.

"One, two, and *three*," Billy T. said.

The door gave at the first attempt. The two police officers had expected greater resistance and stormed into the cramped storeroom. Karl tripped over a pair of skis and stumbled forward.

"*Hellfire*. Damnation! Help!"

Eventually he managed to regain his footing. He brushed dirt and cobwebs from his blue Catalina jacket, which had probably been fashionable when he was fifteen and was so tight and faded that it could easily have dated from back then.

The storeroom was almost empty. Apart from the old-fashioned slalom skis Karl Sommarøy had tripped over, the rectangular room contained nothing other than a bicycle frame with no wheels or seat, a black plastic bag full of old clothes, and a set of worn summer tires stacked in a corner.

"Isn't it possible to get some more light in here?" Irritated, Billy T. stepped over the bag of clothes and tried to wrench off the plywood board nailed over what might be a window. "A crowbar, Karlsen, have you got one?"

"Here," Karl said. "You can borrow my flashlight."

He switched on a foot-long flashlight he had gone to the car to fetch. Billy T. directed the powerful beam at the nailed-up basement window.

"Bingo," he said softly.

Karl squinted at the spot Billy T. was indicating. He could see the hole clearly. He crouched down, and Billy T. shone the light on the floor in front of him.

"Fresh brick dust," the Sergeant said with satisfaction as he licked a finger and dipped it into the dust before resuming an upright position. "That hole is recent."

"And here's our cable," Billy T. said. "But where does it go from here?"

The two police officers followed the slender cable along the wall. It was not even fastened properly but hung in a loose loop across to the side wall, where it disappeared into yet another hole.

"Who owns the storeroom beside this one?"

Karlsen was making an attempt to salvage the remains of the door they had smashed. He had produced a screwdriver from a Swiss army knife and was trying to remove the wood from the twisted hinges. He took his time before coming out with an answer.

"That storeroom isn't Ståle Salvesen's, in any case. That means you can't go in there."

Billy T. and Karl exchanged looks. The man was right. They faced a diabolical amount of paperwork if they wanted to break down the adjacent door. A simpler alternative would of course be to ask the owner for permission.

"But who's the owner?" Billy T. repeated.

"Gudrun Sandaker. She's on vacation."

The old man continued his work with the screwdriver without giving the two police officers so much as a glance.

"Billy T.!"

Karl grabbed the flashlight and held the beam close to the side wall.

"Look here. The planks are old and worn. But look at the nail heads!"

The nails were new. The timber around them had recently splintered, and the paler timber was easy to distinguish from the rest of the dark and dirty wood.

"Give me that screwdriver," Billy T. ordered.

The caretaker stopped working on the damaged door and reluctantly handed over the Swiss army knife.

The first planks were the worst. It seemed that the wall had been insulated with rock wool on the inside, something Billy T. initially found surprising. Why would anyone go to the trouble of insulating the interior wall of a basement? Eventually, four floor-to-ceiling planks were removed and Karl helped him pull out the first insulation mat.

The wall concealed a secret room, barely more than eighteen inches wide. It was insulated in every direction, and now there was no difficulty understanding why. The telltale hum of a computer crept out into the basement storeroom. They tore down the rest of the wall in silence.

"A computer," Karl said under his breath. "A completely ordinary computer."

"But no screen or keyboard," Billy T. said, heaving out the final mat of rock wool.

"They're not necessary," Karl said. "No one's meant to use this."

"What the fuck's it for then?" Leaning forward, Billy T. peered at the green light, confirming that the computer was switched on.

"I've no idea. But I'll bet what's in this computer is extremely interesting. *No!*" Karl Sommarøy grabbed his colleague by the arm and brutally hauled him back. Billy T. had been about to pull the plug out of the obviously newly mounted socket.

"We'll have to take the computer with us, don't you see?" Billy T. said in annoyance, tugging his arm free. "We'll need to get someone to have a look at what's inside it."

"They'll have to do it here. For all we know, it might be programmed to break down if the current is switched off."

"Then you can call in the experts," Billy T. said. "I'll stay here. I'm not leaving here until someone can tell me what this computer contains."

Karl Sommarøy nodded and looked at Karlsen the caretaker. "And you can come with me," he said. "I think you and I have a great deal to discuss."

Billy T. could hear the caretaker's angry mutterings until the basement door was closed. Then he sat down on a pile of wood and rock wool, leaned back against the wall, and fell fast asleep.

88

The man Evald Bromo used to call Kai was busy packing. He had pulled out a suit, two sweaters, four shirts, and a pair of jeans, which he folded neatly and placed in a hard-shell suitcase. On top he added underwear and a toilet bag. He had checked there was nothing in the pockets to betray his identity. Next he emptied his wallet of his personal effects. Photos of the children, a receipt from IKEA, a driver's license, and other cards: everything was cut into pieces and placed in a bag he intended to dispose of somewhere no one would notice.

Then he refilled his wallet and tucked his new passport into his inside pocket.

Now he was called something entirely different.

He felt cold.

The desperation that had almost paralyzed him in recent days had vanished. What remained was decisiveness: what was done was done, and there was nothing left for him to do but flee. The prospect of abandoning the children forever was something he callously pushed aside as he snipped the photographs into pieces. He could not think. He could not afford to feel anything. He had to take action, and do it fast.

He would drive to Copenhagen. From there he would take a flight to somewhere far away, a place where he had friends.

Because he did have friends.

Over the years he had protected a few chosen ones. Always because he had a use for them. Never because he had felt threatened. The only exception had been Evald Bromo.

Snapping the case shut, he left the house and placed his baggage in the trunk of the car. He would go tonight. He felt a strong impulse to jump into the car and drive off immediately, but that would be too risky. His wife would raise the alarm within a couple of hours of him still not being home from work.

By setting off at around 3:00 a.m., he would achieve a head start of several hours. He did not require much more. He lifted the hood, removed the distributor cap, and placed it on a shelf on the back wall of the garage. He could say there was something wrong with the car. Then there would be no chance of his wife going for a drive that afternoon and discovering the suitcase.

89

Karl Sommarøy was one of the few people in the colossal gray police headquarters to have genuinely tried to make his office appear welcoming, decorating it with dark-blue curtains his wife had sewn, pictures of his children in red frames on his desk, and green potted plants on the shelves. On one wall hung a huge poster of a Gustav Klimt reproduction, and on another he had created a collage of children's drawings behind a sheet of glass. It was as if Karl Sommarøy's lower jaw, with its hint of girlishness, was not merely a malicious prank by Mother Nature, but also the expression of a strong feminine streak in his otherwise very masculine body. A rag rug in cheerful colors muffled the acoustics, and the penholder on the desk matched the pale leather of the blotter. Like a sort of masculine counterpoint to all that was a wacky cuckoo clock that hung on the wall. Every hour, a uniformed policeman popped out to raise his baton and cry "You're under arrest!" in a tinny voice.

"You know," Karl Sommarøy said as he sat down on the ergonomically correct office chair, "my grandfather was in the merchant navy during the war."

Ole Monrad Karlsen grumbled sulkily, moving restlessly in his chair.

"He was second mate on the MT *Alcides*. The Skaugen shipping company. Sailed from Abadan with bunker oil en route to Freemantle. Torpedoed in the Indian Ocean in July '43."

"My goodness," Karlsen said, straightening up ever so slightly. "Captured by the Japs, then?"

"Yes, that's right. My grandfather spent the rest of the war in a Japanese POW camp."

"That was really something," Karlsen said, shaking his head. "Those boys who ended up with the Japs, they had it worst of all. I was torpedoed twice myself. But never captured."

He gazed at the Sergeant. His expression had changed somewhat: he was biting his lower lip and no longer seemed so hostile.

"Norway treated you wartime sailors really badly," Sommarøy said sympathetically. "Would you like some coffee, Karlsen?"

Before the caretaker had time to answer, he poured some into a yellow cup decorated with ladybirds and pushed it across to the old man, smiling as broadly as he could.

"But you've managed all right, haven't you? A pension too, Karlsen? You must be . . ." He raised his eyes to the ceiling as he did a mental calculation. ". . . seventy-six?"

"Seventy-five. I signed on at Christmas in '39, when I was fifteen. I was allowed to continue with my work in the apartment block. Don't get paid, you know, but the old woman who owns the whole shooting match lets me keep my apartment in return for doing some work here and there. Cheaper for her, and suits me fine. It was better before, when there weren't as many of those slobs in the place. After the local authority bought up a lot of the apartments, all sorts of strange folk started drifting in. That pal of yours, that tall guy . . ." Karlsen covered his head with his hands. ". . . he's not a nice person. No respect."

"You'll have to excuse Billy T. He's under a lot of stress just now."

"That's no reason to behave like a lout. Police officer and all that. Doesn't look like one, anyway." Karlsen inspected the ladybirds on his cup with some skepticism before taking a tentative sip of the coffee.

"You knew Ståle Salvesen, didn't you?" Sommarøy clasped his hands behind his neck. "Were you friends?"

Ole Monrad Karlsen smacked his lips before putting down the cup and scratching his forehead with his left hand.

"It's not against the law to be on speaking terms with people," he said. The aggressive tone had returned.

"Not at all. I think Ståle Salvesen was basically a good guy. Someone the world had treated badly."

"He was once a businessman," Karlsen said. "Did you know that?"

"Yes. There was some nonsense about an investigation and bankruptcy and that sort of stuff."

"Exactly. They certainly suspected him! Investigating, reporting, digging, and destroying everything, that's how they went about it! But did they find anything? Not on your life—it all came to nothing in the end. And Ståle sat tight, alone and abandoned. His wife left him, and his son never came back from America. Ungrateful lowlife! After all, it was his father who had given him the opportunity to travel and study and all that jazz. Ståle was in much the same position as me, you see. When I came home from the war and was offered—"

Karl Sommarøy realized that this was going to take some time.

Excusing himself, he disappeared and returned with a Danish pastry and two bottles of soda. By the time there was nothing but crumbs left on the paper plate and both bottles were empty, his patience had worn thin.

"You're under arrest!" the cuckoo policeman squawked seven times.

"Heavens, that gave me a jolt," Karlsen said, turning to face the clock.

"That computer system in the basement," Sommarøy said lightly. "You knew about it, didn't you?"

"It's not against the law to have computer equipment in your own basement."

"Not at all. How long has it been there?"

"Why are you asking?"

Karl Sommarøy took a deep breath before getting to his feet and standing with his back to Karlsen while apparently scrutinizing the children's drawings.

"Listen," he said slowly, placing the flat of his hand on what was probably supposed to be a racing car. "We're in the midst of an extremely difficult case. Things would go more smoothly for us if you would just answer my questions. I understand you don't have much liking for the authorities. But you're a decent guy, and to the best of my knowledge, you've never done anything wrong. Let's make sure it continues that way."

He pivoted round to face the caretaker.

"Help me," he said. "Please."

"Since February," Karlsen mumbled. "February."

"Did Ståle tell you why he wanted to hide the computer?"

"No."

"Did you help him build the wall?"

"Yes."

Ole Monrad Karlsen stared at him with an unyielding expression in his eyes. Nevertheless, his demeanor had become more submissive, and he looked as if he had aged twenty years.

"Okay." Sommarøy resumed his seat. "Do you know anything more about that equipment?"

Karlsen shook his head.

"Do you know anything more at all? Something that might give us an answer as to why Ståle killed himself? You talked with him a great deal, he must have—"

"I've already told you. Ståle had nothing left here on earth. Everything he had was gone. I already told you that."

"Does that mean you *knew* he was planning to commit suicide?"

Karlsen's lower lip trembled, and the tremor spread across his face. His botched shave might indicate he had problems with his sight. Sommarøy had never seen Karlsen wearing glasses.

"I didn't know anything," he said so softly that Sommarøy drew closer. "I didn't understand much when you came the first time. I thought he'd just gone on a trip without letting me know. But then . . ."

His hands were shaking now, and he wiped his eyes with his finger.

"But I really should have realized something was going on when he gave me that parcel."

"Parcel?"

"He gave me a brown-paper parcel with an address on it. Stamps and everything. Only needed to be put in the mail, he said, if anything should happen to him. I should wait for a couple of weeks or so. After I'd last seen him, I mean. I asked him if he was thinking of going on a trip. He said he wasn't, and then somehow we were chatting about other things. I didn't even remember about the parcel. Not until some time had passed, and then I thought that the parcel must have been his way of saying goodbye. He trusted me, did Ståle."

Karl Sommarøy gazed down at his own hands, clutching the edge of the table. His knuckles were white. "Did you mail that parcel?"

"Yes, I had to do that."

"Who was it addressed to?"

"I don't think I could remember the address. But the name . . ."

Ole Monrad Karlsen lifted his eyes and looked directly at the police officer. A tiny brown trickle was dribbling from one corner of his mouth, and a tear had come to a halt in the stubble just below one of his nostrils.

"But the name was Evald Bromo, anyway. I haven't forgotten that. That was the man who was lying with his head chopped off in my basement."

"You're under arrest!" screeched the cuckoo clock, eight times now.

90

Margaret Kleiven's parents had died a long time ago, and she had no other close relatives. Admittedly, she had a sister who was four years younger, but they had never had a close relationship. Even as children they were conspicuously different: Margaret introverted, shy, and cautious, and her sister outgoing and charming. After her sister had married an Englishman and relocated to Manchester, they had eventually lost contact. Even the Christmas cards that had been dutifully sent at the end of November for the first few years had failed to materialize in the past six years.

Evald was Margaret Kleiven's whole life. Evald, and her work as a teacher of history and French. She was under no illusions that her students spared her much thought. She was probably too boring and curriculum oriented for that. But she was far from unpopular. In a sense, the teenagers respected her traditional teaching methods, aware that they would pay dividends. Last year, two students had changed classes purely in order to have Miss Kleiven for French. Both had achieved top grades on the final exam. After the results were announced, a little bouquet of sweet peas wrapped in orange cellophane had sat waiting for her in the staff room. Such incidents gave her a sense of cautious anticipation ahead of the next school year.

Margaret Kleiven was not one to indulge in great emotions. When she married Evald, she was old enough not to have unrealistic expectations. Eventually she found some kind of dull contentment in her existence. Life with Evald was quiet. As the years passed, they became increasingly isolated, but in Margaret's eyes, they were fond of each other and had a good life despite the child that never arrived.

Now Evald was gone.

The shock had subsided into a paralyzing despair in the course of the first twenty-four hours. Five days and nights had gone by since the policewoman with the flickering eyes had told her that Evald was dead, probably murdered. Now it was the morning of Friday, April 9, 1999, and Margaret Kleiven was furious.

It was already 6:00 a.m., and she had not slept a wink.

It was of no interest to her who had killed Evald.

The copies of *Dagsavisen* and *Aftenposten* had been lying beside the shoe racks in the hallway for four days and she had not even opened them. On Monday there had been a photograph of Evald on the front page of *Aftenposten*, an old image of a running, slavering man she barely recognized. She brought in the newspapers from the doormat every morning, laid them down on the floor, and returned to bed.

Evald was dead, and nothing could change that.

The mysterious circumstances of his death—which, according to the slightly overweight policewoman, had seemingly happened in Torshov—reminded Margaret that there had been a dark side to Evald's life that he had never shared with her. Of course, she knew that there was something—a burden he carried and could never quite get rid of. During their first years together, she had wondered what it was, and on a couple of occasions had tried to talk to him about it. Her initiatives had only led to him running more and talking even less. And so she had let it drop.

It should be allowed to rest forever.

Margaret Kleiven was angry with her deceased husband. He had gone running at night, despite her repeated warnings. She would never forgive him.

Standing up, she crossed the floor unsteadily.

There was a small chest beside the bathroom door. It was decorated with traditional painting, and it would probably be more accurate to call it a large box. When they had phoned from the nursing home to tell her that Olga was dead, she'd felt nothing. She had never had any feelings for the old woman. In fact, she had not seen her for more than two years. When her mother-in-law had descended into total senility, Margaret had considered there was little point in paying hypocritical visits when Evald already visited her almost every day. However, the nursing home had no one else to contact. They had called Margaret and Margaret had come. Olga Bromo had owned nothing other than a dresser full of linen and a few little silver spoons, and a small chest with her name in blue lettering on the lid. The care assistant had looked down at the floor as he cleared his throat, explaining that they needed the room more or less immediately; there was a waiting list of sick old people and he hoped she would not take offense if he asked her what he should do with Olga's personal effects.

Margaret Kleiven had taken the chest with her and let them do whatever they wanted with the rest.

Now, wearing a pale pink bathrobe, she crouched down in the beam of morning light that had crept into the room through a gap in the curtains, inserted a wrought-iron key into the lock, and turned it.

She was startled when she opened the lid. It was like being struck by a gust of stale air that confirmed what she had always known: she had not really known him. Gingerly, she lifted out two old school report cards. A pink box contained a cameo brooch she had never seen before. There was a stiff speckled red post office savings book in Evald's name, though the dates for the deposits were from when Evald was a small child and could hardly have known what it was to save money.

When Margaret Kleiven was finished looking through the contents of the little wooden chest with blue letters on the lid, she stood up and realized that her legs had gone to sleep. Shaking her legs, she walked slowly downstairs, where she lit a fire in the black stove. It did not take long: the wood was dry and she found plenty of newspapers beside the shoe racks in the hallway. After that, she trudged upstairs to the bedroom to fetch her mother-in-law's chest. One by one she removed the items it contained and threw them onto the flames. Some burned well, such as the report cards and the cardboard box containing an old lock of hair. Other things remained in the flames for some time, like the cameo and a wide gold wedding ring. Eventually even the metal objects blackened, and she knew that if she just left them lying there they would disappear in the end.

At the very bottom of the large box lay a CD case.

Margaret was taken aback: all the other items in the chest were old—extremely old—but the CD looked brand new. Momentarily, it crossed her mind to open the plastic case, but something told her it would be best to leave it be.

She threw it onto the fire.

It sizzled in the blaze and a clear blue flame rose from the plastic. The case crumpled in the intense heat, and the smell of burned plastic stung her nose. A scrap of paper briefly came into sight when the housing cracked, just for a second, and then it too vanished into the flames.

Margaret Kleiven closed the stove door.

She was still just as furious with Evald, and swallowed three sleeping pills before retiring to bed.

91

Evald Bromo,

You have almost certainly forgotten me. In your pursuit of new victims, you probably don't have time to stop and think about the effect you have on the people you persecute. But if you search through your own archives, you'll find my name. Many times. It's true you'll have to go far back in time. In recent years I've not been mentioned in any newspaper. There's hardly anyone who knows who I am.

I ran a company called Aurora Data. It was a promising firm. I won't bother you with the story of how I built up a successful, forward-looking computer company from scratch. You know that story yourself, if you search back far enough in your memory.

The late eighties was a difficult time. When the nineties began, there were many men of my caliber who went to rack and ruin. Companies like Aurora Data fell like dominoes. But not us. Not until Økokrim, the financial-crimes branch of the police, received a message from a former employee of ours, a disloyal worker I'd done a great favor to by only firing him. I should have reported the guy to the police, of course, since he'd embezzled more than 200,000 kroner.

I had actually done nothing wrong. Not then.

It was claimed that my son had bought shares in a company on whose board I sat, just a short time before the same firm went public about a major contract that in a flash doubled the share value. Økokrim got a whiff of insider trading and spent a long time ascertaining what was clear all along: the agreement with the Americans had not taken place when my son bought the shares. But the finance police had got to work. They turned Aurora Data upside down. And me. My enemy, the former employee, had concocted so many stories, muddled up so many facts, and lied so comprehensively that it took years until the case was dropped. Naturally, a number of small anomalies cropped up in the meantime. A company like Aurora Data can't be upended without something or other coming to the surface.

Trifles, of course, and never anything that could implicate me. None of it would have elicited anything more than a reprimand; a small fine at most. But the investigators found just enough to keep things going.

You covered the story. Other media outlets followed. But it was you and your newspaper that led the pack. What you wrote was quoted by the others. You were the prominent voice.

I put up with being investigated. Even today, after everything that's happened, I maintain that the prosecution authorities had to do something about the serious allegations made against me. What I could not tolerate was being condemned in advance.

You condemned me by what you wrote. Halvorsrud condemned me by talking to you so frequently and loosely.

FOUR TIMES I phoned you to explain how it had all actually come about. You listened and feigned interest in my story. Nevertheless, your articles were full of the police's assumptions and beliefs, accusations, and groundless assertions.

I sent SIX LETTERS to Sigurd Halvorsrud. He did not answer a single one. I asked him for a meeting, but was put off with lengthy interviews with the people who worked for him. I never got to meet the man you so willingly quoted, who claimed to know so much about me and my life.

You achieved what you wanted.

Although it was never brought to court, I lost everything. Aurora lost important contracts, and eventually went into receivership. As for myself, I was subjected to "the silent treatment" by increasing numbers of my old business associates, people who had previously expressed such confidence in both Aurora Data and me. I worked twenty-four hours a day in an effort to avert the catastrophe, but to no avail. My wife left me, my son stayed away out of contempt for a father who was no longer someone to admire, and I was left high and dry. When my case was dropped, you saw fit to mention it in just a single column.

Well, I was not entirely without resources. When everything began to collapse around me, without my having done anything wrong, I was sensible enough to stash away a few hundred thousand in cash. I had already been branded and thrown to the wolves. I did not intend to spend the money on myself. I couldn't do that.

For several years I tried to rehabilitate myself. I had created a stock-exchange fairytale in the eighties, and "everyone" knew how capable I was. But no one had really taken in that the case against me had never led to anything. No one would have anything to do with me. In the end I gave up.

That was when I decided to destroy both you and Sigurd Halvorsrud. The disloyal employee who initiated the whole persecution campaign against me was fortunate enough to die in a car accident in 1995. You two have not been so lucky. For three years I have been pursuing you both. Always from a distance, but all the same more closely than anyone would believe. I have moved in the shadows and left no stone unturned in the lives you call your own. For the past three years I have hardly done anything else but watch the two of you.

It was easy to find your weakness, Evald Bromo. With Halvorsrud, it was harder. That is why I have treated you both differently.

You will find a CD-ROM enclosed. You don't know much about IT, so I'll give you a brief explanation of what ROM signifies. "Read Only Memory". That means you cannot manipulate, edit, or change anything whatsoever. The CD contains a recording of myself relating what I have done. Among other things, I make it clear that Halvorsrud is innocent of his wife's murder.

In fact, I have decided to kill her myself.

Not only will I kill her, but I will also take her life in the most spectacular fashion. Halvorsrud will discover how the media operates. By beheading Doris Flo Halvorsrud, I will ensure that the headlines are merciless. The press are going to destroy him, as they once destroyed me.

If all goes well—and it will have been done, if you are reading this—there will be so much circumstantial evidence against Halvorsrud that he will at the very least be dogged by suspicion for the rest of his life. That was how my life was left in ruins, and that is how I want to share my fate with him.

Unless you rescue the man. By now he should already have had a glimpse of the hell that is created by false accusations, a sight that will make him think and may well affect him for the rest of his years.

He will be let off having endured just these few weeks, if you are willing to sacrifice yourself.

The prospect of providing you with a moral dilemma amuses me enormously. Is there any morality to be found in a man who abuses children under cover of having a respectable job? You won't remember it, but when I called you for the fourth time, you spoke of duty. You had a duty to write about the investigation. You had a duty to repeat what the police believed, felt, thought and assumed. Duty!

On the CD-ROM I don't talk only about my extensive and destructive terror campaign against the Halvorsrud family, about the keys I stole from their youngest child while he was at the gym, about the wife's computer whose hard disk I changed one night, just to create a sinister atmosphere, and about the money I deposited in his name and so on and so forth . . .

I also expose you. I talk about the crimes you have committed repeatedly over the past few years. You will be surprised how much I know. A reasonably proficient police force will be able to have you convicted after only a minimum of further investigation.

It is your choice.

When you decide, you should keep in the back of your mind old Pokerface's promise to send a package to your Chief Editor on September 1. Perhaps Pokerface is lying, perhaps not. Since I am Pokerface, I know the truth.

You, on the other hand, can only guess.

You took everything from me. You condemned me to the death I have now sought refuge in. In return, I have sent you both to hell.

Ståle Salvesen

Erik Henriksen was first to finish.

He put down the printout with a gentle shake of the head.

"The eighth commandment," he said darkly. "Thou shalt not give false witness against thy neighbor. It can cost you *fucking* dear."

The rustling of papers became a rising hubbub of shocked voices.

Hanne Wilhelmsen sat at the head of the table in the cramped interrogation room, with the Superintendent flanking her on one side and
Police Chief Mykland on the other.

"Karianne," she said autocratically, raising her hand for silence.

"So," Karianne Holbeck began. "This was the only document that
could be retrieved from the hard disk. It had been deleted, but was still
quite straightforward to find. Salvesen must have used another computer to burn the CD he describes in the letter."

"Does that mean we've no idea what the CD contains?"

Billy T. tried to catch Hanne's eye, but had to abandon the attempt.
Instead he stared at Karianne, who was sitting with a laptop in front of
her and deep red roses on her cheeks.

"It's really quite thoroughly described in the letter, though. But if we
don't find any more of Salvesen's equipment . . . No . . . You see . . . Well,
we might be fortunate enough to track down the actual CD. Or a copy.
The boys have gone out to turn over the whole of Vogts gate 14.
They've been there all night, but nothing of interest has turned up. So
it's fairly doubtful."

"Fuck," Billy T. said, slamming his fists together.

"We don't need that," Hanne said tersely.

"No, but just think! It would've been damn interesting to get more
details! I've never heard the like of this setup. The guy spent *years* of
his life planning his revenge!"

He glanced at Hanne again. He wanted to acknowledge her, to show
her respect. Hanne Wilhelmsen had believed in Halvorsrud's innocence from the outset. Unmoved by other people's intransigence, she
had put forward her own theory logically and clearly to anyone who
could be bothered to listen. Billy T. felt a physical pain in his chest as
he observed Hanne standing there, sallow and pale, wearing no
makeup, looking older than he had ever seen her, slender hands fiddling with the marker and eyes that never made contact with his, no
matter how hard he tried. He wanted her back. He wanted forgiveness, the way he had forgiven her. When he went to bed that night, the
following night, he had lain awake until two o'clock. He listened to the
baby sounds from Jenny, which caused spasms to cross Tone-Marit's
sleeping face. When he felt her hand fumbling in sleep for his, he had
forgiven both Hanne and himself. He knew that everything could be
as before if she could only do the same.

She refused to return his gaze.

"The yogurt in the fridge," she said abruptly, turning to face the flip chart. "Why should Ståle Salvesen go to so much trouble to put his life and his apartment in order and then *forget* the dated foodstuffs in his refrigerator?"

She drew a yogurt carton and a milk carton, not very convincingly. The yogurt carton looked like a damaged bucket and the milk carton like a Danish holiday house.

"Because he wanted to reinforce the weakest part of his plan," she answered herself. "Salvesen did not kill himself on Monday, March 1. It's true he was at Staure Bridge. He parked his car. He went up to the top of the bridge and waited until there were people nearby, close enough to see him, but far enough away not to notice that he never disappeared into the sea. He made it look as if he had jumped, but then he snuck underneath the bridge and returned to the city by some other means."

"Exactly as you thought," Billy T. said, immediately regretting his comment; he felt like a puppy dog wagging its tail and licking the mouth of an old, arrogant bitch.

"How exactly, we'll probably never know," Hanne said, unaffected by the pathetic praise. She drew a car. "However, what never crossed my mind . . ." She lifted a plastic cup filled with water to her mouth and drank deeply. ". . . was that Ståle Salvesen did *not* flee abroad. He did *not* escape to South America or some other place with deficient registration procedures and hostile extradition treaties with Norway."

"He definitely committed suicide, but not until after he had murdered Doris," Erik said slowly, spitting ink: the ballpoint pen he had been chewing was leaking badly. "Ingenious. Halvorsrud would seem crazy when he claimed that a dead man had killed his wife."

"You're right."

Hanne drew wheels on the blue car.

"On Sunday, March 7, a stolen Volvo was found in the parking lot beside Staure Bridge," she continued. "The owner reported it missing on the afternoon of Thursday, March 4. That was the night Doris was murdered. The owner lives in Grünerløkka."

"Five minutes from Vogts gate," Karl Sommarøy said. "Salvesen damn well killed Doris, drove out to Staure in the stolen car, and finally jumped into the sea. Goddamn it!"

"But, you know, it was an incredible gamble," Erik objected. "If he had been found in the course of the first few days, it would have been easy to establish that he hadn't been in the water the entire time since Monday, March 1! And where did he hide in the meantime? Between Monday and Thursday night, I mean? And what if he had been caught while driving the stolen car? What if someone had seen him on Thursday night when he really did jump into the sea?"

"A gamble, yes indeed. Definitely. And there are many questions I'm afraid we'll never be able to answer."

Hanne Wilhelmsen puffed out her cheeks and let the air slowly leak out through gritted teeth.

"But what did the man have to lose? Salvesen had nothing more to live for. His life had no purpose. A few days ago, I met a strange man who said there are no limits to what people are capable of if they feel seriously threatened."

She held back. It seemed so long ago. Eivind Torsvik was of no interest. He was nothing other than a detour on her way home. Closing her eyes for a few seconds, she wondered whether the man himself had been a figment of her imagination.

"Presumably it's even easier to cross the line when you've already lost everything," she said softly. "Salvesen kept himself going for a long time simply on the prospect of getting revenge: the thought that Evald Bromo and Sigurd Halvorsrud would get to experience at least a fraction of the hell he himself had endured. And he hoped that it would take time. The longer it took, the more difficult it would be to establish a precise time of death. The less reason the police would have to doubt the witness reports from Monday, March 1. The yogurt and milk cartons were only tiny pieces of the puzzle. Props, so to speak. A little subtlety we never noticed that gave us a subconscious incentive to see the picture Ståle Salvesen wanted us to see."

"Those delayed emails were really clever," Karianne said, keying in a command on her laptop. "He simply devised a handy little program that sent emails to Bromo long after he himself was dead. The 'sent' mailbox in the computer in the basement was full of emails sent approximately twenty-four hours apart. He had written a couple to the Chief Editor of *Aftenposten* as well, by the way."

"Your lips are blue, Erik."

Hanne rubbed her finger over her own to show him.

"Go and wash it off before it becomes indelibly imprinted."

"But," Erik said, standing behind his chair, trying to wipe the ink off with his shirtsleeve, "think of all that money, eh! A hundred thousand in the basement and two hundred thousand in the Swedish bank. He gave away a small fortune, just to throw suspicion on Halvorsrud?"

Hanne Wilhelmsen shrugged as she struggled to make her hair sit behind her ear.

"What could Salvesen do with the money? After all, we're not talking about enough to settle abroad, start over again, and escape from everything. It was just enough to create a lot of suspicion around Halvorsrud. Naturally he chose Sweden. Just as naturally as he chose to place the money in the basement. We would find it. If he had deposited the money in a bank in Switzerland, we would never have come across a single krone of it."

"And that brings us to a substantial point I can't quite understand." Karl Sommarøy animatedly toyed with a thermos flask someone had left behind the previous day. Suddenly he loosened the lid, and sour day-old coffee leaked out onto his legs. "Halvorsrud would never be *convicted*," he said, without drawing attention to his drenched crotch. "You've said it all along, Hanne. We don't have enough for a conviction."

"True," Police Chief Mykland said, smiling diffidently. "Which of course might explain why Salvesen was willing to let Halvorsrud off the hook if Evald Bromo was willing to sacrifice himself. The point for Salvesen never was to get Halvorsrud convicted. Take the disks we found, for example. Karianne has continually made the point that they were not 'of particular interest to the police.'" Mykland drew quote marks in the air. "Probably Salvesen just put together material he found in the newspapers. All those cases, of course, were discussed at length in the press. He must have realized we might eventually come to doubt the entire chain of circumstantial evidence. But that barely mattered. The point was to give Halvorsrud a sense of what it's like to be under suspicion even when you're innocent. And to be condemned in advance by the media. Salvesen was not a stupid man."

"Go and wash that pen off, Erik," Hanne Wilhelmsen said, sounding annoyed. "You look like a clown. You could get blood poisoning."

"Yes, Mum," he said crossly. "But one more thing first. Does this mean that all the pedophile stuff was just nonsense? That Thea Halvorsrud *is* after all only a daddy's girl?"

"Yes. In all probability."

"Yes? But what about Evald Bromo then? Was *he* a pedophile, or was that a load of bull as well? And who . . . *who the fuck killed Evald Bromo?*"

No one spoke. The room became so silent that Hanne could clearly hear a hungry rumbling in Hasse Fredriksen's stomach; the technician was sitting at the opposite end of the table, holding his breath in embarrassment, as if that would help. The air in the rectangular room was almost intolerably stuffy. Hanne felt her cheeks burning, and the sticky film on her eyes had come back.

Evald Bromo did not concern her.

Evald Bromo's fate had never really touched Hanne Wilhelmsen.

Sometimes it happened. More often these days than a year ago. Before that, when she was younger, stronger—and more naive, possibly—every single murder, every bloody rape, every instance of aggravated assault had felt like a violation of *her* personally. The murders had an impact on her, the rapes hurt her deeply, and knife crime infuriated her. That was why she had spent almost twenty years of her life on a task she knew deep down was hopeless: trying to hold back the tide of criminality in Oslo.

The knowledge settled like an iron fist around her throat, and she suddenly felt sick: she had started to classify people.

Hanne Wilhelmsen had been obsessed with solving Doris Flo Halvorsrud's murder. Doris was a respected professional woman, a mother and wife. Her husband was a competent lawyer. Hanne should, would, and must solve the case.

Evald Bromo, on the other hand, was simply a duty. Evald Bromo was a sex offender who abused unfortunate children.

"I've started to not give a fuck," she whispered to herself, with a sharp intake of breath as she sat down.

"Are you okay?" Mykland said in an undertone, placing his hand over hers. "Are you ill?"

Hanne did not reply. She struggled to pull herself together; she closed her eyes and searched for one last atom of strength. She had to bring this meeting to a close. She had to finish in here, put an end to the Halvorsrud case, and pass responsibility for the Bromo killing on to someone suitable. If she could just make it through this meeting, she could take some time off. Extended leave. She should be at home with Cecilie day and night for as long as necessary, for as long as they had left together, for as long as Cecilie lived.

If she could just make it through this meeting.

She rose again, leaning forward with the palms of her hands on the table, and prepared herself.

"Evald Bromo's death probably has nothing to do with Halvorsrud at all," she said in an unnecessarily loud voice. "I'm still of the definite opinion that he's a pedophile. It's entirely possible there's a connection between his sexual perversions and the fact of his homicide. But in our original case, the murder of Doris Flo Halvorsrud, Evald Bromo was only a detour. Of course, a lot of threads still need weaving together, like, for example, why Halvorsrud's fingerprints were found in the basement in Vogts gate. My personal theory is that in a fit of despair, he tried to find something to prove his innocence. Clumsy and stupid, it goes without saying. But on the other hand—"

"Think how he must have been feeling," interrupted Annmari Skar, who had sat through the entire meeting in silence, leafing through something that looked to Hanne like a novel. "He has been telling the truth all along. No one has really believed him. Not even you, Hanne." She gazed provocatively at the Chief Inspector. "If you had really believed Halvorsrud's story, you would have been more insistent. Put more effort into it. Everybody knows how you've worked your butt off."

"Literally speaking," Erik muttered. His lips were now a lighter shade of blue at least, after his visit to the restroom, and he glanced at Karianne, who used her hand to hide a smile.

"You would have argued more strongly. Persevered more. You would have refused to let him sit there week after week if you'd *really* believed him. He realized that, of course. He was completely alone. He became increasingly hemmed in. His situation must have seemed progressively more absurd. As if he—"

"Besides, he's had to live with having failed his wife," Hans Christian Mykland said. "Amid all the false accusations, he has probably been his own worst critic. He let her be killed. He did not defend her."

"We'll wrap it up now," Hanne said without ceremony.

It felt as if the walls were beginning to close in on her. She lifted the plastic cup to her mouth again, but it was empty.

"But, Hanne," Erik insisted, looking for an argument. "We can't say for certain that Halvorsrud didn't murder Bromo! Salvesen assumes a kind of postmortem responsibility for Doris's murder, fair enough ... but the fact is that the Public Prosecutor's fingerprints *were* in the basement beside the body, he *had* no alibi, and he *didn't* turn up to report at the police station as he—"

"Annmari is right," Hanne said scathingly, fixing her eyes on her younger colleague with the ridiculous baby-blue mouth against a chalk-white complexion and bright-red hair. "I did not stand up for Halvorsrud enough. So I'm doing it now. He's innocent. We all know that. The murder of Evald Bromo was a pathetic copycat execution. It's rudimentary!"

She flung out her arms emphatically, then embraced herself, as if she was freezing in the overheated room.

"Serial murders, or signature murders, are easy to recognize. You find a common denominator among the victims. It is sometimes difficult to discover, but it's there. And how can you tell that a murder has been disguised to look as if it's a link in a serial killer's chain of death? Because the victim doesn't fit! Evald Bromo and Doris Flo Halvorsrud had hardly anything in common apart from both presumably being Norwegian citizens."

She began to pack up her belongings, stuffing two folders and an old leather pencil case into her black backpack. The others in the room watched her closely.

"And on the subject of Norway," she said without a smile as she pointed her finger at Erik Henriksen, "your face looks like a flag—red, white and blue!"

No one laughed. Chairs scraped on the floor. People spoke in hushed tones, and their voices combined into a meaningless buzz that eventually disappeared out through the door. Billy T. lingered for a few seconds in the doorway in the hope that Hanne would follow him, but when he saw that the Chief of Police had laid his hand on her arm, he gave up.

"What do you want to do now?" Hans Christian Mykland said gently to Hanne. "Tell me what it is you want."

"Thanks," she said in a whisper.

"What?"

"Thanks for protecting me recently. I expect there have been complaints."

Mykland gave a broad smile as he smoothed back his hair.

"Three," he whispered. "They're lying at the bottom of my drawer, and they'll stay there for as long as I have any say in the matter."

Leaning on the nylon bag beside her on the table, Hanne suddenly reached out to the Police Chief and put her arms around him.

"Thank you so much," she confided into his shoulder. "I can't fathom why you're so kind to me. So patient. I promise that when it's all over and Cecilie—"

"Hush now," he said quietly, stroking between her shoulder blades.

He did not want to let go. She noticed that; when she made an effort to withdraw, he would not release her. Strangely enough, she found it pleasant.

"Let someone else take over the Bromo homicide," he said. She could feel little puffs of air against her ear as he spoke. "Take some time off now, Hanne. You're entitled to it."

"I will. There are just a couple of things I have to sort out first."

"Don't let them be too many, then," he said, letting her go.

"No," she said, slinging her bag onto her back. "Just a couple of odds and ends."

"Hanne."

She had reached the end of the table and turned to face him.

"Yes?"

"Who should assume responsibility for the Bromo investigation?"

Hanne shrugged. "One of the other inspectors, I would think."

"I was thinking of appointing Billy T. on a temporary basis. What do you think?"

She hitched up her bag and headed for the door.

"It's all the same to me," she said dully, with her back to the Police Chief. "As far as I'm concerned, it's of no interest whatsoever what you do with Billy T."

92

The ashtray Billy T. had given her looked out of place. A simple design in black, it had a steel dish inside that could be tilted and emptied every time you stubbed out a cigarette; it looked like something from Alessi and had probably been expensive. Her office was too drab for that sort of thing. She had never really settled in there, and had never taken the trouble to make the place congenial. She had never had the time. Formerly, she had taken great pains, not only for her own sake, but also because it had a reassuring effect on witnesses and suspects if they were interviewed in a room that did not remind them of a prison cell as much as these rooms certainly did.

She played with the ashtray, repeatedly tilting the movable dish. Since she had stopped smoking, she would not need it. She dropped it into the wastepaper basket, hoping it would catch the cleaner's eye and perhaps be taken home.

There was a polite knock on the door.

"Come in," she said.

Police Sergeant Karsten Hansen smiled at her. Long past fifty, he was never going to earn his inspector's stripes. Round as a barrel, he plodded across to the visitor's chair, snorting loudly. Hanne Wilhelmsen had always found it difficult to imagine that Karsten Hansen had ever been slim and fairly active: he had of course managed to pass the entrance exam for police college, just the same as everyone else. Hansen worked in the Traffic and Environment Department now and was happy to stay there, year after year.

"How are you?" he said cheerfully, wiping the sweat from his brow.

"Okay, thanks. And you?"

"Just fine, thanks. Everything's going well. But you know, I came across something an hour ago."

Hanne Wilhelmsen was extremely uninterested in what a traffic cop had come across. She wanted to go home.

"You know these boxes," he continued undeterred. "Our speed cameras."

"Mhmm."

"I was helping the office staff go through some of the rolls of film in preparation for sending out fine notifications and that sort of thing. And what do I find?"

"I really don't know."

"You're well aware, Hanne, it's not much fun when colleagues crop up in those pictures."

He was sitting uncomfortably and tried to twist his bulky body into a more acceptable position on the narrow seat. Hanne felt a blush spread over her face and tried desperately to remember whether she had been careless enough to exceed the speed limit when driving past one of the boxes. She knew where they all were, so she usually lowered her speed just in time. The journey from Sandefjord, it suddenly struck her. She had driven like a bat out of hell to the hospital at Ullevål.

"I'm terribly sorry, Hansen," she stammered, making an effort to suppress the color in her cheeks. "Of course, there's no excuse . . . how fast was I driving?"

"You?"

He was taken aback, and began to laugh.

"No, no, Wilhelmsen. It's not you we're talking about. Look at this!"

He produced a photograph from a manila envelope and placed it in front of her. She could still feel her pulse racing: speed violations could be a serious matter for a chief inspector in the police. Especially if it was as serious as it must have been that night she had set a new personal best on the stretch between Sandefjord and Oslo.

"The violation is only by four kilometers an hour," Hansen said. "Sixty-four in the sixty zone immediately before the Tåsen intersection, in the westbound lane. But what I was wondering . . ."

He placed his fat finger on the driver's face. The image was grainy and indistinct, but nevertheless more than good enough to identify the driver.

"That's Iver Feirand, isn't it? At least, the vehicle is his—I've checked that already."

Hanne Wilhelmsen did not answer. Hansen was correct. It was interesting. Sensational, even. Hanne had already spotted who the passenger was.

"When was this taken?" she asked, following his finger down to the corner of the picture where the time was shown.

Tuesday, March 30, 1999, at 5:24 p.m.

Grabbing the photo, Hanne held it up close to her face. She must not be mistaken. She could not be mistaken.

"And you know, I was surprised, when I saw that buddy of his there—it's definitely Evald Bromo, who was murdered the other day. There've been loads of pictures of him in the newspapers. I couldn't quite get it to add up that the guy's traveling with a policeman on Tuesday, and then he gets beheaded on the Saturday. But then it dawned on me that there could be a lot I've no idea about in this case, and it might well be that everything's as it should be. However, I'm still a bit old-fashioned and . . ." He gave her a bashful smile. ". . . it's better to make a fool of yourself by asking than to sit on the fence with something that doesn't seem quite right. That's what I think, anyway."

"You're fantastic."

Waving the photo, she grasped his hand and squeezed it.

"You're completely amazing," she said, biting her lip. "I need to make a phone call. Stay there. By all means."

She pulled out a yellow slip of paper she had pushed under the desk blotter and called the number she had scribbled down only a few days earlier.

"Eivind Torsvik," she eventually heard a voice say, after the phone had been ringing for what seemed like an eternity.

"Hi there. This is Hanne Wilhelmsen here. Thanks for your hospitality last time we met."

"You're welcome; it was my pleasure."

She had not even formulated a strategy. The photograph of Evald Bromo sitting beside a man who had asserted he had never seen him before had made her pounce on a lead that could be ruined if she was not careful.

"I'm in a dreadful fix," she said honestly, after a painful silence. "You don't want to hand over any of the material you've gathered. I have to respect that. But I need you to answer one question for me. One single question. Could you do that?"

"That depends. I've promised to give you everything we've got when our work is finished. When we've collected enough evidence. Not before."

"But you *must* . . ."

She glanced at the wastepaper basket, where a brand-new ashtray and a half-full pack of Marlboro Lights had been discarded. Leaning forward, she picked up both, cadged a light from Hansen, who was sitting there in astonishment, listening to a conversation of which he could make no sense at all.

"Do you have a police officer on your list?" she asked, holding the first drag of her cigarette in her lungs for as long as she was able.

"You'd be amazed where sex offenders crop up in society. Did you know that pedophiles are overrepresented in occupations where people care for or have a great deal of contact with children? Doctors. Aid workers in developing countries. Preschool teachers. Scout leaders.

Clergymen preparing young people for confirmation. Handball coaches."

"*I know that, Eivind!*"

She had never before called him by his first name. She had never called him anything at all. It made him stop in his tracks.

"I can't say anything," he said eventually. It sounded as if he was moving around; his breath came in fits and starts. "Not yet. But there's not long to go. I can promise you that."

"Eivind. Listen to me."

Hanne could hear herself talking; it was as if someone else was speaking. There and then, she decided she would set all the IT experts she could find on Eivind Torsvik if he did not answer. She herself would lead the attack, and they would storm into his cottage at Hamburgkilen, ransacking everything they could lay their hands on. If he did not answer her.

"You must give me an answer. It's a matter of life and death."

Hansen stared anxiously at her. Placing her hand over the receiver, she whispered across the table, "Quite a difficult source. Need to exaggerate."

"Yes."

"What? What did you say?"

"Yes, we have a police officer on our lists. Together with two teachers, one dentist, two clergymen who are foster parents in the bargain—"

"Is his name Iver Feirand?"

Silence fell. Hanne closed her eyes in order to hear better: it sounded as if Eivind Torsvik had taken the cordless phone outside with him. She thought she could hear gulls screeching and the distant throb of an outboard motor.

"Yes," he said in a monotone. "His name is Iver Kai Feirand. He was the one who took three years to investigate the case against my foster father. It was Iver Kai Feirand who sabotaged my case."

"Iver K. Feirand," Hanne Wilhelmsen said slowly. "Thanks."

Eivind Torsvik had already disconnected the call.

93

The man who now carried a passport claiming his name was Peder Kalvø was seated on a Lufthansa plane that had just taken off from Copenhagen's Kastrup airport. It was due to land in Frankfurt in an hour's time. From there he would fly on to Madrid, where he would stay for a few days. No more than four.

He had foreseen that something like this might happen.

He had arranged the fake passport and foreign bank account several years earlier. The itinerary had changed slightly in the past couple of years, but not much. Iver Kai Feirand was a highly educated police officer and knew what was required.

He had been attracted to little boys ever since he'd reached sexual maturity. Not men. Never men. If he wanted sex with an adult, it would be with a woman. Never little girls. If he was going to have a child, something he regularly had the urge to do, then it was always a boy. He had two daughters of his own. He had never touched them. Not in that way.

It went without saying that he was a competent investigator of sexual assaults. He knew what he was looking for. He saw it in the eyes of the suspects, and it took him only seconds to decide whether they were innocent or guilty. Methodically and purposefully, he had maneuvered himself into the job he now held. From the time the opportunity arose at the beginning of the eighties, he had known what he was going to specialize in.

It gave him power.

It excited him.

And it taught him exactly where to go to find what he needed.

Seven years ago, a police patrol had picked up two girls aged around twelve in Strøket. They were plastered in hopeless makeup and one was sobbing so violently that a female police officer took her away to speak to a doctor. The other one had stayed in Iver Feirand's office, where she sat bold as brass, chewing gum while they waited for the arrival of the child welfare officer on duty.

Children taken into custody should not be interviewed without a guardian present. However, no one could deny Iver Feirand the chance to make conversation. Perhaps she was already so damaged that sexualized behavior had become normal. In any case, she made persistent efforts to negotiate her way out of the police headquarters: she would not have any objections if he wanted to go with her to an apartment she knew about where no one was living at present.

When the woman from child welfare turned up and took the child away, he noticed a business card left behind on the chair vacated by the slim backside of the girl who had just flounced provocatively out of his office. Evald Bromo's business card. Iver Feirand was keen to know what the man had to do with a twelve-year-old prostitute, and called the journalist in for a chat.

Bromo had broken down completely.

He could not comprehend how the young girl had his business card in her possession. Iver Feirand assumed that the guy had been idiotic enough to drop it in his excitement over a pair of narrow, girlish hips. It surprised him greatly. Everything Evald Bromo said indicated that the man was exceptionally careful, and had managed to be so for an unusually long time. However, Feirand said nothing. Instead, he turned the screw; Iver Feirand succeeded in making most people blab within half an hour or so.

Evald Bromo said too much.

He spoke about a contact Iver Feirand did not want to hear about. A Latin American with some sort of branch in Copenhagen. This was Iver Feirand's own personal connection. Evald Bromo knew about Iver Feirand's own sexual refuge.

Iver Feirand had a unique insight into the psychology of pedophiles. To start with, he was an outstanding police officer, with good instincts and a sharp brain. In addition, he knew himself. And for fifteen years he had been on the receiving end of the best further education the US and European police could offer. He knew everything worth knowing about pedophile organizations, rings, clubs, and individuals. He had never come close to being exposed.

Not until Evald Bromo made him realize that several others knew Pedro Diez and his cellar in the Danish capital.

The interview had taken a different turn.

Bromo was a wimp, one of those people who was continually torn between the paralyzing fear of being unmasked and the underlying need to be stopped from committing what he knew to be criminal acts. When he had first arrived at police headquarters, admissions and confessions, names, addresses, and dates had run out of him like peas from a sack.

If Iver Feirand continued with his investigation of Evald Bromo, Pedro Diez's name would come up in connection with others as well. Bromo had so much to tell that he would keep four detectives gainfully employed for a considerable length of time. That would be the end of the cellar in Copenhagen. So be it; Iver Feirand had other contacts, other names, and other addresses—farther away and even more secure.

What was dangerous was that Evald Bromo put all his cards on the table.

Evald Bromo might give the police a clue that could lead to Iver Feirand himself. If the Danish police were to swoop on Diez's branch in the venerable old building beside the Lakes in Copenhagen, Iver Feirand's identity might come up. Not by name, of course, as he always traveled there without papers, but who knew what descriptions might be given? His extremely tall, athletic body and the almost white, blond hair *could* cause him problems. The best course of action was to let matters lie.

So he let Evald Bromo go.

He not only let the man get away, he subsequently took care to keep him walking a tightrope. He always knew where he had him.

As Iver Feirand sat with a plastic glass of cognac in his hand, surveying the extensive fields of the EU far below, he pictured Evald Bromo in his mind's eye. He had stood by his desk, totally exhausted and blissfully astonished at Iver Feirand's decision to let him off this time, even though he had strong reservations. Perhaps, in his innermost recesses, he had understood why. Evald Bromo was an intelligent man and a journalist to boot. He would naturally have found it surprising that a police officer would let him go after what he had told him. But Iver Feirand was familiar with the psychology of the pedophile. At the very point that Evald Bromo was being allowed to leave the police headquarters as a free man and with an unblemished record, he was already in the process of trivializing the entire affair. Rationalizing it. Pushing everything away.

"I didn't catch it," he had stuttered as he shook Iver Feirand's hand in thanks. "I didn't catch your name."

"Kai. You can call me Kai. If anything comes up, just call me on this number. I'm nearly always in my office. My cell phone's always switched on."

Evald Bromo had accepted the note and left.

It had been an enormous mistake to murder Evald.

But what else could he have done?

When they were parked beside the lake at Sognsvann, behind a delivery truck, he had realized there was no point in trying to talk Evald around. A resolute sense of calm had descended on the man, and he was a completely different person from the desperate, disintegrating wreck who had sat in his office seven years earlier.

Naturally, however, he could not let Evald go to the police. Even if the risk associated with Diez's cellar was no longer so great—Feirand had changed to new pastures since then—Evald would tell them that Feirand had let him go that previous time. Not with the intention of being malicious or to tell tales; probably he still thought that the decision to let mercy temper justice had been entirely reasonable. Evald Bromo would mention the episode because he wanted to confess. He wanted to come out with everything. All the details, all the facts.

Maybe Feirand would be able to talk his way out of it. Maybe not. In any case, the situation would become too hot for comfort. If there was one thing all these years as an investigator had taught him, it was that once a case such as this began to unravel, it would unravel completely.

Since he believed Evald Bromo was entirely unknown to the police, he had felt safe. Stressed and desperate to stop Bromo, admittedly, but safe in the conviction that no one, absolutely no one, would be able to connect him to the murder.

When Hanne Wilhelmsen had shared the information in her possession, it had been like being caught in an avalanche. He had found it difficult to breathe and he'd felt as if he were falling and falling, incapable of grasping at anything to save himself. He had only just managed to avoid letting his mask slip; it had been extremely helpful that she herself had seemed rather out of sorts.

The investigation into Evald Bromo's death would not focus on Sigurd Halvorsrud, apparently. When Iver Feirand had followed Halvorsrud and watched him disappear into Vogts gate 14 in the middle of the night, he had clenched his fists in triumph. Standing in an entryway, he had waited for half an hour until the Chief Public Prosecutor had come charging out again with an old man at his heels. The following day, Feirand had sought out the old man. He needed to know where in the building Halvorsrud had been. When he later learned that there were actually fingerprints in the basement, he was almost unable to believe his own luck. Until Hanne Wilhelmsen had told him what she knew.

The flight must be over Germany by now. Glancing at his watch, he asked the flight attendant for a refill.

The starting point for the investigation would be that the man was a pedophile.

Iver Feirand could no longer take the chance that he would remain in the clear. For two nights he had tossed and turned, considering all the ins and outs of it. In the end his wife had protested: he was twisting and turning so much that she could not sleep. For the remainder of that night he had sat at the kitchen table. When he applied cold logic, he managed to persuade himself he had nothing to fear. Not much, at least. Evald Bromo—despite his pathetic bad luck with the business card seven years earlier—had been extremely careful. It was quite possible that the police would be knocking their heads against a brick wall if they pursued the theory that he had been killed because of his pedophile leanings. On the other hand, Bromo had not been careful enough. Someone knew. Someone had given Hanne Wilhelmsen the information she had in her possession.

A source, she had said.

He must be a good one. God only knew what the guy was holding back.

That a source existed who was so well informed he knew about Evald Bromo made Iver Feirand reach a decision at six o'clock on the morning of the last day he spent at home with his wife and children.

He had to follow his instincts and flee.

He had succeeded in doing so.

94

It was late afternoon on Friday April 9 and no one could find Iver Kai Feirand. His wife could report that both he and his car were gone, and that he had obviously left with a suitcase.

Hanne Wilhelmsen felt it was no concern of hers.

Evald Bromo's death was no longer her case to investigate.

She intended to take an indefinite length of time off, and wanted to go home.

There was only one task left to do, and she was not quite sure whether she was dreading it or looking forward to it.

"I'll speak to him on my own," she said dismissively to the custody officer who had unlocked the cell where Sigurd Halvorsrud was seated on a bunk bed, rocking slowly from side to side. "You can go. Don't lock the door."

She entered the cell. The man inside was murmuring some kind of mantra. She crouched down and tentatively placed her hand on his. She could feel how tense he was: the sinews on the back of his hand felt like sharp edges against her palm.

"It's all over now, Halvorsrud. We've managed to get to the bottom of it all."

He raised his face a fraction.

"What are you saying?"

Smiling faintly, she repeated, "We've got to the bottom of it all. You were right. It was Salvesen who murdered your wife. And Evald Bromo's death had nothing to do with you."

For a second or two, she thought that Sigurd Halvorsrud was about to expire. His face darkened, turning almost lilac-blue around his eyes and mouth. He shut his eyes before suddenly pulling his hand free and getting to his feet. He then adjusted his suspenders and patted his hand awkwardly on his shirtfront.

Hanne had seen the inside of a holding cell countless times. She did not like them, but had never felt as repulsed by them as she did now. She saw Halvorsrud's quick glance in the direction of the open door, as if weighing up the possibility of escape. She watched as he moved with tiny sideways steps in the direction of the exit, until he stopped unexpectedly and covered his face with his hands.

"What have we done to you?" Hanne Wilhelmsen whispered, trying to touch him, a meaningless gesture of consolation.

The man twisted away, convulsed with sobs, as he pressed his elbows into his body and lowered his head.

"What have we *done* to you and your family?" she repeated, inaudibly this time.

She was directing the question at herself.

EPILOGUE

Hanne Wilhelmsen had been on leave for two months. As everything stood at present, she had no idea whether she would ever return to her job in the police force. Provisionally, the Chief of Police had said she was welcome to come back whenever she liked, but she expected that even his authority would come to an end at some point. She would have to make up her mind soon.

Iver Kai Feirand had still not been apprehended. It had taken only a short time to discover that he had traveled to Madrid via Frankfurt on a fake passport. In Spain, all leads came to an end. He was a wanted man in most countries around the globe, and Hanne was convinced he would be caught. If not sooner, then certainly later.

She had been into the office only once in all that time, five weeks ago, and only because Eivind Torsvik had phoned her at home, insisting that they meet. He would not allow himself to be fobbed off on another detective. Since he was willing to make the journey to Oslo voluntarily, it had to be something important.

The material he had presented to her had given the Oslo police their greatest ever triumph as far as the battle against the sexual abuse of children was concerned. Operation Angel had been implemented only a week after Eivind Torsvik had slapped five ring binders and twenty computer disks down on the desk in police headquarters. The material was so detailed, so thorough, and so legally compliant that the police had taken only two days to go through it with a fine-tooth comb. Erik Henriksen, who was Acting Chief Inspector with responsibility for sexual abuse, had gained in maturity from the task. Something new and serious had come over the man. Only thirty-three, he was too young for such a job, but Hanne had always believed him to be capable. She had not been much older herself when she was appointed.

The newspapers had gorged themselves on Operation Angel. There was plenty to choose from. The action had led to nine arrests in Norway alone. One of the people in custody was a well-known politician, two of them established doctors. The story was front-page news for several weeks, until the Whitsun weekend had arrived with a triple homicide in Sørum, forty minutes from Oslo city center, and Oslo Police District got a well-earned break from the intense and sometimes tiresome media focus.

The Kosovo war was now also history.

It was Wednesday, June 9, and almost midnight. Cecilie had been in and out of the hospital since Hanne had gone on leave. She would be up and about for several days and then become so poorly that Hanne would be certain it was all over. But then she'd rally again, remarkably enough, and return home for another week or so.

They were together the entire time.

Friends often came to visit Cecilie, both at the hospital and at home. Hanne never saw anything of any of them: she simply said a hurried hello in passing and headed out the door. Cecilie left it at that. Perhaps she had spoken to the others, because they no longer made any attempt to detain her. Not even Billy T.

It was drizzling.

Hanne had gone for a long walk, through the hospital district, up toward Tåsen, across the intersection where Iver Kai Feirand had been caught by a speed camera, up over Nordberg and all the way to the lake at Sognsvann. She had been away for nearly two hours and was feeling anxious.

"Are you sure you don't want me to call anyone?" the plump nurse had said gravely when Hanne returned.

Her name was Berit, and she was the only person apart from Cecilie whom Hanne had talked to properly in ages.

"Is there nobody you want here tonight?"

Hanne shook her head.

Cecilie was unconscious. As soon as Hanne sat down beside the bed, she realized that. Cecilie weighed barely a hundred pounds now, and had no energy left.

Hanne talked to Cecilie all night long. She stroked her hair gently and told her things she had never before found the courage to say. Not to Cecilie, not to anyone.

When morning came, Cecilie Vibe died.

It happened without a sound, only a tiny twitch of her eyes, and then it was over.

Hanne Wilhelmsen continued to sit holding her beloved's hand for another hour longer, until Berit came and released her grip gently, as she tried to make Hanne stand up.

"It's all over now," she said softly, in a motherly voice. "Come on now, Hanne. It's time to let go."

When Hanne moved stiffly out into the harsh light of the corridor, Cecilie's parents were sitting out there, holding hands and weeping silently.

"Thank you," Hanne said, glancing at Cecilie's mother.

The old woman was so like her daughter. She had the same eyes, set at an angle under broad eyebrows. The same hairline, the same sensual Cupid's bow that had always made it difficult for Cecilie to apply lipstick.

"Thank you for letting me be alone with her."

And then Hanne Wilhelmsen left the hospital with no idea of where to go or what to do.

Turn the page for an excerpt from the next book
in the Hanne Wilhelmsen series

NO
ECHO

*Translated from the Norwegian
by Anne Bruce*

"A nearly pitch-perfect procedural layered over a moving exploration
of rejection and abandonment."

—*Booklist*

"Transcripts of witness statements alternate with Holt's penetrating
psychological analysis of human desires, weaknesses, and essential
decency, unveiling unexpected dimensions of her series characters."

—*Publishers Weekly* (starred review)

AVAILABLE NOW FROM SCRIBNER

S anta Maria, Mother of Jesus.

The picture on the wall above the bed reminded her of one of her forgotten scraps from childhood. A pious face gazing down above hands folded in prayer. The halo around her head had long ago faded to a vague cloud of dust.

As Hanne Wilhelmsen opened her eyes, she realized that the soft features, narrow nose, and dark hair with severe middle parting had led her astray. She saw that now, though she did not understand why it had taken such a long time. It was Jesus himself who had watched over her every single night for nearly six months.

A ribbon of morning light fell across the shoulder of Santa Maria's son. Hanne sat up and her eyes squinted against the sunlight forcing its way through the gap in the curtains. Stroking the small of her back, she wondered why she was lying crosswise in the bed. She could not remember the last time an entire night had been lost in deep, undisturbed sleep.

The cold stone tiles under her feet made her gasp for breath. In the bathroom doorway, she turned to study the picture again. Her gaze swept over the floor and came to a sudden halt.

The bathroom floor was blue. She had never noticed that. She put the knuckle of her index finger against one eye and stared down with the other.

Hanne Wilhelmsen had lived in this spartan room in Villa Monasteria since midsummer. It was now almost Christmas. The days had been drab, just as all other colors were absent in and around this huge stone building. Even in summer, the Valpolicella landscape outside the enormous window on the first floor had been monotonously free from true colors. The vines clung to golden-brown trunks and the grass beside the stone walls was scorched.

A chilly intimation of December struck her half an hour later when she opened the double doors leading out to Villa Monasteria's gravel courtyard. She ambled aimlessly across to the bamboo woods on the other side, maybe twenty yards away. Two nuns stood in animated conversation on the path that divided the grove in two. They dropped their voices as Hanne approached. When she passed the two older, gray-clad women, they bowed their heads in silence.

The bamboo on one side of the path was black. On the other side the stalks were green. The nuns were gone when Hanne turned around, perplexed about what had caused the inexplicable difference in color between the slender plants about the thickness of her thumb on either side of the path. Hanne had not heard the familiar shuffling across the gravel yard. She wondered fleetingly what had become of the nuns. Then she let her fingers brush over the bamboo stalks as she scurried up to the carp pond.

There was something going on. Something was about to happen.

In the beginning, the nuns had been friendly. Not particularly talkative, of course: the Villa Monasteria was a place of contemplation and silence. Sometimes a brief smile, perhaps at mealtime, a quizzical look above hands that gladly poured more wine into her glass, and an odd softly spoken word that Hanne could not understand. In August she had almost made up her mind to spend the time learning Italian. Then she had dismissed the idea. She wasn't here to learn anything.

Eventually the nuns had realized that Hanne preferred complete stillness. Even the astute manager. He accepted her money every three weeks, with no more than a simple *grazie*. The fun-loving students from Verona, who sometimes played records so loudly that the nuns came running within a few minutes, had spotted a kindred spirit in Hanne. But only in the beginning.

Hanne Wilhelmsen had spent six months being entirely alone.

She had in the main been left in peace with her daily battle of not bothering about anything. Recently, however, she had been unable to divert her curiosity from the obvious fact that something was about to happen at Villa Monasteria. *Il direttore*, a slim, omnipresent man in his forties, raised his voice increasingly often to the nervously whispering nuns. His footsteps pounded harder than before on the stone floors. He dashed from one incomprehensible task to another, immaculately dressed and trailing a whiff of sweat and aftershave. The nuns were no longer smiling, and fewer of them assembled at meal-times. However, they sat increasingly often in silent prayer on the wooden benches in the small chapel dating from the thirteenth century, even when there was no Mass. Hanne could see them from the window as they padded, two by two, in and out through the heavy timber doors.

It was difficult to tell the depth of the carp pond. The water was unnaturally clear. The plump movements of the fish along the bottom seemed repellent, and Hanne felt a trace of nausea at the thought of them swimming around in the convent's drinking water.

She sat down on the wall surrounding the pond. Heavy oak trees, almost bare of leaves, were outlined against the wintry sky. A flock of sheep grazed on the northern hillside. A dog was barking in the far distance, and the sheep huddled more closely together.

Hanne yearned for home.

She had no reason to yearn for home. All the same, something had happened. She didn't know what, nor did she know why. It was as if her senses, blunted through a conscious process over several months, were no longer lurking in enforced hibernation. She had started to notice things.

Six months had passed since Cecilie Vibe died. Hanne had not even attended the funeral of her partner of almost twenty years. Instead she had shut herself into their apartment, numbly registering that every-one had left her in peace. No one rang the doorbell. No one had attempted to come in. The phone was silent. Only junk mail and bills in the mailbox. And eventually a settlement from an insurance company. Hanne had had no idea about the policy Cecilie had taken out years before. She had phoned the company, had the money paid into a high-interest account, written a letter to the Chief of Police, and applied for a leave of absence for the rest of the year. Alternatively, the letter could be considered her resignation.

She had not waited for an answer and instead simply packed a bag and boarded the train, heading for Copenhagen. Strictly speaking, she did not know whether she still had a job. It was of no concern to her, at least not then. She had no inkling where she was going or how long she would be away. After a fortnight of traveling haphazardly through Europe, she had stumbled across the Villa Monasteria, a run-down convent hotel in the hills north of Verona. The nuns could offer her tranquility and homemade wine. She signed in late one evening in July, intending to move on the following day.

There were prawns in the pond. Small ones, admittedly, but prawns all the same: transparent and darting by fits and starts in flight from the indolent carp. Hanne Wilhelmsen had never heard of freshwater prawns. Sniffing, she wiped her nose with the sleeve of her jacket and let her eyes follow *il direttore*'s car along the avenue. Four women dressed in gray stood under a poplar tree gazing up at her. Despite the distance, she could feel their eyes on her face, sharp as knives in the drizzly air. When the manager's car disappeared out on to the highway, the nuns wheeled around abruptly and bustled toward the Villa Monasteria without a backward glance. Hanne got up from the wall. She felt cold and rested. A huge raven, flying in oval circuits below the low-lying clouds, made her shiver.

It was time to go home.